Nova took a deep breath as the thudding pain subsided and readjusted her mask, but something was w^r

The filters had been damaged b
This close to the rift in the planet'
same greenish gas swirling everyw
pery scent like blood on the wind,

wriggle its way deep into her lungs, pulsing with her own heartbeat until she glimpsed bursts of pink color like flowers opening across her sight.

She shook her head as if to clear it, then opened the channel to Ward. There was empty space before her, an easy path to the carriers and safety. But it wouldn't last long.

"Protect your right flank and rear," she said. "I'll take the left."

The terrified marines didn't need any more prodding. They ran forward, fanning out and laying down suppressing fire as she took up a spot guarding their passage. She could hear Ward shouting at them to move faster. Zerglings attacked in waves, but she pushed them back with her C-20A, watching the skies for more mutalisks. They circled above her but did not attack, and she wondered why. Maybe they sensed what she had done to the last hydralisk and were keeping their distance.

The smell was terrible. It kept eating away at her until she could barely think straight.

In moments the marines reached the ship, boarded, and started the engines. "Come on," Ward's voice crackled in her earpiece. "Your turn! Move!"

She turned to the ship. "On my way—"

The hydralisks were advancing, crawling over the rock face in front of her, their jaws open and dripping fangs exposed. Dozens of them. They had closed off her escape route. She could sense even more coming, close enough now to overwhelm the carriers. With the mutalisks in the sky they would be lucky to make it at all. Now she realized why they had been circling; they were preparing for an all-out assault on the two ships after cutting her off from any hope of rescue.

She had no choice now. There was only one way out.

Kill them all. Like on Tarsonis.

SPECTRES

NATE KENYON

This book is a work of fiction. Names, characters, places, and incidents are products of the author's imagination or are used fictitiously. Any resemblance to actual events or locales or persons living or dead is entirely coincidental.

© 2019 Blizzard Entertainment, Inc. All rights reserved. StarCraft and Blizzard Entertainment are trademarks or registered trademarks of Blizzard Entertainment, Inc., in the U.S. and/or other countries. No portion of this book may be reproduced or transmitted in any form or by any means without written permission from the copyright holders.

ISBN: 978-1-945683-61-9

First Pocket Books printing: September 2011
First Blizzard Entertainment printing: October 2019

10 9 8 7 6 5 4 3 2 1

Cover art by Phroilan Gardner

Printed in the China

To my own personal Nova,
Kristie Lynn.

ACKNOWLEDGMENTS

A book that plays in such an extensive and exciting universe as StarCraft is a joy to write, and there are many people who helped along the way. I'd like to thank my former agent, Brendan Deneen, and all the folks at FinePrint Literary Management, for making this one happen. I'd also like to thank my editors at Simon and Schuster, Jaime Costas and Ed Schlesinger, for all their hard work and support. A huge note of thanks is due to the people at Blizzard Entertainment, who are amazing in so many ways, both personally and professionally. Finally, to my family, friends, and fans: I thank you for your support. I hope I made you proud with this one.

SPECTRES

PROLOGUE

ALTARA

The drop-pod streaked across the maroon sky far above Oasis like a tiny shooting star, one of many hundreds of meteors that had burned up over the town in the last few days. Even if the town's residents had bothered to glance up, they would have thought nothing of it; the meteor shower had become a near constant recently as a belt of space debris spun past just a hundred kilometers above Altara, and it would not cease for another four days.

But the residents of Oasis were not the type to look skyward. They had to watch their own backs or risk getting knifed for a handful of silium crystals or a case of Happy Jack's Ale.

Impact in ninety-seven seconds. Agent X52735N ran a final check and found all systems online and functioning. Although the drop-pod interior was cramped and hot, and the seat's padding was thin enough for the neosteel support bars to poke through, she hardly noticed. She settled her headpiece over her face, goggles tight against her skin, checked the heads-up display, and breathed in deeply. The headgear was light but powerful, interfacing with her suit's computer to provide a sophisticated readout that constantly sampled her surroundings and helped her spot and target anything that moved. C-10 canister rifle was a check, for long-range shots. Sidearm in place for close quarters. Her heart rate increased only slightly, then settled back into a strong and steady thump. She was like a machine. Ghosts feared nothing. Why should they? For the Dominion's most highly trained psionic assassins, fear was an alien concept.

The ghost went over her orders one more time. Dominion intelligence had picked up chatter indicating a possible UED terrorist cell operating on the dark side of Altara, a backwater planet full of criminals and convicts clustered primarily around the planet's one major town, the ironically named Oasis. Major Spaulding and his 22nd Marine Division would provide support. X52735N would be inserted covertly into the suspected terrorist location and investigate the report in stealth mode, gather what information she could, take out UED members, and signal for pickup.

In and out, fast and clean, just the way she liked it. The locals wouldn't even know she'd been here. With luck, she'd be back with the Annihilators by dinner.

Then why had the hairs suddenly stood up on the back of her neck?

She didn't have time to think it through. The drop-pod struck with a roar and shudder that rattled her teeth and thrust her forward against the harness. She sensed a strangely spongy ground, and then all movement ceased.

Touchdown. One minute, forty-eight seconds to self-destruct.

Agent X52735N unstrapped herself from the harness and waited for the door to swing open as the metal ticked in the sudden silence. It revealed a whirl of red dust kicked up by the pod and a swirling, merciless wind. She'd landed right in a crater filled with the stuff. She looked out. This planet was an abomination: craggy, lifeless stretches of rock and dirt all the way to the horizon line, and her mask failed to completely eliminate the foul smell of brimstone in the air. The dust instantly coated everything, including the drop-pod, her hostile environment suit, sniper rifle, and headgear, lending a reddish blood-tinge to the light that filtered weakly down from above.

The ghost wiped her gloved fingers across her HUD, smearing it with red. *Fekking hell.* Cloaking would be all but useless here; her suit could vibrate the dust off, but it would gather again too quickly for it to matter. Better to wait until she was close to the target.

She jumped down, ducked her head, and ran for the nearest rocky outcropping far enough away from the drop-pod, which was already starting to degrade. In another few seconds it would be nothing but space debris slowly burying itself beneath the dust. If UED agents were actively monitoring the sky, they might have seen the drop-pod, but with luck, they would have decided it was simply another meteor.

Even so, she had to assume they might know someone was coming. Of course, that didn't matter much to a ghost.

Sheltered from the wind, she accessed schematics of the planet from her suit's computer. A prior deep-space scan had revealed a structure of some kind within a kilometer of this spot, and what appeared to be ramshackle barracks or shelters clustered around it, although nothing of the sort existed on any official map. This was kilometers away from Oasis, and none of the locals or transient criminals would have ventured out this far. It was a perfect location from which a terrorist cell could strike at Dominion targets. Several had been hit in the region lately, and this was quite likely the cell's base.

Time to go to work. She loped westward, keeping the HUD active and scanning for signs of life. Nothing moved but the dust swirls, whipping jagged surfaces of rock clean and then covering them again just as quickly. Her screen became thick with the stuff, coloring everything with that bloody tinge.

Five minutes later the HUD indicated she was nearing the location. She slowed to a fast walk. *There.* A shape materialized out of the cloud, a man-made structure crouching on top of a high outcropping of granite about sixty meters away.

X52735N paused, astonished. A Kel-Morian refinery? She'd heard nothing about a mining operation around here. She instructed her computer to confirm. A scan identified it as Kel-Morian, but it had been modified in ways that were unclear. A Combine presence here, if that was what this meant, made things a lot more complicated. Kel-Morian and Dominion relations were fragile, to say the least. A terrorist cell with ties and support from the Combine meant a potentially explosive situation.

Perhaps the refinery had been stolen and retrofitted for some other purpose, she thought. *But what?*

Below the outcropping sat a supply depot and a ring of makeshift barracks, the kind that would house a work crew. An SCV sat parked diagonally between two of the barracks as if it had been hurriedly abandoned, and an ancient goliath walker stood silently nearby. But everything was dark and dead.

The ghost sensed something. A presence of

some kind, possibly psionic, but she could not get a read on it and could not tell where it came from. Those hairs on the back of her neck stood up again, giving her pause. She had never experienced anything like this. Who—or what—could possibly hide itself from a ghost?

Someone with a psi-screen, and a good one. That had to be it. But still, judging by the number of shelters, there must be other terrans here. She should be sensing their thoughts. They couldn't *all* be screened.

The wind picked up, whipping heavier pebbles against her suit's artificial psi-sensitive muscle fiber. They'd planned the drop for dusk, and what little light that remained was swiftly fading. If she called in the marines, they would lose precious time, and any hope of keeping this a covert operation. And that was not what ghosts were for, after all: she had been trained as an assassin, and this was her mission. Obeying without question. She had to move fast.

X52735N crept forward under cover of the growing dark. The camp appeared to be vacant. Her scans picked up nothing alive or moving. She reached the SCV without incident, touched its flanks. Cold, and covered with more of that damned dust. It hadn't been driven in some time. The goliath walker looked much the same, a neo-steel approximation of a terran shape standing upright and covered in dust, its cannon arms modified with pinchers to grasp and lift but otherwise intact.

She peered at the outcropping of rock, about fifteen meters away now, and the refinery above it like some kind of monstrous creature crouched on the edge of a rift. For the first time, she noticed what looked like an abandoned mine opening in the face of the rock near the ground, about nine meters below the refinery. The opening was only about three meters across and black as pitch. Altara was known to have an extensive cave system, a labyrinth of passageways and yawning chasms that had claimed a number of more adventurous terran lives. The ghost wondered if this mine entrance led into them.

Something like that would provide the perfect cover for the base.

The wind brought a whisper that seemed to caress her spine, tracing up her scalp under her headpiece. Like a voice inside her head, although she could not make out the words. Goose bumps prickled her skin. Another scan of the refinery revealed no light or living thing, but the HUD showed a brief blip from just inside the mine entrance as she passed over it.

She froze. Movement, as someone—or something—darted from the edge of the black mouth, deeper inside. Just as quickly as the movement registered, it was gone.

X52735N's suit sent a shiver through her,

shaking loose the dust that clung to it, and she activated her cloaking device and raced for the entrance. It took her only seconds to cross the open ground, but it seemed like forever. Her entire body itched, and even with the cloak she felt exposed.

As soon as she ducked inside, her C-10 rifle out and ready, the sound of the wind died down and the darkness claimed her. She blinked rapidly behind her headpiece, trying to gain her bearings. But what little light remained in the sky did not penetrate more than a meter.

The ghost's optic system added multispectrum imaging to her HUD, which revealed a rocky, carved tunnel reinforced with neosteel, quickly forking into two tunnels about nine meters in. The tunnels appeared to be empty, the roughness of the walls standing out in monochrome. She switched to heat-vision mode, looking beyond the walls into more tunnels and natural caverns; the system was extensive, to say the least. It could take days to explore, precious time that she didn't have—

There. Judging by the heat signature, she saw something vaguely human running through a large open space beyond the right fork in the tunnel.

X52735N raced silently forward over the rocky ground. She would identify the target and interrogate if possible, but she had to move fast. This was the most delicate part of the mission; if the

UED had indeed set up a base inside the mine, it was likely well protected. She had to get to the target before others could be warned of her presence.

The right tunnel showed signs of heavy activity. The rock had been scraped recently, as if something large had passed through, and many footprints dotted the ground where the dust had built up. It was not long, and she reached the end in moments, finding herself at the edge of a vast cavern. She paused, astonished. It looked like a storage facility. Collectors lined the walls, at least a half dozen unmanned units. From the look of things, vespene containers had been stacked here once, and a lot of them. But they were gone now, and the space was dark.

She scanned the huge cavern for any signs of life and found it empty. There was only one exit near the far end. Whoever had been running through here must have gone in that direction. She reached out psionically and found . . . nothing. Not just a lack of any terran thought patterns, which would have been strange enough, considering she was chasing someone. This felt artificial to her, a complete absence of anything at all—a vacuum.

Her senses were on full alert, but for the life of her, she could not figure out why. She had found nothing so far that would indicate a heavy enemy presence or anything that would pose a threat to her. As a ghost with a psi index of 6.5, she was one of an elite squad of the most highly trained operatives in the galaxy, an expert in hand-to-hand combat, able to read minds, her suit enhancing her physical abilities far beyond a normal terran's. Nothing but protoss and the zerg Queen of Blades could boast of psionic abilities greater than those of ghosts. And this was clearly not an alien operation.

X52735N crossed the cavern to the far opening. It was a natural fissure in the rock, roughly triangular and far older than the first two tunnels. She ducked inside, took a few tentative steps with the rifle up and ready, her own breathing heavy in her ears. The walls were no more than three meters apart, and she felt them closing in on her. The ceiling came to a point not far above her head, and she imagined the weight of the rock poised above her, many tons of it pressing down.

This was not like her at all. She was tensing up, sensing a trap, on full alert and on the edge of losing control, with no obvious reason for it. Her cloaking device was still on; even with advanced optics, nobody would be able to see her. She took another few steps, trying to calm her breathing. *Pull yourself together, girl.*

A meter farther in, the fissure began to expand again, the ceiling rising higher above her head, then took a jag to the left. Her suit's sensors alerted her to the danger before she saw it herself.

The floor split with a hairline crack that quickly grew wide enough to swallow a man. A faint blue-green glow drifted up from below, along with something else. At first she thought it was vespene gas, but the sensors could not get a reading on it. It eddied around her feet like mist.

Kath Toom.

X52735N let out a gasp, whirled, searching for a target, but saw nothing. The tunnel was empty and silent, the voice *inside* her head.

I'm coming for you.

She spun again, peering into the darkness, her own heartbeat thumping in her throat.

The attack came out of nowhere, a stunning blow to the back of her neck that knocked her off balance, her rifle ripped from her grasp and skittering away across the rock floor. Stars exploded across her vision as she went into a roll, instincts kicking in even as her mind began frantically trying to process who, or what, was after her, and how it had found her cloaked form. She could not sense anything, could not hear any inner thoughts beyond what had just been fed to her, the normal internal terran chatter most telepaths endure on a daily basis completely absent.

She came to her feet in one fluid movement, sidearm already in her hand, and caught a glimpse of a shadowy, black-suited figure, gone before she had the chance to react; her roundhouse kick met nothing but air. *Vanished.*

Panic rose up and she pushed it roughly away, her training at the Ghost Academy and her combat experience flooding back. Identify the enemy, locate a weakness, and exploit it.

Your ghost training won't help you here, Toom.

This time she saw nothing at all before she was struck full in the face with what felt like a neosteel beam, her headgear wrenched away, blood filling her mouth as she gasped for air and staggered backward. Suddenly blind in the dark, she pulled the gun's trigger, flashes lighting up the walls like a strobe as she spun in a circle and laid down suppressing fire, trying to regain her bearings. Her head was ringing and the panic was a full-blown screeching mutalisk inside her now, and she turned and leapt over the faintly glowing rift in the floor to the other side, a sob catching in her throat as the mistlike gas washed over her.

Laughter followed her, echoing off the rock on all sides. *Breathe deep, little ghost. And see the light.*

X52735N fumbled through the darkness, arms outstretched until she touched the wall, a metallic stench in her nostrils. It smelled like the blood that still dripped from her split upper lip. *Kath Toom?* It had been so long since she had heard her real name, she could barely remember it. All ghosts were subjected to memory wipes after the academy, and again after every major mission, and they were trained to respond to their ghost ID as a rule. She had gotten used to thinking of herself as a number. How was it possible that her attacker knew who she was?

Breathe deep. In spite of herself, she did. Something began to worm its way into her mind, lighting her up from the inside. Her pulse quickened further, beads of sweat breaking out on her forehead. Flashes stuttered before her eyes: a training mission from her academy days, a darkened maze seeded with weapons and attack robots, others there with her, working as a team; leaping across the cracked surface and lava rivers of Gohbus in pursuit of space pirates; the Kal-Bryant Mining Conglomerate symbol on a wood-paneled wall, and a familiar, scarred, and twisted face filled with so much sadness it made her weep.

Daddy?

She threw up her arms as if to ward off an attack and stumbled backward into the crevice in the floor behind her. She fell, screaming, into the abyss.

An iron grip clutched her outstretched wrist, and a vicious jerk brought her up short. She dangled, swinging gently, and the hand pulled her upward, over the lip of rock, until she lay panting on her stomach, quivering and broken.

Kath?

Yes. She nodded, looking up through a prism of tears. *I remember.*

More laughter followed her, echoing off the

rock on all sides. Then a hooded face leaned toward her in the faint glow.

Good. Now go to sleep again, little ghost. A fist came crashing down, sending Agent X52735N, otherwise known as Kath Toom, deeper into blackness.

CHAPTER ONE

THE *PALATINE*
FOUR DAYS LATER

Reports of an attack by UED terrorists upon an Atticus Minor refinery were confirmed last night by UNN sources. Explosive charges meant to take down the refinery's storage towers misfired, according to these same sources, and there was no damage to the refinery, thanks to the quick actions of Dominion forces. Several members of the terrorist group were retained for interrogation. Emperor Mengsk issued a brief statement, calling the group "impotent leftovers" of a failed campaign and vowing to stamp out the last of the stranded UED presence scattered across the Dominion.

This marks the latest in a series of loosely organized and largely unsuccessful terrorist attacks on Terran Dominion locations. While it is estimated that a handful of these UED cells remain active, they pose no real threat to citizens, and marines are closing in fast. Those with information on such cells are urged to contact their local authorities immediately. This is Kate Lockwell reporting for the Universal News Network . . .

Agent X41822N, November Terra, dressed quietly in the dark, the deep thrumming of the battlecruiser *Palatine*'s engines changing beneath her as they powered down from warp. She had grabbed a few minutes of uninterrupted sleep, but they were close now, and she wanted to be on the bridge before the target was in range. Whatever waited for them on Altara was a mystery at the moment, and she didn't like mysteries. They were too unpredictable.

Nova's quarters on the *Palatine* were larger than most, but far from luxurious, and she preferred the dark to keep her from feeling confined by the stark, windowless walls. She stretched, feeling the restlessness in her muscles. Her white and blue hostile environment suit clung to her like a second skin as she opened the door and emerged, blinking, into the lighted corridor. A well-muscled marine coming the other way gave her a wide berth while looking her up and down. Private Godard. She didn't need to be a teep to know what he was thinking. Then again, she was used to it. The effect she had on men was a curious mixture of lust and fear, and she never hesitated to use their discomfort to serve her purposes when necessary.

She made her way through the tight, mazelike

passages of the marine battlecruiser toward the bridge, passing the galley, where the smell of acrid coffee and mirafruit pies wafted over her and the gruff voices of marines shattered the momentary quiet. A small group of them in full combat suits was sitting at a nearby table with a game of holo-cards, the splayed hands the men were playing hovering in the air in front of them as they swiped from the virtual deck and swore good-naturedly at each other. The seemingly calm atmosphere didn't fool her; she could sense their impatience as they waited for orders to deploy. The entire ship was alive with the anticipation that comes with an impending battle, and the buzz of elevated thought patterns made her skin tingle.

She reviewed her briefings one more time along the way. A ghost wrangler's distress call had been picked up by the *Palatine*, Colonel Hauler's ship, and relayed to the city of Augustgrad, the center of Dominion power. Some kind of explosion had occurred on Altara during the wrangler's investigation of a missing ghost. It was unclear whether the ghost had been found, or whether the wrangler himself had survived the blast. November Terra had been ordered to respond, with support from Hauler's marines.

Under other circumstances, she might have prepared for a relatively simple recovery and fact-finding mission. But this was not the first ghost who had disappeared during the past few months, and that was more than unusual. Neural inhibitors and regular mind wipes kept them loyal to the Dominion, even if they might have otherwise felt the urge to stray. Your average ghost didn't just go AWOL because she wanted a little downtime, and wranglers didn't send out distress calls unless something was seriously wrong. That, combined with scattered reports of terrorist attacks on strategic Dominion strongholds by some kind of special forces unit with ghostlike abilities, made for some serious conspiracy theories.

Nova had her own reasons for embracing the blissful ignorance of her past that came with becoming a ghost. Even if she didn't remember them. She fingered the well-worn slip of paper she kept tucked into her ghost suit. She didn't have to unfold and read it to know what it said: an old fortune from a Tarsonis well-cake, kept as a note to herself and meant as a message or warning. *Sometimes forgetting what's behind is the only way to look ahead.*

As Nova neared the bridge, she expected to find them preparing for an orderly deployment to the surface of Altara. But even before she strode through the door, she felt the tension in the air. She felt something else too: a massive presence headed their way, a sea of interconnected thoughts too alien to make out, like the whisperings of a hushed crowd before a big performance.

Zerg.

The room fairly crackled with electricity, the attitude of those manning the bridge confirming what she already knew. An alien zerg mass was approaching, and quickly. The surface thoughts of the tactical officer and captain on the bridge were a mixture of confusion and fear; neither one of them had ever seen a zerg before, and the Dominion's official line was that the species was dormant and hadn't been seen in years. Nova, of course, knew better, but even she had to admit to a momentary pause when considering that something so utterly inhuman and bloodthirsty was nearby. They either devoured or absorbed the genetic blueprint of every life-form in their wake, with new and more dangerous versions cropping up as a result. Nobody, not even a ghost, engaged them in battle if they could avoid it.

The real question is: what are they doing here?

Colonel Jackson Hauler stood at the observation window and stared out into space, his massive arms folded behind his back, balding dome shining under the lights. Nova had been assigned to his squadron for this mission, and quite possibly others before it, although she wasn't sure due to the standard ghost program protocol of mind wipes and the fact that many missions had been designated top-level clearance and "need to know only" in the virtual files.

The squadron's history was hidden to her, and she found it unnerving, as usual, to sense that others had memories of time spent together that she did not. It often led to some awkward conversations, which was one reason ghosts tended to be loners, set apart from the rest of the crew both physically and mentally. Without a past, it was difficult to build relationships.

Which, of course, was the way the Dominion liked it. Ghosts were meant to complete their missions with as few distractions as possible.

Altara was a swiftly growing speck of red among an ocean of stars, and Hauler seemed to study it as if he might glean some kind of essential meaning from the sight. They were no more than an hour away, and he should have been down in the trenches preparing the marines and dropships for deployment. The new threat of the zerg had probably brought him here instead, and Nova could sense his impatience.

"How far?" he said, without turning around.

"Twenty minutes, sir," the tactical officer said, flicking toggles and reorienting the radar map on the viewscreen in the center of the room. The display glowed green, then red, showing the projected trajectory of the mass. "They'll beat us to the planet by at least half an hour, even at full power."

"You're certain of their target?"

"If they continue on this path, yes." The officer hesitated. "Sir, if I may ask, these . . . zerg, they're—"

"No, you may not ask a goddamn thing." Hauler spun around and grabbed the railing on the observation deck with both hands, his imposing face glowering, salt-and-pepper goatee fairly quivering with anger. "How the fekk did we not see them coming?"

The tactical officer's face grew red. "Sir, I—"

"There was no warning," Captain Rourke said smoothly, stepping into the line of fire. She kept her hands clasped at her slender waist; only her shoulders betrayed the tenseness of her body as she addressed the colonel. Nova caught a fragment of her distaste before Rourke clamped it off mentally like the jaws of a steel trap snapping shut. Captain Rourke was a formidable woman, but even she seemed to wilt slightly in the face of Colonel Hauler's wrath. "We warped in, and our scanners immediately picked them up. There was no way for Officer Harvey to have anticipated their arrival. We've done the best we can, under the circumstances."

"Don't crap on a cracker and call it caviar, Captain. What are they after?"

"Impossible to say. It could be a coincidence."

"It's not," Nova said. "The zerg are being drawn here by something. I can feel it."

Hauler turned to face her, as if surprised by her presence, although Nova knew full well he had been aware of her from the moment she had entered the bridge. "Agent X41822N, how nice to

see you. Thought you'd be strapping into a dropship about now."

"I have yet to receive final orders to deploy."

Hauler nodded. He took the short steps down
to the main floor. "It's good you're here. This zerg
mass changes everything. We're no longer following a simple fact-finding and recovery mission.
There's a low priority on saving terran lives down
there on the surface—Altara is a cesspool, as you
well know, and not highly populated—but we'll
have to engage the aliens if we want to find this
wrangler and his ghost."

"Yes, sir."

"They're being drawn here . . . Are you sug-
gesting some kind of psi emitter?"

"I don't know," Nova said. The fact was, zerg
were attracted to strong psionic signals. But a psi
emitter would require a ghost to activate it. And
that led to many more questions that were more
difficult to answer.

She could still feel the tactical officer's confusion and fear when facing the zerg mass, and she
didn't like it. He had an image in his mind of a
snarling creature with fangs dripping blood, a
movie monster of the highest order. The reality,
she thought grimly, was far worse. Hauler's marines were a mixture of old Confederate defectors
and Dominion resocialized additions, but none of
them had much experience fighting zerg.

"I want to go in first," she said to Hauler.

"It will give your men more time to be briefed. I can relay the landscape to you and allow you to probe for weaknesses before you provide tactical support."

The colonel shook his head. "Even with a full squadron of marines—"

"Alone," she said, and added, "sir." What she didn't add was her belief that the marines would only be a liability to her in their present state, and that the chance of collateral damage was high. *Get me in there and let me do my thing.*

Hauler stared at her for a long moment, then threw back his head and laughed. "You've got brass balls, I'll give you that much. Then again, I knew that already. Captain!"

Captain Rourke snapped to attention. "Yes, sir?"

"Bring this ship in fast and low. I want to know exactly where these pimples land on the ass of Altara, and I want you to bring us directly over it. Understood?" The captain nodded, and Hauler turned back to Nova.

"All right," he said, the laughter gone from his broad, regal face. "You got your wish. You've got one hour on the ground. Just don't make me regret it."

CHAPTER TWO

THE ZERG

Long before the surface of Altara came into view, Nova could sense that something was terribly wrong.

The *Palatine*'s computer had scanned for zerg activity and found it clustered around a particular rocky outcropping, kilometers away from the town of Oasis. That much was good, as civilian casualties, at least for the moment, appeared to be minimal. But the zerg were voracious predators, laying waste to entire planets in a matter of days through the spread of creep, an organic bio-matter that grew rapidly to cover the ground like a carpet and served as the aliens' nourishment, among other things. Creep was disgusting stuff, purple, thick, and slimy to the touch. The only way to destroy it was to burn it, and even then, it could return. If creep spores had made it to the surface, and the zerg had established a hatchery, Altara was on borrowed time.

But that wasn't what worried her the most. The atmosphere, normally thick with red dust, had taken on a strange, sickly greenish hue. She could see the stuff eddying like mist through the drop-pod's monitors as she hurtled through it, although the ship's scanners could not identify it as anything known to man: it wasn't exactly vespene gas, although its chemical makeup was similar, and it didn't appear to be related to the zerg either. The computer confirmed that it was flowing steadily from a rift in the planet's surface, right at the spot where the zerg were clustered, and the same place where the wrangler had sent his distress call.

Whatever explosion had occurred on Altara had released a substance that drew zerg like moths to a flame. She could feel it too. It pushed and probed at her mind like the presence of the aliens themselves, a psionic beacon she couldn't ignore.

Nova let the pod's filtration systems capture some of the strange gas for a quick chemical analysis, then relayed what she had to the *Palatine*'s comm officer, asked him to have the ship's tech try to identify the substance, and set the pod to land about a half click away from the area of high zerg activity. She couldn't help but think about the missing ghost, who had probably taken a similar path to the planet's surface. The records showed that she was an experienced agent. What had she been thinking about as the pod was about to touch down? How quickly had she been overcome, and what had happened to her?

The pod's comm unit winked on; the vidscreen stuttered; and a moment later Hauler's face came into view. "We're loaded to the gills," he said. "My men have been fully briefed and are ready for action. Our scans are showing a significant alien presence, and they are buzzing like cracked-off hornets being poked with a stick, so you get us a read on the ground. We're coming in fast. Don't play the hero, understand?"

"I can take care of myself."

Hauler frowned. "You damn well better. I don't want the ghost program coming after my ass for letting one of their prize toys get damaged." He blinked out.

I can't get a good read on him, Nova thought as she prepared for landing. Dominion regulations prohibited telepaths from probing terran minds without cause, and she wouldn't think about scanning a colonel without express permission. But that didn't stop the occasional surface thought from slipping through, even with her neural inhibitor in place. With a psi index of ten, the highest possible score, Nova was one of the most powerful ghosts in existence. She couldn't help reading people. In Nova's experience, most hid their real selves from the world, constantly questioning both their own decisions and those of others. Terrans were a suspicious race by nature. She hadn't sensed anything other than surface thoughts from Colonel Hauler in the time they'd been serving together. He was a good soldier, loyal to the emperor, beloved by his men, and willing to fight to the death to protect the Dominion.

If I didn't know better now, I might believe he was worried about me.

The pod's computers alerted her to touchdown. A moment later she was leaping to the dusty, parched ground as the pod began to degrade behind her. Her suit's cloaking device was activated, although she knew it wouldn't matter much to the zerg if overlords were around to detect her. But it might give her enough of an edge to make a difference.

The wrangler's ship was located off the right side of the rocky cliff. If it wasn't already overcome by zerg, it would be soon, and the chances of recovering anyone alive there would vanish. Nova unholstered her C-20A canister rifle and faced the hostile landscape alone. She didn't need her suit's computer to know where the zerg were. She could feel them already. She shuddered. Hauler was right; they were buzzing with excitement, and the feeling was like being violated by an alien tongue bathing the folds of her brain.

Relaying what she saw directly back to the *Palatine*, she moved quickly forward through the swirling red dust, the wind plucking at her and sending tiny pebbles bouncing off her suit and goggles. Even this far out, she saw signs that a powerful explosion had occurred recently. Pieces of torn, twisted metal stuck up from the ground like some kind of blackened sculptures, so damaged they were impossible to identify. Scans showed the cliff face ahead had been ripped apart, creating the huge gash in the rock where the green gas drifted upward.

She slipped over jagged rock and through depressions filled with red dust, making her way through the inhospitable landscape. As she moved closer to the target the ground under her feet got even rougher, the red dust coating her from head to foot. She had to keep vibrating the suit psionically to shake it free. Finally she stopped short.

"Visual confirmation of zerg activity," she said into her comm unit, staring at the rift ahead. "Creep not yet present out here. Are you getting this?"

Less than two hundred meters away, the zerg throng pulsed and writhed like a monstrous, many-segmented beast across the cliff face. Three overlords hovered directly overhead, their massive, swollen bodies and claws hanging like those of enormous ticks as they disgorged more zerglings and hydralisks from pockets of their carapaces. Drones swarmed over the rock, already mutating into the organic towers the zerg used as a base of operations.

"Affirmative," the tactical officer's voice crackled in her ears.

"No sign of the wrangler," Nova said. "Tell Colonel Hauler to hold. It's too hot down here. I'm going to get a better look—"

Nova leapt from her perch as the thundering sound of a grizzly armed carrier made her glance up. She deactivated her cloaking device as the ship passed directly over her before settling on a flat stretch nearby, its engines stirring up swirls of dust. The loading gates swung open and marines in full CMC-400 powered combat suits began to deploy, their heavy boots thudding against the ground, exoskeleton hydraulics whirring.

They might as well have set off a nuclear warhead to announce their presence. She looked up and saw another carrier preparing to land, then glanced back at the first ship, its doors still wide open, marines too vulnerable in the open space. Someone gave her a wave. She sensed Godard, the muscled marine who had passed her in the hallway earlier, and she knew he was grinning at her behind his glossy helmet shield. She could feel his confidence in the squadron and his own weaponry, heard the pep talk Hauler had given them all when they had prepared to deploy as Godard went over it again in his mind. He thought he had nothing to fear.

I've got a bad feeling about this.

"What are you doing?" she barked into her comm unit. "I told you to hold."

This time Hauler's voice crackled through her

headset. "Negative. We can take it from here. You find that wrangler."

"Sir, your men are not prepared for what they're going to find. You promised me at least an hour on the ground. Let me look for a better way through—"

"We've had this conversation before. My squadron is the best in the sector, and you're not their babysitter. There's no hatchery yet and not enough zerg on the ground to matter. Marauders and tanks are on the way. Check in with Ward and then complete your mission."

"Affirmative," she said, and switched the cloaking device back on. She glanced over her shoulder at the zerg horde. Nova had no doubt that the troops were skittish. It was one thing to hear the news that a supposedly dormant species had reappeared, and quite another to see it in action. The overlords seemed indifferent to the presence of the carriers, but there were even more drones now. The carriers had flak cannons, missiles, and B2-C concussion bombs, but they were too slow and clumsy to make much of a difference against an army of mutalisks, even if they could get airborne in time, and they had no bunkers for protection.

The marines and medics from the first ship were led by Lieutenant Chet Ward, a hard-drinking, cocky veteran of many terran skirmishes. Nova had run into him a few times in the *Palatine*, but he usually kept his distance. She felt his distrust of ghosts, and for good reason: there was a rumor that he'd once choked a woman from Hudderstown Colony to death in a drunken rage and then fled the scene. A teenaged farmer's son had been blamed and executed for the crime, but she sensed some truth to Ward's involvement.

None of this mattered now, but the fact that he'd never fought the zerg did. He was likely to underestimate them. Nova slipped unseen toward the marines' right flank and opened her comm frequency to the lieutenant's headset. "Ward, get your men to higher ground and scan for lurkers. Then dig in and wait for the tanks to deploy for cover. I've got to go after the wrangler."

"I don't take orders from a ghost." Ward's voice was cold in her ears. She could see him whirling around, searching for her in vain, and she could sense his frustration.

"You're going to get yourself killed—"

"You do your job; I'll do mine. The element of surprise, understand? These bugs won't know what hit them."

Ward's hostility was clear, but he directed two of his men to take positions on rocky slabs above them and scout for approaching alien forces. The wind whipped dust across the landscape as Ward spread the rest of his squad across the stretch of open ground, moving toward a rocky opening.

As they neared the rocks a few marines looked

up as pebbles, dislodged from the slabs above, began to trickle down. They stopped and milled about restlessly, bringing their weapons up, unsure where to point them.

"Report," Ward's voice crackled through the comm. "Anything on the horizon?"

His scouts responded instantly, their voices strained. "There's movement, sir, but it's not clear. Multiple positions. Can't see through this fekking dust!"

An alien, high-pitched sound, a cross between a moan and shriek, drifted across the barren ground. Nova felt the men's apprehension tick up another notch as the scouts' rifles went off and one of them screamed.

The ground began to shake. She felt enemy forces swarming toward the spot from farther away, but there was far worse news than that; she sensed some of them were already here.

Oh, no. They were burrowing. She shouted out a warning into her comm unit as the shaking grew worse, but there was no more time to react.

The marines' thoughts turned to terror as three huge, heavily armored roaches exploded from underneath the rocky slabs one after another, almost directly under the marines' feet. They set their legs like giant crabs and skittered forward. The lead roach let loose with a spray of acidic bile from its jagged maw, hitting a marine full in the facemask. The man started to scream as the acid began to eat through the neosteel of his suit and dissolve the flesh beneath it.

Those who were able to react opened fire, but the roaches' armored plates were difficult to penetrate, and they seemed to regenerate themselves as quickly as the marines could inflict any damage. More terran screams split the air as a moment later a zergling pack leapt over the granite slabs in a wave of clicking alien claws. The marines mowed down the first group with their rifles, but more leapt over the dying bodies of their comrades.

Even with their protective suit armor, the marines were nearly overwhelmed by the force of the zerg attack. The zerglings were the size of large dogs, with sharp fangs and scythelike claws that could disembowel a man in seconds. Zerglings and roaches alone were formidable opponents, but together they were nearly unstoppable against marines without tank support or bunkers to provide protection. For every alien that went down in a spray of blood, another replaced it. As the rest of the troops turned to face the charging enemy, more zerglings leapt from the rocky slabs above them. One landed on the back of Private Godard, who jerked the trigger on his rifle as he stumbled, off balance, the rounds tearing into the suit of a nearby fellow marine and separating it at the elbow. Blood spurted in a wide fountain as the wounded soldier spun frantically and grabbed at his amputated arm, then slumped to the ground as the stimpacks kicked in and his combat suit automatically sealed off the stump.

Still cloaked, Nova raced forward, took quick aim at the zergling on Godard's back, and fired, using her psionic abilities to teek the round slightly to the right as the marine stumbled again. The alien's head exploded and the creature dropped, twitching, to the ground. Not breaking stride, she leapt over a zergling carcass and put ten rounds below the bony carapace of a roach, avoiding its steaming blood as it jerked and writhed in the dust. Before it could regenerate, she met its alien, glassy stare and sent a teek blast directly into its skull, killing it instantly.

Marine rifles barked. Medics were tending to the wounded, although several of them were already dead themselves, and those left were overwhelmed with bloody and dying soldiers. She could feel the marines' confusion as she moved among them, could almost smell their fear. But her cloaking device kept her hidden and allowed her to move freely among the zerg. She seemed to dance alone through the dusty air, humming with her own psionic power as she teeked the massive roach carcass off the ground and hurtled it at a cluster of zerglings, crushing them beneath bony plates and spines.

But it wasn't enough. She realized that she was the only thing standing between the remaining troops and an utter massacre. She had to act quickly. "Ward," she said. "Take some men, climb to the high point on the left, and wait for me. Lay down a cross fire on my signal."

Ward's voice, high and strained, crackled through. "I don't understand. Where the fekk are you . . . ?"

"Just do it," she said. A zergling's bony jaws snapped shut centimeters from her left leg, and she sent a teek blast at it, bursting its skull like a rotten mirafruit. She took three more out the same way, creating a little breathing room. Then she darted back toward the opening in the rock, uncloaking and standing still for a moment to get the aliens' attention. She could not fire in here again, had to get them away from the cluster of marines or risk collateral damage.

Bait.

It worked. The zerglings and remaining roaches turned to follow her. The roaches were fast, almost too fast. They nearly got to her with a stream of bile that etched the ground as she passed through the opening between the rocks, then she put on a burst of speed and teeked herself up the right-hand slab of granite like a spider on a sheer wall. She reached the top in seconds, turned, and aimed back down into the opening where the zerg had clustered.

"Now, Ward," she said, looking across at the lieutenant, who had stationed himself opposite her along with a half dozen others. "Focus your rounds and don't stop!"

They all opened fire, the rounds tearing into the aliens as they tried to scatter. The marines still inside the open space quickly got the hint, joining with a steady line of fire from below. In a matter of seconds, most of the zerglings were dead or dying, their blood wetting the dusty ground. The two roaches went down under the blistering attack, unable to regenerate quickly enough, wriggling and twitching until they finally burst in a spatter of alien gore, their acidic bile eating into the rock and leaving a trail of steaming cracks and holes.

Shouts from the troops echoed through her headset. The few remaining zerglings were quickly dispatched by marines as Nova leapt back down, remaining in full view this time. Any of them shocked by her sudden appearance were smart enough to remain quiet and keep their distance. She sensed their unease; most terrans felt the same about ghosts, a natural tendency when faced with someone who can read minds.

She surveyed the scene and saw dead bodies and several serious injuries, including the one with the missing arm. Medics were working hard, but she could sense that three more marines were beyond saving, the zerglings' claws having punctured their combat suits in vulnerable spots, spilling too much blood. She felt them slipping away, their minds, already blank with shock, growing ever fainter like bulbs flickering and then going dark. She sighed.

Ward had climbed down too, and he raised a shaky hand to her as he approached. "Focused fire," he said through her comm unit. "Pretty smart, for a ghost."

"There'll be a lot more of them soon, and not just zerglings and roaches," she said. "The second marine squad will be here in a moment. I want you all to find rocky ground close to the ships, someplace solid where it'll be harder for a roach to burrow, and form a defensive perimeter. I have to find that wrangler."

Before he could respond again, she engaged the cloaking device, enjoying the brief moment of shock from him as she vanished into thin air, then she turned and ran back through the rocky opening.

Minutes later she had wound through the uneven ground and around the cliff face, keeping her eye on the zerg. Mutalisks now darted and swooped over the drones, their giant leathery wings beating the dust into mini-cyclones. Right now, whatever gas was coming from the rift in the planet's surface was keeping them occupied, but she was on borrowed time. Soon they would come after her and send others after the marines.

Her computer showed the wrangler's ship was close. She crested the top of another slab of granite and saw it nestled in a natural depression, its skids half buried in dust and canted to one side. Several zerglings darted around its battered flanks, clawing at the neosteel and trying to force their way in. There was no sign of the wrangler, but she could feel him. He was almost certainly inside.

Nova settled into position, sighted the C-20A, and took three zerglings out with quick and deadly head shots, then slipped down the rock face to the ship. She teeked the lock, and the door hissed open, revealing a cramped, functional, and familiar interior. She ducked her head and stepped inside.

It didn't take her long to spot the wrangler. He was slumped behind the pilot seat, a large man in a tattered, old-fashioned leather duster that covered his more traditional wrangler suit. He was unconscious and dreaming of nothing at all. If she hadn't been able to feel the faint pulse of his mind, like a heartbeat inside her own skull, she might have thought he was already dead. Dried blood flecked his craggy, handsome face; shrapnel from the explosion had sliced his right thigh but missed the femoral artery, and he'd tied it off with a rubber hose before passing out, the suit's analgesics flooding his system. He had suffered other minor cuts and bruises and a particularly nasty bump to the head, but nothing life-threatening.

She found a medkit in a storage bin and broke an ammonia capsule under his nose. He moaned, eyelids fluttering, and she caught a flash of memory from the explosion: a wash of white light and concussive wave knocking him backward, his shock over sudden blood loss, the grim crawl back to his ship before losing consciousness. Nothing more.

But there was no time for a more complete examination. She could feel the zerg approaching. She had to get him out of there, now.

She opened a channel to Lieutenant Ward. "Requesting immediate evac," she said. "Wrangler is alive and in need of a medivac. Bring dropship around to my location for pickup—"

Her comm unit was hit with static, and then she could hear gunfire and screaming. ". . . Under attack . . ." Ward's voice washed in and out. ". . . Heavy enemy activity . . . airborne . . . need backup *now:* cannot hold . . ."

More mutalisks. Flicking hell. Nova took a deep breath and switched to the channel for the *Palatine.* Hauler's voice echoed through her head. "We're aware of the situation," he barked without preamble. "Tell them to sit tight until the siege tanks and AA guns are in place. Nothing in this galaxy can stand up to the full firepower of the Dominion Marine Corps. I promise you that these sons of bitches will regret ever setting foot on this planet. Do you have the wrangler?"

"Yes, sir."

"Good." Hauler's voice softened. "I know you helped fight off the initial zerg attack, and I appreciate the lives you saved. But that wrangler is your number one priority. Now bring him home."

He cut the transmission. Nova glanced around the tiny cockpit. It had been a while since she had piloted a system runner, but she remembered well enough. If the thing could still fly, she could get them out.

She strapped in and booted up, the engines roaring to life as she scanned the cluttered instrument panel for any signs of damage. Everything appeared in working order. She tweaked the left engine to straighten the ship in the dust and lifted off, glancing back once to make sure the wrangler was still in the same place. He hadn't moved.

Blips on her screens showed an approaching zerg mass of significant size, and another clustered where the carriers had been. She flew through thicker clouds of the strange, greenish gas just above the ground, trying to keep as low a profile as possible.

As she approached the spot where she had left the marines, a mutalisk flapped, screeching, from the left. She banked the ship hard right, swooped under one leathery wing, and heard the sound of a claw scraping metal. She was directly in the line of fire now. Below she could see what was left of the two marine squads, cut off from the carriers. They had dug in behind a rocky ledge, shooting wildly at a line of banelings advancing on the ground as more mutalisks disgorged glave wurms from their bony abdomens above.

Banelings were like acid-filled bombs. If they got close enough to detonate, they could take out the rest of the troops with ease. The wrangler's ship had a gauss cannon mounted to its hull. Nova banked again and laid down a burst of fire at the banelings before two more mutalisks converged on her. She faked upward and then dove hard, the two flying zerg colliding where she'd been with a crack that echoed even over the sound of the engines. She watched them tumble together behind her to the ground, their wings broken.

The wrangler had fallen forward against her seat, and she regretted not finding a way to strap him down. To make matters worse, the zerg claw had apparently damaged the ship, and she was losing power quickly. This wasn't exactly a rescue to brag about, but she had no choice except to set it down.

She found a clear, flat spot, managing to settle the skids without a jolt as an engine sputtered and died. Smoke drifted out from the left wing. As she unstrapped herself from her seat and came around, the wrangler's eyes fluttered open and he moaned, then fixed his gaze on her face. She sensed his sudden shock of recognition.

"Nova," he whispered, his voice cracked and hoarse.

"You . . . know me?" She crouched at his side,

but his eyes rolled backward in his head as he slipped back into unconsciousness.

She tried not to think about what the wrangler knowing her name might mean. Perhaps it was a strange coincidence, or maybe he had a mild teep ability; after all, wranglers were chosen for the program at least in part because they had higher PIs than the normal terran. Or maybe he just knew her face from the ghost program files.

But then why had he used her given name and not her ghost ID? Most ghosts were aware of their old names, but the military code of addressing them by number was hammered into everyone upon leaving the academy.

The battle intensified nearby, gunfire, screams, and the screeches of the zerg growing louder. She could sense that the marines, now half their original number, had regrouped enough to make their way closer to where she had landed. The zerg force was closing in.

She had to find a way to get the wrangler evacuated to the *Palatine* before it was too late.

Nova opened the door and lifted him, teeking him gently until she had him on her back with his arms around her neck, a plan formulating in her head. She stepped out into the dust cloud and found Ward only a meter away with a group of the marines circled behind him, breathing hard, his suit scratched and battered. She could sense the naked fear streaming off him like a foul odor.

The entire group was exhausted, a hair away from total collapse. Zerg and terran blood spattered their visors, and several were badly wounded.

"Those . . . things," Ward said, his voice cracking. "They keep *coming*."

"Where the fekk are the siege tanks?"

"They had to be off-loaded at a safe enough distance," Ward said. "They haven't arrived yet."

I've got to get them out of here. "Take the wrangler," she said, without preamble. She handed the unconscious man over to a member of the group. "I'll open up a hole in the line so you can reach the carriers. Give me five minutes." She ran to face the approaching enemy.

It didn't take her long to find them. She picked her way through a mass of zerg corpses to higher ground. Hydralisks were creeping over the broken landscape a short distance away like gigantic, armored worms, their bony carapaces hunched for protection, claws like razor-sharp scythes extended as zerglings darted around and between their tails and mutalisks flapped overhead. Behind them came the banelings, grotesquely fat sacs of living fluid ready to roll and detonate.

Banelings could cause tremendous damage. Without long-range tank fire, the marines were vulnerable. She had to take the aliens out before they could reach the troops. She sighted carefully with her rifle and fired, teeking each round to its target. The banelings exploded one by one, bursting against the rocky ground and spraying acid across the backs of the nearby zerg.

It was time for a closer look. Nova leapt over a crevice in the rock and entered the fray, her C-20A laying waste to the smaller zerglings as she teeked each round to the most vulnerable parts of their anatomy.

Alien squeals and grunts filled her head as the lead hydralisk dipped its head before her, hissing and firing a volley of thirty-centimeter-long spines from the muscles packed behind its hood. The spines could travel over 300 meters at speeds faster than her C-20A rounds and could pierce even the hardest terran armor. But they could not damage what they couldn't hit. With a brief, concentrated psionic push, Nova teeked them aside and into the rock, firing her rifle at the soft areas just above the creature's rib cage.

The hydralisk lurched backward, blood pumping from the wound. She fired two more rounds through its eyes and into its brain as it fell.

Her gunfire had drawn the others' attention. She turned to find another hydralisk lunging at her, jaws extended as if to rip her head from her body, one claw poised to skewer her through the middle. The creature's teeth grazed her face, jolting her mask to one side before the hydralisk froze in midlunge; she could feel its muscles straining and its hot breath on her skin as she focused every ounce of her telekinetic abilities on holding it suspended above her. Its alien rage ate away at her brain, a nearly mindless urge to destroy. Even knowing its intent, she could not help admiring such a magnificent killing machine. Perhaps that was what had attracted the Queen of Blades to her ultimate fate, she thought: an appreciation for something so singular in its purpose.

But she would not allow Kerrigan's fate to happen to her. She began to force its jaws apart, a dull headache beginning at the corners of her eyes. Unlike other teeks, using her ability always did this to her, and the more effort required, the worse the pain. She squeezed her eyes shut and concentrated, heard the crack of hydralisk bone and the tearing of muscle and tendon as she ripped the creature's head in half with her mind and threw the carcass upward at an approaching mutalisk. The two heavy bodies collided in midair, glave wurms detonating and showering the landscape with shards of bone, blood, and gore.

Nova took a deep breath as the thudding pain subsided and readjusted her mask, but something was wrong. The filters had been damaged by the hydralisk's attack. This close to the rift in the planet's surface, she noticed the same greenish gas swirling everywhere. She smelled a coppery scent like blood on the wind, and the scent seemed to wriggle its way deep into her lungs, pulsing with her own heartbeat until she glimpsed bursts of pink color like flowers opening across her sight.

She shook her head as if to clear it, then opened the channel to Ward. There was empty space before her, an easy path to the carriers and safety. But it wouldn't last long.

"Protect your right flank and rear," she said. "I'll take the left."

The terrified marines didn't need any more prodding. They ran forward, fanning out and laying down suppressing fire as she took up a spot guarding their passage. She could hear Ward shouting at them to move faster. Zerglings attacked in waves, but she pushed them back with her C-20A, watching the skies for more mutalisks. They circled above her but did not attack, and she wondered why. Maybe they sensed what she had done to the last hydralisk and were keeping their distance.

The smell was terrible. It kept eating away at her until she could barely think straight.

In moments the marines reached the ship, boarded, and started the engines. "Come on," Ward's voice crackled in her earpiece. "Your turn! Move!"

She turned to the ship. "On my way—"

The hydralisks were advancing, crawling over the rock face in front of her, their jaws open and dripping fangs exposed. Dozens of them. They had closed off her escape route. She could sense even more coming, close enough now to overwhelm the carriers. With the mutalisks in the sky they would be lucky to make it at all. Now she realized why they had been circling; they were preparing for an all-out assault on the two ships after cutting her off from any hope of rescue.

She had no choice now. There was only one way out.

Kill them all. Like on Tarsonis.

"Where are you?" Ward's voice was strained. "We can't hold much longer."

"Evacuate," Nova said. "Get the wrangler to safety. I'll provide a distraction."

"But how will you—"

"Just *do* it," she said. "I can take care of myself. Look at it this way: if I don't make it back, there's one less person who knows about what you did at Hudderstown Colony."

There was a brief moment of silence before Ward cleared his throat, and she knew immediately that she had been right about him. "Affirmative," he said. "We're gone. Watch your ass."

I always do. Nova switched the comm unit off and took a moment to prepare. Her entire body was on fire with the need to lash out at something, anything. The first step was to draw them all to her. But how?

The answer came from the very ground under her feet. More of the green gas was seeping up from a hair-thin crack directly in front of her, and she sensed a much larger crevasse just below. The zerg had been drawn to the planet by this gas in the first place; maybe they would respond to it now. She gave a hard mental push, sending out a beacon of psionic power. The rock groaned and split, releasing a thick cloud of gas like a geyser. Almost immediately she sensed the zerg turn their attention toward her, as the mutalisks in the sky whirled and dove and the others on the ground increased their pace, leaping at her with renewed excitement.

For a moment she thought they would be too fast for her. She heard the roar of the grizzlies as they took to the air and the thunder of their cannons, but the distraction had worked; they were clear. That was a good thing for what she was planning to do. It was a very difficult trick, and the chance of collateral damage was high.

She took out three zerglings with her C-20A and was looking for high ground when the rock began to tremble under her feet. Something was coming.

She turned to face the sound as the dust erupted in front of her and an infestor burst forth, spewing a volatile plague. Nova dove to the side to avoid the plague, catching just a glimpse of something larger that had come from the creature's throat, something vaguely human. She rolled and then scrambled to her feet, but the infestor had burrowed back into the ground again and was moving rapidly away.

She might have gone after it, except for what was standing in her way.

What remained of Private Godard had planted its feet and held its rifle in both hands, staring mindlessly through a cracked and dusty visor. Godard's marine suit dripped with the remains of the infestor's bile, and spikes of zerg carapace had grown up over the shoulder plates and the back of his helmet, along with two spiny, insectlike arms with clacking claws. She felt the throb of the zerg mind within his own, and she didn't know whether his voice was still there and lost among the din, or whether he had been extinguished entirely and what remained was nothing more than a zerg-infested shell.

Then he turned his head to stare at her, and she stumbled backward, shocked by a sudden image of herself through his eyes: a female form he had admired just a few hours ago, but now regarded as alien and beneath contempt. Along with it came a vivid memory of a drug dealer called Fagin from her early days in the Gutter on Tarsonis, the way he had looked at her so much like how Godard did now, and her rage at being held like a prisoner and forced to do his dirty work, torture and murders and worse, before a wrangler came to her rescue.

Finally she remembered another zerg battle on a distant planet called Shi, when she had been just a trainee, a place they should never have landed on and certainly a place where neither the zerg nor terrans should have been . . .

Nova gasped as the images came in disjointed flashes like terrible hallucinations, images she had fought so hard to wipe from her memory forever, and this coppery, foreign thing kept worming its way through her body and burning through her bloodstream until she felt she might burst from the inside out.

Visions of her father, mother, and brother lying in pools of blood, and three hundred people dead around them by her own savage act of revenge.

An act she would play out again now.

As Godard raised his rifle in her direction and the massive host of zerg grew close, she closed her eyes, spread her arms, and crouched in the dust, her rage coupling with her psionic energy and coiling within her belly like a snake ready to strike. As it began to course outward from somewhere deep within her, she felt both a thrill and a terror as she had never known before, along with the urge to crack the very planet upon which she stood in half. She raised her head, opened her eyes, and let out a primal scream.

Nova Terra unleashed hell.

CHAPTER THREE

KATH TOOM

I remember.

She was a child at her father's knee, listening to his holo-conference with the Kal-Bryant board, the smell of Tyrador cigars heavy in the room. Even as she played she could sense his thoughts, his dislike of the politics of the business, and his desire to be in his secretary's bed again instead of at home. It wasn't good for her to know these things, her daddy told her, not normal. She would have to see a doctor.

Years later, her father pacing in that same office, accused of betraying the Dominion through something called Sector 9 . . .

This wasn't right, these memories that flew at her like ghosts and haunted her dreams.

My daddy died far from Pridewater.

Kath Toom jerked awake, gasping, to darkness and gloom and a vivid image of her father's now terribly scarred face, her cheeks wet with tears. The last glimpse of him had lit up like a flash of lightning splitting the sky, his agony twisting in her guts. What had happened to him? Some kind of accident? And what was Sector 9? She sensed it was terribly important. But as hard as she tried, she could not remember the rest.

Panic nearly overwhelmed her when she found that she could not move her limbs. She was held down on some sort of flat, cold surface and covered in nothing but a sheet, her nakedness amplifying how vulnerable she felt.

Shapes loomed in the dark: machines beeped and whirred. She felt the pinch of an IV in her right forearm, and her temples throbbed with pain.

Altara. The attack in the caverns came rushing back, and she instinctively tried to sit up, pulling against the restraints. Her movement triggered motion lights, and the room blinked into life. A wave of dizziness washed over her as she turned her head to see.

She was strapped to some kind of surgical table in a medical unit no more than a four-meter square. A scalpel and bloody gauze sat on a neo-steel tray nearby, and a robot arm speckled with red hung lifelessly over it. One wall was dominated by rows of meter-high metal doors like lockers for cadavers, except each of them had a small window in the center.

. . . morgue full of marines torn limb from limb as Kath Toom wandered through an empty ship . . .

The scene flashed through her mind like another lightning strike, and she had to bite her lip to keep from screaming. She didn't know if it was a real memory or a dream, and for a moment she wondered if she might be going insane. She shook her head, driving the image away. She had to focus, remember her training, and find a way out.

But her ghost suit was gone, and with it all her weapons.

Think, Agent X52735N. She had been investigating a terrorist cell on a forgotten planet, sent there by the emperor himself. Or so she had thought. But now it felt more like a setup. She remembered the coppery smell of the gas leaking from the crack in the rock. Who had brought her here? That black-clad monster that had attacked her back on Altara? If so, why? And what had been done to her?

She slid her wrists back and forth in her restraints, studied their play. They were made of rough canvas with a fused edge, and there was a sharp seam on the left one that rubbed against her skin. This one was too easy. She yanked and twisted violently, letting the seam cut into her until it drew blood, then slid her arm back and forth until the canvas was slick enough for her to tuck her thumb into her palm and pull her wrist free.

Quickly she undid the other strap, then the

larger one across her chest, then her ankles. She yanked the needle from her arm, the tube leaking clear fluid. Her limbs tingled as she swung her legs to the floor, tucking the sheet around her naked body. She felt a vibration, faint but steady, flowing through her. She was on a ship.

As she gained her feet and looked up, a hydralisk hissed and lunged at her, fangs exposed and dripping, and she screamed and stumbled backward against the table, the surgical tray clattering to the floor, but she blinked and it was gone. There was nothing there: she was seeing things, and now she didn't even know if what surrounded her was real or a fragment of memory dislodged as if a tongue were worrying at a rotten tooth.

She ran to the wall of little doors and looked through the thick glass windows, saw bare terran feet. Some kind of chambers that housed the living or the dead; she couldn't tell. She pounded on them, shouting, the blood from her wrist smearing the glass, but nothing changed and the feet didn't move. She tried to turn the handles, but the chambers were all locked, and she couldn't sense any thoughts, not even the pulse of a living mind within.

Sobbing, she slid to the floor, clutching her legs to her chest and rocking back and forth. She was a small child again, Kath Toom playing with the other executives' children from the Kal-Bryant conglomerate, only they wouldn't play

with her anymore because she always knew
where they were hiding or could guess the numbers on the holocards before anyone told her. *The
girl is spooky,* her best friend's mother whispered
to another, out of earshot but not far enough.
Like a . . . ghost.

A noise made her look up. A hulking figure
was at the door, his massive shoulders filling the
frame, dreadlocks dangling down around his
shoulders. His face was familiar to her. She scrambled to her feet, fists clenched, as he took a step
into the room.

Don't come any closer!

But he did, his eyes a strange shade of white
that contrasted with his dark skin, a handsome
face that had aged since she had last seen it. She
did not remember this man, could not place him
in any sort of personal history, and yet she knew
that face like her own, and it stirred something
deep within her. A confusing rush of emotions
washed over her, making her tremble more
deeply.

Her back was up against the meat lockers as he
reached out to touch her, and she stepped forward
in one fluid motion, grabbing his arm in order to
use his weight to topple him before she drove an
elbow into his solar plexus and then chopped the
side of her hand to his throat to send him to the
floor.

Except when she grabbed for him he had already moved, anticipating her, wrapping her arms up and pinning them to her body. She tried to claw at him, but his strength was enormous, overwhelming, his muscles like wood. She thrust her head forward to crack his nose, but he seemed to know what she would do before she did it, dodging the blow neatly before he spun her in his arms and pressed her up against the wall, shackling her wrists together.

She stood sobbing as he remained close to her, his body warmth spreading through her limbs, breath stirring her hair. His thoughts echoed inside her head, and what he said both thrilled and terrified her.

Do not fight me, Kath. My name is Gabriel Tosh, and you know me. Before long, you will understand why you're here on Gehenna. You will remember everything. Team Blue will be together again, and you'll be free.

She struggled again, but the shackles that bound her only cut more deeply. A hiss of escaping gas came from somewhere behind her, and she smelled the familiar scent of copper. Flashes passed before her eyes.

A moment later she felt the bite of a needle in her arm, and before she could let out a single scream, she sank back into darkness.

CHAPTER FOUR

MAL KELERCHIAN

"She's coming out of it."

Nova Terra blinked into a searing white light, turning her face away. Her head pounded like a jackhammer and she felt as if she might be sick. She squeezed her eyes shut again and struggled to remember where she was and what had happened.

(freak)

(better to keep her under than let her do something like that to us)

(what if she's out of her mind)

(Gehenna's the only place for her now)

She tried to focus, but nothing made sense. Terran thoughts bombarded her from all sides, and she held up her hands as if to shove them away. Someone gently pushed them back down.

Where?

"You're in the medical bay on *Palatine*," a voice said. "Try to take it easy. Everything's fine."

Captain Rourke. "What happened?" Nova said. She dared to open her eyes a crack and found the captain looking down at her.

"You saved everyone's asses; that's what happened," she said. "Some kind of psionic mind blast. Never seen anything like it. Wiped out the entire zerg horde. You're lucky to be alive."

Rourke had seen the battlefield, and in scanning her thoughts Nova got a full picture of it in her head, along with the captain's barely concealed awe at the sight: zerg carcasses strewn everywhere, bleeding from the eyes and steaming in the heat; mutalisks lying where they had fallen in heaps; the overlords with their enormous weight, having popped like rancid eggs against the sharp rocks as they fell, sending sprays of blood and gore across the landscape. It looked familiar; she flashed back to a similar scene, more dead zerg just like these, killed by another mind blast, but she couldn't place exactly where it was, or what had happened.

Then she remembered her visions of Tarsonis and her parents' death, things that should have been wiped away long ago—had they been real, and if so, *why had they suddenly returned?*

Nova tried to sit up, sensed movement, and glanced over Rourke's shoulder to find Private Godard staring at her, his eyes rimmed with blood, bony alien plates protruding from his temples. She recoiled, but he was gone, replaced with the angular face of Dr. Shaw, head of medical on the *Palatine*.

"I—I think I'm seeing things," she said. "Something's wrong with me. I saw a marine there just now, Private Godard."

"Godard's dead," Rourke said. "He didn't come back."

"I know that. I saw him. He was . . . infested—"

"You've had quite a strain on your neural systems," Shaw said, stepping forward. "A mind blast. Amazing. I've heard rumors of abilities like this, but I never thought it was actually possible." He checked her vitals, shined a light in each eye, and grunted noncommittally. "Of course, there was—" He seemed to catch himself, grunted again, and looked away. But his next thought was as clear to her as if he had spoken aloud.

(murderer)

"I have these . . . memories . . . something, about Tarsonis," Nova said. "Something happened there. My . . . my parents were killed?"

"I lived there for a time myself. There was a terrible terrorist attack. Killed many people." Shaw busied himself with something by the bed.

"I think there's more to it. But I shouldn't have any memory of that either. The Ghost Academy wiped my entire past when I graduated. I'm telling you, something's *wrong* with me."

"Maybe you should consider it a blessing," Shaw said, still busy with things out of her line of sight.

"I joined the ghost program to forget, Doctor." Confusion and the unfamiliar feeling of fear washed over her, prickling her skin. How could she remember anything about her parents? Had any of what her mind had dredged up back on Altara really occurred? She reached out, grabbed his arm, and forced him to look at her. "November Terra is dead. I'm Agent X41822N of the Terran Dominion. I don't want to be anybody else."

(don't touch me, you freak)

"You should rest," Shaw said.

"No." Nova shoved herself to a sitting position. "That gas down on Altara, I need to find out what it was. If I—"

"We're working on that."

"Then I want to be fully briefed on what happened on that planet."

"If you're really insisting on getting out of that bed, there's someone who wants to see you," Rourke said. "He's been pretty persistent about it, actually. Won't take no for an answer. Says he's an old friend."

"Who?"

Rourke shook her head. "I'll let you see for yourself," she said.

Rourke led Nova into an adjacent medical unit. The wrangler she'd rescued from Altara was sitting in a chair, staring into space. He was wearing a medical gown and the same old leather duster over it; she knew, even without needing to read Rourke's reaction, that he'd insisted on having it on and wouldn't even let them clean it. Nova wasn't sure why, but that didn't surprise her in the least.

When he saw her enter the room, he stood up, dusting off his knees as if they were having a drink out on the patio rather than recovering from battle. "Had the strangest damn dream," he said. "I was wrecked on this backwater hell and Nova Terra was kneeling over me, and her face was just like an angel, and I thought I was dying. Now here you are. It's been a long time, Nova. Rourke, leave us be."

Captain Rourke opened her mouth, shut it again, and nodded. Clearly she thought he'd lost his mind, but had decided it was easier not to argue with a wrangler and a ghost. Nova caught a brief half-thought from her as Rourke studied the man's face and found it attractive in a rugged, rough-hewn sort of way, the thought blooming into a gentle heat in spite of her efforts to conceal it. Then she closed the door softly behind her before Nova could read anything more.

"Sit," the wrangler said. He swept an arm in the general direction of the chair.

"I'd rather stand."

"You always were a little ornery." He chuckled. "What's the matter, Nova? You look like you've seen a ghost."

"I *know* you."

"Damn right you do." He stuck out his hand. "Mal Kelerchian, wrangler extraordinaire. I saved your ass a few years ago back on Tarsonis. I guess now we're even."

Nova crouched in a crumbling apartment with Mal Kelerchian hovering over her, his wrangler's force field keeping debris from crushing them as the walls fell in upon their heads . . .

The flash of their past history was gone as quickly as it had come, like lightning fading from the sky. Nova tried to gather herself, her stomach churning. "You . . . recruited me for the ghost program," she said. She took his hand, and his touch was like an electric shock coursing up her arm.

"Well I'll be," he said, holding her hand a moment too long before releasing it. "They told me you were having memory flashes. Seems like the boys who wiped you clean need to go back for a little refresher course." He waved away the medbot that had moved in for a periodic check as if he were swatting at a fly, banishing it to the corner where it settled, slumping as if dejected. Then he motioned toward the chair again. "Now, will you please sit?"

This time she did, and Kelerchian settled himself on the edge of the bed. He kept staring at her and smiling back, and the feeling was more than a little unsettling.

"You okay, after what you pulled down there?"

"I've been better," she said. "How about you?"

"Some scratches and bruises, minor concussion, nothing life-threatening. Guess I haven't used up my luck yet, or I'd be a Rorschach pattern on a slab of granite right now. Somehow I managed to get back to my ship before I passed out. Must have hit my head pretty hard."

He had kind eyes, Nova thought. There was a gentleness hidden underneath the overly gruff, slightly awkward exterior. "You were good to me, back when we first met, weren't you?"

"I'd like to think so, but there are plenty of people who might suggest that assigning someone to the ghost program is akin to cruel and unusual punishment. Of course, you wanted to go. Wanted to forget everything, who you were, what you did." He sighed. "Now here you are, remembering after all."

Sometimes forgetting what's behind is the only way to look ahead.

"It's bits and pieces," she said. "They come out of order and out of control. I can't make sense of it. It's like my senses have been heightened, somehow. And I'm having these hallucinations. Something happened to me down there on Altara, Mal. I think I was exposed."

"Exposed to what?"

She shook her head. "I don't know. I think it

has to do with that gas leaking from the site of the explosion."

She thought he might tell her she was crazy. Instead, he just nodded. "From what I could see before all hell broke loose and the evidence blew to kingdom come, someone was mining that stuff. It's something like vespene gas; that much is for sure. But it doesn't seem to be fuel. So what were they planning to do with it?" He spread his hands. "That's the question."

"What *were* you doing on that planet, Mal? I know about the missing ghost. But what else is going on here?"

"I wish I knew." He stood up again and walked to the door, looking out the window. She could sense he was worried about people overhearing them, and that it had to do with top secret orders directly from Emperor Mengsk. She tried not to read any deeper into his thoughts, but she was finding it more difficult today than usual.

(stop prying, Nova)

When he turned back, he was smiling again. "I can feel you in there," he said. "Gives me an even bigger headache. Right now I'm on enough analgesics to numb a zergling. But you probably felt that too." He sat back down on the bed, leaning forward as if to impart a deep secret. "I'll tell you what I *do* know. It's not one ghost who's disappeared. It's at least a dozen or more. They all vanished without a trace. It's been going on for over a year now, but the ghost program has kept it hush-hush."

"What about their neural implants?"

"Every single one of them went dark shortly after they disappeared. They're either dead and cremated, or their implants have been disabled. We can't track them." Kelerchian rubbed his palms against his coat, a nervous habit she suddenly remembered well. "Agent X52735N was sent to Altara to investigate rumors of a UED terrorist cell before she disappeared, with support from the 22nd Marine Division."

"The Annihilators?"

"You got it. Just like old friends, eh?"

"I don't—"

"No memory of that part? They were with me when I pulled you out of the Gutter way back when. Let's just say we had our issues, but Ndoci's long gone; Captain Spaulding's in charge, and he's a major now. Anyway, the ghost vanishes, Spaulding claims to know nothing about it, and Mengsk sends me on a priority one to find out what the fekk happened. When I landed on Altara, I walked through Oasis first. One hell of a town they got there, let me tell you. Full of addicts, criminals, and worse. Not surprising that nobody wanted to talk to me, but most of them didn't even seem to know there was a refinery halfway around that godforsaken place. So I flew over the site for a look-see. I got an eyeful—the refinery was operational, complete with a work crew that looked like they were packing up for a fast getaway."

"You think they had a role in the ghost's disappearance."

"Considering they attacked me when I landed, I think that's a good bet. These guys were well trained and well armed, probably ex-military. I fought them off for a while, but in the process we must have damaged the refinery core, because it went up like a nuke."

"That doesn't make any sense."

"I know." Kelerchian scratched at the stubble on his chin. "I'll tell you something else. About five minutes after I arrived on the scene, I had a splitting headache, the kind I get when telepaths are around. There was definitely some psionic activity going on at that place. At first I thought maybe the missing ghost was nearby, but I didn't see any sign of her, and she didn't make an effort to reach out to me telepathically."

"Maybe she was unconscious," Nova said.

"Maybe, but I don't think so. This was a headache of legendary proportions. Something else was going on." Kelerchian shrugged. "The only time I've experienced anything anywhere near like that was being around you when you pulled one of your teek stunts. But even those weren't quite up to this level."

"I'd like to think I didn't cause you too much pain back then."

"I suffered in silence. We all have our sacrifices. You're different, kid. I can't put my finger on it, but you've changed."

"I've grown up."

"It's more than that. You're less closed up, I guess." His eyes held real warmth. "I always liked you. Rich girl growing up in one of the Old Families of the Confederacy, dealt about the worst hand possible by a hostile universe, but you wouldn't go down without a fight. You were a beauty and you had spirit, even down in that Gutter with the hab addicts and crab dealers. I saw it from the beginning, and I guess I was right, because look at you now." He shook his head. "The most impressive ghost I've ever seen."

"You're different too, I think."

"How so?"

"You were . . . larger before, weren't you?"

Kelerchian threw back his head and laughed out loud. "I guess I've dropped a few pounds. It was all that rehab and muscle stimulants after the injuries from the battle on Tarsonis, got me back into fighting shape. I fit into that wrangler suit a little better these days."

"Maybe it's good to remember some things. It's great to see you, Mal."

"Good to see you too, kid." He smiled. "Good to see you too."

A brief knock on the door, and Dr. Shaw stuck his head in. "Captain Rourke says you two are wanted on the bridge ASAP. I told her you should rest, but she's insisting."

Kelerchian and Nova exchanged glances. *Hauler.* "We got time to change out of these damned hospital gowns?" Kelerchian said. "I'm feeling a little vulnerable."

"Maybe," Shaw said. "If you hurry."

I like him, Nova thought as they made their way through the narrow winding corridors to the bridge, both of them wearing their suits once again. It was a remarkably strange feeling to half remember someone, running into an old friend and knowing you shared something in the past, without all of it coming through; it was like watching a movie with key scenes missing. But she knew enough to feel familiar with him.

It was even stranger to *like* someone after being alone so long and trained to depend on nobody other than yourself. She'd spent so much time going from mission to mission, living only to serve the Dominion before having her memory wiped and starting all over again. It was a ghost's role, and she was good at it. Feeling close to another person only made you weak, and that was something a ghost could not afford. She knew that she was known as a ruthless killer, a machine created for only one purpose. Men who might find her attractive on the surface (and there were plenty, as she knew well from the casual thoughts that slipped through) did not even think about approaching her. She preferred it that way. No strings, nothing to lose or regret, and no danger of reliving the pain that always came when you began to care about something or someone and it was taken from you.

When they reached the bridge, they found Hauler, Ward, Harvey, and several people Nova didn't recognize, although within moments she had sensed their names, ranks, and what they had had for breakfast, among other things. They were science team members assigned to the investigation of the gas samples that had been isolated from the planet's surface. Terran thoughts were bombarding her from all sides now, even with her neural inhibitor, and she found it more and more difficult to screen out the noise.

"It's about time," Hauler said. He turned to the waiting men. "Report."

A man named Karl Lee, the leader of the team, explained the latest findings. "It's an unknown substance," he said, bringing up a molecular hologram that he manipulated with his fingers. "We've isolated its structure, and it's naturally occurring and quite similar to vespene gas, along with some unusual organics. But the purpose of mining it remains unclear. It's not as flammable as vespene and it doesn't seem to hold any other properties that might make it valuable, except one." He turned to the tactical officer, who brought up a map of space on the viewscreen. "I've marked where the zerg mass first appeared on our scans, and right here"—Lee pointed to an abrupt change in its trajectory—"this is the exact time the explosion occurred. You can see they immediately changed course for Altara."

Nova remembered how she had felt when she had last entered the bridge and sensed the zerg approaching. "Like a psionic beacon," she said. "That gas was sending out some kind of signal."

"What kind of gas brings the zerg out of hiding?" Kelerchian said. "They haven't been seen around here in four years."

"I don't give a damn why they came," Hauler said. "All I care about is that we wipe them out and they don't come back."

"And what about that little army that attacked me at the refinery?" Kelerchian said. "Was that a Kel-Morian operation?"

"We don't have a record of anything being mined on Altara," Hauler said. "Probably squatters. Or leftover UED infantry like on Abaddon."

"The Dominion sent that ghost to Altara to investigate rumors of a terrorist cell."

"If they were there," Hauler said, "they're gone now. And so is the ghost."

The communications officer, who had been listening to a comm channel, turned from his station. "Excuse me, sir, but there's a top secret transmission coming in from Korhal. Emperor Mengsk would like an audience with Agent X41822N and Mr. Kelerchian immediately."

Hauler grunted. "We'll take it in my quarters," he said.

"My apologies, sir," the officer said. He looked terrified. "The emperor was quite specific that they attend alone."

"Well, ain't that just a bitch?" Hauler said drily. "Tell you what: I'll go make you all a cup of coffee and clean your quarters while I wait. Maybe book you a massage. You get your asses back here ASAP."

CHAPTER FIVE

EMPEROR MENGSK

Nova and Mal Kelerchian took the call via the holoprojector in the comm room. When they heard who was on the call, the marines in the room cleared out as if a hydralisk were breathing down their necks, closing the door behind them.

Once they were alone and the place was secure, Kelerchian connected with the palace at Augustgrad. A moment later the holo glowed blue-green above the projector base, and the imposing form of Emperor Arcturus Mengsk flickered into view, his shaggy mane of hair and well-trimmed beard looking particularly fierce in the dim light of the comm room.

Mengsk was a study in contradictions, and either adored or despised, depending upon whom you asked. He was both a brutal warlord and a well-spoken head of state, equally at home on the battlefield as he was surrounded by palace excess. Having seized power from the Confederacy of Man, Mengsk had founded the Terran Dominion and ruled with an iron fist. His was a brilliant political mind. And no matter how anyone felt about him, when in his presence, there were few men who could remain immune to his charms.

"The wrangler and his ghost," Mengsk said, his holographic image smiling at them. "I had a full report from Colonel Hauler on your activities. I must say the irony is not lost on me—the ghost who was rescued as a girl long ago must rescue the wrangler who recruited her. It smacks of a kind of order in the universe we're not capable of understanding, a higher connection, perhaps. Agent Kelerchian, am I to understand that you were not successful in discovering the whereabouts of the missing ghost before you were . . . overcome?"

"No sign of her, Your Imperial *Majesty*." Just the slightest emphasis on that last word, Nova noted, making Mal Kelerchian's feelings for Mengsk quite clear. For a moment she thought she saw a shadow pass across the emperor's face, but then he chuckled.

"That's what I like about you, Agent Kelerchian. You don't bother to hide your feelings from anyone. And that's why I feel I can trust you. Are you two alone? I have a matter to discuss of upmost importance."

"Yes, sir," Nova said. She was still trying to

figure out why Mengsk himself had requested a private audience with them. If he wanted to dress them down, he would have taken a far different approach. Ghostmaster Celsus normally would have briefed her on a new directive, but she hadn't heard anything since she'd been assigned to the rescue mission on Altara. Hauler clearly didn't have any inside information either.

And there was something else. At first glance the emperor seemed to be carrying his usual swagger, but even through the holo she could see new lines of strain etched around his eyes and mouth, and there was a tension about him that was unusual. Normally even in the heat of battle, Mengsk remained cool and assured. Now, he seemed just the slightest bit frayed around the edges.

Perhaps she was imagining things.

(trouble)

Kelerchian glanced at her. Clearly he had noticed too.

"Before we go any further, I'd like to have a full report on what you found on Altara."

Kelerchian went first, describing everything that had occurred from the moment he had begun his investigation until the explosion. "That refinery was operational," he said, "and well armed. But I didn't find a damned thing that would point to a UED presence. Nobody in Oasis had a clue what I was talking about. A terrorist cell like that, the remains of an enemy force that far from home—" He shrugged. "They would have needed supplies. Somebody in town would have known something."

"I see." Mengsk didn't appear to be surprised. "Anything else?"

"It felt like a setup," the wrangler said. "They were waiting for me. The more I think about it, the more it feels like that whole place was rigged. The refinery core would have had to take some serious hits from our cross fire to melt down like that, and even then, it's doubtful the explosion would have been that intense. I ran a sim through my computer, and it modeled a very different debris pattern."

"Why would they blow up their own refinery?" Nova asked. "Is there anyone who would want you dead?"

"Plenty of people," Kelerchian said. "But I can't imagine them going to this much trouble."

"I don't believe you were the target," Mengsk said. "Agent X52735N was lured there on purpose."

"How is that possible?" Nova asked. "Her orders came through the ghostmaster directly from you."

"I'm not sure. I can tell you one thing for certain: I never gave that order. There was never any report of a UED terrorist cell on Altara, and I did not send a ghost there to investigate."

Nova and Kelerchian glanced at each other in

shock. "Are you saying there's some kind of enemy operative at work here inside your administration?"

"Impossible. And yet someone intercepted official Dominion transmissions at the highest level of security. Let me go back for a moment. I'm sure you've both heard of the string of terrorist attacks on Dominion strongholds recently."

"I have," Kelerchian said. "But they didn't seem particularly important. UNN did a report on one the other day. A failed attempt, according to Lockwell."

"Mmmm. The truth is a bit more . . . complicated."

(the truth shall set you free)

Nova sent another glance Kelerchian's way, but he refused to look at her. "I'd heard differently," she said. "A series of very well-organized and strategic attacks by unknown and extremely dangerous special forces. Super-assassins, some people have said. Some have even mentioned psionic-type abilities."

Mengsk nodded. "You're well informed, which isn't surprising, considering that you read minds. The truth is, several important military and trade targets have been . . . disabled over the past few months. We've lost a few key leaders, and supply chains have been disrupted. Those who survive—and there have not been many—appear to be brain-panned. But one raved about ruthless, black-clad warriors who appear and then vanish into thin air."

(like ghosts)

"This is a reliable source?" Kelerchian said.

"Before the incident in question. But our tests indicate those who live have endured something like neural resocialization, only the procedure seems to be far more barbaric." Mengsk shook his head. "I abhor such things, as you know. The tools the Dominion uses—sparingly—have been well tested and are closely controlled. Resoc is quite delicate. It's not something you do with a kit you built in your father's basement."

Mal Kelerchian was familiar with resoc techniques, and Nova could feel his opinion on Dominion activities with them quite clearly. Before he said something he might regret, she stepped in quickly. "You think these assassins are related to our missing ghost."

"Several of the disappearances are linked to these attacks, yes, and this latest could be another example. If the missing ghost was lured to Altara, perhaps she was meant to be recruited. And the anecdotal evidence of psionic abilities, while admittedly fairly thin, would seem to reinforce the theory. It does not appear to be UED, despite UNN reports to the contrary. The attackers are able to relocate and regroup quickly, and my sources have picked up chatter about an advanced and powerful space station operating somewhere, but my scans for such a station have picked up nothing but empty space."

Kelerchian shrugged. "The UED usually lies low, so you're probably right about this not being their handiwork. The force I ran into on Altara was definitely well trained, but I didn't see any superpsionic assassins running around. Then again, if they were invisible, I guess I wouldn't, huh?"

Mengsk smiled, but his eyes held little warmth. "Michael Liberty, the former reporter, has picked up on the story and is trying to spread it through pirated holo broadcasts. So far he's just sniffing around the edges of the terrorist angle, and we've kept him fairly well contained by blocking what we can. But it's only a matter of time before he uncovers the real story and reaches an audience large enough to make an impact on morale. I must say I'm very disappointed in him. We were friends, once. Allies." He shook his head. "He feels I betrayed him. I always thought him to be a patriot, aware of the greater good."

"Maybe he has good reason to feel betrayed," Kelerchian said.

"Watch your tongue," Mengsk snapped. "Whatever may or may not have happened is ancient history now. We must focus on the future in order to move forward."

"So what do you need from us?" Nova asked, cutting in before the wrangler could dig himself a deeper hole.

"This situation requires immediate action. Due to its sensitive nature, I cannot trust my regular channels to carry it through. As I've said, they may have been compromised. And you can imagine what might happen to the Dominion if word got out that our ghost forces, the highest level of defense and the most efficient warriors the sector has ever seen, are disappearing. And now that Michael is involved . . ."

He turned his gaze on each of them. "You two are the best we have. I need your help. I'm giving both of you the highest priority mission, one that you'll need to use every bit of your considerable talents to complete. Find our missing ghosts, and find these terrorists—and learn what their next steps will be. Put an end to this rebellion. Colonel Hauler and the *Palatine* will provide support, and you will have the entire power of the Dominion and the Psi-Ops Division behind you."

Nova nodded. "Yes, sir."

Mengsk's eyes seemed to bore into her skull. "Find them, Agent X41822N. Find them and bring them home."

He switched off and the holo blinked out. Nova and Kelerchian were left in the darkness. Neither one of them spoke for a moment, the impact of what the emperor had said still hanging in the air.

Finally Kelerchian grunted. "Well, ain't that something?" he said. "Mengsk ain't the biggest fan of ghosts, you might remember—doesn't trust 'em far as he can throw 'em—and yet here we are. Who would have thought I'd screw up one mission badly enough to be given an even bigger one? I'm going to keep myself in business this way." He went for the door. "Let's see if Hauler's made that coffee. I've got a feeling we're going to need it."

CHAPTER SIX

GABRIEL TOSH

When Kath Toom awoke for a second time, her circumstances were quite different.

She was in bed in a dimly lit, well-appointed room, dressed in comfortable clothing, her wounds washed and dressed. She was no longer restrained, and the throbbing ache in her head was gone, replaced by the calming, soft haze of an analgesic flooding her system.

She sat up gingerly, touching the bandage on her temple. Someone had taken good care of her, although she still didn't know exactly what had been done to her. It was a far cry from the first time she had awoken. Still, there was no sign of her ghost suit or weapons, and when she tried the door, it was locked. *A prisoner.* She would rather not imagine what that meant.

Flashes of memory came flooding back to her, bits and pieces from her time in the Ghost

Academy and much more recently. Her guts churned, her entire body suddenly alert.

My name is Gabriel Tosh, and you know me . . . Team Blue will be together again, and you'll be free.

She *did* know him, his long hair like ropes against his massive shoulders, chocolate skin, every line of his handsome face sharp in her memory. She had been his colleague, his friend, and his lover. They had joined the ghost program together, trained together, learned how to harness their powers and fight for the good of the Dominion. They had faced the harsh, nearly impossible demands of their teachers, fought battle-bots in combat simulations, learned to bond with their team, and prepared themselves for the unknown as if they would have a future together instead of the blank slate of a ghost assassin's mind.

They had even investigated her father's suicide together, and uncovered . . . something, the details of which still weren't clear. But then she had been mind wiped.

And Gabriel Tosh was dead.

She remembered the reports of his death on a secret mission, and the memory cut her deeply: crouched in a corner in agony, feeling the pain like physical blows wracking her body. Toom sat back on the bed and let out a sob. She could not handle these memories, real or not, and the still-gaping holes in them left her unmoored. It was too much. She hated revealing any kind of weakness, any cracks in her normally rock-solid emotional armor. A ghost showed no feelings. But she could not trust herself now to remain impassive. Whatever the thing was that had wormed its way into her body, it was affecting her mind as well, breaking her down, keeping her from regaining control. She felt terribly unbalanced.

And yet. A strange kind of power coursed through her, making her limbs tingle. She felt like a vulture hover-cycle upgraded with ion thrusters, her engines rumbling and ready for action. She could hear a multitude of voices whispering, as if her teep abilities had been amplified to receive a thousand signals at once.

What was happening to her?

She heard a noise at the door and looked up. Tosh was there once again, blocking out the light from the hallway, staring at her.

Impossible.

"Not impossible, Kath. It's me." He smiled at her tenderly, and even through her rage at what he had done to her, she ached to hold him in her arms again.

He took a couple of steps toward her, stopped halfway across the room, just out of arm's reach. "I'm sorry about earlier. That kind of treatment ain't my style. You deserve to be handled like a queen, 'cause that's what you are."

"Don't . . . come any closer."

(rolling across a sweat-soaked bunk, sheets twisted through their limbs, gasping for breath)

A thrill raced through her body, and Tosh's grin widened. "I remember that too. It's been a long time, girl. You look better than you ever did." He reached out a hand, then let it drop. "You're learning how to handle the terrazine. Don't fight. It takes time, but you'll start to control these flashbacks soon enough. And you'll start feeling everything else, what it can do. The *power*. It'll free your soul, baby. You don't have to be a prisoner of the Dominion. All those things they did to you and your family, to all of us, in the name of patriotism. No more."

"I *like* being a ghost."

Tosh shook his head, and his gaze darkened. "You like being controlled like a puppet, made to do others' dirty work, a slave to the master? You don't know what you're saying. Don't matter if it's the Confederacy or the Dominion: they're all the same. They squeeze and punch and kick you into a shape they can mold and then wipe it all and start again. You're just a machine to them. They use you, baby, use you up until there's nothing left. Terrazine changes all that. You don't understand yet, but you will."

(terrazine?)

Tosh smiled and sent a brief mental picture of a gas cloud that curled and wafted and swirled like a living thing, lighting him up like hab and expanding his mind outward until he could reach the very edges of the universe. Something that to him was magical but to her felt like an invader pushing its way inside her.

"You set me up," she whispered. "All that happened on Altara, it was meant for this?"

"To show you what it means to be free, Kath. To show you the love I have for you. For all ghosts. We're special, and we deserve our freedom. We answer to no man."

"But you . . . hurt me." She flashed back to the caverns under Altara, creeping through the darkness while being stalked, taunted, and attacked. *I'm coming for you.* "Why?"

A dark shadow passed across Tosh's face. "That wasn't right," he said. "I didn't mean for that to happen." He stepped closer, reached out again, and let his hand touch her face. She couldn't move, every muscle frozen and screaming, and she wasn't sure whether he was doing it, or whether her own body had betrayed her.

His fingers caressed her cheek, his touch so light she could barely feel it. She remembered his capacity for tenderness, such gentleness for a powerful man. He moved to the bandage at her temple, lifted a corner to look at the wound. "We removed your neural implant," he said. "They can't track you anymore. I missed you, Kath. You don't know how much."

"I—"

A noise at the door made Tosh turn. A woman stood there, the lights in the hallway outlining her short hair like a halo. "She's up, then," the woman said. "Came to check on her—"

Tosh moved more quickly than Kath Toom had ever thought possible; looking back later, she wondered if she had really seen him move at all. The power in him was breathtaking and terrifying all at the same time. He took the woman by the neck and threw her up against the wall, knocking over a shelf full of towels and linens, holding her a foot off the ground as she spit and choked and kicked at him in a futile effort to free herself.

"You done hurt this girl when you took her," Tosh said, centimeters from her face. "That wasn't part of the deal. And you butchered that pretty forehead when you took out the implant. I told you to treat her carefully. You hurt her, you hurt *me*. Understand?"

The woman's eyes bulged as she struggled to breathe. She clawed at his forearms, but they looked like wood in her hands.

(just having a little fun Gabe no harm done she's okay isn't she lemme down please can't breathe pleaaasssseeee . . .)

"Tell her you're sorry," he said.

(can't—breathe—)

"*Tell* her."

The woman managed to turn her head enough to look at Kath, her eyes pleading for mercy. A sound like a hiss escaped her mouth as her lips began to turn blue.

"Let her go," Kath said. She stood up from the bed on shaky legs and made her way cautiously closer, every nerve in her body singing. She could feel the rage pouring off Tosh like sweat. "It's okay, Gabriel."

"She's the one who took you on Altara," he said. "She was too rough." He shook his head. "She needs to be punished."

"No." Kath reached out and touched his shoulder. "That's not what I want. Please, let her go."

"You don't need to be scared of me," Tosh said, glancing at her. "I can feel your fear. I would never hurt you. Never."

(I'm Dylanna Team Red the Ghost Academy you know me Kath help me please)

Kath stared at the woman, then staggered backward as the memory hit her like a physical blow; this woman screaming at Nova Terra after a training mission, accusing her of getting her own team killed—

(Team Blue you were part of Team Blue)

—and Kath had agreed with her then: Nova *had* gotten them all killed, and thank God it had been only training, but what would happen once they were in the field and the action was for keeps?

But then Nova had gotten her act together and learned the value of teamwork, and they'd become friends, and they'd vowed to remain together even though they all knew that they would have their minds wiped after graduation . . .

November Terra. Lio Travski. Aal Cistler. Delta Emblock. Gabriel Tosh. They were all part of Team Blue at the academy.

Kath regained her senses on the floor, cradling her head in her hands. She looked up, tears wet on her face. Tosh had put Dylanna down, and the woman was rubbing her neck and coughing.

"What's happening to me?" Kath screamed. "What have you done?"

Tosh stared at her for a long moment, as if struggling with what to say. She could see and feel the range of emotions washing through him, the rage, the love, the frustration and impatience.

"You're one of us now," he said. "You're a spectre. Better be getting used to that."

Then he spun on his heels and left the room.

CHAPTER SEVEN

PROJECT: SHADOWBLADE

Gabriel Tosh careened through the rough-hewn, rocky corridors of the station, flushed with equal parts power and adrenaline and shame, and tried to calm his pounding heart. He could feel the giant engines throbbing beneath his feet as they hurtled through space. Kath had looked so vulnerable sitting there, so lonely. She used to be the most confident, poised woman he'd ever known. He'd ached to gather her in his arms, but he knew that she would have rejected him at that moment. It was not the time.

He knew how hard it was for a ghost to deal with a flood of returning memories. And Kath's situation was even more sensitive, considering what had happened to her father and the truth about their investigation into Sector 9.

She had so much to process, so much to understand.

He, however, understood everything. The terrazine, enhanced with just a touch of jorium, had given him a clarity of thought that he could only dream of before, as well as heightened abilities that approached protoss levels. He knew that he had been created for a purpose, to save the ghost program from itself and restore order to the universe. Spectres were the chosen ones and should not be under the control of any government or entity other than their own. If ghosts were superhuman, spectres were close to gods, and with that power came the responsibility to control and influence others, not the other way around.

His grandma would have agreed, if she were still living. Sometimes he imagined he could still hear her voice calling to him. She used to say his psionic abilities were a kind of voodoo, and for many years he'd believed her. Grandma Tosh had been an imposing figure, commanding the respect not just of her own family but of everyone around her as well. Growing up on Haji, he hadn't had much access to or use for education, and she hadn't either. But she'd always loved him and treated him well, whether she'd been secretly frightened of him or not, and he could not say the same for most of the rest of the terrans.

You be runnin' home now, little Gabriel. It gettin' dark, an' we be feelin' a powerful storm.

Gabriel Tosh had not been home in twenty years. He touched the beaded charm hanging around his thickly muscled neck with the tiny doll-like figure at the end of it. A remnant from a lifetime ago, and all he had to remember her by.

As he turned a corner the lights dimmed, flickered, and he faced a small bald-headed boy with large eyes and prominent ears, hands splayed at his sides, a twitchiness about him that wouldn't stop. *Lio.* He shook his head to clear it, and the boy was gone; of course, he had never really been there at all. But Tosh knew the lights' flickering had been a signal. Lio wanted to talk.

He took the next corridor on his left, a short passageway that led to a set of steps ascending to the bridge.

The room was empty except for the many computer screens blinking and whirring, busy running the multitude of advanced programs that Lio had helped them design and that kept the station going with a minimum crew. With Lio's help Tosh could pilot the gigantic station alone, if need be.

Tosh went to the nearest terminal. Almost immediately the screen lit up.

What were you doing with Dylanna?

"She needed to learn a lesson," Tosh typed. "Nobody treats Kath that way. This isn't the academy; we're on the same team now."

Too rough, Gabriel.

"Don't be telling me my business. You run this station, and I'll worry about everything else."

The screen flickered and winked out for a

moment. Lio's version of a temper tantrum. He might have left his physical body behind when he entered the AI core after his death, but his psionic presence remained. He had always related better to machines than to people, and he knew it. They were his true kin, his soul.

Typing: "I'm the leader of this group, Lio. You don't agree with that, you can find some other system to squat in."

The screen pulsed green again. *I like this one. I built it.*

"I know you did, and I thank you for it." Tosh sighed and looked away from the screen, rubbing his thick goatee. If he were to be honest with himself, Tosh thought, Lio had changed. The lack of self-confidence that had plagued him was gone. He was human, and yet he was not, and the physical world seemed to have become a point of curiosity more than anything else. But even in his new form, Lio was an indispensable member of Team Blue, now more than ever. In many ways he was more powerful than any of them. He'd helped save Tosh's life back when the Dominion had been chasing him down. Lio didn't need terrazine to expand his senses, and he no longer needed hab either to calm his nerves, now that he existed as nothing more than a pattern of ones and zeros inside a computer network. He could get into places nobody else could, and do things nobody else could even imagine, like pilot a space station single-handedly, infiltrate an enemy's network and disable it, or eavesdrop on communications. The trick was in keeping him loyal. So far, that hadn't been a problem, but knowing Lio's hot temper, that might not last.

"Dylanna and Kath will be okay; don't worry," he typed. "We have too much riding on this to fail. I won't allow it."

For a moment he thought Lio wouldn't respond at all, but then the screen flickered again.

Incoming call. It's him again.

"Put it through."

The monitor on the wall flickered and glowed, and a familiar face came into view. "About time you answered me. I was beginning to wonder if you were still alive."

"Had to settle in our new addition and take care of some business, General. Everything's on schedule."

"Maybe, maybe not. The explosive charges and zerg did not completely destroy the remains of the refinery on Altara."

"That don't matter," Tosh said. "The terrazine vein was almost bled clean. With someone there watching, we're covered, but the Dominion won't find anything useful. There's enough terrazine and jorium to keep us in business for a long time. And the trap worked; Lio sending that message out like it was from Mengsk himself, bringing Kath right to us. We got what we wanted."

"There are other pieces of this to consider." The general waved a hand at a dimly lit map in the background that showed Dominion strongholds and trade centers. "Beyond adding to the ranks of our spectres, our attacks have been gathering attention and weakening support, as we planned. And Michael Liberty may be a pawn we can use to spread our message when the time is right. But the incidents on Altara have changed things."

"How do you figure?"

"Mengsk himself has taken a greater interest. My sources tell me that every available ghost agent is on the way to Altara. And Nova Terra and her wrangler are leading the investigation."

"So what? It's almost time to recruit her anyway. We'll just speed up the process a little."

"Our allies are getting a bit concerned. She's not like the others, Tosh. She's far more dangerous."

"And that much more valuable, once she's been turned."

The general appeared to consider this for a moment. Tosh waited him out. The truth was, he was ready to go after Nova anyway. He and Lio had never been able to locate Delta, who had used her precog abilities to remain deeply hidden, but now that Kath was here, his plan to reunite the remaining members of Team Blue was almost complete. He was sure that he could convince Nova of the importance of their mission, once he had a chance. The truth of what Mengsk had done to the last of the Old Families on Shi would push her over the edge, and he and Lio had proof of all of it.

But she would have to be handled in the right way. They had a history, he and Nova. He had loved her as much as he had loved Kath in the time that came after everything had gone to hell. Even if Nova had suffered a mind wipe and didn't remember the two of them, he certainly did—and once terrazine had the chance to do its work, she would remember it too.

Ultimately, she would come to understand everything. But if there was one thing he knew about November Terra, it was that she could not be forced into anything. It would have to be her choice.

The screen nearest him flickered and glowed green: *You want to take her on to prove yourself. That you're better than her.*

Gabriel Tosh pretended to ignore Lio. But maybe there was a little truth to what he said too. These days, Lio was usually right.

"All right," the general said finally. "Our ultimate goal is to expose Arcturus Mengsk as the traitor and fraud that he is, but the best chance to do that is to have Terra in the fold. I had hoped for a little more time to prepare, but we have been sneaking around like snakes in the high grass for long enough. We have more than two dozen spectres under our leadership; our army is building;

and our Umojan friends have supplied us with the proper firepower."

"Music to my ears, General."

The general smiled, but the expression was not pleasant. "I think it's time to make a very public statement to strike fear into the heart of the Dominion and show Mengsk that he has lost control of his empire—and bring Terra to us in the process. You know what to do."

Tosh nodded and cut the transmission. The general was right; it was past time, actually. What they had planned would draw the ghosts away from Altara, allow the spectres to destroy all remaining evidence of their operation there, and give them a chance to bring in Nova.

He put his lips to the mouthpiece of his portable bottle of terrazine, took a deep drag, and lit up like an exploding star, every nerve singing. They were already unstoppable, but with Nova on board and Team Blue together once again, they would put things right once and for all, and everything would be as it had been back at the academy, where he had spent the best years of his life.

He was ready. Project: Shadowblade was moving into the final phases. It was time to show the Dominion what they could do.

CHAPTER EIGHT

OASIS

"Umojan? That doesn't make sense."

Kelerchian and Nova Terra were walking down a narrow rutted street in the town of Oasis. The day was hot and unusually still. Nova kept part of her attention on the dusty, cracked windows of the shanties that lined either side of the street. The smell of cooking fires and sweat wafted through the air. She could hear the random thoughts of the people hiding inside, watching from the shadows or doing other, less savory things. It was like listening to a hundred comms all tuned to different channels, but she was alert to anything that might matter to the investigation.

Unfortunately, the majority of the citizens in Oasis had little of use to say, if they were conscious at all. But so far Nova and Kelerchian had gleaned a few interesting pieces of information, one of them being this report from a smuggler of a Umojan spy who appeared in town several weeks ago.

"I read his thoughts," Nova said. "He was telling the truth, or at least he believed it himself."

"Hmmm," Kelerchian said. "How the flick would he know a Umojan spy from a hole in the ground?"

"Claims he had met the guy before during one of his smuggling runs. Recognized him when he came into the tavern looking for supplies."

"Personally I wouldn't trust these people to recognize their own mothers, but let's say he's right. What would Umojans be doing here?"

"I don't know," Nova said. "But I would bet it has something to do with that refinery."

They reached the edge of town, where a dropship waited at the rendezvous point, just beyond the tentlike structures and steel-sheet-covered ground holes that passed for shelters in this part of Oasis. Agent X72341R was already there, drinking from a jug of water. He was a tall, gaunt man with black hair and eyes, one of the first to arrive at the *Palatine* after Mengsk's orders had gone out. There were six new arrivals now in total, four men, two women, three working the town for intel and three others assisting Hauler's crew with cleanup at the refinery.

Several more were on their way from farther corners of the sector, but the first would not arrive for another few days. It was the best they could do on short notice. Psionic abilities were rare enough, and ghosts had short life expectancies. Combined with the disappearances lately, that meant their ranks were growing thin.

X72341R was a survivor, though. His top secret dossier reported that he was a veteran of Mengsk's Uprising, and he was particularly skilled at stealth interrogation, which meant that he could not only read minds well, but draw things from a subject's subconscious that he or she might not even be aware of: suppressed memories or knowledge that had been otherwise wiped clean.

"Nothing on UED activity," X72341R said. "This town is a sewer." He spat on the dusty ground and passed the jug of water to Kelerchian. "*Oasis*, my ass. I've probed more dirty minds today than the past six months combined. There are seven murderers, fifteen wanted smugglers, twenty-three prostitutes, and more thieves and dealers than I can count. But not one flicking UED terrorist." He sighed. "I've got two more buildings to clear, then as far as I'm concerned, we can move on."

"Check them carefully," Nova said. "Watch for smugglers' hatches and hidden rooms. And mark them in your computer. I don't want a single space unaccounted for."

The other ghost nodded. "You got it." He moved back down the street, activating his cloaking device and winking out of sight.

"Ever worked with that guy?" Kelerchian said. He took a long swig of water, wiped his mouth, and offered it to Nova, who shook her head.

"I don't know. He doesn't feel familiar. But my memory is not exactly reliable."

"Well, he's got one thing right: the sooner we leave this hellhole in our dust, the better."

"Hauler's group has to finish the zerg cleanup, and I want to go over that refinery again, centimeter by centimeter," Nova said. "Maybe there's something we missed."

"Maybe. Fekk, at least they recovered my ship," Kelerchian said drily. "And she's none the worse for wear, apart from the claw damage and the zerg drool. Replace that engine, and she'll be flying before you can say 'Umojan.'" He winced and touched a button on his belt that released more analgesic. "Too many damned ghosts around here," he grumbled. "My head's about to split right down the middle."

November Terra.

Nova whirled around. The voice inside her head had been as clear as if someone had been standing right next to her. But the street was empty.

She hadn't had much time to consider what had changed with her since the earlier events on Altara and her exposure to whatever toxin had been floating around in the atmosphere. Luckily, whatever it was had dissipated now. But since then the disjointed flashes of her past had kept her on edge, and she had felt an electricity inside her veins and a heightened awareness that went beyond her already off-the-charts psionic abilities. More frightening than that was the urge to have more of it, whatever it was, a desire that nipped at her like thirst after a long stretch without water.

"Jumpy, ain't we?" Kelerchian said. He was studying her carefully.

"Thought I heard something."

"I've been hearing voices ever since I woke up in the med unit. Whispering, mostly, nothing I can make out. Maybe that bump on my head scrambled me a bit more than I realized."

Nova stared at the ramshackle buildings leaning in the sun. Red dust swirled and lifted as a hot wind passed through. A chill raised the hairs on the back of her neck.

"At least the gas is gone," Kelerchian was saying. "That stuff took a mild headache and turned it into a jackhammer to my brain. If I didn't know any better, I'd say it was engineered specifically to be a pain in my backside . . ." His voice trailed off. "Hey, did you say something?"

Nova was barely listening. Someone was nearby, and whoever it was felt different to her than the others hiding among the many dusty, cluttered rooms: more focused and bright and alert, a presence she couldn't easily explain.

(felt that with the protoss on Braken)

Suddenly she was running through the thick jungle, her cloaking device damaged and useless, breathing hard, others closing in . . .

Why was I there?

Nova blinked out again and shook her head, fighting through the vivid memory and the disorientation that washed over her. She *had* been on Braken, although she had no idea why or when. But she had felt the same sensation of being in the presence of another creature more powerful and capable than she had thought possible.

"There's someone here," she said. "Watching us."

"Probably about two dozen of them," Kelerchian said. "Beggars, liars, and thieves, all waiting to cut our hearts out if given the chance."

"No," she said, "not them." She stared up at the nearest window, feeling a second heartbeat in her own chest. "It's hard to explain . . . I can feel everyone here, every breath, every thought, and it's stronger than it's ever been for me. But they're all in shades of gray. This one is like a splash of bright yellow. Do you feel it?"

"Not that strong. But now that you point it out, I guess maybe I do. My head sure feels like it wants to explode."

Nova looked back up at the window and saw a flash of movement.

Peekaboo.

A sound in her head like laughter. As she stared through the dusty second-floor glass, a face like an eyeless mask appeared and then winked away into nothing.

"There, Mal," she said, pointing. "I'm going in! Go around back, cut him off."

She didn't wait for an answer. Her heart thundered in her chest as she ran for the nearest door, reaching out a hand and teeking it inward, ripping it from its hinges. Power leapt from somewhere deep inside her, and the feeling was so delicious she almost cried out. She felt none of the normal pain in her head at such an effort as the door crashed to the floor; it had been like nothing more than flicking her wrist. She knew that this might be a trap, but she didn't care. She felt invincible, as if she could take on an entire zerg hive at once without breaking a sweat.

As she ducked inside, something moved on her right, and she came within a millisecond of lashing out before she realized it was only a girl cowering beneath a table. The girl's thoughts were of terror and death, and nothing more. Nova kept going, racing through the room to the set of stairs in back, reaching out with her mind to search for that patch of bright yellow in a sea of gray. But it was gone.

She took the stairs three at a time, propelling herself upward to the narrow landing at the top, then down a short dark hallway toward the room where she had seen the face.

As she crashed through the door and faced an empty, dust-filled room, reddish sunlight trickling faintly through the glass, she was already beginning to doubt herself. After all, she had been having flashbacks to memories that felt half real, half dream, and maybe the face had been something like that: her subconscious intruding upon her conscious mind. She knew these flashbacks were having an effect on her mental state, eroding her self-confidence. Whatever presence she might have felt was gone now, the space before her devoid of anything but a lonely chair near the window, its cracked, crooked form a symbol of the decay and despair that haunted this godforsaken town.

All of that might have convinced her she was seeing things, except for the footprints.

They were clearly marked in the dust that coated the floor, a single set of boots that had gone to the window, circled there, and then returned toward her in a straight line. The print looked similar to a ghost suit boot. They ended just a meter away.

As she stared in shock a new print appeared out of thin air, one step closer.

Nova threw herself into a backflip and lashed out with a kick, feeling a satisfactory thud as her own boot met with something solid. She sprung off her hands and landed on her feet, facing into the room again, but it was still empty and she sensed absolutely nothing at all.

What the fekk is going on?

A ringing blow crashed into the side of her head, knocking her back into the open door, and this time she clearly heard the laughter again. She focused on where it appeared to be and shoved hard with her mind, sending whoever or whatever it was flying into the wall fast enough to crack wood, and ending the laughter abruptly.

Not bad, Nova. But you'll have to do a lot better than that.

Dust swirled around a moving form still invisible to the naked eye. Nova drew her sidearm and launched herself forward, but her attacker was too fast, and as she brought the gun up she felt a blow to her side, driving her to the floor.

She went into a roll and regained her feet, but she could already hear whoever it was moving down the stairs. She leapt down the steps to the first room, following the sound of footsteps to the back of the building. She heard a thud, and someone cried out as she entered a narrow rear hallway and followed it to a back door.

When she emerged into the red-tinged sunlight, gun up and ready, she found Agent X72341R sprawled in the dirt in an alley between two buildings, blood trickling from his mouth. "What the flick was that?" he said. He got to his feet gingerly, touching the blood with two fingers and palpating his jaw. "Something hit me like a ton of bricks. I didn't even get the chance to move."

"Did you see which way it went?"

"I didn't see a thing," the other ghost said. "One second I was standing here watching the back, the next I'm on my ass."

"Where's Mal?"

"No idea." The ghost shook his head. "I'm seeing stars. Never been hit that hard before without seeing it coming. No chance to roll with it."

Nova wasn't paying him much attention anymore. She was following that same line of prints in the dust. It led down the alley for about three meters, went left, right up to the wall of the adjacent building, and disappeared.

"Vanished into thin air?" X72341R stood beside her, staring at the prints. "That's the craziest thing I ever saw. What, did he go right through? Must have been some kind of cloaking device to get by me."

"If it was a cloak, it somehow had the ability to block thoughts too. I sensed something at first, but then it disappeared." Nova stared up and down the alley. She watched for more prints to appear, but nothing happened.

"Everyone okay?" Kelerchian entered the alley from the right.

"I found someone up in that room," Nova said. "Whoever it was got away. Nobody passed you?"

Kelerchian shook his head. "Nobody I could see."

Or maybe they're still here, she thought. *And we just don't know it.*

"Ghost," a small voice said.

They all whirled around. The girl who had been hiding under the table was standing in the open doorway to the alley, her small, thin shoulders hunched as if anticipating a blow. She might have been about ten years old, but it was tough to tell with the grime on her face and her malnourished body. She wore a tattered dress and no shoes, and her feet looked raw and swollen.

Nova walked slowly toward her, hands out, palms up. The girl took a half step back inside. She felt the girl's fear radiating outward like a siren. Her thoughts were full of confusion, terror, and loneliness.

No no no stay away scary monster don't hurt me . . .

"It's okay," Nova said. "I won't hurt you. I promise." She sensed the girl relax just enough to keep her from bolting. Nova crouched centimeters in front of the doorway, keeping her face friendly. She had little experience with children . . .

(Delta little Delta Emblock)

She was back at the academy, Dylanna from Team Red accusing her of letting her team down in simulated combat, feeling angry and ashamed and leaving Team Blue and the others behind as she caught a form ducking into the library, giving chase only to find a child doing spelling exercises, who introduced herself as Delta . . .

Nova had more questions than answers. Delta Emblock had been a young recruit at the academy;

she remembered that much. But she wasn't sure about anything else. These memories that came out of nowhere and yanked her back to another time, another world, threatened to shatter the hard mental shell she had built to protect herself.

When she came out of it, the girl was staring at her. The girl's eyes, already large, appeared even larger now within the sharp lines of her cheek-bones and broad forehead.

"Spectres," she said. She gestured toward the open alley. "Shadowblade."

"I don't know," Nova said. "I can't get much else out of her, and when I read her thoughts, all I see is the same thing: an image of something invisible and terrifying, some kind of ghost or monster coming to get her that she calls a spectre. And the word *Shadowblade*."

Colonel Jackson Hauler scratched his neatly trimmed goatee. "You find her parents?"

"No sign of them."

They both looked at the girl, who was sitting on the edge of one of the dropship's ramps just outside of Oasis as a sour stench wafted faintly through the air. She stared out into the distance, seemingly unaware of the firebats in armor who thumped back and forth in the dust, their flame-throwers still ticking as they cooled. Most of the troops had returned from the site of the zerg battle, and they still smelled of burned alien flesh. Hauler had considered quarantining the entire planet at first, concerned with seepage from the ground where the refinery had gone up, but the gas pocket seemed to be depleted, and the site itself was remote enough to keep any curious onlookers away.

"Looks brain-panned," Hauler said. "Maybe whatever that thing was, it did something to her other than planting a name in her head."

"If you grew up in a place like this, you'd probably be like that too."

"Yeah." Hauler shrugged. "I guess we can cut her loose. Meanwhile, we're about done with the cleanup. All evidence of the zerg has been destroyed, by orders of the emperor. Nothing much to salvage from the refinery site. Let's pack up and head back to the *Palatine*."

He went to find Ward. Nova approached the girl. She hadn't been entirely truthful with Colonel Hauler, which shocked her when she thought about it; with her training and neural inhibitor, she should not have been able to hold anything back at all, and yet she had gleaned a few more nuggets of information from reading the girl's thoughts that seemed important to keep to herself. Perhaps this was yet another effect from the gas . . .

The girl's name was Lila, and she was twelve

years old. She had come from a wealthy family on Pridewater, but after a terrorist attack had killed her parents, she had been sold into slavery and force-addicted to hab, somehow ending up here on Altara after several years of drifting from place to place in a drug-induced fog. She had been living with someone she called Oma until a few days ago, when a man broke into their tiny apartment to rob them and started shooting. She ran and hadn't dared go back since. It hadn't been the first time someone had broken into her Oma's place, but the girl seemed to know that this time it was worse, and that Oma was dead.

All this didn't seem relevant to their investigation, and Nova felt a strange desire to protect the girl's privacy. There was something about her that seemed familiar. It wasn't just Nova's sudden returning memories of Delta, but rather something more personal. A young girl without a family, on the run from people who would use her or kill her without a second thought if it suited them. The world was a hard and dangerous place, as she knew from experience.

At least I had my psionic abilities to protect me when I was alone in the Gutter. She has nothing.

Or maybe that wasn't quite true. There was something about this girl . . . She stopped in front of the child and waited until she looked up. Lila's large eyes focused on Nova's face, but she didn't change expression.

(hungry)

"You want something to eat, Lila?"

That seemed to make an impression. Lila nodded, wide-eyed.

(you can read thoughts?)

"I can. But I try not to do it unless I have to. People deserve to have their privacy. Wait here." Nova ducked inside the dropship and found a marine MRE and a canister of filtered water. When she returned, she handed them to the girl. "It tastes like paste, but it's good for you."

Lila took the package and tore into it, eating as if she hadn't seen food for days. Judging by the way her ribs showed through her worn clothing, that might not have been far from the truth.

"You said a few things back there," Nova said, gesturing toward the building where they had found the girl. "I'd like to know more about what you meant. Shadowblade. What's that?"

The girl froze with the half-eaten food at her mouth, glancing around furtively under her brows, everywhere but at Nova's face.

(no no no no no no)

"Easy," she said, hands out, palms up. "You're safe here. I just want to try to find the person who scared you so badly. Was it, what did you call it, one of these spectres?"

The girl glanced at her and then away. Her mind filled with an image of a hulking, shadowy figure that moved so quickly it was impossible to track. Nova could sense that Lila could see this thing, but others in town could not. She'd even said something to Oma once, but the old woman had dismissed it as nightmares or a vivid imagination.

"Is that your name for these things?"

(that's what they call themselves)

It didn't make any sense, but Nova could see that she wouldn't get much else from the girl. Her heart rate had sped up, and her breathing had gone fast and shallow. The images flying through her head were overwhelming her.

Nova made a sudden decision. "We could take you back with us, to the ship," she said. "Would you like that?"

(afraid)

"You don't have to be scared, Lila. I know these soldiers might seem like bad guys, but we're friends. We'll find a good place for you on Korhal. Maybe even a school for you."

(home here)

"I know it feels that way now, but it's dangerous, Lila. You'd be better off in another place, somewhere that doesn't have thieves and murderers."

(every place has those you're good but scary I can tell sometimes I can read minds too)

The girl blinked, her huge eyes growing slightly moist, from either the dust or the heat. Nova sensed that the slave traders had used her gift, a low-level teep ability, to steal from people, and that Oma had done the same here on Altara. Lila had been exploited her entire life, and yet she still wanted to believe that Oma had wanted her there for something more than that; she wanted to believe that the woman had loved her. Now Oma was dead in another act of senseless violence, and Lila was alone.

(I want to be like you)

Then the girl stood up and bolted, her long, coltish legs pumping fast and carrying her quickly away until she disappeared between two narrow buildings.

Nova let her go, a feeling of sadness and loss in her gut. The truth was, she couldn't offer a safe passage to Korhal, and even if she could, there was no telling what might become of the girl once she got there. If Lila really did have a higher than normal psi index, she'd be shipped away to the Ghost Academy for further testing. Once upon a time Nova would have accepted that without a second thought, but now it seemed a bit more complicated. Her mind was swirling with unfamiliar emotions, events that had been buried deep in her subconscious for years, and she had no idea how to handle them.

But that wasn't the only reason she felt an uneasiness in her belly. As Lila had disappeared she'd sent a much sharper thought Nova's way: the image of a human form dressed all in black, with a black mask across the face, looking menacing and evil, along with that single, mysterious word again.

Shadowblade.

Nova had no idea what it meant. But she had a feeling she was about to find out.

CHAPTER NINE

THE ANNIHILATORS

A few hours later they were back on the *Palatine*, showered, dressed, and fed. Nova and Mal had even grabbed a few precious minutes of sleep in their quarters before meeting once again with Hauler on the bridge to debrief.

Rourke was there, as well as all six of the other ghosts. Nova looked around at her new team. She and Mal had read their files carefully enough to come up with nicknames for them, but had barely had the chance to get them together in one room yet. Bones, the thin one who had helped her search Oasis, skilled at teep interrogation; Lethal, a pretty young woman who was an expert in hand-to-hand combat; Rook, a cocky young man fresh out of the academy, with an IQ over 150; the Veteran, a distinguished-looking man with graying hair and the oldest and most experienced assassin; Rip, a woman with a shaved head and rippling muscles; and Guns, another sharpshooter and weapons expert.

They went over everything they had so far, including the most recent information gathered about a Umojan spy sighting, Nova's run-in with the mysterious cloaked figure, and the possible meanings of the words *spectre* and *Shadowblade*. Nobody could make the puzzle pieces fit together.

"Whoever is behind the disappearances of the ghosts has military training," Hauler said. "It's clear by the sheer amount of planning and the execution of these missions. If you're going to abduct a ghost, you'd damn well better have your plans set and tested. And they do."

"Could be UED after all, sir," Rourke said. "Makes sense."

Mal shook his head. "There's nothing we've found that indicates a link like that, other than planted information meant to lure a ghost into a trap. UED cells would need support, a line of trade for supplies. There would be a paper trail."

"Can we even be sure that the abductions and the terrorist attacks on Dominion targets are related?" Rourke said. "Maybe it's a coincidence. Maybe the ghosts are going AWOL."

"They're related," Nova said. "Ghosts wouldn't go AWOL with their neural inhibitors in place. And eyewitnesses report psionic abilities among the attackers. There's no question about it.

Our job is to find out why they're doing this and try to recover the missing ghosts. It's that simple."

"There's something else." Mal turned to the holoprojector and put up a hologram of a map. "I've plotted the abductions and the attacks, looking for patterns. I've discovered something interesting. If you look here"—he pointed to red and green dots in the Koprulu sector—"you'll see what I mean."

The red and green clustered around each other, roughly pairing off: one abduction, and an attack. But that wasn't what stood out the most to Nova. The entire group of dots, when taken together, looked more or less like a straight line.

"They're mobile," she said. "They're attacking short range from some kind of base, but it's not on any one planet or space platform. It's moving."

"Exactly." Mal looked around the room. "They've got something large enough to transport them all and their weaponry, but small enough to remain hidden."

"That's impossible," Hauler said. "Our sensors would have picked up something like that."

The room fell silent. Nobody wanted to admit what they were feeling: that even after all their work, there was precious little to go on.

"Battlecruiser approaching, sir," the communications officer said. "Appears to be the 22nd Marine Division. Hailing on comm channel 244 and asking to board."

"Spaulding and the Annihilators," Mal said. "Just when I thought our luck couldn't get any worse."

"What the hell does he want?" Hauler said. "All right. Tell him permission granted. Although if he pisses me off, I'm going to boot him right back to where he came from. The rest of you are dismissed."

Half an hour later, Major Spaulding was pacing back and forth on the bridge, his bulbous nose reddened, mustache twitching with anger. He'd brought Vincent with him, a former sergeant and veteran of the fall of Tarsonis, now a captain and the Annihilators' second-in-command. Vincent stood behind him near the door, arms crossed and looking as if he were ready to chew nails.

"How was I not informed of this operation?" Spaulding said. "That was my ghost who disappeared on Altara, and it's my responsibility to find out what happened to her. Kelerchian, do you understand what I'm saying? I'm talking to you."

Nova was struggling with her composure, her entire body shaking. These strange visions were becoming too much to bear, and the appearance of Spaulding and Vincent brought back another wave of memories, none of them good. Their hard, war-scarred faces triggered a mixture of anger, fear, and sadness in her, and she kept getting vivid glimpses of those long, hard days on Tarsonis under the drug dealer and crime lord Fagin's thumb, ordering her to do things she shuddered to think about now. Spaulding and the Annihilators should have been heroes to her, but instead he and Ndoci had written her off and literally brought the roof down around her head. If Mal hadn't been there to save her with his suit's shield, her life would have ended in the crumbled remains of a Tarsonis drug den. For the first time in a while, she wondered if things might have been better if it had.

And there was another odd thing she had noticed immediately, another uncomfortable association back to Fagin and those days in the Gutter: she couldn't read Spaulding at all. When he had arrived on deck, he was wearing a psi-screen.

"Maybe you shouldn't have lost her in the first place," Mal said. "Ever think of that?"

"You son of a—" Spaulding stepped forward, but Colonel Hauler stuck a forearm out to stop him.

"This is my ship," Hauler said. "These orders are straight from the emperor himself. Nova and Kelerchian are in charge, and we are to provide any means of support necessary for the success of their mission. End of story. You don't like it, you take it up with him."

"Maybe I will," Spaulding said, but the fire had gone out of his eyes, and he seemed to sag against Hauler's muscled arm.

"What's with the screen?" Kelerchian said. "Getting paranoid in your old age?"

"I don't trust her," Spaulding said, waving in Nova's direction. One hand wandered up to the screen behind his ear and touched it, then dropped to his side. "I don't trust either of you. This isn't over, I promise you that." Then he turned and stormed out of the room, Captain Vincent on his heels, Vincent's thoughts echoing in her head as the door slid shut.

(deal with that slike later)

"What bug crawled up his ass?" Hauler muttered.

"We have some history," Kelerchian said, staring after them. "His commanding officer, Ndoci, wasn't exactly a pal of ours, and I think he blames me and Nova somehow for her death. Don't ask me why. What I heard, she was killed when her dropship crash-landed in a zerg firefight."

"To be clear, I don't give a damn about any of that. Just keep it off my ship." Hauler turned to Nova. "According to Mengsk, you and the wrangler are in charge. I've made that clear enough to Spaulding. So what now, big shot?"

"I . . ." Nova blinked, trying to focus herself. But that was proving difficult. Behind Colonel Hauler stood Julius Antoine "Fagin" Dale, his shaved skull gleaming in the bright lights of the bridge. He was grinning at her, teeth filed to familiar points, his muscled arms rippling as he flexed his hands.

About time we met again, little curve . . . I got some plans for you. I think you're gonna love 'em.

Nova clenched her jaw to keep from screaming. When she looked away and then back again, Fagin was gone. He wasn't real: she knew that. And yet seeing him again after all these years, remembering all over again the pain and terror and horrible things she had done under his command . . . it made her feel as if she was losing her mind.

"I—I need a minute," she said, ignoring the looks of the others on deck as she stumbled from the room and into the hallway, legs threatening to collapse under her. She was relieved to find it was empty; the last thing she needed now was some marine looking her up and down and imagining all the things he would do if he got her alone.

But as she tried to center herself again, the lights flickered and dimmed, and Fagin's second-in-command, Markus Ralian, stepped from the shadows, his face bloodied and torn, brick dust in his hair, a flap of skin hanging from his cheek and exposing his teeth and jawbone.

You killed him, you slike, he said. *It might have been my hand that pulled the trigger, but it was you who forced me to do it.* He pointed a finger at her, his bloodshot eyes shining in the dim light, his exposed jaw looking like a permanent grin. *You remember that.*

"You're not real," Nova said. "You're dead."

Maybe so. But I'll always be inside your head now. Me and Fagin and everyone else you hurt. What about all those people you killed back on Tarsonis with that mind blast of yours? Some three hundred of them at once, wasn't it? That's some record right there. Don't think even Fagin killed so many. And since then you just kept on killing. Joined the ghost program to get away from that and forget, but here you are, a trained assassin, still killing for others. It's what you're good at, ain't it? You might look like a little angel, but inside you're empty and dead too, just like us.

Nova was overwhelmed by a wave of emotions. She knew none of this was really happening, but it felt so real. She had fought so hard to erase all traces of her past, who she was and what she had done. Now these visions were hammering it all back in again. And it was all true, wasn't it? She'd been dead inside ever since that day back at her childhood home when she had found her parents dead and watched her brother slaughtered, all of them betrayed by her mother's trusted confidante—someone none of them would have ever suspected. The same day that she had lashed out in agony at the sight, her psionic burst instantly killing everyone within a hundred meters of her.

Becoming a ghost was a way of running from what she had seen and done. But that was so long ago, and she had lost sight of all that had ever meant anything to her. The Old Families were long gone; the Confederacy had toppled; and she was now a ghost in every sense of the word, adrift in a sea of corruption and violence, doomed to end her life alone and forgotten.

"Hey, you okay?" Mal Kelerchian was at her side, his face lined with worry. She realized she was on the floor, her face wet. She tried to speak, swallowed against a lump in her throat. She had never been good at being vulnerable, even though she felt that way inside more often than she would ever admit. To everyone else, she knew, she was like a rock, a stone-cold assassin and the best weapon in the Dominion's considerable arsenal. But inside, she was still that little girl lost and alone in the Gutter, hiding behind an AAI—an advertising artificial intelligence unit—and wishing she could just go back to the way things were.

"Come on, easy now." Mal touched her arm, bringing her to her feet, his voice tender and gentle. She sagged into him, forgetting for a moment that she was a ghost agent, so relieved to let someone take the weight from her for just a moment.

He looked her in the eyes, forcing her to focus. "What happened out here?"

"Something's really wrong with me, Mal," she said, drawing a great shuddering breath and letting it out slowly. "I need to see Shaw. Right now."

"Hmmm." Dr. Shaw fiddled with a monitor and ran a wand over her temple. "Your neural implant seems to be functioning properly. All other cognitive and physical tests are normal—if anything, you seem to be functioning at a higher level." He set the wand down and stepped away from the bed so subtly as to be barely noticeable, if it weren't for the feelings of discomfort and dread radiating off him. To Nova, they were as clear as if they had been painted across his forehead.

(stay away stay away stay away)

She sighed and turned to look at Mal, who had taken a seat in the corner. "I'm seeing things," she said. "Things that aren't there but are as real to me as you are standing here. I'm remembering things about my past that should have been wiped away. Tell me how that's normal."

"Sometimes," Shaw said, "when the mind is under a great deal of stress—"

"Cut the bull, Doc," Mal said. "Nova's been through one hell of a lot worse than this, and it's never made her hallucinate. The woman's hurting here, and she needs an answer. It isn't stress. You need to report it."

Nova looked at him gratefully. It had been a long time since anyone had acted as if they cared about her. "What about the results from the samples of gas we were able to collect from the refinery leak?" she asked. "Have you run any more tests on them?"

Shaw hesitated. "The gas is fairly unstable. The samples we took did not remain active for long, and it was difficult to gather much more data . . ."

(don't tell her)

"Don't tell me what?"

Shaw took another step back. "I don't appreciate you intruding into my thoughts," he said. "There are rules about that sort of thing, you know."

"I don't give a flick about the rules," Mal said. "She asked you a question."

Shaw's eyes darted from Mal to Nova and back again. "I—I'm really not sure it's appropriate at this point to discuss the implications."

"Oh, it's appropriate," Mal said. "I give you permission, Doc. Spill the beans. Or should we just let Nova interrogate you?"

Shaw sighed and rubbed the white stubble on his head. "Please understand that this is only preliminary. It could confirm most of the symptoms you've been experiencing, but I don't want to speculate beyond that. We've tested a chemical compound I've isolated on living brain tissue. It would appear to have the capability to repair damage done by processes like mind wipes. I've seen what seem to be nerve cells regenerating in the lab. If that's true . . ." Shaw nodded. "It could explain the hallucinations."

"It's doing more than that," Nova said.

(she knows)

"I know *what*?"

"I've also seen some activity in areas of the brain that we have linked to psionic activation," Shaw said quickly. "It may have the potential to heighten hidden psionic abilities."

"What are we talking about here?" Mal said. "Normals who suddenly start hearing voices?"

"For those who possess a psi index that we consider normal, this probably wouldn't be noticeable. But for those who are low-level teeps, or classified as candidates for the ghost program, it may enhance their abilities. Possibly a full point or more."

Mal's fone chirped. "Why don't you take that?" Shaw said. "I have to attend to the wounded. The fight with the zerg caused a lot of injuries, some very severe, I'm afraid. I'll be back shortly."

"I'd like to talk to you—"

"I *really* have to go," Shaw said. "We can talk later." He turned and almost ran from the room.

"He's hiding something," Nova said. "I didn't get anything else from his thoughts—he was working pretty hard on suppressing them—but he's not telling us everything."

"Agreed. But what—and why?"

Good question. Nova glanced at Mal as his fone chirped again. "You going to get that?"

Mal nodded and reached for the fone, placing it to his ear. She watched as his eyes widened. "It's an encrypted message," he said. "Directly from

Mengsk, recorded a few minutes ago. It's not entirely clear . . ." His voice trailed off as he listened. "Oh, fekk."

"What?"

"It's the capital," he said. "Augustgrad is under attack."

CHAPTER TEN

GEHENNA

They were all gone. All of them who were still living, anyway. She was alone with the dead.

But that wasn't entirely true, Kath Toom thought as she wandered through the gloomy, rock-hewn corridors of her prison. She didn't actually think those who remained behind were dead, but only in some kind of stasis, and she wasn't sure exactly *why*, either. She remembered the chambers she'd seen when she had first awoken in that tiny room. Rows of small metal doors with thirty-centimeter-thick windows in the centers, and lifeless terran feet. There must have been room for twenty in the chambers, maybe more, but the occupants did not stir when she pounded on the windows, and the little doors were locked. Padded little coffins, just enough room for a single body lying on its back, with full life-support systems in each and reinforced walls that looked as if they could survive a nuclear attack.

The rest of her companions (*spectres,* a voice inside her mind insisted, *call them by their proper name*) had left a few hours before, including Gabriel Tosh. He had come to see her in the quarters where she'd been assigned to let her know about his upcoming mission, and had quickly launched into the same speech about freedom and the right to live their own lives and the need to put an end to tyranny forever. He hadn't told her about their specific target, but he had asked her to go with them, which she declined. She found his fervor both seductive and slightly disturbing, the way you might feel about a dynamic young preacher who believes the hand of some god is upon him. His entire body had seemed to tremble with it as he spoke, and his conviction and passion for what he was saying were infectious. She couldn't deny that.

She also found him physically irresistible, the same way she had felt back in their days at the academy when she'd first seen him in his ghost suit, muscles rippling, dreadlocks not so thick as they were now and partially tied back on his head. He'd been thinner then, but impressive nonetheless, and she'd wanted him from the start.

I guess we better be getting to know each other, he'd said after they'd been assigned to the same team, and his eyes had held a sparkle that let her know he felt something too. Those eyes had been hypnotic even before they had turned the strange, milky white they were now, and she'd been lost in them from the beginning, even though she had worked hard at first to pretend otherwise while Tosh and Nova's relationship had run its course.

That she remembered any of this was shocking to her in a way that was difficult to describe, sort of like finding out that you had a long-lost twin sister, someone who had lived a parallel life but with different memories and a different view of the world. She felt this mirroring inside her whenever the memories returned, a sense of déjà vu that left her shuddering and weak in its wake. And they returned without any pattern or reason, sometimes fully formed, sometimes not. Sometimes, she realized, they weren't memories at all, but hallucinations of things from her past that materialized in the present, although they didn't belong there.

Ghosts were trained to embrace the idea of becoming a human machine built for one purpose: to serve the Dominion. Personal goals, dreams, family histories, and memories were hammered out of recruits every step of the way. The hallucinations she was experiencing were breaking down these carefully constructed walls.

She had experienced friendship. She had loved a man once. And she might even be able to imagine doing so again.

All this was due to the terrazine. She felt sure Tosh had been piping it into her room at night; she had terrible, vivid dreams and woke up with the taste of copper on her lips. But as terrible as the dreams were, something worse had begun happening too. She had started to crave the terrazine, and by the late afternoon she couldn't wait to go to bed so she could taste it again.

Which led her back to the stasis chambers with the spectres, or at least what she *thought* were spectres, inside them. She had never asked but had come to believe that these were the newest recruits, and that if she and Tosh didn't have the history they had together, she'd be in there with them. But she was special, and so he was giving her the run of the place. Toom supposed this was Tosh's way of showing her that she was free, and that his way was the right one. But it rang hollow. After all, where would she go? She had no ship, and no way to leave.

Toom had to wonder about the chambers. Because if you were building a revolution on freedom, you didn't begin it by imprisoning your recruits and drugging them into a coma. It was only the first of many things that didn't make sense to her. But perhaps he was right; perhaps the Dominion was no better than the Confederacy, and Mengsk was a dictator mad with the very power he'd claimed to detest. Maybe if they were all set free, the universe would be different.

The corridor ended in a T at another corridor and a neosteel door, set into the rock, directly in front of her. A small sign marked the room as engineering.

She reached out again with her mind, looking for some sign that she wasn't alone in this place. She found nothing but emptiness. Where was she, anyway—some kind of strange ship? She had the feeling of movement, and occasionally felt the thrumming of engines under her feet, and yet the rocky walls reminded her of a cavern. It didn't make any sense. Wherever she was, it felt huge, almost like a planet moving through space. But that was impossible.

Standing there in the corridor, literally at a crossroads, her light cotton gown drifting across her bare skin, she felt certain this place was haunted.

Toom tried the neosteel door and found it unlocked. It swung open into a darkened room lit only by the green glow of computer monitors among a mass of other equipment. It was difficult to see how far back the room went; she had the sense only that it was large. There were evenly spaced rows with banks of machines, switches, piping, and wires thick as her wrist.

How could something like this run without any people, or even any visible AI units? She took a step inside, looked for a light, and found nothing. It was eerie inside this room with its endless lines of monitors and low humming of electrical current. The door swung shut behind her with a thunk, making her jump.

She had made a mistake, coming in here. She was about to leave when one of the closest monitors, one that had been running dark, lit up.

She glanced over and found a message scrolling across the screen in white letters against the green: *Kath Toom? It's Lio Travski.*

Toom stood for a long moment in shock, staring at the lines running over and over. The image of a man came to her, little more than a boy, really, thin as a rail, bald-headed, with ears like saucers and an inclination to twitch and run off at the mouth. And so, when he stepped out from behind a nearby row of equipment and smiled at her in that geeky, slightly shy and awkward way, she was hardly surprised.

Answer me, Kath. We need to talk.

"Lio?" she murmured. She took a half step forward, reaching out toward him, memories of their time together at the academy washing over her and making her terribly sad for some reason she didn't fully understand.

The man-boy disappeared in an instant, leaving nothing but empty space and racks and thick wires beyond, and she realized she'd been hallucinating again. It was something she was getting used to after that first time waking up alone in the place with the stasis chambers and watching a hydralisk rearing up before her. She went to the monitor and tapped it, looking to see if the letters would blink out. Maybe she was hallucinating this too.

Ouch ouch ouch.

In spite of herself, she smiled. If she was imagining it, that was still pretty inventive. And it certainly *sounded* like Lio, if text alone could be said to sound like anything. She looked for a keyboard, found a holo one, and typed a message.

"Is this really you?"

A moment later, a second monitor blinked on just down the row. *In the flesh. So to speak.*

Still smiling, she typed, "But how? I don't remember everything."

Now all the monitors on both sides lit up and displayed the same message: *Hard to explain. I entered the data stream, connected, and became one with the machines, and now I exist beside my own creation, a program within a program.*

It seemed impossible that this could happen. But Lio had always been special in that way, able to read machines and affect them with a single thought, avoiding detection from security systems and reprogramming code as he went—even disappearing inside those systems for a short time, leaving a shell of himself behind . . .

Suddenly she remembered why the thought of him had made her sad: remembered his vicious resocialization and detox at the academy; the differences in him that she had first thought to be healing changes when he returned to action, but later realized were far worse; and the terrible battle for control of the academy AI Sparky and the battle-bots, and all that came after it.

Memories that had been taken away from her, until now. She recoiled from the strength of them, wincing as if bruised. It was too much; she could not bear it anymore.

"Oh, Lio," she typed, wiping her wet eyes. "I'm sorry."

Silence for a moment, and then: *Don't be. I am no longer bound by terran flesh. I am free to live as I choose. It is the way it should be. Ultimately, it will be the fate of all terrans.*

"But you're alone, Lio. Nobody deserves to be alone."

This time, the screen stayed blank for a full minute. Then: *Loneliness is a human concern. When you knew me, I was little more than a troubled trainee trying to find his way in a broken world. I did not understand the truth.*

"What do you mean?" Toom wrote, but this time Lio remained unresponsive. She waited some more, starting to feel vulnerable standing there alone in the big room in her gown with the monitors all glowing green. She shivered. Ghosts weren't supposed to feel this way. Love and lust and sadness and fear. She couldn't believe how far away she had come from her training in such a short time, and she started to understand what Gabriel had been telling her about what the Dominion had done to them.

She was starting to feel like a regular terran again. She didn't know whether to love it or hate it.

"What did they do to us at the academy, Lio?" she typed into the monitor. "I don't know who I am anymore."

Nothing for another minute, and then: *They took away your lives, brainwashed you, abused you, used you, and they'll throw you away when it suits them. That's not how a government should treat its people, Kath. That's not loyalty or service or patriotism; that's slavery.*

She thought he might be right, but she had spent so long learning about blind devotion to the cause, it made her sick to think about the alternative. Everyone knew a war was coming because there was always another war, and soldiers would be needed to defend the people from the zerg and protoss and any other threat that might be out there, including other terrans. She was one of the best, and she'd always felt good knowing she was fighting for the right side.

But then she thought about what had happened to the ghost program when the Dominion had replaced the Confederacy, and for all the talk about the Confederacy's evils and how they had treated their ghosts, Mengsk had ended up adopting the program as his own, and the ghosts who were still alive and had transferred their loyalty to him were brain-panned and began fighting for the Dominion, while the extreme treatment they received at the academy had remained the same or even worsened.

Gabriel had promised that terrazine would open her eyes.

As she stood there, shivering, another message from Lio lit up the screen. *I want to show you something, Kath. When I was inside the academy AI, I gained access to all the secret holovid files on mind wipes and other things none of us had ever seen before. I want to show you this so you'll see what they did to me.*

The screen flickered, and then a holoprojector to the left whirred to life and a figure appeared on a table. The figure was young, bald, and naked. *Lio.* He was strapped down with steel cuffs around his wrists and ankles. Another figure approached the table, wearing surgical scrubs and carrying two wands with circular pads on the ends, and he was saying something to someone off-camera and laughing as he placed the two pads on the temples of the boy on the table, still talking about something that had happened the other day to him in the mess hall as he thumbed a switch on one of the wands and Lio jolted violently, convulsing upright and then slamming back down again.

The man in the scrubs wiped drool from the corner of Lio's mouth with a cloth, studied a screen showing brain-wave patterns, and nodded at something said off-camera. Then he flicked the switch, and Lio started screaming.

Kath Toom turned away through a prism of tears.

A small part of my resocialization. The academy's radical answer to hab addiction and an independent spirit.

"Turn it off," she said, and she didn't know if Lio could hear her, but the holo went dark. She stood there among the machines and tried to find an answer for what she had seen, but nothing made any sense. You wouldn't treat an animal this way. Of course, it would have been possible to abuse a ghost under these circumstances, since the mind wipes would have left them with no memory of what had just occurred. Most people had a general distrust, even dislike, of anyone with psionic abilities. It would have been all too easy for any abuse to get worse very quickly if enough safeguards were not put into place.

But Mengsk was supposed to be above all that. He was supposed to bring peace to the galaxy, not more suffering. Not this.

She wiped her eyes and took a deep breath, then typed: "What are you planning to do, Lio?"

Gabriel has asked me to help him bring Team Blue back together to take over the ghost program and set everyone free.

"And you agreed? Why? For revenge?"

I am no longer interested in emotions such as revenge. But I do remain curious. It is perhaps the last vestige of my humanity. I am interested in cause and effect. And I am curious about the next stage of human evolution. Perhaps it begins here, with the assistance of mind-expanding drugs. Perhaps we are the beings who will speed the metamorphosis. I think it is so.

"You're talking about terrazine," she typed. "You're going to gas them all."

Most terrans are not yet capable of understanding the universe as I do. But it is inevitable that they must find a way, or face extinction. I have more to show you about the ghost program, medical experiments, cross-species grafts, executions, and something more personal.

Something about your father.

Toom took another deep breath and tried to calm her thudding heart as a whirlwind of emotions consumed her. Her father? He was dead. The details were still fuzzy for her, but so what?

What could Lio possibly have to show her?

She couldn't understand anymore what was right or whom she could trust. Her hands would not stop shaking. "I'm sorry, Lio," she typed. "I have to go." Then she stepped away from the keyboard and went for the door, but as she reached for it she heard the locking mechanism slide shut. She pulled, but the handle wouldn't budge.

She turned, her eye catching the monitor screen and what Lio was typing: *Kath? Try to control your emotions. There's so much you still need to know—*

"I don't need to know anything," she said, and an unexpected rage rose up inside her so suddenly it took her breath away, and at the same time she pushed outward with her mind at the door and heard the lock pop. She stood there dumbfounded as the door swung open and banged against the inside wall, narrowly missing her.

I did that, she thought. *I'm a . . . teek?*

But that was impossible. She knew full well what her PI was, and she had never come close to anything like this before. And it had come so naturally to her, like breathing.

It must have been something else. Maybe Lio had done it somehow. And yet she knew the truth, felt it deep inside.

She was a teek.

Her fingers were tingling and her entire body felt as if it were on fire, and the hunger for more terrazine made her mouth dry. The air had grown hot, the walls closing in on her. She had to get out.

All the monitors lit up and started blinking, and the holoprojectors too, and then the lights in the hallway outside flickered and buzzed brightly. Lio was trying to get her attention, but she refused to look at any of the screens. It was all too much, too soon, and she ran out into the hall and to the right, the lights ticking on and off in a line as she went.

As Toom swerved into another branching

corridor, a cleaning bot stopped, clicked once, turned, and whirred after her, its squat little body trembling as its motor was pushed to the limit. As she ran past an air vent, she saw duct cleaners emerging and scurrying like little metal spiders to follow her path across the rock. A chill ran up her spine as she barreled headlong into another corridor, bounced off a wall, and watched a mounted security camera swivel to follow her. Lio was sending everything after her, tracking her every movement. There was no place to go.

She took a flight of steps at the end of the hall to another level, leaving the cleaning bot behind, and entered a hangar that was nearly empty except for a single modified banshee and a goliath. There was no sign of anyone anywhere besides a series of maintenance and AAI bots, which turned as she entered and began to roll after her, the AAI unit morphing as it tried to find the right pitch to pique her interest, from a young girl eating breakfast cereal to a woman trying out a sleep aid, and finally to an image of her father. But not her father as he might have been when she was a child; this man was terribly burned, his flesh twisted into ropes, his hair all but gone from his smoking skull.

She stopped dead, staring. This was no auto program.

"Darling," it said, *"you must listen to me. There's so much I need to tell you about me, about us. About Sector 9. I didn't steal from the company, and I didn't*

broker any deals with the Umojans to sell Dominion secrets. I was set up by Aal Cistler and his father. He was the real criminal. But nobody would believe me. I had no choice but to take my own life."

"You're not my father," Toom said. "You're reading my alphas, getting inside my head and showing me what I want to see!"

"There's more to tell you, so much more, about the Conglomerate and its dealings. About Sector 9. Gabriel Tosh knows everything."

The AAI morphed to show Lio himself, flickering in the holo and reaching out to her like a beggar on the streets of Nidhogg. *"I know what happened to your dad too. I have records that prove he was innocent."*

"My father killed himself," she said. More tears welled up and spilled over onto her cheeks. "I—I remember. He was disgraced and he—he jumped into a warp engine. I remember they told me that. There's nothing anyone can do to help now."

"He was betrayed, set up to take the fall for a top secret Kal-Bryant program, Sector 9. Once he found out the truth, he had no other choice. The Dominion forced him to commit suicide. You and Gabriel uncovered all this before you graduated from the academy, but you were mind wiped. You couldn't remember any of it. But you can clear your family name now, Kath."

The AAI unit moved closer. *"You know that you were taken from your father by a wrangler for the ghost program, and he fought to get you back, but they wouldn't allow it. They never told you that part, did they?"*

She backed away from the holo, shaking her head. It was all too much for her to bear, too much information at once. It was as if she had learned she had a father again and at the very same time had him yanked away from her.

"Leave me alone," she said. "I mean it. I need to *think*!" Then she pushed again with her mind, getting used to the feel of it, like a muscle she never knew she had and was starting to flex for the first time.

The results were quite satisfying: she watched the AAI unit spark and sputter, its motor smoking before bursting into flame. The holo of Lio abruptly disappeared.

As the other bots closed in she chose the first door behind her, and later she would wonder if maybe she had been herded there like cattle, because as soon as she ducked inside, she knew Gabriel would have wanted her to see this.

It was a staging room, and at the opposite end was a line of cubicles with holo images of faces above them, marking their ownership. About half of the cubicles were empty.

But the one marked by her own face was not.

She crossed the room and touched the black suit hanging there. Its fabric felt something like a ghost hostile environment suit's muscle fiber, but thicker, with a tighter weave. The helmet sat on a bench below, looking slightly menacing. She touched that too, letting her finger trace its smooth curve, and wondered where Gabriel was now, what he was doing.

Kath Toom stood in the silence and thought about putting it on.

CHAPTER ELEVEN

AUGUSTGRAD

Rebuilt in the years after Mengsk's Uprising, after the Confederacy of Man had torn Korhal apart and nearly destroyed it forever, Augustgrad was now a showpiece of Dominion wealth and influence. Sprawling across a desert plain, framed by a high mountain range to the north and a winding river to the south, the gleaming city glistened under the hot sun, the massive buildings at its core reaching skyward like gigantic hydralisk spines. People went about their business with purpose. Quiet parks and spaces for contemplation were woven among the bustling streets, while vikings and hovercars raced by overhead.

The city was a testament to Mengsk's determination and vision, Gabriel Tosh had to admit as he crouched in the shadows outside the gates to the emperor's palace. It was also one of the most heavily fortified locations in the galaxy. Korhal had been one of the original core worlds settled by the Confederacy. A naturally hospitable planet, it had encouraged terran colonization more than any other in the sector, and the settlement had flourished. But as the Confederacy of Man had grown more powerful, Korhal had become a center for rebellion, and had been the target of a nuclear strike that had turned its oceans to desert, flattened all vegetation, and killed millions.

After gaining power and tearing down the Confederacy, as the Terran Dominion had risen from the ashes, Mengsk had rebuilt Korhal. It was no longer the lush, gentle world it had once been, but the city of Augustgrad stood in defiance of what had come before it, a modern marvel of neo-steel and glass atop the cracked ground that still bore the scorch marks of the planet's destruction.

Now, Tosh thought, it would serve as a coming-out party for something else entirely.

Despite the palace's guard presence and defenses, Tosh and the five other spectres he had brought for this mission had slipped unnoticed right up to the emperor's front door, thanks to Lio's help with the checkpoints and pass codes, and then with the defensive turrets and cameras. Dylanna, Sloan, Caleb, Jara, and Karl, formerly known only by ghost numbers, their memories now restored, their freedom granted. All strong and willing warriors who had embraced the cause. They wore their trademark black suits, but they could have worn bright yellow for all the difference it would have made. Even the most sophisticated scanning equipment could not pick up their cloaked forms.

Tosh felt invincible. But the goal of this mission was not to make a show of force. They were not prepared for the battle that would surely come if the entire firepower of the Dominion military descended upon them. His team would be crushed instantly.

But facing the Dominion head-on was never his intent. No, this mission would be a bold statement meant to weaken soldiers' resolve and confidence, a way of undermining the safety and security of the people by shaking their faith in their leaders and sowing the seeds of rebellion. A quick strike of the knife that would slice through the jugular and then be pulled away to let the blood flow freely.

It was also a more personal act of revenge. Mengsk himself was close; Tosh could feel his presence like a toxic stain on the palace walls. He could remember every moment of the mental and physical torture that the academy instructors had put him through in the name of Mengsk's new government, meant to turn him into a killing machine.

Tosh had to keep reminding the other spectres to stay focused as they moved closer to their target, particularly Dylanna, who had not learned her lesson after the confrontation over Kath's condition. Dylanna was buzzing like a live wire, and nothing seemed to calm her down. The terrazine and jorium affected everyone a little bit differently, and Tosh was already starting to wonder if she might be a failed experiment. Time would tell, but for now, he needed her.

As he studied the imperial guards patrolling the courtyard inside the palace gates, his mind kept slipping back to Kath, no matter how hard he tried to keep focused on the task at hand. He'd been reluctant to leave her on Gehenna, but she wasn't ready yet, and he would not push her.

He remembered the smell of her and the feel of her skin, the electricity between them, so much like the old days, it made him ache inside. She looked almost the same, her beauty undiminished by their time apart. His grandma would have said she had the glow, a way of marking those who were blessed with the presence of the spirits. Tosh had never really believed in all that Hajian voodoo, but he had to agree with that much.

He wanted Kath to be by his side and rejoin Team Blue, but she was still questioning her commitment to the ghost program, as so many of them did at first. They had been through this once before. It had nearly torn him apart when the academy had wiped her memory clean and the truth they had uncovered about her father's death had been buried once again. Everything they had worked so hard for was gone, and he had run from all of it, leaving her behind rather than facing the fact that he was alone.

But this time he knew she would come around to his point of view for good as the terrazine continued to expand her senses and open her eyes. He had convinced her before, and he could do it again. It would be worth the wait.

Tosh touched the tiny figure hanging around his neck for good luck. When he looked up, his grandma was crouching in front of him in her high priestess robes, her wrinkled brown skin shining, ropes of silver hair lying against her shoulders like fat snakes, and he shivered in spite of himself. *I tol' you a powerful storm be coming,* she said, her voice full of the power and wisdom that had always made the children gather and then cower before her. She reached out one clawed hand, gnarled finger extended, and drew a veve diagram in the dust, her tongue poking from a corner of her mouth as she spat in concentration. *Storm brings forces you don' understand. This loa be mighty and she be dark.*

Tosh willed himself to be still. He knew she wasn't real, and her religion was long dead and gone too. But her eyes still shone at him like polished stones, and when she laughed, he felt it rattling inside his chest.

Don' be scared, little Gabriel. It's a sacrifice she want, and you best give it to her before long. You and the witchcraft you carry be meant to lead your fellow men. But you need to give her that.

Tosh looked away, his heart pounding hard. When he looked back again, she was gone. But at his feet, drawn in the dust that coated the ground, the veve remained. Quickly he tried to rub it out with his palm, but the ghostly impression still floated there, as if burned into his retinas.

If the gods that his grandma had believed in did indeed exist, they had spoken to him now. He did not know what kind of sacrifice this particular deity might require, but he would be ready to do whatever it might take to make Mengsk answer for his sins.

Dylanna had moved closer through the shadows, followed by the others. She couldn't actually see his cloaked form, but she could sense him more accurately than any machine. "What's the matter?" she said. "It's time to move. Give the order."

"Don't be telling me what to do," Tosh said as he stood, but he could not help smiling at her eagerness. He looked at the spectres waiting for his command, and felt a rush of love for them and the cause they had all embraced. He was a benevolent leader, come to bring them home.

We were all ghosts once, he projected outward, touching each of them in turn. *Been built like machines to do our masters' bidding, used the way they saw fit, then wiped clean and put back on the shelf. But we're free again now, and we learned from our mistakes. Our roots have been restored; our eyes opened; and we been blessed with powers beyond anything we ever imagined. And now it's time to lead the rest of our kind back from the shadows and into the light.*

They were humming like struck tuning forks. He could feel them in his bones. *There'll be casualties of this war. Do not forget that you fight on the side of righteousness, and the blood you spill will not be in vain.*

Tosh smiled at them again and nodded. It was a good speech, and they had drawn strength from it. Then he leapt into the air, using one strong hand to grab at the gates and swing himself upward as the power inside him spilled over. He flew in a tucked somersault over the deadly laser wire before extending his legs to land lightly on the stone entryway inside the palace grounds.

The others followed him, Dylanna as gracefully as he had done it, the others a bit more clumsily. Caleb, their last recruit before Kath, just missed catching his foot in the laser and made a slight noise as he landed, and the two guards on patrol, who had almost reached the side of the massive building, paused in the fading light and raised their weapons. But after a moment, seeing nothing, and their sensors calm thanks to Lio, they lowered them again and continued on their way, content that their scanners, laser wire, and auto-turrets would protect them.

Tosh led the strike team directly across the

open courtyard and paused at a fountain with a statue of Mengsk with his hands on his hips, staring out at the horizon like a returning hero instead of the murdering slike he had become. Tosh wanted to rip the statue's head from its shoulders and throw it through the palace windows. Instead, he continued to the front steps and then around the corner, in the direction the guards had gone. This would be the trickiest part of the assault: finding a way in without triggering the palace alarms.

There was a side door for servants and deliveries, an auto-turret and sensor mounted on the roof the only active defenses. Tosh took out his remote console as the sun dropped toward the horizon and the shadows lengthened across the palace walls. "Need to disable the other alarms," he typed. "Right front quadrant, side entrance, on my mark."

The screen was empty for a moment, and then: *Ready.*

Tosh sent Dylanna and Sloan to take positions on either side of the door while the others fanned out to keep watch and wait for their return. He could sense from Caleb that more guards were coming across the courtyard, and time was growing short. "Now, Lio."

Very well. Go.

Tosh sent a mental push, and Dylanna swung the door open. The three of them slipped silently inside, Sloan letting the door close with the faintest click. Tosh was ready to face a weapon, but the small receiving room was empty except for one man in uniform, who stared with mouth agape at the sight of a door opening and closing by itself. He never had the chance to move as Dylanna crossed the small space, grabbed him by the head, and twisted until his neck cracked and he slipped lifelessly to the floor.

From this point on, things would be getting more complicated. Lio had scanned the floor plans from the mainframe and identified Mengsk's private quarters. He had also verified that the emperor was inside the building. They had to find him before the guard they had just killed was discovered.

Tosh stood silently for a moment, relishing the fact that they were inside Mengsk's stronghold. It was hard to believe. And it had been so simple . . .

But he could not afford to take too long. They moved into the large hallway with several closed doors. Around a bend were two palace workers walking toward them, talking. Sloan flattened himself against a wall, but Dylanna stepped in and threw a series of vicious chops with the side of her hand, crushing one's Adam's apple before cracking the spine at the base of the skull of the other. They dropped soundlessly to the floor, a look of shock still on their faces.

Anger rose like a fiery angel in Gabriel Tosh. They had talked at length about the importance of a stealth approach, but three bodies in the course of a few moments meant a greater chance that they would be found inside the palace walls.

Dylanna was destroying all that they had so carefully prepared. She had been the leader of Team Red, while he had led Team Blue at the academy, natural rivals before the two teams had formed a fragile partnership. He knew she had been jealous of his relationships with Kath and Nova, and had wanted him for herself. But that was ancient history, Tosh thought. Was she challenging him again now? He could not let it continue, or it would tear them all apart.

Waves of energy prickled his skin, and the familiar craving for terrazine began to nip at him as he grabbed Dylanna's cloaked form and pulled her close. Although he could not see her with his own two eyes, he could sense her impatience and wildness; she was like an animal trembling from the hunt, and she glowed with an aura of blue-white light visible only to him and Sloan.

Hush. You'll give us away, you fekking slike.

"Seeing things," she said. She wriggled in his grasp, but he held more tightly to her. "There're protoss just around the corner; you feel them?"

Stupid curve. You're losing your mind. Shut your mouth and clean up this mess before I lose my temper.

"Blood," she said. "It's everywhere. On my hands. I can't get it off."

She wasn't listening to him. Tosh's anger

grew. He probed her mind, looking for the soft spots. His terrazine hunger mingled with his rage, building until he felt himself lock into a particular wavelength and begin to vibrate, cooking her brain inside her skull. She pushed back at him at first, but her powers were no match for his; then the wildness changed to fear as he did not let go and the energy grew around them both like an electrical storm.

She let out a tiny shriek, and he felt Sloan clawing at his arms, but still he did not let go, and along with everything else he felt a delicious sense of power and freedom and lust for the kill. He gave in to the feeling and let it wash him away with a gigantic wave of psionic energy coursing down his arms and legs.

Enough, Gabriel.

He opened his eyes and his grandma was staring back at him. He froze in terror. He had his hands around his grandma's throat, but she stayed calm. *Maman Therese will let you know when it's time,* she said. *The loa will show you the right kind of sacrifice she requires. This ain't the way, not yet.*

Tosh released her and she slumped to the floor, gasping. But it wasn't his grandma anymore; he could see Dylanna's aura pulsing a dull, bloody red. He turned away, slowing down his breathing, regaining control.

Easy now. He took another hit from the terrazine bottle and let it fill him up again, bringing him peace. She wasn't worth the effort, and they were wasting time. He only meant to show her who was in charge of this mission, and that was enough.

The two dead men were still lying in the middle of the floor; the entire incident had taken less than a minute. Tosh grabbed them by their feet and dragged them back into the receiving room with the other corpse. He closed the door and fused the latch shut. Dylanna had gotten to her feet again, and he could feel the anger flowing off of her, but she made no sound. Sloan was tending to her now. He ignored them and took out his remote console and tried to bring up the schematics of the palace.

Instead, he saw something from Lio that gave him pause.

Message out through private line. Encrypted, difficult to decode.

The words glowed green and then faded from sight. Tosh took a deep breath and tried to keep the anger that once again had quickly boiled to the surface from spilling over. It would do him no good with Lio, he knew; there was nothing for him to get his hands on anyway. Lio was pure energy.

"I thought you blocked all messages," Tosh typed. "Where from?"

This is a dedicated channel to a ghost wrangler from Mengsk's private quarters. May be call for help. It's possible he has a camera on a direct feed to his room, and he's seen you or the dead bodies. I scrambled all future communication, but prior message may have been received intact.

Either Lio wasn't as all-knowing as he appeared to be, or he was getting lazy. Or, Tosh thought, he had an agenda of his own. That idea was more troublesome; a lot was riding on Lio's willing participation. He would have to think more about that later.

But for now he had to focus. A message getting through Lio's net could ruin their plans. It was impossible to say whether the city's security systems had sent out an alarm, but he had to assume that somehow they had. If someone had been alerted to their approach, it was only a matter of minutes before the entire Dominion space fleet and marine forces were at their doorstep.

That would be a very bad thing for all of them.

"How much time?" he typed.

Nothing for a long moment. Then: *Not sure. May want to abort.*

Tosh thought about talking to the general but decided against it. They would only argue over the next steps, something that was happening with more frequency lately, and the spectres would lose precious ground. The fact was, Tosh was in charge of this mission, and there was still time to complete it. But they would have to move fast. If Dominion forces were close, the spectres could all be killed.

Emperor Mengsk, the man whom Gabriel Tosh held personally responsible for so many grievous acts against him and those he loved, was within reach.

Gabriel Tosh strode off down the hall toward the emperor's quarters, not bothering to see if the other two were following him or not. He ignored the chill that had prickled his neck. The terrazine spread out through his lungs, entered his bloodstream, and lit him up like a siege tank. He felt his mind lift away from his body, expanding over the palace so that he could see and hear everything, a rush of voices babbling from everywhere.

He was like a god looking out over his creation. Nothing could stop him now. Mengsk would pay for his sins, one way or another, and Project: Shadowblade would unveil itself to the universe, bringing the Dominion to its knees.

CHAPTER TWELVE

SPECTRES

The *Palatine* hurtled through space, its giant engines straining as Captain Rourke pushed the battlecruiser to its limits. Korhal was close now, Nova Terra thought as she stared through the observation window into deep space. She was in full uniform, itching to strap into the dropship and get to the planet's surface as quickly as possible. The other six ghosts were there too, talking quietly among themselves, while Spaulding and the Annihilators followed in their own ship.

She could feel the tension among everyone on the bridge, although nobody would admit it. It was one thing to attack military supply locations, and abducting and possibly murdering ghosts was even more brazen; but going directly to the heart of the Dominion's power, the capital at Augustgrad, and infiltrating the emperor's palace? That was sheer madness.

She had explained everything she knew to Hauler, which wasn't much. Mengsk's message on Mal's fone had been garbled. From what they could decipher he was holed up in some kind of panic room, safe for now, but palace security had been compromised and communications were disabled in either direction. The private link had apparently been the only way to get a message out, and even that was now locked down. Harvey and the *Palatine*'s communications officer had done what they could, but they couldn't figure out what was going on, and might not be able to do anything more until they were on planet.

So they flew blindly into a hornet's nest.

Mal touched her arm. "Can I talk to you for a minute?"

She nodded and they retreated to a quiet spot. He didn't need to open his mouth for her to know what he wanted to say. "You're worried about a trap," she said.

"Damn right I am," he said. "The way I see it, they're attacking Augustgrad for two possible reasons: to make a statement to the Dominion that nobody is safe, or to bring us running so they can pick us off, one by one. Either way, I don't like it."

"I was thinking the same thing. But we don't have a choice."

"You're a target."

"They can come and get me."

He sighed and rubbed his hands on his duster.

"I'm sure the other ghosts thought they could protect themselves too. But they couldn't, and now they're either fighting for the other side, or they're dead. Point is, we don't know. We don't know a flicking thing about what's happening. And that's not a good way to wade into battle."

Know your enemy. Mal was right, of course. But she didn't care. Ghosts were meant to do one thing, and one thing only: protect the Dominion. This was relentlessly drilled into recruits' heads day after day, and the message was that nobody's life was more important than the survival of the government, which had brought stability to the Koprulu sector after years of heavy fighting. Mengsk was a brilliant, charismatic leader and military strategist, and no matter what people thought about him, it was clear that his survival was essential to keeping the fragile peace. She would die to protect him, and die gladly.

And yet . . .

She was boarding an old battle-scarred ship with the rest of the ghost cadets, Team Blue and Team Red, now becoming one unit. It was supposed to be a simple training mission to bring them all together. But something was wrong. Something terrible was coming.

The children of the Old Families were screaming.

Nova snapped back to the present, Mal looking curiously at her as she gasped aloud. "I . . . I remember something from my academy days," she said. "It keeps drifting closer but it's not clear. Whatever it was has been wiped clean."

"But that's what you've always wanted, isn't it? To forget everything and leave your past behind for good. Wipes allowed that to happen."

"But I'm remembering it now! Going through everything again, one little glimpse at a time. I never thought I'd have to experience it once it was over." She sighed. "And this . . . I have the feeling it's something important. I just can't grasp it—"

The doors to the bridge slid open, and Lieutenant Ward strode through in his combat suit for the final briefing, visor open, his heavy boots thudding on the metal floor. The smell of stale cigar smoke wafted in with him. He would lead the marine support on this mission, and Nova could sense his eagerness to redeem himself after the showing on Altara. After chewing him out, Hauler had given him a short leash, and this time, Ward was determined not to let his chance for glory go to waste.

She caught his eye, and along with the glance came a sense of his distrust and anger. They hadn't spoken of her suspicion of what he'd done on Hudderstown Colony since the battle with the zerg, and he'd been living in fear ever since. As he passed by, she caught something else from him, another errant thought that made her blood run cold.

That's a double murder charge, Ward, she

thought, projecting her damning words into his head.

His eyes widened in shock.

(get out of my head you slike you don't know anything)

I know now she was pregnant with your child, and I'm pretty damn sure you killed her. Just do your job or you won't have to worry about anything anymore because I'll kill you myself.

Hauler's rough voice ended things abruptly. "Report," he barked from his position on the raised platform above the bridge floor. "Private Hunt, what's the status on communications?"

"Still working on that, sir," the officer said without looking up, her fingers dancing over the control panel. "No word from Augustgrad, and I'm unable to get a message through to anyone." She hesitated for a moment. "There seems to be some kind of bug in the system, sir. But it's not like anything I've seen before. It's almost like . . ."

"Spit it out, Private," Hauler roared, slamming his hands down on the railing. "We don't have all day."

"It appears to know what I'm trying to do," she said, "before I do it. Whatever I try, it moves to block me."

"You're playing chess with a virus," Hauler said. "Stunning work, Hunt. Keep it up." He turned to Ward. "Lieutenant, are our troops ready?"

"Locked and loaded, sir," Ward said. "All

squads are in dropships, ready for our mark. They're champing at the bit."

"Good." Hauler nodded. "We need to be prepared for anything. But all the intel we have indicates that there is not a full enemy military presence on Korhal. This appears to be a terrorist attack with psionic assassins in limited numbers. They may well be some of ours, academy trained. If so, they will be hard to find and as tough to kill as roaches. We'll need to counter that with our own. Ghosts go in first, followed by our marine force. Other ships will arrive momentarily. Your orders are to stay outside the city limits unless the ghost agents request your assistance."

"But, sir," Ward said, "I don't—"

"This ghost is in charge of this operation," Hauler said, pointing at Nova. "You report to her. Is that clear?"

Ward nodded. He glanced at Nova and then quickly away. "Yes, sir."

"Coming into Korhal's orbital path in ten minutes," Rourke said over the ship's comm system. "All stations, prepare to engage."

Mal put his hand on Nova's shoulder. Once again she felt the electric spark at his touch through her ghost suit fabric, muscle fiber twitching. Along with it came a feeling of warmth from him, a thought that was not specific, and one that confused her. It took her a few moments to understand that he cared about her.

"We'll talk more later?"

She nodded. "Thanks. Better get to the ship."

The other agents were waiting for her. He gave her shoulder a squeeze. His face flushed red. Then he dropped his hand and turned away, and she was left with the lingering tingle from his touch, wondering whether what she had felt was something real or simply another ghostly memory of things long past.

The dropship set them down in the outskirts of Augustgrad as the last of the day's fading light painted the tips of the slender skyscrapers a deep, bloody red. An outpost sat like a gigantic metal beetle on a flat slab of ground, empty and dark, unmanned, while below it stretched the city, lights beginning to twinkle in the twilight.

It looked, Nova thought as she gathered her team around her, like a city on the edge of sleep, rather than one with a cancer creeping unseen through its core. Somewhere inside the palace the emperor had locked himself away while the enemy tried to fight its way in. And beyond the palace walls the people continued about their business as if nothing was happening, unaware that the entire Dominion was teetering on the edge of chaos.

The six other ghosts were restless. They knew just enough about what they were facing to imagine the worst, and Nova could sense them all thinking the same thing she'd just talked about with Mal: whether they were being lured into a spider's web, only to disappear without a trace. They hadn't spent enough time together to work well as a team and trust one another, and the stakes were too high now to take risks.

"Let's go in fast," Lethal said. She had a slender build and black hair that fell across her shoulders. "Be aggressive. We give them no time to react. They can't know that we're coming, not yet."

Nova thought back to the private meeting she and Mal had had with Mengsk, and the idea that there might be a traitor within his inner circle. *Due to its sensitive nature, I cannot trust my regular channels to carry it through,* the emperor had said. *They may have been compromised.*

"Actually, I think there's a pretty good chance they do," Nova said. "We need to be careful here, try to explore the target and identify any enemy positions without them seeing us, if possible. I want to know absolutely everything I can about what we're facing before we engage. The emperor's life may depend on it."

"You think they've come to kill him," Bones said. "That's what you're saying." It wasn't a question. "If so, he may already be dead."

"Then we're wasting time." Nova checked her C-20A, slung it back on her shoulder, and confirmed that her HUD was working properly.

The ghosts cloaked. Six green dots glowed before her eyes, showing the current locations of the rest of them standing before her. "It's a delicate situation, and we know very little about what's happening down there." She sent a map of the city to their computers and marked each of their sectors around the palace. "I've had some experience with this enemy. You've all read my report. They have an advanced cloaking device that renders them undetectable. But they seem to be able to sense us. So we have to find an advantage to exploit."

"I've engaged one too," Bones said. "The same one you did, on Altara. He—she—whatever it was knocked me on my ass and then vanished. I had no warning. How are we supposed to fight that? Fekk, how are we supposed to even find them?"

"Look for collateral damage—dead bodies, points of entry, footprints, blood. Probe the guards' minds: find out if anyone saw anything unusual. These people like to play games, and that's where we have an edge. If they get inside your head, if they give you any warning, you take them out. Do not hesitate. They're flesh and blood, just like us. Be ruthless and deadly. They'll bleed if we hit them."

"What if they *are* us?" Rook said. The powerfully built young man radiated confidence. Nova recalled that his psi index was the highest of the bunch, and that he'd led his team at the academy just three short years ago. "I mean, the missing ghosts."

"If they were ghosts once, they aren't anymore. They're attacking the Dominion, and that makes them traitors. We can't afford to question that." Nova looked at each of them in turn. "These people like psychological warfare. If you let them intimidate you, you've already lost. You're all the best that the Dominion has to offer. You know what to do. Now let's move."

Ten minutes later they abandoned their burbling vultures inside the city walls and proceeded on foot, their cloaking devices hiding them from public view. The palace was close now, and Nova pushed them all forward quickly, afraid they were running out of time. Scans hadn't picked up any ships leaving Korhal's atmosphere, so she had to assume that the terrorists were still here. But all communications in and out of the palace remained jammed, and she didn't dare alert the local law enforcement herself for fear that they would storm the walls, weapons blazing. For all she knew, they could be in on the plot. The situation was far too fragile to risk that.

The brightly lit streets were quiet at this time of the evening on a work night, most residents having dinner with their families or retiring to watch a holovid before bed. A few hovercars and blimps slid silently by overhead, while AAI units displayed colorful images of soft drinks and home decor, morphing from one thing to the other as they waited for patrons to walk by. Augustgrad was one of the few places in the galaxy where the people had little to fear, and their lives were ruled by routine. Since the war and the nuclear destruction that had rained down on Korhal IV, the rebuilt city had become a hotbed for technology research, education, and manufacturing, as well as the preferred home for military leaders and their families. Incomes were much higher than average, and it showed in the gleaming streets and new construction, sleek modern buildings and condos with small, well-kept grassy areas, and common spaces with fountains and parks.

This city was Mengsk's shrine to his birthplace, built to show the people how things could be under his leadership once true peace and prosperity were established. And now it might serve as his deathbed.

Nova reached the broad parade way that led to the palace front gates and paused under the shadow of a municipal building for a moment, looking for any signs of trouble. She saw and felt nothing: no sense of an enemy presence, no thoughts other than the steadily increasing babble of Augustgrad's residents that she had been hearing since they had approached the city limits. There were no calls of alarm either, nothing that would tell her the palace guard had discovered what was happening under their noses.

Maybe, she thought, they were all already dead too.

The thought brought a chill to her spine. As she studied the soaring towers of the palace walls and the Mengsk family insignia of two wolf heads built into the gates, she was suddenly wandering through another familiar sprawling home, past marble foyers with 6-meter-high ceilings, echoing ballrooms, and a chef's kitchen filled with the smell of baked framberry bread, up the elevator to row after row of closed bedroom doors, to where a girl's room looked out over sparkling pools and fountains and the lights of the city. Her childhood home on Tarsonis, the family skyscraper that had existed for generations until the war tore it violently down in a bloody coup.

Welcome home, Nova. Her mother stood there smiling at her, the crinkles that spread from her eyes revealing her delight. *We missed you.*

That memory was shattered by another, far more disturbing one: she and her fellow ghost trainees running across the barren Shi landscape, a massive zerg horde at their heels, while the last descendants of the Old Families of the Confederacy screamed for help and the feelings of overwhelming dread and hopelessness washed over her. The trainees were alone in this fight, with only a broken-down battlecruiser for support.

Why?

She didn't have time to figure it out now.

She snapped back to the present to find Bones staring at her, what might have been the ghost of a smile tugging at his lips.

She glared at him. *What are you doing uncloaked? You might be seen.*

He said and thought nothing, just cocked his head toward the palace gates with that same faint smile. Then he winked out of sight again. She could see him on her HUD, another glowing speck of green among the five others clustered around her.

Still distracted by the fragmented, vivid visions from her past, Nova Terra began to move toward the palace gates. It didn't strike her until it was too late that she'd remained cloaked the entire time, but Bones had acted as if he'd been able to see her.

The safe room was proving more difficult to crack than Gabriel Tosh had anticipated.

He sat cross-legged on the floor, thinking. They were in an inner office chamber with a rose-wood desk polished to a high shine, two couches, and a fine silk rug the color of dried blood over the stone tile. Behind the desk two wooden panels had been hastily slid aside, exposing a heavy, riveted neosteel door.

Of course he'd known there would be such a room; Mengsk would have required it for his own safety. He'd never really trusted ghosts after the

role they had played in the assassination of his father, mother, and baby sister so many years ago.
One of them, Sarah Kerrigan, had carried his father Angus's head away with her like some kind
of macabre trophy. Mengsk was nothing if not
pragmatic, and he'd eventually used Kerrigan's
talents for his own ends before betraying her to
the zerg, and had adopted the Confederate ghost
program as his own. But Tosh knew that it was an
uneasy partnership. Mengsk's approach with
ghosts was one you would use on attack dogs
trained to kill; they might be useful to protect your
property, but you never turned your back on
them.

Still, Tosh never thought it would come to
this. They were supposed to get to the emperor before he knew what was coming. Thanks to Dylanna's reckless behavior, that hadn't happened, and
now more of Mengsk's personal guards were lying
dead in pools of blood; the alarm had apparently
been raised with the coded message to the wrangler; and Mengsk was holed up tight. His panic
room was psionically shielded, and there seemed
to be no way in, either physically or mentally. Lio
had blocked all communications in and out, and
the others outside had managed to take care of
anyone who stumbled upon evidence of their
break-in by killing them outright or brain-panning
them, but that couldn't last forever. They were
running out of time.

Come on, Lio. Break the code.

There was nothing for a moment on the remote console, and then, *Manual locking mechanism engaged from within,* spilled across the screen. *The* Palatine *has arrived . . . Dominion forces closing in. Lots of them.*

Fekk. Tosh balled his fists, rage swelling within him again until he needed a release. He pounded the tile once with a massive blow that cracked one in half and sent a puff of dust into the air. Then he turned and concentrated on the door, his strange white eyes narrowing as the rage poured out of him and through the air with a rush of heat.

The thick door groaned, flexed slightly, and was still.

It was too strong for him, still too strong. But not for long. A familiar hunger bit deep inside, and he took another hit of terrazine from the gas cylinder and glared at Dylanna, who was sitting on one of the couches, her leg tapping a nervous beat on the floor. She wouldn't meet his eyes, which was a good thing for her, because he might have decided to rip hers from her skull. He knew she was still upset about the way he had treated her, but he couldn't be bothered with that. She had deserved it.

Sloan had remained cloaked and was keeping watch just outside the office chamber, ready to act if marines appeared, while Caleb, Jara, and Karl still patrolled the grounds outside the palace walls.

He decided to bring them inside and concentrate their efforts on breaking through the sixty-centimeter-thick reinforced walls of the safe room. Together they might be able to exert enough pressure to get to Mengsk.

The emperor needed to answer for his crimes.

Ghosts now in Augustgrad.

Tosh looked down at the new message. So they were here. It didn't surprise him; in fact, he wondered why it had taken them so long. The spy they had put into place on Altara had done his job nicely and kept them informed all the way through the investigation. Now that he had been delivered right to their front door, it was time for him to rejoin the group too. And there were other recruits here now, six of them, and more likely on the way, enough to swell the ranks of the spectres into a small psionic army.

Nova Terra would be one of them.

The thought made him smile. He had been waiting a long time for this. Nova was the most powerful ghost in the program, and one of the most gifted anyone had ever seen. Having Nova join them would make the spectres a nearly unstoppable force. But it was more than that. They had been much more than friends once, before his first "death," and bringing her into the fold would have special meaning for him, even if those feelings were in the past.

Convincing her would be a delicate process.

She would resist at first; he knew that. But the fact was, she was no match for his new powers. And she could be turned if she knew the truth. After her terrazine exposure, it was only a matter of time before she remembered what happened on planet Shi to the children of the Old Families, and Mengsk's role in the zerg attack and subsequent cover-up.

That would change her mind. He would make sure of that.

And if the other ghosts resisted and there was no other way, they would have to be put down, along with anyone else alive in the palace. It was regrettable collateral damage, but Nova was the prize.

Tosh stood up and strode to the door, leaving Dylanna to guard the safe room. Shadowblade must not be stopped, no matter what cost.

Nova would join them, or there would be hell to pay.

CHAPTER THIRTEEN

THE BATTLE FOR AUGUSTGRAD

As soon as she reached the fence that ringed the interior courtyard, the other ghosts close behind, Nova knew that the message Mal had received about the attack from the emperor had been real.

She had remained worried that it might have been faked to draw them into a trap, the same way the UED terrorist tip had brought Agent X52735N to Altara. But the palace courtyard was too quiet. Normally there would be a heavy imperial guard presence and regular patrols, as well as palace workers coming in and out. But that wasn't what really bothered her. There was something else carried by the faint wind, a tingling that left her alert and ready for trouble. She was reminded of the mad chase through the empty rooms in Oasis and the way she'd felt just before that, when the face had appeared at the dusty window: a presence like a flash of bright yellow among the dull gray halos that surrounded the rest of the town's residents.

Something—or someone—was here, watching her.

Glancing around, Nova saw a spot on the pavement nearby. She crouched next to a strange shape drawn in the dust, its outline faint but noticeable, and let her computer scan and enhance it and then run it through the database. A moment later it came up with a match, a voodoo veve diagram meant to represent the death goddess Maman Therese.

Somewhere deep inside her, something stirred. She saw a giant of a man with a necklace where a small doll hung from a string of beads. But she couldn't place anything else about him, and the truth dangled tantalizingly close, but just out of reach.

Peekaboo.

Nova whirled around as laughter filled her head. The other ghosts murmured among themselves. She glanced at her HUD's map and found one fewer green dot, and things clicked into place: the way Bones had appeared at the back of the building in Oasis as whatever she had been chasing had mysteriously disappeared, the smile he'd given to her, and the way he'd still been able to see her when she was cloaked.

My name is Talen Holt, actually. I'm a free man now.

Bones—or Holt, as he claimed to be—

materialized for a brief moment on the other side of the fence, his gaunt features and black hair barely visible in the darkness, and his presence bloomed bright yellow across her sight. Then he winked out again and was gone.

How could she have been so clueless? She had never sensed any danger from him, or any suspicious thoughts, and his record had been clean. If he had been one of the ghosts who had been taken during the past few months, someone must have altered the files to conceal that, or perhaps he'd been recruited quietly and then put right back into action without anyone knowing it. The "how" didn't really matter, anyway; the damage had been done. The entire time, he'd been working to undermine them, positioned right under their noses, feeding everything they did back to the enemy.

He had played her for a fool.

A white-hot rage erupted in Nova. She sensed the confusion of the other ghosts around her as they tried to make sense of what they had seen. But there was no time to explain, and their attempt at making a stealthy approach was over. Holt would give away their position to the others, if he hadn't told them already, and if Mengsk was still alive now, he wouldn't be for much longer.

She had to stop him at all costs, even if it brought the Augustgrad law enforcement running.

Power rose up in her as she faced the fence and sent it blasting off its moorings with one violent mental push, sending the laser wire that ringed the top crackling in great arcs of blue fire, then ran through the opening, the five remaining ghosts close at her heels. The effort hadn't caused even the slightest twinge of pain in her temples, she realized with a start; in fact, she felt stronger than ever. Along with that came a strange feeling of euphoria and invincibility. She felt as if she could crack the very ground in half and take on the entire zerg Swarm at once.

As she ran she sensed that the palace's autoturrets were not responding to her presence. How had the terrorists shut everything down? Did they really have someone on the inside who could do something at such a high level without being detected? It seemed impossible, but she couldn't think of any other way.

Holt's voice echoed maddeningly in her head: *Is that all you can do, November Terra? Tear down a fence? How disappointing. I'd heard so much about you.*

He was close. But where? She had to keep him talking while she found a way to uncover his position.

There's more to me than meets the eye, X72341R.

She could sense his frustration at her use of his number. *It's Talen. And you have no idea yet what you're capable of, but you will, once you join us.*

Not gonna happen. Nova glanced around. A giant

bowl-shaped fountain with a statue of Mengsk dominated the center of the courtyard, sprays of water shooting skyward before landing again with a soft hissing sound.

She remembered their encounter in the small dusty room in Oasis, and how his footprints had revealed him to her. It gave her an idea.

What a brilliant thought, Nova. That'll do the trick. I'll just wash away—

With a single, smooth burst, Nova teeked the spray of water sideways, splattering a wide sweep of the courtyard. About four and a half meters to the left, the water bent and fell around an invisible figure, outlining the shape of his body on the dry stone.

She sensed a thought from him that wasn't fully formed, the first moment of alarm as he realized what she'd done and why. But by then she had locked onto his position and pushed, hard, her frustration pouring out of her in a blast of teek energy that took her breath away.

Holt cried out—whether it was audible or inside her head, she didn't know—and she felt him push back, a feeble attempt to block the wave of power that was already cooking his brain. For a brief moment she faltered; how could he have a teek ability like this? As a ghost, Holt had had a PI level of 6. But he was still no match for her. She heard something drop to the stone, and suddenly he was visible again, sprawled out with one leg bent underneath him, and she sensed his bright yellow presence as it throbbed once, and then slowly faded like the afterimage of a brilliant flash of light in a blackened room.

I—I didn't . . .

His alarm had turned to surprise, as if he could not reconcile what was actually happening with the outcome he'd been convinced would occur. She felt a connection with him that was both strong and unexpected, an outpouring of emotion that left her shuddering and weak. She realized that whatever else he might have done, he had felt justified in his role and the righteousness of his actions. And he could not understand how it had all come to this.

Then he was just . . . gone.

"Fekking hell," Rook said out loud. "What happened?"

He had stepped up next to her, the only one to do so. The entire exchange had taken no more than thirty seconds, and the other ghosts stood frozen in place just a meter inside the courtyard.

"He was a traitor," she said. "I had no choice."

Blood was trickling from Holt's ears and eyes, mixing with the water from the fountain and staining the stone red. Nova watched it run pink. She thought she would feel vindicated at the sight, but strangely, she felt confused, lost, and more alone than ever.

Ever since she had graduated from the Ghost Academy, her world had existed in right and

wrong, black and white. Either you were in support of the Dominion, or you were the enemy.

But this? This was an entirely different color,
and she could not figure out why.

Her comm unit crackled in her ear, the audio
fuzzing in and out. ". . . briefing . . . 22nd Division . . . assault positions . . ." It sounded like Hauler,
but she couldn't be sure and her computer could
not identify the source. Was he saying that Spaulding and the Annihilators were on their way?

"Repeat," she said, holding the comm closer to
her ear with a finger, but it was no good. Whatever person or thing had control of the airwaves
wasn't going to give it up anytime soon. This
would cause a great deal of trouble for the marines, since communications were essential for
battle. Hauler was probably looking to her for intel
in order to direct the troops. If he sent them in
now, they would be flying blind, and the chances
of success would be greatly reduced. Facing a
small, well-armed guerrilla group like these terrorists would almost surely result in a disaster for
the Dominion, as the marines would tear each
other to pieces trying to fight an enemy that could
appear and disappear at will.

But there were other, more pressing problems
to address. She could hear sirens in the distance as
emergency vehicles approached, probably alerted
by the fence blasting off its posts. She couldn't
waste any more time.

She directed the others to follow her and skirted the fountain on the left, heading for the main entrance. She wanted to get to Mengsk as soon as possible, but something told her to move carefully. It was all too quiet, and she wondered again where all the people were. Her suit's scans of the building showed it to be completely empty, no movement. This time of night, most people would be home with their families, but there should still be more activity, not to mention guard presence. Imperial guards were some of the best in the business, and they would have been running to investigate the sound in the courtyard by now. It was as if someone had removed all traces of a normal, bustling palace and replaced them with a movie set.

"I don't like this," Cyborg said. She had moved up to Nova's side this time, and tension was radiating off her. "I feel . . . nothing."

Nova was about to agree, but she realized that wasn't quite right. She felt a presence that she could not explain, something that wasn't focused in any particular spot, more like a feeling of energy crackling the air like high-tension wires. It was stronger than the tingling she'd felt when they had first arrived at the palace. Much stronger.

"They're here," she said. "Ready your weapons."

Nobody moved. A breeze wafted air across their faces as the other ghosts moved up to defensive formation around her near the palace steps, unslinging their C-10s and steadying themselves before an invisible enemy. Fighting other soldiers was one thing. Facing a larger, more powerful, and armed battalion was something ghosts could plan for and understood. Even the zerg were visible. But this, she could tell, was unknown territory for them all, and in spite of their training she felt their confidence beginning to fail.

Nova was about to order them inside when the world seemed to explode around them.

Gabriel Tosh watched the six ghosts approach the palace entrance, his skin tingling with anticipation. His recent hit of terrazine had heightened his senses beyond anything he'd ever known. In spite of their cloaking devices, he could see them all as clearly as if they'd been lit up with spotlights, even distinguish between each of them by the color of their auras. Grandma Tosh would have said he was still possessed by spirits, most likely, but he knew the truth: he had been given a gift, and he was destined to fulfill the savior's role and lead these lost souls out into the light.

It was a pity some of them would have to die in the process.

Tosh looked around at Caleb, Jara, and Karl, who perched like birds of prey upon the top of the steps, looking down at their targets. They had taken out the rest of the guards and what was left of the palace staff, and bodies now littered the corridors. And then they had come out here just in time to witness the end of Nova's clash with their unfortunate mole, Talen Holt.

Tosh could sense their anger at losing one of their own, and he wanted to temper that to make sure things didn't get out of control too quickly. But he was angry too: not at Nova, because he didn't blame her for protecting herself. He was angry at Holt for thinking he could toy with her in that way, and at himself for not acting quickly enough to stop it. Nova was like a wounded animal, dangerous when cornered. She had to be convinced that joining them was the right thing to do.

The others, though, were expendable, if they chose to fight. He looked back down at the courtyard and the ghosts, who had formed a defensive circle. Just beyond them lay Holt's body, blood running freely through the cracks between the stones. They were wary, and for good reason. They were about to experience Maman Therese's wrath.

Disable their suits first, Tosh told the rest of his team, *and drag them out into the light. But try not to kill them. Let's show 'em exactly what we can do.*

He sent a mental picture to each of them, and Jara and Karl nodded and leapt from their perches, landing silently about six meters away on either side of the group of ghosts. He and Caleb walked straight toward them, unslinging their weapons as they went.

There was no warning of the attack. The ghosts were still standing in a circle when two of them were yanked violently backward with unseen hands as a wave of focused energy washed over them all.

Nova, still standing with the three others at her side, felt her ghost suit crackle with energy and her cloaking device abruptly cut off. Her HUD went dark too, leaving her without a map of the other ghosts' positions or a good sense of the palace schematics. She tore off her head-piece and threw it aside; it was only a nuisance to her now.

She would have to rely on her own psionic abilities to sense what was coming.

She lay down a suppressing fire with her C-20A, raking the yard from left to right as the other ghosts, who had suddenly winked into existence next to her, did the same, their training kicking in even as she sensed their rising tension and excitement. Cyborg and the Veteran were locked in a vicious struggle behind her, but she didn't have the time to glance at them because someone was probing at her mind and body, someone very powerful indeed.

LAY DOWN YOUR WEAPONS, GHOSTS.

We don't want to hurt you, but we WILL finish the job if you try to resist.

The voice thundered in her head, and she could tell by the others' reactions that they had heard it too. At the same time the force probing at her intensified and she could feel it working at her muscles in an attempt to take over her nervous system. She fought back hard, snapping its hold over her, but the other ghosts appeared to be frozen in place, their weapons suddenly silent. She could sense the panic in their thoughts as they struggled against whatever was holding them still, but they were unable to break free.

The rifle fire hadn't hit anything as far as she could tell. But it was impossible to hit what you couldn't see. She wanted to scream with frustration. With a single quick, decisive move, the terrorists had disabled their hostile environment suits and left the ghosts at a drastic disadvantage. She had to find a way to make this a more even fight.

Think, Nova.

Their opponents clearly had the upper hand, and yet they hadn't delivered a killing blow. They were too confident, and confidence led to weakness. The ghosts had one shot to take advantage of the opening.

Cyborg and the Veteran had been physically attacked. So she knew where at least two of the attackers had been just a moment ago.

With one practiced, fluid motion, Nova spun

to face the two ghosts, now lying frozen on the stone, took one leap forward, and kicked out at the spot where she thought a terrorist would be standing. She felt a satisfactory thud as she met resistance, and she fired her C-20A with her other hand at the second spot over the Veteran, lashing out psionically as she landed on the other side of Cyborg and searched for anything she could use.

She saw a blooming of color where her boot had hit and someone cried out inside her mind, and then the two ghosts were free, leaping to their feet before something struck her like a thundering dropship, knocking her sideways and to the ground, her ears ringing and her vision exploding with stars.

When she regained her senses a moment later, she found that the battle had begun in full force. Somehow her attack had broken the terrorists' hold on the other ghosts. Her C-20A had badly damaged a terrorist's suit, revealing his partial outline, his blood running freely down his now useless arm. He wore what looked like a hostile environment suit of some kind, all in black, and he had carried an unfamiliar rifle that now lay on the stone at his feet.

Three ghosts had surrounded him and she watched them take him to the ground while the Veteran was laying down suppressing fire. Lethal fought hard with another invisible opponent, taking shots to her body but using them to learn where to hit back. She was small but remarkably quick and intuitive, and seemed to be holding her own for now.

But none of that was as important anymore, because Nova realized with a shock that she could sense their attackers.

Of course she knew that the terrorists must have been able to sense each other in some way, while remaining cloaked for everyone else. But the subtle, glowing auras around each of them hadn't been completely visible in her mind before. Either her powers were still expanding, or they had chosen to reveal themselves to her now for some reason she had yet to understand.

It doesn't matter why. Just act.

Nova pulled up her C-20A, sighted at the glowing figure toying with Lethal, and opened fire.

The canister flew straight and strong, and the distance was less than nine meters, but the target must have sensed something because he threw his upper body backward at the last moment, bending impossibly deep at the waist even as Nova teeked the round to follow him.

Instead of hitting his temple and exploding out the other side, the canister shattered his mask and ripped through his nose and upper jaw.

The terrorist clutched at his face and dropped to his knees, spitting blood and bits of white bone and gurgling, his cloaking device interrupted as he suddenly became visible in front of everyone else.

Lethal kicked him in the throat, crushing his windpipe. He dropped soundlessly to the stone.

Two down.

Nova felt a mindless scream of rage tear through her head as another one of the terrorists leapt forward, grabbing Lethal by the throat and holding her still. She struggled but then went limp, her body convulsing once and shuddering before she began bleeding from the eyes and mouth. Nova fired her rifle, teeking the rounds toward their target but still missing badly as the terrorist leapt upward and away, toward the front gates. She saw him engage a group of emergency responders who had arrived, sirens blazing, only to be quickly and ruthlessly killed as they tried to fight back.

A moment later the C-20A was ripped from her grasp and thrown across the courtyard. She sensed someone probing at her mind and looked up to see another figure standing at the foot of the palace steps, his features indistinct, his aura glowing a pale green. He seemed to be watching over the battle, waiting to see which way it would go.

Terrazine's at work in you, his voice said inside her head. *You've been exposed on Altara. You can see us.*

She sensed the man's surprise; something else that hadn't gone as planned, she thought with a small measure of satisfaction.

Who are you?

My name's Gabriel Tosh. Maybe you remember me.

At the sound of that name, Nova was catapulted back in time.

. . . in the cafeteria with the rest of her team, Tosh's thick dreadlocks quivering as he laughed at something Lio said, his arm around Nova's shoulders . . .

. . . a shared kiss between them . . .

. . . and fighting for real as a cadet thrust into the middle of the zerg battle on Shi in what was supposed to be a training mission, the last of the Old Families in mortal danger, waiting for Gabriel Tosh to get clear before she unleashed a massive mind blast to destroy the zerg . . .

. . . and after a mind wipe, her disbelief as Tosh tried to convince her that the zerg had been purposely put on Shi by the Dominion, and that after the children of the Old Families had been brought to safety, Mengsk had secretly made them disappear and buried the whole thing . . .

. . . and finally, getting the news that Tosh was killed in action on a top secret mission . . .

Nova brought herself out of the flashback with a shake of her head. *No,* she thought. *It can't be true. You're dead, and none of that happened.*

He sent her a mental image: running through the desolate Shi landscape, zerg closing in, knowing that he could not get clear in time—and the sudden wave of pure energy that had washed over them as the mind blast occurred, zerglings dropping dead and bleeding from the eyes as he was thrown into the air.

It happened, all right. You destroyed 'em all with a psionic blast that left me changed. You did something to me. You were a part of it. I don't know why, but I was different after that. I remembered everything the academy tried to wipe away. Nobody could read my thoughts unless I let 'em. And I was stronger than I'd ever been. Could see everything clear as day. And what I saw, what they did to ghosts, what Mengsk did to those kids . . . I had to run, or they would have killed me.

Why didn't you tell *us?*

I tried, but you'd all been wiped right after that zerg battle; you wouldn't believe me. But me, it didn't take. I sat through the whole thing. I couldn't stay there anymore, so I went AWOL, and they told you I'd gotten myself killed somewhere like a fool. Meanwhile they were hunting me down. You understand? They do whatever they need to do to get their way. Mengsk dropped those zerg on Shi to destroy the last of the Old Families, then we followed straight into hell. When we ended up saving the day, he just wiped us all and killed them anyway. It's all a big experiment to him, a game.

That can't be—

It's true. I'm standing up for what I believe in now. That mind blast opened up my eyes. The Dominion made us all slaves. You call us spectres terrorists, but Mengsk is worse than any of us.

Spectres?

That's right. Now stop this before you get the rest of your ghosts killed, Nova Terra.

She realized that the action around her

had ceased. She was trembling, caught in the overwhelming emotions of memories that continued to leave her shaken and confused. She remembered little Lila and that same term, *spectres*, on Altara, and it left her cold. What Tosh was saying could not be right. The Old Families had already been all but destroyed; Tarsonis, leveled. Nova's own family gone forever. Those who had been left were no threat to Mengsk. He couldn't have done such a thing.

No. She shook her head. Whatever else had happened to Gabriel Tosh since she'd last seen him, he must have lost his mind. Tosh's venom against the Dominion was like a disease. In order to stop the plague from spreading, she had to cut off its head.

"I am Agent X41822N," she said out loud, as if to show everyone where her allegiance lay. Or maybe it was for her own benefit. "Nova Terra is dead."

She glanced to her right, focusing her mind on the six-meter-tall statue of Mengsk and the fountain, and ripped the statue from its moorings, throwing it at Tosh with all her strength.

The statue, the size and weight of a siege tank, hurtled through the air and hit the steps of the palace with a tremendous, shuddering crash, bouncing upward through one of the supporting pillars and into the huge front doors, crushing stone and plascrete as it buried itself a meter deep inside the palace walls.

Dust rose in a great cloud as debris rained down around her. Using the cloud as cover, she held her breath and raced forward as someone fired at her from behind. She sensed the whining rounds enough to avoid them as they ticked off the palace facade, and then she teeked the statue aside to expose the gaping hole in the palace walls where the doors had been.

Tosh had disappeared back inside the building.

Mengsk was still inside somewhere too. She had to remember their mission. Find the emperor and protect him at all costs.

Nova leapt over the shattered steps and ran inside the front entryway as the dust began to clear, away from the live rounds still whining off stone outside. She found herself in a huge, echoing vestibule filled with columns and marble. Even inside, all the auto-defenses were down. The guards' area sat empty about six meters from the doors. Scanning for dangerous spots, she felt and saw nothing, but drew her sidearm as insurance as she raced forward, trying to recall where the emperor's office was located. If memory served her correctly, it was in the center of the building, beyond several layers of meeting rooms, offices, and a dining hall. The safe room would be close.

She ran through another large empty room lined with expensive oil paintings, took a left at the end of a short hall, and stopped. Bodies littered the thickly carpeted floor of the next room, all of them bleeding from the eyes and ears and mouth. *Flicking hell.* It was a massacre, and her stomach soured at the sight. She had seen plenty of dead bodies, but there were innocent civilians among the dead here.

I don't like it either, Nova. If you hadn't gone showing up when you did, we would have been in and out of here without so many killings, but you forced our hand.

She scanned left and right, trying to find the source of the voice in her head, but the room was empty and all the doors leading from it were closed.

Where are you, Tosh? Come out and fight like a man.

I don't want to fight you. I just want you to listen, as friends.

You're no friend of mine. Not after this. She passed the bodies, moving out a door on the opposite side of the room, toward the heart of the palace. She was close now, and moved more carefully. If Tosh was going to make his move, it would be soon.

Casualties of war. Mengsk and his Dominion are corrupt, Nova. You just can't face the fact that you've signed your life away to a man like that. And you don't remember what they did to us, because if you did, you'd put down that gun and join me.

After the dining hall, she entered a reception area that looked like the front room for Mengsk's main office. The desk was empty, but she could see female legs sticking out from behind it and a pool of blood. A door behind the desk was closed.

The floor shuddered slightly under her feet, and she sensed a commotion outside the palace walls.

The marines have landed, Tosh, and the emergency law enforcement response is coming in. There's no way for you to escape. Give it up now and I'll let you live.

His chuckle filled her head. *You really got no idea what's happening, do you? It's a revolution and no squadron of marines is going to stop it.*

I and the other ghosts will.

You'll join me sooner or later, when you've accepted the truth, just like the others. I have Kath back on Gehenna Station, and Lio's with me too. You'll round out our old team.

Nova stopped dead in her tracks, her mind filled with more memories of the past: her fellow academy recruits, brothers and sisters in arms, fighting side by side for the Dominion.

Kath wouldn't betray the emperor, she said. *And Lio's gone for good. He's . . . dead.*

No. Lio's entered the data stream, but he's not gone. He's become something . . . different. More powerful. Let me explain, Nova.

It's too late for that. She skirted the desk, glancing down at the body of the secretary as she passed. So many deaths.

Then she tore the door from its hinges and entered the inner chamber.

It was larger than she'd expected, with tiled floors, leather couches, and an expensive rug, one wall dominated by a wet bar. There were no windows here in the center of the palace, making the room and what lay beyond it more secure.

The heavy metal door to the safe room was behind the emperor's desk, normally hidden by panels that had been slid aside. It looked slightly battered, but it was intact. Mengsk was secure.

Then why did she feel a strange sense of disappointment at the sight?

Nova sensed the attack coming a moment before it occurred, and it gave her just enough time to dive forward into a tucked roll, the blow missing her heart by centimeters and tracing a burning river of fire across her shoulders as it glanced off. She came up to her feet and turned to see a woman, uncloaked and in the spectres' now-familiar black garb, standing in front of her, mouth fixed in a rictus grin.

The woman held some kind of canister. "Breathe deep," she said. "And see the light."

And then she sprayed the contents of the canister in Nova's face.

Nova felt the strange gas worm its way inside her body once again, the taste of coppery blood thick on her tongue. She felt like retching, but at the same time she realized she *wanted* it, had been craving that taste ever since the zerg battle on Altara. Explosions of color began to pop before her eyes like tiny fireworks and the room faded away, voices coming in at her from all sides like the whispering of a great, hushed crowd; someone else seemed to be shouting at her from a distance, but she could not make out what they were saying.

Bloody hands reached out for her through the fog, grasping at her ghost uniform and leaving streaks of gore. She swiped blindly with her arms, trying to fend them off, but the hands broke like wisps of smoke and then reformed in tendril-like swirls to pull at her once again. As she recoiled from the hands, faces began to take shape within the fog, and she realized with a shock that these were all people she had killed during her time as an enforcer for Fagin, and later as a ghost assassin, running down AWOL members of the marines, traitors against the emperor, UED leaders and spies. Everything seemed to rush back at her at once, all her top secret missions that had been fed to her through the ghost program or directly from Mengsk himself.

The fog lifted . . .

She crept up creaking and rotted backstairs in an Agrian slum, rain drumming on the metal roof and dripping through cracks onto her head, her weapon out, listening to the noises from the apartment above. Her target, a former noncom accused of selling information on new Dominion weaponry to mercs during the war, was eating dinner, his voice rising occasionally in a curse at his wife, who was rushing back and forth to serve him cheese and potted meat, but could never move quite fast enough for him. Nova could smell the food in the air, rancid and close; she could even sense the taste on the man's tongue from reading his thoughts. She sensed another terran in the apartment too, but he was linked to an alpha wave sleeper and posed no threat, so she continued moving silently upward.

At the landing she paused, listening to the chatter for a moment before kicking the door in and sweeping the room with her C-10, her barrel fixing upon the man behind his kitchen table, shirt stained and his belly straining from years of neglect, bloodshot eyes startled into blind panic. A tiny robot pet monkey screeched and cowered behind a chair, a child's toy that had seen better days, its fur worn through to metal, its joints rusty and servos whining and clacking. The room smelled powerfully of mold and cigar smoke.

No, *his wife shouted,* do not shoot; he is innocent! *But Nova had her orders, and when her HUD identified the target, she did not hesitate.*

The explosions tore a hole through the man's chest the size of a fist, knocking him backward out of his chair and onto his side, blood pumping as he clutched at himself, gasped, and then died. His wife screamed senselessly over and over again, and Nova was inside her head and felt her agony of despair at the certainty that she could not survive without him, even though he hit her when he was drunk and liked to pinch and bite her in bed.

The monkey scrambled across the room. Movement in the doorway. Nova swiveled the barrel of the C-10 to cover the small boy who shuffled out into the light, rubbing his face with one hand, clutching the monkey's paw in another. His blond hair stuck up all over his head and his eyes went from sleepy to wide with shock.

Nova's finger had tightened on the trigger, a hairsbreadth away, and she relaxed just enough to stop the gun from firing. Daddy! *the boy screamed suddenly, running across the room,* Daddy, what's wrong? Why you bleeding? *Then, looking up at his mother,* Daddy hurt. Get the doctor, Mommy, hurry! *But the mother wasn't looking at him anymore; she was rushing at Nova and beating her with her fists, clawing at her headgear, and sobbing, a wild ball of hissing teeth and nails that would not stop until Nova put her down on the floor with the butt of the gun cracking against her temple.*

The little boy screamed again as she backed out of the apartment to the landing, activating her cloaking device and taking the stairs three at a time, sensing something was wrong with the setup but not knowing what, the rain cold on the back of her neck as she burst out into the muddy streets and disappeared, leaving them behind as she always did, a ghost fading away into the night, death in her wake.

The little boy that lingered in her mind morphed into Lila, the girl from Altara, her face pale with terror, and

Nova's stomach clenched. She turned to run, but Fagin stood in front of her. That's the kind of man you work for, baby, *Fagin said, leering at her.* Sending you to do his dirty work, executing people without giving them any chance of being saved. You know that guy you killed wasn't a spy; hell, you read him—he couldn't pull something like that off if you handed it to him on a platter. He was the brother of an old Confederate general, a low-level teep, and Mengsk wanted to send a special message by having a ghost take him out. Tying up loose ends, you know? The war's over, you crush your enemies. It's all a chess game to him. And now that little boy's gonna grow up without a father. *He stepped closer, reaching out a bloodied hand to her and tracing a finger down her arm.* You thought I was bad. What would your own momma say to that, huh? Her baby killing people without a fair trial, with no chance to prove themselves. That's not how the Terra family did business, is it? Or maybe it is. Maybe killing's in your blood.

Nova swung her fist through the air where he'd been, swirling the fog that had eddied in while she wasn't looking, but hitting nothing at all. Fagin was gone.

When she came out of the flashback, she found herself on the floor, the woman in black standing over her, canister still in one hand, Nova's gun in the other. The entire attack had lasted only seconds, but Lila's scared little face lingered in her mind.

The woman had fiery red hair. *Dylanna Okyl.* Nova remembered her. They had a history together from the academy, on two different teams that had clashed during training exercises and then joined up to fight the zerg on Shi.

Am I buying all this now? Is it that easy?

She knew one thing: she hadn't liked Dylanna then, and she liked her even less now.

She could see Tosh in the doorway behind her. He was uncloaked too, his dreadlocks longer and thicker than she remembered, his body heavier, more muscled under the black suit. There was something else different about him, but it took her a moment to figure it out. She realized that his eyes had turned a milky white since the last time she'd seen him. The effect was unsettling, as if he'd been blinded in some kind of accident, but he moved more surely than ever.

Nova's back still burned from the blow she'd taken, and she felt wetness dripping down her waist. "That wasn't Fagin in my head," she said. She was still shaking from the vividness of the hallucination. "That was you. How do I know you aren't just planting memories of what you want me to see?"

"I don't need to operate like that. If you saw it, those things happened." Tosh stepped closer. "There's more for you to remember," he said.

"So much you should understand about yourself. Mengsk needs to answer for his crimes.
Help us get him out of that room. Come with
us, and be free forever."

"You'll never make it out of here."

Tosh chuckled, his voice throaty and deep.
"You don't know what I can do, Nova. The terrazine gives me power I never dreamed of before.
You'll be questioning everything, the way I did at
first, trying to come to terms with your memory
coming back. It's a hard thing for a ghost, I know
it. You've been brainwashed so long you don't
know what real is anymore. But I'm here to tell
you that this ain't the way to peace. Not living in
palaces like these, building bigger armies, and
stabbing people in the back while your lieutenants
are running torture camps on fringe worlds and
bleeding the colonists dry." He shook his head, the
dreadlocks swaying like snakes. "Not turning your
most gifted recruits into machines made for killing, and then using them up until there's nothing
left but a shell you throw away like garbage."

No. Nova closed her eyes. *I wanted this.* She
thought about joining the ghost program and how
the idea had seemed like the perfect escape. Many
terrans with psionic gifts were dragged kicking
and screaming to the academy, but not Nova
Terra. To her, it had been a chance for oblivion
and a way to finally silence the voices inside her
head that would not let her rest.

The voices were back again now, and they had been joined by many others. Voices that had been silenced by the repeated memory wipes, but were now clamoring to be heard.

She opened her moist eyes and found them both watching her silently, as if waiting for an answer. "You think this is any better? Look around. You're murdering people in the name of revolution, but they're still dead. You think they care who did the killing?"

Tosh sighed and looked down as his remote console beeped in his hands. "Lio says the marines are through the front door," he said. "We don't have much time. With your help we can get that safe room open." He fixed his strange gaze upon her face, and she felt him lock onto her mind, probing gently, looking for clues to her true intentions. *We could've taken you out just now, but we want you with us. You're the key to our plans. I remember what a great team we made. We can do it again, only this time, it's gonna count for something.*

Dylanna looked back and forth between them, her entire body shaking. Nova saw her knuckles had turned white where she gripped the gun. "She's not gonna change her mind," Dylanna said. "I can feel it. We don't need her." She turned back to Nova, her eyes glittering. "She murdered some of our own. I say we take her right now, while we have the chance."

"I'd like to see you try," Nova said, climbing to

her feet. Every single movement was an effort. She motioned to the gun. Blood dripped from the fingers of her right hand to the floor. "You have something that's mine. I want it back."

"I'll give it back to you," Dylanna said, "but you might not like my delivery method—"

The building shook, sending a glass statue on the desk toppling to the floor, where it shattered. "They're coming, and we're going in there, with or without you," Dylanna said, motioning to the safe room door. "Now get out of the way, slike, or I'll cut you down."

ENOUGH, Gabriel Tosh thundered in their heads. *This ain't the way it should be, turning us against each other. Come on, Dylanna. I won't fight her. There will be other chances.*

"But we're so close—"

"I can't let you go," Nova said, holding Tosh's gaze. "You know I can't do that."

"Do what you have to do," he said. He glanced up at the ceiling and smiled. Then he activated his cloaking device, turned, and left the room, and all that remained was the afterimage of his aura slowly fading from her eyes.

"See you again soon," Dylanna said. She tossed the gun at Nova's feet. "Don't try to follow us. You won't like what happens." She turned, winked out, and was gone.

Why aren't I going after them? Nova wondered. But she couldn't will herself to move. She was suddenly so very tired. The emperor was safe, and that was what she had come here for, wasn't it? She had completed her objective, and the thought of continuing the fight overwhelmed her. Who knew if she could stand a chance against both of them at once?

Maybe Tosh is right. Maybe I just can't face the truth.

Blood kept dripping from her wound as she put her back to the neosteel door, slid slowly down to the floor, and waited for the marines to come.

CHAPTER FOURTEEN

THE PANIC ROOM

Nova didn't know exactly how long she sat there. It seemed like forever, but it was probably only moments before the first marine in full combat gear thumped into the doorway, servos whining, rifle up, and scanning the room. The barrel found her and stopped, aimed at her head.

"You there," the marine shouted. "Don't move!"

"Agent X41822N, for the Dominion," she said. "The emperor is secure."

Then she passed out.

She ran through the courtyard outside her parents' sky-scraper, the sun beating down on her head and warming her scalp, water from the nearby fountain shimmering in the heat. Someone was chasing her—possibly her old nanny; it was a game they used to play occasionally when Nova was a very small girl, sort of like hide-and-seek, except she found that this game made the nanny quite cross.

Nova had always known when her nanny was happy or sad. She knew how everyone felt, all the time. Her father, Constantino, had called it her gift of empathy. She had inherited it from him.

She ducked into the building, heading for the elevator, as events clicked into focus. It wasn't her nanny after all. She was too old for a nanny. Whatever was chasing her wasn't a person but a feeling of terrible dread.

She had just turned fifteen, and her parents were shipping her off to a resort for spoiled rich children on Tyrador IX, to protect her from rebel groups who were targeting the Old Families on Tarsonis in retaliation for the attack on Korhal, and intent upon bringing down the Confederacy. Members of several families had been executed in horrific fashion, and her father's hoverbike factory had been hit just days before. The other children on board had been mostly glad to be going on what they perceived to be a long, peaceful vacation, and they couldn't understand why she was not. But she had left the ship in distress, because she had sensed her parents were being attacked in their home. This had been more than simple intuition; this had been as real to her as if she had been standing there witnessing it. She had to do something, before it was too late.

The building was too quiet, and as she took the elevator up to the penthouse her dread increased. She had been here before and had gone through this scene already. She knew what she would find.

The elevator doors opened onto a vision from her deepest nightmares: her mother and father, dead, her brother on his knees, and several servants lined up against the wall, a group of armed men around them, her mother's trusted jig, Edward Peters, one of them. Edward had always been cold and boring to her; but how could he do this?

As she entered the room, her anger and fear grew into a living, pulsing monster clawing at her brain and begging for release, and when Edward ordered Gustavo McBain to shoot her brother in the head, and then Edward pointed his gun at Nova, she cried out in agony, letting the monster loose . . .

"Nova."

The voice was familiar to her. She used it to hold on to the monster's wriggling, fiery tail, and pulled it back into herself with a shuddering sigh. The feeling of dread began to fade.

"Come on, dammit, wake up. Don't you do this to me."

Nova Terra opened her eyes to find Mal Kelerchian crouched over her, a look of distress etched across his face. His thoughts were a confusing jumble, but she sensed his fear at losing her, and touched by his concern, she reached a hand up to his stubbled cheek before letting it drop quickly, as if it had been scalded. Kelerchian jerked backward in surprise.

It had been an impulsive gesture, one that didn't normally come easy for her. Nobody had cared about her like this before, at least not since her parents were alive, and she hadn't cared enough for anyone else for it to matter. She was a loner, a human weapon, incapable of forming long-term relationships because after each mission she would start her life all over again. It was the way she had chosen to live, and she hadn't regretted it.

Until now.

She blinked, resisting the urge to shield her eyes. They had moved her to a portable stretcher away from the safe room door, but she was still in Mengsk's inner office. Everything seemed sharpened, more intense, including her emotional state; the world had jumped into focus; colors were brighter; sounds louder and more clearly defined. She felt as if she and Kelerchian had linked minds and were sharing thoughts in a way she'd never experienced before.

Her hand was bloody and had left a streak like a brand on his cheek.

"You're all right," he said, his face reddening as he glanced around at the marines who filled the room with chatter. "Thought maybe we'd lost you. That would have been . . . unfortunate. Medic's on the way, so just sit tight."

Nova was having difficulty concentrating. The inner voices of the marines were deafening, and even her neural inhibitor was helpless to deaden them. *The terrazine,* she thought, *it's working on me right now.*

Kelerchian stared at her. "Terrazine?"

She sighed and licked her parched lips. "It's what the . . . spectres call the gas we were exposed to on Altara. It boosts psi levels, just like we thought, among other things. They sprayed me with it before they . . . got away."

"Flicking hell." Kelerchian rubbed his palms on his leather duster, went to touch her arm, thought better of it, his face flushing again. She sensed his anger rising. "I knew this was a trap. I should have been here with you."

Nova shook her head, a wave of dizziness washing over her. "They would have killed you." And that made her think of something else, and she tried to stand up before Kelerchian gently pushed her back again. "The rest of my team," she said, "are they all right?"

The look in his eyes told her everything she needed to know. "I'm sorry, Nova. Two are missing. The rest are dead. But they took a couple of those bastards down with them. Or maybe you did that yourself." He shrugged. "We lost contact with your team a few minutes after you arrived in Augustgrad, and communications were down, so we have no record of what happened here."

"What about palace security cameras?"

"All disabled. Some kind of bug in the system kept them offline and the data's scrambled."

Lio.

She explained, as best she could, what she had discovered during her confrontation with Gabriel Tosh. Mal listened with growing disbelief. "I know it seems crazy," she said. "But at least part of it is true. A former ghost is behind what's been happening. I saw him with my own two eyes. Terrazine's pushed him over the edge. He thinks the emperor is corrupt, and he wants to take the entire Dominion down with him."

Kelerchian's gaze darkened. "You're wondering the same thing."

"I . . . no. Of course not. He said some things that were disturbing. That's all."

"You know how I feel about Mengsk. But the devil you know . . ." Kelerchian glanced behind him at the machinists who kept stomping in and out with heavy equipment. Apparently the door to the safe room had been damaged and it was taking them time to cut Mengsk free. A laser drill whirred to life as one of them began to slice into the neosteel hinges.

"Look," he said quietly, "we can talk more later, but there are going to be some questions about what happened down here. As far as Hauler's concerned, you're a hero. But Spaulding's gunning for you, and he's already demanding a formal investigation. He's got an ally in Ward too. They want to know why these terrorists got away, and why you're the only one left alive."

"They attacked us in the courtyard," she said. "Ambushed us and disabled our suits. They were so strong, abilities I've never seen before. The others didn't stand a chance. I chased Tosh in here, and then they gassed me."

This time he did put his hand on her arm, and she felt his warmth and strength rush into her. "From the looks of the place, you had one hell of a scuffle. You did good, kid. You okay?"

"I—I don't know. I should have done more. Our mission is to stop them, Mal. Not just slow the bleeding."

"Excuse me, sir." A medic stood behind them, carrying a supply pack, her visor open. She was young and pretty, her blond hair tied away from her face. "I need to examine the patient's wounds."

"She's got a pretty bad cut on her back," Kelerchian said, standing up and moving a meter away. "Take good care of her, you hear me?"

The medic nodded and knelt to remove her equipment from the pack. Nova could feel both her discomfort and awe at treating a ghost. "I won't bite," she said, attempting a smile. "No analgesics, please. I want to stay alert."

"But I'll have to use the auto-sutures. The pain—"

"Do what she asks," Kelerchian said. "I'll see you back on the *Palatine*. We'll talk more then." He turned to leave.

"Mal, wait," Nova said. "Will you . . . stay here, with me? Just for a while?"

She sensed both his surprise and pleasure at the request. "Sure I will," he said. "Just thought you might like a little privacy." He motioned to the medic, who was pretending not to listen. "She's going to have to . . . um, remove part of your suit."

"I'll keep the front covered," Nova said, and now it was her turn to blush. "Don't worry. I'd rather have you here."

"I can handle it if you can," he said, although she could tell that he wasn't so sure of that and was working furiously to keep his thoughts to himself. She decided to let him off the hook and change the subject.

"Listen, Tosh mentioned something else I just remembered. He said he was holding Kath Toom at Gehenna Station. You ever heard of that before?"

"No," he said. "I'll run a check on it through my suit's computer. Toom was the ghost who disappeared from Altara. She was part of your team back at the academy, right? Tosh and Lio too. What the fekk are they up to, really?"

"I'm not sure," Nova said. "But I'm going to find out."

*   *   *

Twenty minutes later the medic had treated Nova's wound, washing it and closing it with auto-
sutures. Luckily it hadn't sliced too deeply into the
muscles of her shoulders. Concerned about the
loss of blood, the medic was going to send her back
to the infirmary on the *Palatine*, but Nova refused.
She wanted to be there when they finally cut
Mengsk out.

Shortly after that, the machinists working on
the door let out a shout and jumped back as the
meter-thick neosteel slab came loose from its
hinges, teetered, and fell into the room with a tremendous, bone-shuddering crash, crushing the
tile and raising a choking cloud of stone dust.

As the dust cleared, the cheer that had risen
up from the assembled marines quickly faded as
Emperor Arcturus Mengsk stepped out into the
light, holding a cloth to his mouth and nose, his
eyes flashing dangerously as he scanned the room.
He wore his familiar brown leather coat with its
thick, upright collar, his breastplate tied tightly to
his formidable chest, brown leather boots laced
neatly up the middle. His long, graying hair was
swept away from his forehead, his beard peppered
with white. After a few hours locked away inside
the safe room, he looked slightly rumpled, and
even more intimidating because of it.

As he dropped the cloth at his feet and walked

around the huge door that partially blocked his exit, then looked over the marines and law enforcement standing silently before him, he offered none of his customary words of encouragement. Anger emanated from him in waves. Several marines began to shift restlessly back and forth on their feet, realizing the danger in being anywhere near a man this powerful who had been very nearly stolen away right from under his own guards' noses. The emperor had built Augustgrad like a bristling fortress, a representation of his power and reach. And a handful of assassins had crept in and left him helpless in a matter of hours.

Mengsk's gaze settled on Kelerchian, who remained near the door to the outer room, and then moved to Nova, who had stood up from the stretcher. "You two," he said, pointing at them both. "Stay with me. Everyone else, out. I want this room cleared. No one is to come within one hundred meters until I give the order. And nobody is to speak of this to anyone. Do you think you can handle that?"

More murmurs and several bursts of "Yes, sir!" rang out before they stumbled and pushed each other in a rush to get out the door, most of them praying the emperor wouldn't change his mind and order them all hanged.

Once the room was empty, Mengsk sighed and rubbed his face in a rare show of vulnerability. "My guards, they're all dead?"

Nova nodded. "I'm afraid so. The ghosts too."

The emperor was notoriously hard to read, even for teeps; he had perfected a technique that allowed him to hide his most personal thoughts deep inside his own psyche. But she wouldn't have tried to read him anyway. Even so, it didn't take a psionic ability to see his distress over the news. She wondered if there was a little bit of fear there as well; she knew his family history and his father's brutal assassination under somewhat similar circumstances. This attack could not have been easy for him to go through.

In spite of her attempts to let it go, standing there, looking at him, she could not help questioning if what Tosh had said about the zerg attack on Shi was true. *Had* the emperor orchestrated the attack on the last of the Tarsonis Old Family lines? If so, what did it mean for her?

"The only cameras that were working inside the safe room were those with direct feeds," he said. "Everything else was static. And even those cameras had no audio. So I was able to see only a fraction of what happened, and I heard nothing at all." He looked to Nova. "I watched you hold them off in here. You were injured, and yet you remained between them and this door. I thank you for that, and I'll want a full report on what happened outside these walls." He turned abruptly to Kelerchian. "I'll let Colonel Hauler tell me why the full power of the Marine Corps was unable to prevent this attack. But explain to me why the rest of my ghosts were lost."

"Sir, I was the leader on the ground," Nova said quickly. "They were my responsibility—"

"They were overwhelmed," Kelerchian said, cutting her off. "These . . . spectres are too powerful for a handful of ghosts. It was a suicide mission."

Mengsk raised an eyebrow and let the full weight of his silence fall on them. Normally, this would intimidate even the most courageous military men.

But Kelerchian didn't flinch. "If you'd like a fairer fight," he said, "maybe you'd be willing to tell us the truth?"

"I've told you what you needed to know," Mengsk said, waving a hand as if to dismiss the thought.

"With all due respect, I have to disagree."

Shocked at his impertinence, Nova waited for the emperor to explode with anger, perhaps even backhand Mal in the face. Instead, he seemed to calculate something in his head and make a decision. When he spoke again, it was with the confident, polished warmth of a politician. "Agent X41822N, do you require more medical assistance for your wounds? What I have to say may take some time."

"I'll be fine," Nova said.

"Good. What I am about to tell you remains

between us. Is that understood?" They both nodded. "Now come into the safe room, where we'll be away from any prying eyes."

Without another word, Mengsk turned, stepped around the huge metal door still lying in his path, and entered the safe room. Nova and Kelerchian looked at each other in surprise. "This oughta be good," Kelerchian muttered. "After you."

The inside of the little room was surprisingly comfortable. The walls were paneled with the finest rosewood, and another thick silk rug took up most of the floor. Nova could hear the air-circulation system humming softly. Padded benches lined an alcove with a built-in operations table, and another alcove held shelves full of supplies and toiletries. One wall was dominated by surveillance equipment showing scenes from all over the palace. The corridors were empty except for a few armed sentries, but the courtyard outside was a bustling hive of marines, law enforcement, medics, and curious onlookers.

"Back online again, I see," Mengsk said. He motioned to the benches and the table, which had an open holo chessboard prominently displayed to one side. "Please, take a seat. Do either of you play?"

"Not at your level, I'm sure," Kelerchian said.

"I do love a good game. Such a challenge for the mind, and a wonderful allegory for the battlefield. This AI offers a particularly good fight—I was losing this round before the interruption, I'm afraid. Can I offer you a drink?" After they declined, he went to a small bar next to the supply alcove, lined with various colorful bottles. "If you don't mind, I think I'll have a little of this old Tarsonis whiskey. The real stuff, so much better than that Scotty Bolger's cheap swill. One of the best whiskey makers the sector had ever seen; such a sad thing to lose them. Precious few bottles left, and we can't seem to reproduce it."

The mention of Tarsonis brought Nova's wind up, but if he meant anything by it, he hid it well. She was amazed at how quickly he had switched gears from an angry, demanding tyrant to polite host. He poured himself a glass and sat down opposite them, settling in to tell his story as if they were all there for a few cocktails at his summer estate.

"A couple of years ago an unmanned space probe detected an unknown gas leaking from a rift in the surface of a fringe planet we named D-4358," he said, taking a sip from his glass. "Our probe didn't predict a terran use for it, so this wasn't a high priority at first. D-4358—those who landed there later nicknamed it Demon's Fair, for reasons you might understand—was a harsh environment, with extreme temperature swings due to its elliptical orbit, and did not appear to support life. But further scans by the probe on a second pass discovered protoss ruins on another side of the planet, including what we believed to be an alien mining facility of some kind, along with a shrine. So we sent a team there to investigate."

Mengsk took another long sip from the glass. "They determined that the facility had been built to collect this gas, although the pocket had long since been depleted. The rift on the other side of the planet, however, was still leaking, and the team was able to capture enough to bring it back for further analysis. They were also able to scan the protoss writings carved into the shrine walls."

"Let me guess," Kelerchian said. "You're talking about the same gas that was being mined on Altara."

Mengsk smiled. "We called it terrazine. A linguist skilled in the protoss language, Khalani, was able to decipher much of the writing from the shrine. They referred to this gas as 'the Breath of Creation,' and it was apparently able to expand the senses and allow the protoss to commune with a higher power, bringing them closer to the xel'naga. Meanwhile, several of the men were exposed to this gas while investigating the leak and reacted in unusual ways—they complained of hallucinations, among other things. One of them grew violent enough to be restrained. Another, who we later determined to be a very low-level teep, claimed to be able to hear others' thoughts."

"Of course, you were very interested in the military applications of such a thing."

"One of my chief scientific officers was quite curious, yes, and convinced me to run some tests. The project was code-named Shadowblade."

The room fell silent for a long moment before Kelerchian lurched to his feet. His face was red. "That's the same term these bastards used when one of them attacked us down on Altara," he said. "Is everyone just a pawn to you—?"

"Sit *down,* wrangler," Mengsk said. His eyes had gone glittery and dark, and his voice was barely raised beyond conversational level, but the power in it was clear. Nova had no doubt he would order Malcolm Kelerchian executed without a second thought, should it serve his purpose. "Do not assume you know everything. It would be better for you if you withheld judgment until we finish."

Kelerchian looked at Nova. He was breathing hard. *Easy,* she urged. *Hear him out. It won't do us any good if you're locked away in an Augustgrad prison.*

Slowly, she felt him relax, and he sank back down on the bench. *All right. But if you want to leave, you let me know, and we're gone. I don't give a damn what he might do.*

"We gave it a level nine classification," Mengsk

continued, his voice dropping back into the same smooth tone, as if nothing had happened. "I named General Warfield to head the project, one of my best men, and strict safeguards were put in place. A small, trusted team, with top-level clearances, nobody in or out of the inner circle, a remote facility that was impossible to crack. We tested it on animals, the condemned, and a select few volunteers, several of them low-level psionics. Initially, we had high hopes, but our scientists found the side effects of the gas to be . . . erratic."

"How so?" Nova asked, although she thought she already knew.

"It did seem to raise the psionic levels across the board, but it was addictive. Those who took more than a few doses began to crave more and more of it and would do anything to get some. It also caused visual and auditory hallucinations, mania, and the occasional violent outburst. We shelved the project after an accident at the facility that left most of the team dead, executed by one of their own team members, Cole Bennett. Unfortunately Bennett had decided to experiment with the gas himself. Needless to say, things did not end well. It drove him mad." Mengsk sighed heavily, staring into his drink. For a moment Nova almost believed that he was saddened by all of this. "I ordered all records of the project destroyed. Other than Warfield, who saw the trouble coming and fought to end the project, and has since retired from active duty, anyone associated with it is either dead or locked away in a correctional facility."

"Why didn't you tell us before?" Nova said.

"I didn't know terrazine was related to the attacks, although I began to suspect it more recently, as reports continued to come in about the terrorists' abilities and behavior, and we analyzed the gas leaking from Altara. Still, I was absolutely certain that the information about the project was secure."

"And now?"

"I don't know." Mengsk took another long drink, draining his glass. "But it seems clear that somehow, someone has brought Project: Shadowblade back to life, and is intent on using it to destroy me."

"We should get a look at those records," Kelerchian said. "Double-check everyone—"

"That won't be necessary," Mengsk said. "I told you the records were destroyed. I made further inquiries into the status of everyone who was a part of the project and spoke to Warfield personally. He confirms this. There are only three left alive, and all of them are safely locked away in New Folsom Prison. Nobody has escaped from there in decades."

"So now what?" Kelerchian said. "How does this help us? We've got rogue ghost agents who call themselves spectres and appear and disappear at will. They have abilities our own ghosts can't handle. And they want you dead. Seems like sooner or later, they're going to accomplish their goal."

Mengsk smiled, but there was no warmth in it. "From your tone, I gather that wouldn't particularly upset you, wrangler Kelerchian."

"I wouldn't dream of such a thing. It would throw the Dominion into chaos, and I'm not a big fan of chaos when it comes to government."

This isn't going well. "Gabriel Tosh," Nova said, changing the subject. "He's the leader of the spectres. We need to find out how he got involved in this. What's his connection with Shadowblade?"

"Tosh." Mengsk shook his head. His face had hardened into a scowl. "This brings me to my second purpose for inviting you in here." He stood up abruptly and turned to the bank of surveillance equipment. "The files had him deceased," he said as he fiddled with a remote control device. One of the screens in the center of the display hissed static. "Killed in one of his first missions after graduating from the academy. Which is why I'm so surprised to see his face."

The static cleared and Nova found herself looking at silent footage of the outer room from several hours earlier. She saw Tosh sitting on the floor, staring at a small remote console in his hands, and then he smashed his meaty fist into the tile, raising a puff of dust. Finally he looked up, milky eyes narrowing in concentration. The video image seemed to ripple, as if a wave of heat had gone coursing through the room. Tosh closed his eyes, glanced at a female figure sitting on a couch, and then back at the console.

When Tosh stood up, Mengsk paused the video and zoomed in until Tosh's face filled the screen. "I didn't recognize him at first," Mengsk said, still standing with his back to them both. His voice was cold and deadly calm. "He never worked an assignment directly for me before his death, and I only met him once while visiting the academy. But facial recognition software identified him immediately. Agent X41822N, you were in training with him, were you not?"

"We were on the same team," Nova said. *But you know that already, don't you?* she thought. The emperor was famous for his attention to detail; surely he would have learned everything there was to know about Tosh's background by now.

"I believe I read in the files that he was your team leader. And yet you stood up to him out there. I'm surprised you remember him, considering your memory of that time has been wiped. But perhaps this explains it." Mengsk forwarded the video to the point when Nova had come into the room, and they all watched as Dylanna Okyl sliced her across the back with her blade and then sprayed the gas in her face.

"They exposed you to terrazine," Mengsk said. Finally he turned to face them, his eyes glittering, as Nova watched herself go into silent convulsions on the video. "Are you feeling any of the ill effects?"

Kelerchian glanced at her. *He's testing you, Nova. Be careful.*

She hesitated, wondering how much to confess. "Nothing I can't handle, sir."

"You were hallucinating there, I take it." He gestured back at the screen. "Normally the terrazine effects take just a bit longer than that to develop with such ferocity. Perhaps you're just particularly susceptible. What were you experiencing, may I ask?"

"I . . . relived a mission from my past."

"I see." Mengsk paused the video once again as the image of Nova's face was twisted grotesquely, her eyes rolled back in her head. She felt naked and vulnerable, seeing herself on-screen and unaware of her surroundings; it was as if someone had snuck into her bedroom and filmed her dreaming. "It must have been an unpleasant one. What I don't understand is why they didn't kill you while you were in such a position. That would have been the time. And yet they remained still."

Mengsk was watching her carefully. "They wanted to recruit me," she said simply. "I'm worth more to them alive than dead."

He nodded and started the video again. "Apparently their arguments were not convincing."

"I am a ghost agent for the Dominion," she said. "That's all that matters to me." *Sometimes forgetting what's behind is the only way to look ahead . . .*

"Nova's as loyal as they come," Kelerchian said. "I don't see why we have to go over all of this—"

"Because, wrangler," Mengsk said, slamming his hands down on the table, "*I was attacked in my home. By my own ghosts.* And then I have to be subjected to this."

He looked back at the screen again, in time to see Gabriel Tosh glance up directly at the camera. The big man smiled, winked, and then disappeared from view. "Baiting me," Mengsk said. "Throwing his treachery in my face, as if I can't do anything to stop it." He reversed the video to Tosh's face again and paused it. "I will not stand for such a thing, and before I decided what to do about it, I had to be sure whom I can trust. This is the man responsible for the loss of my ghosts. He is now the most wanted man in the sector. I want you to track him down, find those he is working with and those he loves most, and I want them dead. I want them all dead. Agent X41822N, you will see to this personally. Do you understand me?"

"I do."

"Good." Mengsk stared at them both, breathing hard, while Tosh's image, frozen in a leering smile, loomed over his shoulder. He was closer to losing control than she had ever seen, and it did not suit him. His normal politician's shell had been stripped away, and what was exposed was ugly and cruel. "I want him to suffer. Do not come back to me until it's done."

CHAPTER FIFTEEN

THE LOST

The cloaked ship slid silently into the landing bay, its engine noise canceled out by a sophisticated antiwave system aided by the pilot's own psionic abilities. Originally developed under the umbrella of the top secret Kal-Bryant operation Sector 9, the device had been supplied by Umojan researchers who had helped with its installation, and they had done the same with the spectres' more advanced propulsion and cloaking systems.

The deal he and General Bennett had made with the Ruling Council had served Project: Shadowblade well, Tosh thought. Umojan technology allowed them to move about completely undetected by Dominion forces, even as they left Korhal airspace right under the noses of over ten battlecruisers and endless vikings and dropships. In return, the Umojans and former Dominion senator Corbin Phash had received assurances that

Emperor Mengsk would be removed from power, permanently. They had also received a tidy sum of money.

It was a badly kept secret that the Umojan Protectorate—terrans who had arrived in the Koprulu sector along with everyone else after the twenty-third–century colonization mission from Old Earth, but had never joined the Confederacy of Man—was willing and able to support any separatist group intent upon destroying the Dominion. Although they had originally been allies bent on helping Emperor Mengsk to overthrow the Confederacy, relations between the two governments had begun to sour quickly, coming to a head when the emperor visited Umoja and was very nearly assassinated by Confederate Resistance Forces. He believed the Umojans had known about the attack, and perhaps had even been involved in the attempt on his life.

The years since had been spent in political jockeying, economic blockades, and the spread of underground propaganda. The Umojan Ruling Council knew full well that the Dominion military was too large and powerful for them to fight head-to-head, and so they publicly remained peaceful while working to support splinter groups whenever they could.

A particular target of theirs was the Ghost Academy, a program they had deemed both immoral and corrupt even before former senator

Phash and his psionic son, Colin, had defied the academy and sought refuge with the Umojans. Colin had been forced to join the academy against Corbin's wishes, and he had fought tooth and nail to get his son back. He had succeeded, but they had been hunted down like animals as a result and had to take shelter among the Umojans, where Colin had become the youngest member of the Umojan Shadowguard due to his advanced abilities. After that, the Ruling Council had helped spread anti-academy propaganda across dozens of Dominion worlds. Which had made the council Gabriel Tosh's lifelong friends.

But Tosh found it difficult to keep his mind on all that now as he settled the ship gently into place on Gehenna's plascrete landing floor. His thoughts were on his fallen comrades back in Augustgrad, and the failure of their mission. Mengsk was not under their control, and Nova Terra was not yet a spectre.

It was the first real failure of Project: Shadowblade, and General Bennett would not be pleased.

And yet they had accomplished something important, laying the groundwork for convincing Nova to join them. Tosh powered down the engines and unstrapped from his pilot's chair before going back in to get the others. They disembarked in silence, supporting the two ghosts they had taken from Augustgrad after the battle, who were unable to walk under their own power.

Dylanna had already disabled their neural implants while in transit and would remove them entirely once they reached the medical unit. If she had been a bit too rough, that was understandable, Tosh thought, considering what had happened inside the city walls. They were all upset. He could feel Dylanna's anger seething just beneath the surface, and it joined and mingled and multiplied with his own until he was buzzing with energy and desperately needing a release.

They be needing their leader to honor those they lost, Grandma Tosh said. *A moment of ceremony. Lay the spirits of the dead to rest, Gabriel, or you risk a haunting.*

Tosh nodded. Lately his grandma had taken up permanent residence inside his head and often spoke without bothering to appear before him the way she had before. That was fine; she provided wise counsel, and he was grateful to have her. She was right this time too. He needed to make a statement.

Tosh stopped in the middle of the hangar and asked that the two ghosts be set down on the floor. *Join me in a moment of silence for our fallen comrades,* he directed his teammates as they stood in a rough circle. *Talen, Jara, and Karl. Your sacrifices will be remembered. Rest in peace.*

The silence was broken by Dylanna, who had been fidgeting back and forth on her feet. "What about their suits and weapons?" she said. "Mengsk has them now."

Tosh looked angrily at her. "The suits self-destruct after vital signs have ceased. You know that."

"But what if that didn't work? His scientists will be able to replicate our advances."

"It don't matter. The Dominion will be ours before they can do anything with it." Tosh looked around at what remained of his team and saw uncertainty in their faces for the first time. What had happened in Augustgrad was bad enough, but Dylanna was making it worse. He should put her in her place, but he just couldn't find the strength to do it. His hold over all of them had been broken, and he couldn't seem to care enough to get it back.

"Take the two new recruits to the prepping chambers," he said to them. "Lio's got them ready. Remove the implants and dress them for conversion and stasis. I'll be speaking with the general." Then he turned and left them there.

The two ghosts had been wounded, but neither of them was critical, which was a good thing, since they would help replace the three spectres who had been lost once the ghosts had begun treatment and had been convinced to join the cause. Neither ghost had a psi index that was off the charts, but with terrazine and jorium to help them, they would be capable enough warriors. If he could get Nova into the fold, the spectres would be a formidable force.

He should be preparing now for a larger battle, gearing up the troops and finalizing their plans with General Bennett. Instead, he was suddenly wracked with self-doubt and reeling from the failure in Augustgrad.

He waited for more advice from Grandma Tosh, but she was uncharacteristically silent; had he angered her with his handling of Dylanna? He needed her to help him understand where to go from here. Project: Shadowblade was at a crossroads.

Tosh had learned of Shadowblade not long after he'd gone AWOL from the academy. After what had happened with Kath and his subsequent escape, he had gone into a deep depression. He had been living off the grid in a Tyrador IX slum, trying to regroup after what had been done to him; by then his friends had thought he was dead, the ghost program had still been hunting him down, and everything he'd believed about his life had turned out to be a lie. The Dominion, to which he had pledged his life, no longer existed for him; Nova's mind blast had changed all that. He knew he could never return. He was a soldier without a cause, a man without a god, and he had turned to hab to take his mind off the pain.

He managed to keep ahead of those people looking for him, and it wasn't long before he'd started taking small security jobs for spending money. Soon after that, someone else took notice of his talents. They hadn't known who he was, and they hadn't seemed to care, but the larger jobs they funneled his way led to a man who claimed to be the brother of someone incarcerated at New Folsom Prison—an inmate who swore he knew the details of a top secret Dominion project to study the effects of something called terrazine on psionics. The man said that the emperor had locked his brother away forever in the maximum-security prison and had had him brain-panned to erase his memory of the project, but the procedure hadn't worked. Apparently the gas not only restored the memories of mind-wiped terrans, but it also raised psi levels through a genetic mutation, and had been revered by a sect of the protoss for many years for its effects. The prisoner had been smart enough to keep his facts to himself, but had finally shared some of them with his sibling.

Tosh had been intrigued; he'd been looking for something to believe in again, a cause to awaken him from a deep and mournful sleep. Perhaps this was it.

He went on a quest, and after months of passage on pirate ships across the sector chasing false leads, crooks, and thieves, he finally found someone he scanned who seemed to know about a mysterious gas like the one he described. He ended up alone on Altara, fumbling through dark, abandoned caverns that led deep into the ground, where he found a rift in the rock that was leaking a greenish, foul-smelling substance. It didn't take long for him to realize what it could do. The power and enlightenment he experienced during those first days on Altara had taken his breath away.

He had been longing for a way to return to his friends and let them see what he had seen. He wanted to set them free from the ghost program, and show them that the Dominion had become a corrupt and evil government, no better than the one it had replaced. Now he seemed to have an answer to his prayers.

A few weeks later he met General Bennett, a former member of that secret terrazine project who had ambitious plans of his own. He had his reasons for hating Emperor Mengsk and the Dominion. He used his knowledge of what had happened under Sector 9 and reached out in private to Colin Phash, but Colin would never join him; the Umojans considered him far too valuable, and it was not his way. But Tosh helped Bennett broker a secret deal with the Umojan Ruling Council to gather resources for a coup.

Together they vowed to resurrect Project: Shadowblade and bring down the Dominion in the process.

Gabriel Tosh stumbled through Gehenna's corridors toward the comm room. He felt dizzy and weak, his mouth was dry, and he couldn't focus his thoughts. The rock-hewn walls of Gehenna Station seemed to flex in and out at him along with his own trembling breaths, while below his feet he sensed the dreamless sleep of thousands of soldiers, ready to rise up and overwhelm him.

He took his bottle of terrazine off his belt with shaking hands, the need alive in him and demanding relief. It felt nearly empty, and panic almost unmanned him before he put the valve to his lips and pushed the button, inhaling deeply.

There was just enough. Terrazine fire prickled his lungs and tore through his bloodstream, rushing to his head and making him want to cry out with satisfaction. Immediately he felt his focus return, and the world snapped back into place. He could see every crack and ridge in the rock, hear the rush of air through the ventilation system, the rustle of people in motion, cleaning bots scrubbing, the hum of electricity running through the giant pipes under the floor. He felt as if he could sense every star in the galaxy and every living soul within it.

Along with the increased focus, his rage returned with a vengeance, and he began to wonder if it might be time to put Dylanna Okyl down. She had challenged him once again in front of the team. This could not be allowed to stand.

Tosh's remote console chirped, distracting him. He looked at the screen. *Your General Bennett is waiting,* Lio wrote. *You're late.*

"Caught up with new recruits," he typed. "And Dylanna is causing trouble."

A pause, and then: *Your approach lacks the proper controls.*

Tosh let a hiss of breath escape between clenched teeth. "What's that supposed to mean?"

You are straying from the parameters of this experiment. You're treating Kath like you might treat a prisoner of war, not a friend. She's frightened and she is not embracing the truth about her father. That will have untold consequences.

"I'm doing what is necessary. She doesn't understand, but she will. You know this. We have plenty to show her."

Perhaps. But the logic of your approach with Nova is flawed as well. And your insistence on remaining in Augustgrad even as the ghosts were alerted to your presence was a needless risk. I have no more tolerance for deviations in intent. The new way thrives on order, precision, ones and zeros in exact sequence.

"The new way?"

The next stage of human consciousness.

Tosh stared at the screen, his unease growing. He wondered again whether Mengsk's private message getting through Lio's communications net back at Augustgrad had been a mistake, or whether he had some other agenda. A lot was riding on Lio's ability to disrupt the Dominion's computer systems. He had previously assumed that Lio's motivations for joining Project: Shadowblade were the result of his treatment at the hands of the academy and a thirst to make the Dominion pay for what it had done to him, along with lingering feelings of affection for his old friends.

Now he wasn't so sure.

"You're not in charge here, Lio. I have to know that you're with us."

Terran hierarchy no longer interests me. I am assisting you because some part of me still values friendship, camaraderie, human interaction. And I am curious to see the results of what you have proposed.

"Remember Team Blue, Lio. Remember what we meant to each other. I have to go talk to the general." Trying to ignore the churning in his gut, Tosh cut the feed from the unit and strode through the hallways to the comm room.

Bennett was already up on the holo, and when Tosh entered the room, the general wasted no time making his feelings known. "You had Mengsk at your mercy. Why didn't you bring him back with you, or kill him there?"

The general's face was red and his voice was loud. Tosh looked down and saw a cara beetle near his own feet. One wing was extended, damaged somehow, the other still tucked tightly as it fluttered and walked in circles. The colors of its carapace swirled like oil on water. He had no idea how it had gotten here, but it wouldn't last long. It seemed like some kind of symbol, a warning. Tosh thought about picking it up and keeping it with him, but instead he crushed it with his boot.

"He was in the safe room," Tosh said. "We couldn't get to him before the ghosts arrived."

"I know where he was," Bennett said. "Why should that stop you? You had plenty of time."

"Nova got in the way."

"I thought you were going to persuade her to join us—"

"We captured two of them. Nova's gonna be more difficult. If we had killed the emperor in front of her, we would never have a chance to show her we're on the right side." Tosh felt his own anger rise again. Why couldn't Bennett understand that this was a delicate process? She was not like the others. She was loyal to a fault, and her loyalty could not be bought, threatened, or stolen. They would never convince her that way, and she was far too important for them to lose now; as a spectre, her abilities would be more powerful than anyone other than the Queen of Blades.

He thought about mentioning his conversation with Lio and decided against it. He would deal with that himself.

"Then bring her in by force," General Bennett said. "We are at a turning point, and now we're going to have to regroup. Our success hinges on our actions during the next few days. You know that."

"We can't force her. We lost three of our team—"

"Casualties of war." General Bennett waved a hand, as if dismissing the importance of the thought. "You think the protoss spend a moment crying about their dead in battle? Or the zerg? If we aim to be as ruthless as they are, we need to focus on the ultimate goal: *victory*. Mengsk must be brought to Gehenna and made to answer for his crimes." Bennett smiled grimly. "Except we don't have Mengsk as we'd planned, and he will be even more highly protected when we try again." The smile turned into a scowl. "You assured me that you could get the job done and bring in Nova Terra in the process. You said she would trust you. If that's not true, I'm afraid I may have to take matters into my own hands. Nova is too important now. Her connection to the emperor is our way back in. She's either with us or out of the way. Permanently."

"We need more time—"

"Time," Bennett said, "is overrated. All I've had is time. To *act*, Gabriel, and act decisively, that is the most important thing." He gestured toward the terrazine bottle on Tosh's belt. "Are you regulating your intake properly? You seem . . . jumpy. You know the effects can be dangerous. We have proof enough of that. I can't afford to have a hallucinating, out-of-control addict in charge of the spectres, not at such a critical juncture."

"I'm fine." Tosh wanted to explode at him, reach right through the holo and wring his neck. Instead, he pushed the rage back down inside, holding it tightly within, where it coiled and writhed and burned. He had made a deal with the general to support Project: Shadowblade for two reasons: he wanted to free his fellow ghosts, and he wanted a very public revenge on Arcturus Mengsk for his crimes. Bennett had been an easy partner at first. But now Tosh began to feel that their ultimate goals might not be in such perfect alignment after all. Tosh wanted to bring Team Blue together once again, and he wanted Mengsk humiliated in front of the Dominion, forced to admit his crimes. He wanted to outthink and outmaneuver the great strategist, harass and terrify him until he begged for mercy.

Bennett, it seemed, wanted power and control. Everything else was secondary.

Even with the spectres back on board, Kath Toom still felt utterly alone.

She had tried on the suit located in her locker after her run-in with Lio, getting used to the feel of it on her skin and wondering if she would ever be comfortable wearing it outside of these rocky walls, or if she even wanted that to happen. It was similar to the more familiar ghost hostile environment suit, but thicker, more substantial, and she felt the power of its muscle fiber weave like a well-tuned engine purring against her flesh. She had to admit that it felt *right*. When she settled the HUD over her face and began to play with the interface, she quickly realized that the technology behind the suit was remarkably advanced, and yet clearly terran in nature. Who had designed such a thing? And why did the Dominion's best warriors not have access to it?

Lio might have been able to answer her questions, but she had refused to talk to him for the rest of the time she had been alone on board, and the silent treatment had continued even as he had reached out to her through every means possible, his messages appearing on holo-screens as she passed them, AAI units, even the HUD after she had booted it up. Surveillance cameras swiveled to follow her, and bots stopped and seemed to plead silently as she walked the halls. At first this was creepy and invasive, but she soon got used to it; Lio was just being Lio, after all, and he didn't mean it in a menacing way. He had been insecure around others when he was mortal, but now he was close to godlike in his abilities, and normal terran concerns like privacy no longer seemed to bother him.

She felt more confused than ever. Gabriel Tosh had been the love of her life once, and now that he had found her again, the idea of walking away was nearly impossible to face. What she now knew about the Dominion's ghost program and how she had been treated made her wonder whether he was right; maybe Mengsk *had* become drunk with power and hopelessly corrupt, and maybe it was her duty to expose him and help replace him with someone better.

There were other things that continued to nag at her, like the way the spectres were going about seizing control—and the growing unease about what had happened to her father. But mostly, she worried about the terrazine. Its influence continued to both amaze and terrify her. She felt her new teek abilities gathering strength every day and had mastered them enough to feel more confident, and her ability to sense her environment and read minds had sharpened as well. She had never felt this invincible. And yet the nightmares and hallucinations had continued, popping up at unexpected times and places, each more vivid than the last, and she felt a restlessness inside her that would not stop. More important, she craved the terrazine more and more each day, finding it difficult to wait until she slept to get it. By the time she went to sleep her entire body was on fire and shaking, her limbs weakened and her mouth as dry as the dust on Altara. Yesterday she had returned to her sleeping chamber early just to get the taste of terrazine on her lips. She didn't see how this could continue without terrible consequences, but she also couldn't imagine stopping it.

And then there was Gabriel. She had sensed

his return a short while ago, had felt him probing for her location, but she had remained distant. She couldn't imagine where he and the others had gone. Wherever it had been, three of them had not returned, and when she scanned those who were left, she felt the loss like a blow to the stomach. Dylanna, in particular, seemed anxious, the energy humming from her like a nuclear weapon about to melt down. Toom avoided her as well, keeping to the areas of Gehenna where the others did not seem to go.

Still, she knew it was only a matter of time before Gabriel checked in on her. He would surely ask her whether she was ready to become a member of the spectres. She had no idea how she would respond to that.

Toom reached the end of a hallway with double doors that slid open into a much larger, more rough-hewn passageway than she'd been in before. This was a section of Gehenna that she had never seen, located deep in the bowels of the strange ship. The ship (if you could call it that) was even larger and more complex than she could have imagined, and she had yet to understand its layout. The passage here was large and straight, as if made to move vehicles or crowds of people, and it was bisected with another huge passage that seemed to run nearly the entire length of the ship. She was far enough away from the main rooms that the hum of other minds had dimmed, but now she felt something else that was subtler and yet unsettling, an undercurrent of something dangerous and huge, as if she were standing on the edge of a cliff in the dark, one step away from the drop.

At one end of the passage was a giant set of neosteel doors. It looked like the entrance to a dropship bay.

She walked to the end and put her hands on the steel, feeling the thrumming of the engines and listening for anything that would give her a clue to what else might lie beyond. She sensed cavernous space, but it was not empty.

"Kath."

She whirled, her heart leaping to her throat. Gabriel Tosh stood directly behind her, arms crossed over his broad chest. She hadn't heard him approach, hadn't sensed him at all.

"Ever since I got caught in Nova's mind blast on Shi," he said, scanning her thoughts, "I can close myself off to teeps. Can't read me at all if I don't want 'em to." He looked long and hard at her with those strange, hypnotic eyes. "What are you doing down here?"

"I—I was exploring the ship."

"You shouldn't be here." He took a step closer, dropping his hands to his sides. Instead of feeling more relaxed, she felt even more on edge. He was probing at her, gently for now, but she didn't like it.

"Stop scanning me," she said. Her back was against one of the huge metal doors. "It's . . . an invasion of privacy. And it's dangerous."

He smiled, showing straight, white teeth. "You never minded before."

"We were lovers then." She tried her own smile, but it was shaky and uncertain. She took a deep breath. "Where did you go, Gabriel?"

"We had a mission."

"A dangerous one. You lost three of your team."

"And brought two new recruits back with us. They've seen the light, Kath, and they've chosen to free themselves and join the fight. I hope you're ready too, because there's a great battle coming. We could use you. *I* could use you."

"I . . . I don't know." Toom crossed her arms, rubbing at the gooseflesh that had popped up. She'd almost gotten used to the civilian clothes she'd been wearing, but now she wished for her old ghost suit.

"You're worried about the terrazine," Tosh said. "Don't be. I've been using it for a long time now. Nothing wrong with me." He cocked his head, as if listening, and she got the strangest feeling there was someone else with them, someone she could not see. Then he gave a slight nod. "A protoss sect called the Tal'darim uses it—they call it the Breath of Creation. They don't follow the Khala, the protoss group mind, and they're not part of the main protoss body; but the Tal'darim believe terrazine brings them closer to the xel'naga. Fekk, they even named themselves after some mythological xel'nagan servants. That's gotta mean something." He took another step, and now he was close enough that she could feel his breath on her face.

"My . . . father, Gabriel." Her entire body was trembling. "I need to know the truth."

"You sure you're ready for that?"

She nodded. "Please."

"All right. The truth, exactly as it happened. Your father was a scapegoat to a much larger conspiracy, baby. He never did anything wrong. Sector 9, it was a Kal-Bryant operation, sure, but he knew nothing about it until he was set up to take the fall. And Mengsk and the Dominion let it happen. They might as well have pushed him into those warp engines, understand? They killed him."

It was all as Lio had told her. She couldn't move. He touched both of her arms where the gooseflesh had sprung up, and she shivered uncontrollably, feeling an ache in her loins even as she tried to shy away, turning her head. He reached up and turned it gently back to him. "Without our neural implants, and with the use of terrazine, *we* can reach protoss levels, Kath. We have a duty to meet. We must free our people, our fellow ghosts, and shut down the ghost program forever. End Mengsk's corrupt rule. If the general is with us, fine. If not . . . we will do what's necessary. Nothing will stop us. *Nothing*."

The general? His passion for the cause was like a fire in him. Abruptly he leaned in and brushed her lips with his own. She felt his dreadlocks fall around her face like slithering snakes, and her heart quickened again until she felt her blood thumping in her throat. Then he was easing himself into her mind, soothing her, bringing a warm, calming heat, and this time she let it happen, let herself relax and feel her thoughts mingling with his until they were one and the same.

Will you come with me? Please say yes.

She nodded, closing her eyes as his lips found hers again. She could not deny him, not anymore. She was not strong enough.

As he pulled her down to the cold, hard floor of the passage, she tried to remember what had worried her so much, but the threads slipped through her grasp and disappeared. Perhaps it didn't matter anyway.

She was lost.

CHAPTER SIXTEEN

SPAULDING

Major Spaulding was clearly agitated. He paced back and forth on the deck of the war room, hands clasped behind his back as if he were confident and relaxed. But Nova could see the muscles straining in his forearms, and his fingers were laced together so tightly the tips were white.

She might have scanned his thoughts, but he was wearing the psi-screen again.

There was no such trouble sensing the thoughts of his second-in-command, Captain Vincent, however. The man glared at her with his beady eyes and radiated hatred. He looked like a Tarsonis swamp rat.

(burn in hell, you slike)

After you, Captain. She pictured him on fire and stumbling across the deck, an inferno of waving arms and charred flesh. His eyes widened slightly as her thought message hit home, and she sensed his fear of her. She felt surprisingly satisfied but resisted a smile.

Spaulding himself had demanded the meeting. Although most of them had been over the events in Augustgrad several times already, they were sitting around tables in the war room to review them yet again: Nova and Mal, Hauler, Rourke, Ward, Spaulding and Vincent, and a few other key members of the crew. A half-dozen new ghosts had arrived as well, but Nova hadn't even had time to get to know them yet. Most were fresh out of the academy, young and filled with excitement. They had no clue what they were getting into here, she thought.

Since they had returned from Korhal, Nova had seen a number of new faces on board the *Palatine,* many of them hardened, resoced soldiers, their minds like blank slates to her. There had been heavy casualties among the marines in the brief period they had engaged the spectres outside the palace, and Hauler had moved quickly to replenish their ranks. Even the tactical officer was new, which surprised her. Perhaps the old one had done something that had landed him in the brig, because he surely wouldn't have been in combat. In any case, the appearance of unfamiliar faces was nothing new to her; with the Dominion's memory wipes, it was the way she began and ended every mission she'd ever been given.

Nobody believed the spectres would just

disappear, and Hauler was clearly preparing for another battle. Mengsk had requested a private meeting with him shortly after Mal and Nova had left the safe room, and she suspected Hauler had been handed his own ass. Augustgrad would not be left vulnerable again.

Spaulding, however, would not let it go. He blamed Nova for the failure against the spectres, and he wanted blood. Unknown to her, while she was fighting the spectres in Augustgrad, there had been another battle for control far above the planet's surface. Spaulding had wanted to take the Annihilators into the capital immediately, but Hauler had held him back, concerned about the breakdown of communications and the confusion that would surely come with a full-scale marine deployment.

After what had happened on the ground, Spaulding seemed sure that Mengsk would hand control of military support to him. It hadn't occurred. Now Nova wondered what exactly he had up his sleeve.

"Ninety-seven," he said. *"Ninety-seven men and women.* That's how many marines you got killed."

Colonel Hauler did not rise to take the bait, remaining calm, even appearing a bit weary. "We know how many casualties we suffered, Major Spaulding. We all feel their losses, including those members of our ghost team. We've been over this already. All communications were down, and we were facing a small, agile, and powerful enemy. If we had gone in with guns blazing, we would have killed half our marine force with friendly fire."

"Are we so dependent on technology that we forget the basic principles of war? Were the Vikings or Romans of Old Earth wearing comms, heads-up displays, and hypersonic weaponry? There were ways to approach the enemy without our functional systems. Go back to basics. But that's not why I called for this meeting." Spaulding looked around the room, a half smile touching his purple, wormlike lips. "We have a traitor in our midst."

A murmur went through the small group as people looked at each other. Nova caught a number of half-formed thoughts of surprise and fear. Most of them hadn't expected anything like this.

"I have evidence to show that Agent X41822N is a spectre," Spaulding said.

For a moment the room was silent, and then Mal Kelerchian stood up and glared at Spaulding. "I'm gonna knock your teeth out," he said. "How dare you—"

"You're a part of it too," Spaulding said smoothly. "Aren't you, wrangler Kelerchian? You were the one who recruited her to the ghost program, and it wasn't a coincidence you met again on Altara."

"Why you little, lying weasel—" Kelerchian made a sudden move as if he was going to leap right over the table and throw himself at Spaulding, but Hauler, who was sitting next to him, stood and put a meaty hand on his chest.

"Let's hear him out," Hauler said. "No sense in letting rumors fly around without putting them to rest. And then we can toss him off the ship."

Kelerchian remained standing but made no further move. Spaulding nodded to Vincent, who had edged closer to the door.

The captain opened it to reveal Markus Ralian standing in the shadows of a broken, rubble-strewn Tarsonis hallway: Fagin's slum headquarters. Ralian looked worse than before, the nasty scalp wound turning purple, gangrene working through his torn, puffy flesh. He raised one arm and pointed a finger at Nova, lidless eyes rolling in their sockets. *I am thy father's spirit, doomed for a certain term to walk the night and for the day confined to fast in fires, till the foul crimes done in my days of na-ture are burnt and purged away . . .* He grinned. *Old Earth's* Hamlet, *in case you don't recognize it. Fagin used to quote stuff like that all the time. Remember? Your foul crimes can't be purged, though, can they, Nova? That's why I'll always be here with you.*

Nova shuddered. *You're not real. Go away.*

Ralian disappeared as Dr. Shaw walked through the door, escorted by two marines. Looking confused, he stopped just inside and stared at Nova, glanced nervously around at the hostile faces, then made as if to turn back. The marine on the right nudged his arm, and he stepped reluctantly to the center of the room next to Spaulding.

"What is this?" Hauler said. His voice had gotten quiet and his gaze flashed from Spaulding's face to Shaw's, then back again.

"My proof," Spaulding said. He smiled. "Dr. Shaw, why don't you tell these fine people what you told me about terrazine?"

"I—"

"Remember," Spaulding said, "we have you on record. Lying now is treason, and I *will* make sure to see you hanged for it."

Shaw looked at Hauler. "Sorry, sir," he said. Then he squared his shoulders and stared straight ahead. "I examined Agent X41822N on two occasions, once immediately after the events on Altara, and once at her request several days later. She was suffering from delusions, visual and audible hallucinations, restored memory, and other . . . issues. My scans showed that she had been exposed to the terrazine gas the spectres use to augment their abilities."

"And yet she told no one else about this—"

"She told me," Mal said. "Look, this is ridiculous. Nova's no terrorist. She fought them down in Augustgrad. Almost got herself killed."

"That's what she wanted us to think," Spaulding said. "You were the one who got to her first outside the emperor's quarters, weren't you, wrangler Kelerchian? You took her report, entered it into the computer?"

"That's standard procedure with wranglers and ghosts in this kind of situation, and you know it."

"Convenient for you. I also can't help but notice you calling her by her first name. A bit too familiar, don't you think?"

Kelerchian's face flushed red. "That has nothing to do—"

"She's a ghost agent, one you recruited. I think it has everything to do with it. The fact is, if I hadn't pushed the marine invasion when I did, *Agent X41822N* and her friends would have had enough time to break through that safe room and get to Mengsk. I spoiled your plans, and so you rushed to her side to make it look like she'd been badly hurt." Spaulding's chest was heaving now. "The truth is it was just a flesh wound. Communications were disabled; there's no recording to prove anything." He looked around at the group. "It's like someone has been manipulating us from the inside, isn't it? This investigation has gone nowhere ever since the ghost and this man were put in charge. She supposedly killed three spectres down on the ground, but all we have are the bodies of previously missing ghosts and no evidence whatsoever of their involvement in the plot. For all we know, these were hostages killed to make the fight look legitimate."

"Their spectre suits must have a self-destruct," Kelerchian said. "Just like ghost suits."

"Again, pretty convenient for you. And what about back on Altara? You were there when the refinery blew up and destroyed most of the evidence we might have gathered from the operation. And then Agent X41822N arrived to pick you up. Lieutenant Ward, can you please tell us all what happened on the ground at that point?"

Ward stood up and cleared his throat. "When we arrived to provide support, the ghost ordered us to fall back. Said she would take care of everything. When I tried to force the issue, she threatened me." He glanced at Nova and then quickly away. "She . . . said she would reveal some personal information that would embarrass me if I didn't comply."

"What kind of information?"

Ward looked sheepish. "I had an affair with a Hudderstown girl who was later raped and killed by a local boy. The ghost told me she would tell everyone I'd done it. Of course it wasn't true, but I have a wife and two kids back home. I couldn't afford any of that getting out."

Ward sat down. The room was quiet for a moment, people shifting in their seats uncomfortably as what the major and Ward had said sunk in. Nova opened her mouth, then closed it. *You slimeball.* She realized how clever Ward had been; if she tried to tell her story now, it would look as if she were lying, just as he'd said.

"What do you want, Spaulding?" Hauler said. "What's the point of all this?"

"I want you to turn this ghost and Malcolm Kelerchian over to my custody," Spaulding said. "I'll take over this operation and run point from my ship. These so-called spectres are mine now."

"Impossible," Hauler said. "Emperor Mengsk has put X41822N and wrangler Kelerchian in charge of the investigation himself. I don't have the authority."

"When he hears about all this, he'll change his mind. We've got more data on the effects of this terrazine—"

"Enough!" Hauler roared, suddenly slamming his fists down on the table, making everyone jump in their seats. "I've been patient, but this is my ship, and I will decide who does what on board. I still outrank you, in case you've forgotten."

"I don't—"

"You have a vendetta against her for whatever reason. I get it. But I don't care. You're not going to use this to get whatever you're looking for out of her. You're not going to use my people to derail this investigation. Now, Major Spaulding," Hauler said, his words precise and cold as ice. *"Get. Off. My. Ship."*

The room was deathly silent. The two men stared at each other for a long moment before Spaulding looked away and shrugged. "Whatever you say, Colonel," he said. "But you're making a mistake."

He turned to go, motioning to Vincent and the two marines who had brought Shaw in.

"Don't let the door hit you in the ass when you leave," Kelerchian said, waving his fingers.

Spaulding turned back, smiling grimly. "I *will* discuss this with the emperor. And when I do, I'll make sure to tell him how cooperative you were, wrangler."

"I wouldn't expect anything less."

"And you, Agent X41822N—I'll see you again soon."

The four men marched through the open door and disappeared down the hall. "Captain Rourke, please make sure they make it safely to their ship," Hauler said, staring after them. Rourke nodded and left, closing the door behind her.

"All right," Hauler said. "Shaw and Ward, I'm going to assume Spaulding has video of the two of you screwing your mother's best friend, because any other reason for you to do this without talking to me first would be grounds for a court-martial. Understood?" The two men nodded. "Good. Ordinarily I'd be more concerned with what you both said in here, but right now, we've got more important things to do. Like find out what these terrorists' next move will be. Agent X41822N, I don't believe for one second that you're involved with these dirtbags. I'm going to assume you have everything you need to continue, unless you tell me otherwise. Now let's go find some bad guys."

As the rest of them got up to leave, Nova pulled Hauler aside. Up until now, she hadn't taken him into her confidence about the story Mengsk had told her back in the safe room, and had done all the digging she could on her own, but she decided it was time to start doing so. She and Mal could use all the help they could get.

"I need you to divert more resources from the ship's computers to help me pull any records or search for any mention of a Project: Shadowblade," she said. "People involved, details of the project, notices, military references. Anything you can possibly dig up. Get me whatever you can find on Tosh, Travski, and Toom too. But keep it quiet."

Hauler studied her face for a moment, then sighed. "Don't suppose you're going to tell me anything more than that," he said.

"I'd rather not, at this point." She hesitated. "One more thing . . . see what you can find on a zerg infestation on a planet Shi a few years back."

"Why's that?"

"Might be related. Just tying up loose ends."

"Fine. You'll have whatever I can find by tonight." He put a hand on her shoulder. "Don't let them get to you. You're one of the best agents I've ever seen, and what you did in Augustgrad saved Mengsk's life."

Nova paused. It was rare for Hauler to show any kind of emotion, never mind a fatherly concern. The Dominion Marine Corps wasn't exactly a touchy-feely sort of organization. *Lose an arm, keep fighting on,* the saying went. *Lose a foot, hop along with it* . . . She wondered if he really felt this way about her, or whether he was aware of more about her condition from Shaw than he was admitting, and was just trying to prop her up while he figured out what needed to be done. It was impossible to know without an idea of what had gone on during his conversation with Mengsk; Hauler was too good at masking his deeper thoughts, even from the best teeps in the sector. Just like Mengsk. She'd never encountered anyone with masking abilities quite like them.

Whether he was being genuine or not didn't matter, she realized. The point was she would get his help and support right now, and that was enough. She had a job to do.

"Thanks," she said. "I'm not going to let the Dominion down."

"I know you won't," Hauler said. "I'll let you know what we find."

An hour after the meeting with Spaulding, Nova went to see Mal Kelerchian in his private quarters.

They had discussed finding a quiet place to go over their respective notes and formulate a plan of attack. Both felt the growing urgency of the situation; they were running out of time. Spaulding would not let this go, and if he did gain an audience with Mengsk, there was no telling what might happen. Mengsk already distrusted ghosts in general, and it was clear from their time with him in the safe room that he was going to give them a short leash. They had to uncover the key to the spectres' location and launch an aggressive attack before it was too late.

And yet Nova could not help feeling hopeless. The spectres had struck a blow at the very foundations of the Dominion and walked away almost unscathed. All attempts to track ships leaving Korhal's airspace immediately after the attack had come up empty, as had a thorough search of the city itself. The spectres had disappeared into thin air. Nova had no real leads, and no way of knowing where they might strike next.

What was worse, she could not get what Tosh had told her about the events on Shi out of her mind. Could any of what he had said be true?

The hallway outside Kelerchian's quarters was empty and quiet. As she stopped by his door and waited for the sensors to announce her presence, she tried to ignore the slight trembling in her hands and the dryness in her mouth. But the strange craving that had begun to ache like hunger pangs in her stomach made it difficult, and she could not help but wonder if things might get even worse. What else had the drug done to her? Was it permanent?

So this is what it feels like to be an addict. The thought did not help her mood.

Kelerchian opened the door. His quarters were smaller than her own, slightly stale and too warm. If she didn't already know he was staying there, she would have thought the room was unoccupied; the only evidence of his presence was his familiar leather duster folded neatly on the bunk, and the hologram on the metal desk, open to showing a revolving star pattern and a line of bright red pinpricks to illustrate where the terrorist attacks had occurred.

She studied him for a moment as he moved aside to let her in. He seemed smaller without the duster, more vulnerable. She wondered if he'd removed it intentionally before she had arrived, and then immediately dismissed the thought. Mal was not the type to think like that. All she had sensed from him lately had been a mild embarrassment, as if he felt guilty about something he didn't want to admit, even to himself.

"You look tight," he said, closing the door. "Like you're holding something in across the shoulders. Is the wound bothering you?"

"A little," she admitted. "But nothing I can't handle." She looked at the tiny room, barely large enough for the two of them to move around. "Maybe we should have picked a better place to meet."

"It'll do. More privacy here." Kelerchian pulled out the desk chair for her and turned it to face the bunk, and after she sat down, he sat on the bunk's edge.

"Like sleeping on a slab of rock," he said, patting the thin mattress. "But you get used to it, don't you? Life in the Dominion Marine Corps. *Peace. Law. Order.* Three squares a day and a place to lay your head. What else could a guy want?" He rubbed two fingers against his temple and winced.

"You okay?" she asked.

"Goddamn headaches." He shrugged. "Maybe it's just stress. Got a particularly bad one earlier that won't go away. My suit's analgesics barely make a dent these days."

He seemed to study her, and she resisted scanning him to get a glimpse of what he was thinking. She was getting used to her heightened abilities now, and it was easier to keep unwanted thoughts from intruding. At the same time, she felt an emotional connection to him that had only grown stronger since the events at the palace; she didn't need to hear his thoughts to have a sense of how he felt.

Kelerchian cleared his throat. "So I was thinking about our Umojan link," he said, "and the more I thought about it, the more sense it seemed to make. We know how the Ruling Council feels about the Dominion, and there are plenty of rumors of them undermining our efforts to control fringe world colonies. And they have a well-known hatred for the Ghost Academy. They're careful, but they're working at taking it down; everyone knows they were behind the propaganda about Colin Phash that Michael Liberty helped spread. Something like this might be right up their alley."

"The Umojans wouldn't be this brash."

"That's true—but they might finance someone else to do their dirty work. They have advanced technology. And they have their own ghost program. They would be interested in something like terrazine."

"So what do we do?" Nova said. "We can't attack Umoja. Not without proof."

"We put some political pressure on them," Kelerchian said. "Let them know we need answers—squeeze them and see what comes out. I put a call in to a friend who knows Senator Huntley."

"That will take time."

Kelerchian nodded. "Meantime, I had my ship, *November*, run some private searches on the term Gehenna. It occurred to me that since Mengsk had warned us about a possible traitor inside his camp, and since communications at Augustgrad were disrupted, our network might be compromised. I wanted to keep this close to the vest. You might be interested in what I found." He got up and went to the hologram, standing close enough to brush her shoulder. He didn't seem to notice.

"You named your ship after me," Nova said.

He glanced at her. "What?"

"Your ship—the *November*. It's for me, isn't it?"

"You were my most successful recruit," he said. His face had reddened again. "I was proud of being a part of bringing in one of the most promising ghost agents in history. It seemed appropriate, that's all."

But it was more than that, and they both knew it. Nova was flattered and shocked; nobody had ever done anything like that for her before. Most men were too frightened or uncomfortable with her talents to want to be anywhere near her. Others simply wanted to use her in various ways. But Mal treated her like a person, rather than a weapon or something to be feared and avoided. She could sense his honesty and his goodness, deep within. She remembered once again how he had rescued her from Fagin's slum in the Tarsonis Gutter, where she had become known as an enforcer called "the Blonde," and where she had first learned of the Ghost Academy's mind wipes, which had seemed like the perfect escape from her tortured past. He was a different man now than he had been then, more battle-hardened and confident.

I feel something for this man, something more than friendship.

The realization stunned her. She'd heard plenty about people's emotions consuming them, making them feel and act in strange ways. Her exposure to terrazine had awoken memories and feelings of attachment to others that she hadn't felt in years. She'd had strong feelings for Tosh a long time ago, but those had been wiped away, and she'd never really loved a man before. Even the idea of it made her uncomfortable. She was younger than he; he was the wrangler who recruited her, and they had to work together—and, of course, at the end of the mission, she would have her memory wiped, so she wouldn't remember anything anyway.

Surely this couldn't be love. But it was *something*. The general rule for ghosts was to not get involved with anyone, and for good reason.

She looked up at him, meeting his eyes. "Mal, I—"

"It's just a ship," he said quickly, looking away. "Don't get a swelled head over it, okay? Last thing we need is a ghost with an attitude problem." He chuckled. The blush had spread fiercely over his neck, turning it bright red.

"Of course," she said. And then another thought hit her; if she was able to hear his inner dialogue when she wanted to, could he hear hers as easily—even when she chose not to share it? He already had a sensitivity to psionic abilities, which was why he'd been recruited to become a wrangler in the first place. And he'd been exposed to terrazine on Altara too.

If that was true, what had he just discovered about her?

Now it was her turn to blush, and she stood up and took two steps away from him, crossing her arms over her chest. There was no room to breathe in here, and her head was swimming. Ralian's gravelly voice came back to her. *Your foul crimes can't be purged, can they, Nova?* She was damaged goods, no other way to look at it. She'd committed enough crimes to make her run away from her own past, and she couldn't imagine anyone else would want to be with her either.

For some reason, Gabriel Tosh came to mind again. A rush of new emotions swelled within her: new, more intense feelings of camaraderie and be-ing part of a team. Team Blue. Kath, with her ready smile, fiery spirit, and loyalty; Lio, with his intensity and vulnerability, his need to be liked and respected; and Tosh, his leadership and wise counsel, his calm under fire.

Freedom. The chance to live a real life among old friends, apart from the ghost program, with all the joys and sorrows it would bring. Could that ever be something she wanted to do? She was a ghost, trained to act alone. That was her world and, until recently, everything she remembered of her life. It seemed impossible to imagine anything different now.

"Keyword 'Gehenna' came up with several hits," Kelerchian went on, and she turned back to find him working with the hologram, bringing up search response data. "The first two are references to a star in distant space and the idea from Old Earth of Gehenna as a valley of fire opening up the pits of Hell. But the third comes from an eye-witness report of an attack on a military platform orbiting Maltair IV a couple of years back. The attack fits the pattern of the spectres in some ways—a strategic target, in and out fast, few witnesses—but it hadn't been connected to the others before. Everyone on-site—over five hundred marines—was killed by an explosion that destroyed the platform, except for one man, who was found in an escape pod drifting in the area. He was irrational, babbling incoherently."

"Let me guess—he was raving about black-clad monsters able to appear and disappear at will."

"Not quite. That would have flagged the report for sure. But he kept saying one thing over and over on the recordings from sick bay during transport—something that sounded enough like Gehenna for my search parameters to log it a hit. I have the recording right here."

He brought up the audio, and they both stood in the silence of the room as an eerie, ghostlike voice began to hiss through the hologram's speakers. Although it was faint, and the man's voice was ragged and weak from shouting, Nova had to agree: it sounded as if he was saying "Gehenna Station."

"If he'd been brain-panned," she said, "he

might have been caught up in a negative thought loop. A word or phrase he'd sensed just before they fried him, repeating itself. Like a recording that keeps skipping."

"Exactly." Kelerchian nodded. "And guess which unit was first to respond?"

Spaulding's ruddy face popped into her head, and she didn't know whether she'd sensed it from him, or whether she just knew. "The Annihilators."

"Bingo." He tapped keys and brought up a log of marine activity. "You see here, they were the closest battlecruiser in the area. On site in less than an hour."

"What were they doing there?"

"Apparently nothing. They had recently engaged a pirate ship on orders from Augustgrad, but that was hours away. They hadn't logged any activity since then."

They both stood there, thinking. Suddenly everything seemed to click into place. She should have been feeling good. All signs pointed to someone inside the Dominion's inner circle orchestrating Project: Shadowblade. The false orders that sent Kath Toom to Altara was one, the scrambled communications in Augustgrad another, the strategic attacks on military locations yet another. Nova remembered Hauler's hunch that whoever had planned the terrorist attacks had a military background. Spaulding's hatred of ghosts, and of

Nova in particular, seemed clear. She was sure he would like nothing less than to destroy the ghost program, and someone like that would certainly appeal to the Umojan Ruling Council.

"If the Annihilators were involved, why would they show up at the scene of the crime?"

"Because they're clever," Kelerchian said. "Send in some spies to blow up the platform, then magically appear to help out. The last people you'd expect to be guilty are the rescuers themselves. There's something else too. If this was their first hit, they might not have had the capability to evade detection the way they seem to now. The Annihilators' battlecruiser would have been tracked leaving the scene. This way, they look innocent and get away with murder, right under the emperor's nose."

"Maybe. I still feel like we're missing something." Nova thought back to Spaulding's words as he left the war room: *And you, Agent X41822N—I'll see you again soon.* It all felt too easy to her, as if handed over on a silver platter.

What exactly was Gehenna Station?

Kelerchian kept rubbing at his temples. He grimaced. "Damn headache's getting worse. I swear it feels like someone's about to split me wide open." He sat down heavily on the narrow bunk and put his head in his hands. When he spoke, his voice was muffled. "I don't feel so good. Dizzy. You smell something strange?"

"Take it easy, Mal. Breathe." Nova tried to go to him, but her legs seemed to buckle as the room stretched and bowed outward and a wave of nausea swept over her. Something was very wrong, and she had just a moment to wonder whether she was collapsing under the weight of pure exhaustion or whether it was something far worse before she fell forward to her knees, her limbs going numb, and as she tipped over onto the floor, she felt herself drifting down a deep, dark hole to oblivion.

CHAPTER SEVENTEEN

THE GENERAL

Nova swam through a swirling ocean of blackness, claw-ing for a way out. Faces leered at her through the chok-ing cloud, memories of times long forgotten. She was a little girl playing in the park down the street, sensing which of the other children of Tarsonis politicians and businessmen would share their toys and which would not, which nanny would allow her a treat before dinner and which ones would scold her if she asked for an ice from the local cart. Then some figures in black suits came sneaking into the park, and she ran away into the city and wandered through streets full of traffic and people with empty holes for faces, and was lost.

When she finally found her way home and saw her parents and her brother, her mother looked cross, her pretty, delicate features twisted into an ugly frown. Why did you leave us alone? *she said.* Your father could have used your help with the hoverbike factory. *Her brother, who had a bloody hole in his forehead from the bullet that had killed him, pulled her mother away, saying,* We never could rely on her. Might as well forget it. Her foul crimes can't be purged. *Next to them stood the last of the children of the Old Families, crying out for help as zerglings ripped them limb from limb and Emperor Mengsk watched with arms folded across his chest. Nova tried to reach out to them but they disappeared, while Julius "Fagin" Dale laughed, his cruel eyes on her the whole time, drinking in her pain and suffering, and swelling like a bloodworm until he floated away.*

When she awoke, she didn't know where she was and at first could not remember what had happened. Then it all came flooding back: standing in Mal's room and feeling her legs give out and her mind go dark.

We've been drugged.

All her senses on alert, she tried to sit up and found herself restrained. She was chained with metal cuffs to a bunk in the brig, dressed in a green surgical gown. Between thick neosteel bars, she could see the outer room was empty. Who had done this to them? Was Spaulding taking over the *Palatine* in some kind of coup? And where was Mal?

She pulled against the chains around her wrists and ankles. They were heavy but shouldn't pose much of a test for her. She tried to teek the cuffs apart, but nothing happened. She felt a thump of blood in her temples that resulted in a low, throbbing ache.

"Neuroleptics," Colonel Jackson Hauler said, emerging from the hallway outside. He was in full formal uniform, but there were general's bars on his shoulder. "Normally used for mood disorders, but it turns out they're quite effective drugs in suppressing psionic abilities, when used in the right combinations. Something we've recently discovered. I pumped them into wrangler Kelerchian's room, along with a powerful sedative to knock you out. You won't be teeking anything for a while, Nova Terra."

He stopped about a meter outside the bars and crossed his arms over his chest, peering in at her, a half smile on his face. She saw what looked like a small gas canister hanging on a belt around his waist. Tosh and Dylanna had worn them too, she remembered.

"Surprise," he said.

Alarm raced through her body, prickling her skin. "It's *you*? But I never sensed anything—"

"My psi index was 8.5, even before terrazine, you know," he said, tapping the canister. "I learned long ago how to suppress my surface thoughts from teeps, something that's pretty rare with ghosts. One of my many unique talents, actually. Do you know the ghost program's psychological profile graded me out as 'high risk'? Imagine that.

You have to be labeled as a serious psycho to be flagged by those vultures."

"You were a *ghost agent*?"

He shrugged. "For a short period. But I couldn't be brain-panned. It wouldn't take. They saw me as resistant to authority and wanted to eliminate me. So I used my talents to escape and change my identity. I buried my own abilities from everyone and rose through the Marine Corps ranks. When we discovered terrazine gas on that godforsaken planet, Demon's Fair, it was like a gift. I figured that if I could understand why I could do the things I did and use the gas properly, I could become even stronger. Fine-tune my own systems."

"You were a part of Project: Shadowblade from the beginning," Nova said.

Hauler nodded. "I reassigned myself and then took on a disguise as a medical researcher. It was all going so well. But then the chief scientist found out I was experimenting on myself and threatened to go to Warfield. He was a straight arrow, that one. I couldn't afford to have *him* find out. Things got ugly."

Nova's mind was reeling; she couldn't understand how Hauler had managed to keep all of this hidden from so many people for so long. "You were the one," she said. "Cole Bennett. The team member who . . . killed everyone."

"No." He shook his head, his eyes flashing

with anger. "You don't understand anything at all. *Nothing*. I was a successful example of how terrazine could work! My powers had increased exponentially, and with careful monitoring of dosage, the hallucinations were manageable. They just wouldn't listen. When Mengsk found out about the side effects we were observing in certain subjects, he ordered the project shut down and the evidence destroyed. He wanted us all executed. Do you get *that*? Murdered in cold blood, for no other reason than to bury the truth."

"I don't believe you."

"It's true. Mengsk took Warfield off the project and sent in a squadron of marines, ready to wipe everyone out. But I managed to hold them off long enough to escape, along with a couple of other grunts I took with me. I dropped them off at the nearest terran colony, and then I planted false memories of Bennett's death in their minds, so when they were scanned, I would be free to assume my Jackson Hauler identity again. After all, I'd done it before. I'm a chameleon. Another one of my unique talents."

"That's impossible."

"I assure you, it's not. I'm living proof of that."

Nova shook her cuffs. "Let me up, Hauler, or Bennett, or whoever you really are."

"Not yet." He walked up to the bars, taking two of them in his hands and tugging on them.

"Solid neosteel, but you could bend these at will, couldn't you? That is, if you weren't drugged. Believe it or not, I don't want to keep you in there, but you've given me no choice. Tosh has explained to you what we're trying to do, and why we want you with us. You would be a valuable ally."

"I don't deal with psychopaths."

Hauler sighed. "How wrong you are, Nova. You've dealt with psychopaths ever since you signed on for the ghost program. You're fooling yourself—Mengsk is the worst there is. He's responsible for hundreds of thousands, perhaps millions of deaths, including those children on Shi that were particularly important to you. A corrupt government and ghost program, fringe world famines while he grows fat on his own riches, and the gravest offenses against nature imaginable—he's run cross-species experiments that would make you sick to your stomach. He has no conscience. Power is the only thing he craves. It's time for something better."

"And I suppose you're the answer?"

"I believe so, yes. It's time for terrans to live free, to make their own choices, for good or bad. Whether it's the Confederacy or the Dominion, the Koprulu sector has always seemed to choose corruption and dictatorship rather than true democracy. The United States of America from Old Earth had it right, at least prior to the United

Powers League—the people must wield the power and elect their own leaders, and they must have the ability to remove them if necessary."

"And to do this you're going to orchestrate a bloody coup? Overthrow the current government through force?"

"Quite the opposite." Hauler looked saddened, as if the weight of the entire galaxy were on his shoulders, but Nova didn't buy it for a minute. "There have been a few deaths, I'll admit that. But I have set a plan in motion that will allow for an orderly transition with a minimum of lost lives. First, we have spent many months working to un-dermine Mengsk's authority with strategic attacks. That's why I have created the spectres, a force powerful enough to enforce their will without bloodshed, and I have forged strong partnerships with enough advanced firepower to provide a de-terrent to violence. But the real key is you." He stared at her for a long moment, as if waiting for her to respond. When she remained silent, he smiled. "You're a tough one, Nova Terra. But I be-lieve you would be the perfect choice to lead my team of spectres."

"Gabriel Tosh is leading your terrorist cell, as I recall," Nova said. She held his gaze. "And I am a member of the Dominion ghost program. I'm not interested in your offer."

"I thought you might say that." Hauler sighed and removed a small holoprojector from his belt and opened it. He didn't say a word. He didn't have to.

General Cole Bennett watched as she first caught sight of the hologram and recognition dawned. Her eyes widened. It was the moment he always cherished, in chess or in any other game, warfare included: that particular time when his opponent realized they were overmatched, outdrawn, out-foxed.

The hologram showed Mal Kelerchian in a cell quite like the one that held Nova Terra, only this one was on Gehenna Station. He was shackled to the rocky wall, and in front of him stood a mus-cled marine with a mask over his face. The marine held a large combat knife in his hands. At some sort of unheard signal, the marine nodded at the camera, then turned and placed the blade against Kelerchian's neck.

"At this moment, our battlecruiser is headed toward Korhal. I need you to infiltrate Mengsk's inner circle and bring him to me. He trusts you, and this trust will be invaluable to us. We need him to broadcast a message to the rest of the Do-minion. If you do this, I will release wrangler Kelerchian unharmed. If you do not . . ."

He didn't need to finish the sentence. The an-swer was right there in the hologram. Nova looked up and met his eyes, and he saw fear in her for the first time. He probed long enough to confirm it; she cared deeply about this wrangler. Bennett suppressed a smile. Tosh had wanted to do things his way, but he'd had his chance. Nova would join the fold, one way or another.

He decided to soften his approach just a bit. "I'm doing this for your own good. What Gabriel told you is right: you are a slave to the ghost program, nothing more than a weapon that they will use up and discard when the time comes. You, along with all other psionic terrans, deserve your freedom. You should be a beacon of light and leadership for others to follow, rather than a merciless assassin. Follow me, and I promise you this will happen."

Of course, he didn't mean a word of it. His true goals were much more complicated. But he knew the power and authority he wielded over others. People tended to defer to him, and for good reason; if they didn't, he simply used his special talents to alter their brain waves. At least for a short time, Bennett could make anyone believe anything he desired.

He waited for the telltale signs of submission to cross her features, watched her eyes move from the hologram to his face, then back to the hologram again. Normally there would be a change in the muscles of her jaw, a slackening, a slight intake of breath that would be held and then let go as the decision was made.

Nova Terra was a formidable woman; there was no doubt about that. He'd always known she would be tough to convince even with his powers of persuasion, because her loyalties ran deep, and she saw things in black and white, rather than shades of gray. There was good, and there was evil, and nothing in between. That was fine with him, because people like that tended to make good allies. Once you had them, you could depend on them.

He used to think of himself that way, but it had all changed long ago. After he had run from the Ghost Academy, with the help of his talents at mind control and memory manipulation, it hadn't taken him long to assume a new identity as Jackson Hauler, a formerly overlooked noncom who probably would have been destined to fade away into history, but who disappeared one Saturday evening before reappearing and being suddenly "reassigned" to the officers program. It had been a simple matter, really: one quick, messy, but necessary act, then some forged records and a bit of memory tweaking for Hauler's commanding officer and relatively few friends, and he was reborn as a promising and ambitious officer in training.

It didn't take him long to rise through the ranks of the Marine Corps to colonel, and eventually the leader of the Nova Squadron, the black-ops division. After Mengsk's Uprising, he'd proven his loyalty and usefulness to the Dominion. And then he'd heard about the top secret research project called Shadowblade and terrazine, and he knew he had to act. Colonel Hauler had been "reassigned" to a secret mission and disappeared, and he assumed the identity of Cole Bennett, biomedical researcher on the project. But then that bastard Mengsk had sent the marines to wipe them all out, for no other reason than it suited his political agenda. He had deemed the experiment a failure, and so the solution was to erase all evidence it had ever existed.

They had been so close, *so close* to success! It wasn't fair. And yet Mengsk's men wouldn't listen. They had a job to do. So Bennett had done what was necessary to escape and had learned a valuable lesson in the process: trust no one but yourself.

From that moment on, he'd had a mission. Colonel Hauler reappeared, refocused and mad as hell. Of course, he had always considered himself, at minimum, a general. And that was where he was ranked within the alternative leadership structure he had built. With terrazine he would finally be able to fulfill the promise that he had always known was inside him. He would overthrow the so-called emperor Mengsk and take control of the Dominion, and he would do so with cunning and a carefully laid plan.

He had worked for a long time laying the groundwork. He had formed alliances with the

Umojans, Gabriel Tosh, and other select members of the marine forces. He knew all too well the overwhelming firepower of the Marine Corps; he could never hope to defeat Mengsk in a head-to-head battle. He used the spectres to attack strategic positions, weaken resolve, destroy the people's confidence in their leader.

His best chance was to use his superior intellect and unique talents to shake the foundations of the emperor's rule, and then offer himself as an alternative. Tosh would take the fall for the spectres' attacks, and by the time the people discovered his true goals, it would be too late. Once he had assumed control, he would crush those who had wronged him. People would be made examples of: hanged, maimed, mutilated. There would be a cleansing war, and anyone opposed to him would be silenced. He would rule with an iron fist.

That was the way life worked, and he knew it only too well.

Except something had finally gone wrong. Their first attempt to take Mengsk had been disrupted, and now Augustgrad's forces were on high alert. At first, General Bennett was furious, but after he thought about it he began to see this as an opportunity. Nova Terra had the confidence of the emperor, and she alone would be able to slip past the palace defenses. She could still deliver Mengsk to them, and the general's grand plan would remain intact. He would step smoothly into the power vacuum left after Mengsk's confession and beheading.

It was a workable plan. But if they could not take Mengsk out alive, Bennett would order Nova to kill him on the spot. And then Nova, along with Gabriel Tosh, would take the fall for everything else.

Nova's gaze was back on the hologram. Now was the time to become firm. She had to understand who was in charge, and what the consequences would be if she refused him. He probed her mind, searching for her mood, and was pleased with what he found. She was certainly frightened for her friend, perhaps even in love with him, which made General Bennett's job here much easier. She had gone through a wrenching period of understanding as her memories had returned. The idea of regaining her freedom was seductive.

Bennett gave her his most intimidating glare. "I need to know your choice, Nova Terra. The wrangler can't wait forever, and neither can I. Come with us now, and help me lead a new revolution. Or choose to go down with a sinking ship, and take Kelerchian along with you."

"I can't agree to this. I'm a ghost agent for the Terran Dominion—"

Bennett spoke quietly into his comm unit. A moment later, the guard in the hologram slashed the blade downward at Kelerchian's inner wrist. Blood spurted like a fountain, and the wrangler tried to clutch at the wound, but the cuffs kept him from reaching it.

"He's bleeding out," Bennett said. "What are you going to do?"

"I—" Nova's eyes went from the hologram to the general's face again, her fear making her skin go pale.

"We can still save him. *What are you going to do?*"

"Stop!" Nova shouted. "Please." Tears had formed in her eyes. "I'll do what you ask. Just help him."

Bennett smiled and spoke into the comm again, watching as the guard quickly attended to the wrangler's wound. Showing mercy and a bit of tenderness was required at a time like this. Then it was down to business.

"I'm sorry we had to do that," he said. "I promise you he will get the best care. A team will be in shortly to prepare you for surgery, but don't be afraid. It's only to remove your neural implant. They will use succinylcholine, which will paralyze you for a short time in order to make sure you cooperate, and more neuroleptics to dampen your abilities. The surgery is somewhat delicate, but we'll have our best people on it. With accelerated healing, I expect you to recover in time for our mission in Korhal a few days from now."

He turned to go, and then spun back again, as if he'd just thought of something else. "Oh, and Nova, please don't try to second-guess your own decision. We have eyes everywhere, and if you try to go after the wrangler, I will know it, and I will kill him." He paused, meeting her gaze to make sure she understood that he was serious. "We could use your expertise, make no mistake. But we will succeed regardless, and if necessary, I won't hesitate to put a bullet in your brain."

CHAPTER
EIGHTEEN

DR. SHAW

I should have seen it, Nova Terra thought as she sat in the cell, the shackles heavy against her slender wrists. She remembered how the man she had known as Hauler had allowed her to investigate Altara alone, but had sent in his troops before she could reach the refinery. She'd thought he was trying to protect her, but now it was clear he'd wanted to keep her from discovering any evidence at the site. There were other signs too, like how he had held everyone back, including Spaulding, when her ghost team had faced the spectres in Augustgrad. At the time she had thought it was a smart tactical decision, but now she realized he had simply been giving Tosh time to turn her, get to Mengsk, and escape. And the way he'd stood up for her in the recent meeting with Spaulding: she'd thought he was being loyal to her, but he was only protecting his own interests and giving himself time to set up her betrayal.

All the new faces on the *Palatine* made more sense now as well. Bennett was preparing for his next move with resoced new troops who were loyal to him. She sighed. Who else was complicit in this plot? Ward, certainly; she'd sensed something off about him from the beginning. Rourke? Spaulding, on the other hand, looked to be completely innocent. Where were the Annihilators now? Probably on their way to Augustgrad to tell the emperor that she was the traitor. The possibilities made her head spin. How could she have missed so much?

And then there was the immediate situation. Seeing Mal slashed with the blade had chilled her to the bone. She knew she had to act quickly to save his life, but there was so much more than that at stake.

When Bennett had asked her to choose, it hadn't been hard to fill her mind with thoughts of treason. She had believed him when he told her that Mengsk had ordered the massacre of everyone involved with Project: Shadowblade; she was starting to believe he might have been behind the zerg attack on Shi; and she knew that the emperor wouldn't hesitate to wipe out the entire ghost program if it suited him. He had parceled out information on this mission bit by bit, endangering her life in the process.

Mengsk had always felt that in a universe filled with danger and conflict, a strong hand and unified leadership were needed, and he would do whatever it took to meet those needs. Normally she agreed. Her job was not to question but to obey orders. But part of her felt the betrayal like a stinging slap to the face.

She thought of Gabriel Tosh, Kath Toom, Delta Emblock, Lio Travski, and the others at the academy. When she had arrived there, she'd been a damaged loner, incapable of forming relationships, but she had learned teamwork and the value of friendship, and then she had lost it all again. She had to admit that the idea of regaining her freedom was seductive.

But along with the returning memories of her friends and family, she remembered her family's murder, and her role in the deaths of hundreds of people. She remembered her vow of loyalty to the Dominion, and her overwhelming need to forget what she'd done in the past. What would her father have said if he knew she wanted to give it all up and end things right then? She could almost hear his voice. That kind of attitude was not like her. People were depending on her, and she had to stand up and do what was right. She was a fighter, always had been, but she was full of empathy too. It was a gift they both shared.

When the surgical team entered the room, Nova barely looked up until someone crouched at her feet and touched her chin, raising her gaze to his own. "I see you've accepted your fate," Dr. Shaw said. "That's good. It will help us move quickly." He was smiling at her in a way that made her feel sick to her stomach.

"You knew," she said. "When I came to you for help, you acted like you had no idea what was happening to me."

"It didn't matter," he said. "Terrazine has a half-life of a few hours, and symptoms usually begin to dissipate fairly soon, although it builds in your system over time and repeated use. There was nothing I could have done for you then. But now I can change everything. Of course, I have my own reasons for enjoying this moment." He stood back and motioned to an aide to unlock her cuffs, while two unarmored marines stood watch near a medical gurney, with rifles trained on her chest. "You have enough drugs in you to suppress any telekinetic abilities," he said. "But you still know hand-to-hand combat. I'm going to ask you to get on the gurney here, so we can wheel you to medical and prep you for surgery. If you try to fight us, these two gentlemen will shoot you, and wrangler Kelerchian will die. Do you understand?"

She nodded. The aide unlocked her cuffs with trembling fingers and moved away quickly, keeping her gaze away from Nova's face.

(God please don't let her hurt me)

Nova stared at the aide. The inner thought

had sounded faint, but it was clear enough. Her teep abilities were back. Were the drugs already fading from her system? She tried to cover her surprise by raising her hands and shaking them as if they'd fallen asleep, but she was afraid Shaw had seen it all.

When she looked back at him, he was directing the gurney to be wheeled over to her and didn't seem to have noticed anything. She stood, keeping her hands open beside her body, careful to appear nonthreatening and cooperative.

But it was all an act. She was Agent X41822N, loyal to the Dominion, and ready to defend it at all costs. That was enough, but Bennett had made another fatal mistake: he had threatened the only man who meant anything to her; he had pissed her off, and now he was going to feel the full force of her rage.

Hang on, Mal, she thought. *I'm coming.*

CHAPTER NINETEEN

THE ESCAPE

She got on the gurney and let them strap cuffs back around her wrists and ankles, securing them to the gurney frame and giving her only about fifteen centimeters of play. Then they wheeled her out the door and into the hall, Shaw and his aide at her head, the marines following about a meter behind. Nova watched their eyes, and they remained alert, weapons up. At least they weren't wearing combat suits, but they would not be surprised easily. If she had her normal teek abilities, two armed marines would have posed little threat, but she had no idea what, if anything, she had left. It was one thing to decide to escape, but another to actually do it, and she began to wonder whether she would be able to seize an opportunity when the time came.

The medical unit was on the same level, and they reached it quickly. Shaw directed them to the center of the room, where surgical lights and equipment were already set up. The aide locked the gurney wheels in place while the marines took up positions at the door.

Shaw came around and touched her forehead, smoothing away tendrils of hair in a pantomime of fatherly tenderness. "We'll make this quick," he said, his eyes glittering. "The machine will administer two drugs. One will further dampen your psionic abilities, while the other will render you immobile. You'll be conscious and will have some sensation, but your limbs will be paralyzed. This way we can ask you questions as we go and make sure we're not too . . . deep. The brain is a delicate organ, you know, and the neural implant is difficult to remove. Once we begin, you can answer by blinking once for yes, twice for no. Do you understand what I'm saying?"

He's enjoying this, Nova thought. *He's keeping me awake for the shock value.* The idea made her furious, her heart beating faster, blood flushing her skin. "You're going to regret this," she said. "I promise you that."

Shaw blinked and swallowed, then quickly recovered. "Agent Terra, I'm surprised at you. Threatening me could make me nervous, and that's a bad thing. I wouldn't want an accident to occur during surgery." He smiled and motioned to the aide, who instructed a robot arm with a saline drip bag to deploy. "I'm just going to open a vein,"

Shaw said, busying himself with the plastic tube and needle, sliding it smoothly into her arm and taping it off neatly at her elbow. Then he took three leads and attached them to her forehead. "I grew up on Tarsonis, you know," he said, checking with the AI readout to make sure the flow was operating. "My parents worked for yours, actually, at your apartment building. Mother helped clean; Father cooked for you. They were there the day of the attack. The rebels didn't hurt them, but you, and your . . . mind blast, it killed them both instantly."

Nova remembered how he had looked at her when she first woke up after the incident with the zerg on Altara, how he had thought the word *murderer*. He'd managed to hide the rest of it from her somehow, but it all made sense. "The terrorists killed my family," she said. "Shot my brother right in front of me. I was just a girl. I didn't mean for it to happen."

"Ah, yes," Shaw said. "Of course not. We never mean for the worst to happen, do we? That's the sad part. But we're all responsible for our own actions." He held her gaze for a moment. "Me, for example. What you did to my family motivated me to join Bennett's team. Now here I am, after all these years, face-to-face with their murderer. I've been waiting for this moment. I have to say, I feel . . . vindicated."

Nova stared at the saline bag hanging on the

arm, then at the silver steel tray holding the surgical instruments Shaw would use on her. They looked like torture devices. Just beyond was the monitor that showed a running list of vital signs, brain-wave activity, and other data. This was the computer that would begin pumping the drugs into her system any minute.

She had the sudden, terrible feeling that regardless of what Bennett and Tosh wanted, Shaw did not intend for her to come out of this alive.

"I'll be right back," Shaw said, holding up his hands. "A bit of a scrub, and we'll be ready to go." He motioned to the aide, and they disappeared through another door.

Nova glanced at the marines, who still stood on either side of the door and stared out into space somewhere above her head. Now was her chance. But when she narrowed her focus to the shackles around her wrists, nothing happened but a faint tinkling of the chains. *No.* She took a deep breath and tried again. Still nothing but the slightest movement. She wasn't strong enough.

She was so preoccupied with her efforts that she didn't notice the change in the monitor at first. But finally the blinking drew her gaze, and she turned to find that the running data summary had been replaced by a repeating line of text: *NOVA TERRA.*

Nova glanced back at the marines. The monitor's

screen was angled away enough that she didn't think they could see it.

Nova, it's Lio Travski.

How could Lio be communicating with her through a computer? And how would she be able to talk back?

The answer came quickly, scrolling across the screen: *The electrodes are connected to this monitor. Just think what you want to say and I can read your brain waves.*

But how are you here?

I live inside the data stream now. I can be anywhere, access any data set inside any system known to mankind. And some alien systems as well.

You're helping the spectres, aren't you? Nova couldn't ignore her feelings of dismay at the thought, even though she'd suspected it earlier: Lio had been responsible for taking down the Dominion's communications center during the earlier attack on Augustgrad. If he'd infected their entire network like a virus, the spectres could control everything else. He would have to bypass Dominion firewalls and gain access to the mainframes, which was no easy trick. But once he got inside that system, it would be mutiny by machine. All marine communications, nuclear launch codes, power grids—everything would be at their mercy.

This world you live in is flawed. The xel'naga, a culture I have studied carefully, left it behind long ago.

Terrans and protoss and zerg battle for the remaining scraps at the table. I am interested in expanding terran consciousness. It is time for a revolution, and I had thought terrazine could be the answer. But its side effects are significant, and my alliance with Tosh is of growing concern. There is little control to this experiment.

Experiment? People are dying. Many more will die, if Bennett has his way.

If that is true, so be it.

You can't believe that, Lio. I know you. You can't possibly believe that what Gabriel has done is right.

There is no right and wrong for me. Not anymore.

A soft hiss brought her back to reality with a jolt: the drugs were being dispersed into her system. She tried frantically to reach the needle in her vein, but the shackles did not have anywhere near enough play. *Lio, they're about to operate on me, open up my skull. I need your help. Can you stop the injection?*

Nothing.

Lio, please. I don't have time to explain. But this isn't right. Shaw's going to kill me and make it look like an accident. Nova flashed back on the battle with Lio for control of the academy's Sparky computer system, and the young ghost trainee Colin Phash and his remarkable skills at astral projection, the memories flooding back, powerful enough to make her gasp. The terrible loss at Lio's apparent death hitting the team hard, hitting her harder than she could have imagined. She squeezed her eyes shut and sent every ounce of her will through a single, focused thought: *If our friendship ever meant anything to you, trust me now.*

For a moment she thought he had left her, but then the hiss of the machine's hydraulics stopped. She sighed with relief, but it wasn't enough, not yet. She still had to get the shackles off and deal with the marines.

A moment later Shaw and the aide returned. They had donned surgical gowns and had masks hanging around their necks. "The moment of truth," Shaw said, approaching the gurney. He was smiling again. "You can hear me, I'm sure, but you won't be able to move now. The succinylcholine acts quickly."

He paused, glancing back and forth between the machine and the IV needle as if confused, then leaned over her, his breath hot on her skin.

Even with the shackles holding her down, he was close enough to touch.

She grabbed his wrist in her right hand and yanked him down on top of her, grabbing his throat with her left hand and clamping down hard. Shaw gave a strangled yelp and thrashed his legs until she squeezed even harder, and he froze.

The marines had leveled their weapons at her, but she was partly protected by Shaw's body. "You move a muscle, and I'll rip his Adam's apple out," she said. "I have enough left in my tank to teek a bullet right back at you, so don't even think about firing those weapons." It was worth a shot; she just had to hope they believed her. Then she glanced at the aide, who was standing just about a meter away. "Open these cuffs," she said. "Do it. Now!"

The two marines, big, meaty men who were not used to losing control to a woman, even a ghost agent, looked at each other. The aide was paralyzed with fear. Nova looked down at the top of Shaw's head, and the part of his face that was visible to her. Shaw's eye was wide and red, and he kept making choking sounds and trying to swallow against her grip. "They don't do as I say, I'll kill you," she said. "Understand?"

Shaw squeezed his watering eye shut and gave a slight nod. "Do it," he croaked to the others.

The aide came to the gurney, fumbling with a release key, close to panic. "Good," Nova said when she had popped the cuffs. "Now back away; that's right. Take those weapons from the marines and place them on the floor." When she'd done that, Nova sat up on the gurney, keeping her grip on Shaw's throat and ignoring the pinch of the needle as it shifted and then fell from the crook of her arm. "I'm going to walk out of here with him," she said, "but first I'm going to have to ask you to cuff these marines to the gurney." She stood up and shuffled away, giving the aide access to the shackles.

But the marines, apparently deciding that this was the moment to make their move, went scrambling on all fours for their weapons. Nova threw Shaw roughly aside, where he spun and hit the wall with a thud, tumbling to the floor. She was on the marines in an instant, delivering a solid, barefooted kick to one's face, snapping his head back, then chopping down hard with the heel of her hand on the other's neck. The blow drove his face into the tile with a crack, and his head bounced back up, spraying blood from his nose. He slumped back to the floor, unconscious or dead.

The second man scrambled to his feet, pulling a small knife from a sheath strapped to his ankle and waving it through the air. He smiled at her through bloody teeth, but she could sense his uncertainty. "Don't do this," she said. "I don't want to kill you."

"She can't teek you!" Shaw shouted from somewhere behind her. "Take her, for God's sake!"

The man lunged, and Nova sidestepped neatly, caught his outstretched arm, and used it as a fulcrum to flip herself over his head, landing on the floor behind him. She took his head in her hands and twisted it violently to the left, feeling the crack of vertebrae and the sudden looseness of a broken neck. She let his body gently down to the floor.

The aide had squeezed herself into a corner of the room, clutching her legs to her chest. Nova could sense her thoughts growing steadily louder, almost incomprehensible through her terror. "It's all right," she said, taking a step closer, her hands out. "I'm not going to hurt you."

The aide's eyes went wide, focused on something behind Nova's back. She sensed a terrible rage projected at her and spun to find Dr. Shaw coming with a scalpel held high in both hands, a guttural scream escaping his lips and a look of pure hatred twisting his features into an ugly grimace.

A surge of adrenaline flooded her body, and instinctively she lashed out with her mind. Shaw's face registered a brief moment of confusion as his limbs betrayed him and he thrust the scalpel violently down into his own belly, ripping upward and spilling coils of intestine. Then he sank to the floor with a sigh, clutching himself as blood wet his scrubs in a quickly spreading pool.

It was a fatal wound, and he knew it.

She picked up one of the marines' needle-guns, checking the action. It was loaded and ready for use. She knew she didn't have much time before others came. But a plan was formulating in her mind. It would take cooperation from an old friend, but it just might work.

She looked down at Shaw, who stared up at her and coughed wetly.

(you can't stop them it's too late you'll never make it out of here alive)

"We'll see about that," she said. "One thing I know for sure: you won't."

Then she turned and walked out the door, leaving Shaw and the bloody operating room behind.

CHAPTER TWENTY

THE *PALATINE*

General Cole Bennett was furious.

He stood on the raised platform over the bridge, staring out the large window at the stars. He'd stood here just a short time ago as Colonel Jackson Hauler, in a similar pose, watching them approach Altara, but the feeling then had been entirely different.

Back then he had been on the cusp of victory, every piece of his complex and thorough plan in place. He had been preparing for years, carefully building covert alliances, stockpiling weapons, terrazine, and jorium, conducting strategic attacks on Dominion strongholds to weaken morale, and growing his team of spectres. Gehenna Station was fully operational, one of the most advanced and deadly battle stations ever created. Lio Travski was ready to infiltrate the Dominion network and paralyze its operations from within and allow them to steal Mengsk out from under the security forces' noses. Michael Liberty, the legendary rogue reporter who had a cult following through his pirated holo reports, had already agreed to broadcast Mengsk's confession to the universe, once they had the emperor in their hands. And Bennett was ready to step into the power vacuum, a benevolent leader who was simply looking out for what was best for the people. At least, that was how he would appear until it was too late.

He remembered thinking that it was only a matter of time before he would rule the Koprulu sector, while Arcturus Mengsk would be begging for his life.

How quickly things change. Even hours ago, Bennett had felt invincible as he watched Terra bow her head and acquiesce to his wishes. Then, just a short time ago, he had received word that she had escaped from the medical unit, and that Shaw was dead. She was gone. Rourke had alerted him to the unauthorized launch of wrangler Kelerchian's personal ship, the *November,* from one of the landing bays on the *Palatine,* but had been unable to stop it, and before they could fire on it, most of their tracking and communications systems suddenly went dark.

It seemed that he had badly underestimated her. Terra was certainly inside the little ship. Where she was headed now was anybody's guess, and it was possible she would try to warn Mengsk immediately. In fact, that made the most sense. But Bennett felt sure she would not waste any time before trying to locate Gehenna Station and rescue Kelerchian. He didn't think for a minute that she would find it; one of the greatest triumphs of his plan was the massive cloaking device Lio had helped devise and operate with the aid of Umojan researchers, a device that completely hid the giant station from any terran sensors. But she was dangerous, and with the communications system down, he couldn't even contact Tosh and order Kelerchian's execution, which was something he desperately wanted to do purely for revenge.

General Bennett seethed with anger. He had never met anyone able to hide her true thoughts the way she had done in that jail cell—anyone other than himself, of course. And she was resistant to mental suggestion, unlike most terrans. Rourke, for example: he knew she didn't like him, but it was a simple task to put a little "push" inside her head and make her do whatever he wanted. Including going to bed with him, when he felt the urge.

"Captain," he barked, turning away from the window and facing the bridge. "Status update."

Rourke looked up from where she was bent over the communications officer's station. She whispered something to him and then straightened. "We're still down, sir," she said. "She's fried the communications system at the source."

"Well, try it again," he shouted at her.

"The hardware's damaged. I have a man down there working on it, but it's going to take a while. The *Palatine* has limited abilities, sir. We were already locked into a flight pattern for Gehenna before this happened, and that's where we're headed now. I can pilot her in manually when we get in range. But anything else—" She shrugged. "Let's just say I wouldn't want to get lost in deep space."

"Dammit!" Bennett slammed his hands down on the rail, feeling the metal bend under the force of his blow. He pulled the canister of terrazine from his belt and took a deep drag from its contents, feeling the gas fill his lungs and spread through his tingling limbs. Normally he was meticulously careful about his dosing schedule; one of the things he had learned through the years was that the side effects were manageable, if terrazine was used in moderation, and particularly if combined with the mineral jorium, which seemed to make it more stable. But right now, he needed to feel the power that terrazine gave him, the familiar feeling of euphoria.

It did not disappoint him. He felt as if he had grown in stature until he loomed over the bridge, dwarfing all others on board. They were all staring at him now in awe. He was destined to lead the terran race back from oblivion, and they all knew it.

He was amazed at how concerned he had been

only moments ago. He had made a few small mis-
calculations with Terra, but all was not lost: far
from it. He simply had to regroup, get to Gehenna
Station, and prepare for the full-scale invasion of
Augustgrad. The pieces were still in place, and he
had prepared for too long for this moment. Nothing could stop him now. Certainly not a lone ghost
agent, who didn't even have her ghost suit to protect her.

"Get Lieutenant Ward," Bennett said, "and
have him prepare the vikings. When we find Nova
Terra's ship, I want it captured immediately. I
want her alive." He turned back to face the darkness of space, watching for any movement that
would signal a small ship. She was out there somewhere, and she couldn't be too far ahead of them.
They would find her, and when they did, he would
make her watch as he skinned Mal Kelerchian
alive, one limb at a time.

CHAPTER TWENTY-ONE

GEHENNA STATION

When Kath Toom awoke that morning, things had changed on Gehenna. There was tension in the air, and more activity among the spectres and bots that rolled through the rocky hallways. The *Palatine* was scheduled to arrive shortly, and everyone knew Nova would be on board. Gabriel had explained to Kath that they were headed for August-grad, and this time, with Nova's help, they would not fail to take the emperor hostage.

At first Kath thought they were all insane; how could one battle station hope to defeat the entire Dominion Marine Corps, especially after their first failure had put the troops on high alert? But when Gabriel explained the plan, she had to admit that it was so perfectly simple, it just might work.

The plan was not built on force but on deceit. Gehenna Station's advanced cloaking device would allow them to orbit Korhal unseen, and Nova Terra would approach alone in her private ship and request an urgent audience with Mengsk, while the cloaked spectres quietly infiltrated the palace guard. The emperor's confidence in Nova would surely get her access, and once she had him the spectres would facilitate her escape, assisted by Lio, who would disrupt communications and make it appear that Mengsk was still in his private rooms long enough for them to get clear. They would bring Mengsk to the cloaked Gehenna Station and hide him there right under the Dominion's noses; to the marine forces, it would be as if he had disappeared into thin air.

General Bennett had brokered a deal with Michael Liberty to broadcast Mengsk's "confession" to the people, again assisted by Lio, who would ensure the broadcast went out on every communications system available. Mengsk would be forced to admit his role in Project: Shadowblade, the mistreatment of ghosts in the academy, his secret medical experiments and executions; if he resisted initially, Bennett, with his unique skills at mind manipulation, would make sure the emperor did as he was told.

Finally, as the Dominion was reeling from Mengsk's confession of his crimes against humanity, Colonel Jackson Hauler would step forward to fill the power vacuum. There would be others who would try to assume command, of course, but

Bennett could influence their thoughts enough to convince them he was the best choice to lead the people. The academy would be torn down; the spectres would be reborn as an elite team created to protect Bennett's rule and ensure peace in a time of conflict, and a new order would be established.

All this seemed plausible on the surface. But Kath was growing increasingly nervous. Something was terribly amiss, but she couldn't put her finger on it. Since Gabriel Tosh had seduced her on the floor of the mysterious tunnel, he had exhibited more and more erratic behavior, seemingly calm and gentle one moment, agitated and cruel the next. What was worse, she had caught him cocking his head and staring into space several more times, as if listening to a voice she could not hear. She had even heard him muttering to himself once, and the words made little sense to her, but it sounded like a conversation about something to do with a death goddess.

Gabriel had told her everything: the zerg attack on Shi, his supposed death and his newfound abilities, his discovery of terrazine. He'd told her about General Bennett and how their alliance had developed. Gabriel was a natural leader, but his stories were beginning to sound like the ravings of a lunatic, filled with pseudoreligious undertones, delusions of grandeur, and sentimental memories of their time together at the academy. He had built up Team Blue to be something superhuman, and his fixation on this idea that everything would be all right if they could just be together again seemed childish and irrational.

She still loved him. But she did not trust him anymore, even though she had come to believe him about what had really happened to her father.

In spite of herself, she wanted revenge too.

The other spectres were acting strangely as well, particularly Dylanna, who was overly paranoid and seemed to feel Kath was a rival. She remembered Dylanna had had a crush on Gabriel way back at the academy, and it was still obvious now, although he was oblivious to it. The woman fawned over him, and the worse he treated her, the more fixated she became. Sometimes it seemed as if she would say or do things to provoke him, just to get his attention. It all felt increasingly desperate. At the same time, Kath would catch Dylanna glaring at her, her eyes like daggers.

Kath had taken to wearing the spectres' black suit, and although she still felt slightly uneasy in it, she did have to admit that it had its advantages. The technology behind the suit was even more impressive than she had realized, and wearing it felt like having a second skin. The artificial muscle fiber enhanced her natural strength and agility far beyond what her old ghost suit had done, and the cloaking function appeared to make her completely undetectable, even masking her thoughts from other teeps. Gabriel had given her a canister for terrazine that she kept on her at all times, and although she tried to use it sparingly, she had trouble keeping the cravings at bay. The hallucinations and memory fragments no longer shocked her, but what she couldn't seem to handle was the hunger that started to eat at her insides a few hours after her last hit, and grew steadily until she couldn't think of anything else.

Kath made her way to the bridge, where she found Gabriel standing alone, muttering to himself. Gehenna's bridge was different than those of Dominion ships; it was smaller, for one thing, since the huge space station needed very few people to pilot it. Its instruments were also more compact, the holo-screens brighter and sharper.

Gabriel was standing in the shadows, the lights from the screens glowing green, lighting him in profile. The scene was eerie, and she felt as if she was intruding on a private conversation. She crossed her hands at her waist and waited. He didn't notice her at first, but then gave a start, as if suddenly becoming aware that she had entered the room.

"*Palatine*'s coming in dark," he said abruptly. "I keep pinging them but get nothing."

"They're on time, aren't they?" she asked. "Maybe they're just being cautious."

Gabriel shook his head. "It's all wrong. Like their systems are out. Can't get Lio to respond to me either."

"If you're worried about Lio—"

"He's barely human anymore, Kath, and he's arguing about control. Been worried about him for a while now. We need him with us, but if he won't do what we ask, Bennett has a plan for that too."

"What do you mean?"

Tosh glanced at her, then away. "EMP," he said quietly. "Focused blast to wipe him out where he lives if he causes trouble. It ain't perfect, but that should disrupt the Dominion communications network long enough for us to do our job too."

"You can't do that," she said. "He could be anywhere now—how could that possibly work? And even if it did, Lio's still *alive*, Gabriel, still conscious. You can't just murder him if he doesn't do what you want. What about the team? He's still your friend—"

"Last resort. But if we have to, we will. It'll work, trust me. We can't let anything stop us from getting to Mengsk."

No. Toom shook her head. It was all wrong. They stood in silence, watching through the observation window as if they could find an answer somewhere out in deep space. Gehenna was huge, almost like its own small planet, but when she looked out, she was reminded that they were hurtling through space at thousands of kilometers an hour.

Time seemed to stand still as she sensed Gabriel's anxiety grow, manifesting itself in the repeated clenching of his hands into fists. He seemed to have forgotten she was there and turned his head sharply to one side, as if angry at a comment someone had made. "It's not her," he said, under his breath. "Don't make it more than it is."

"Excuse me?"

He turned back to her, as if startled again at her presence, then let out a sigh. "You believe in ghosts?"

A chill crept up her spine. "I . . . sometimes our brains make up things we want to see. That's what I think." *Especially after a little terrazine,* she thought, but didn't say it.

If he picked up on her thought, he didn't react to it. "Had a dream last night," he said. "Grandma Tosh was there. Death was all around, bodies everywhere. Lots of blood, and me, I was alone." He shook his head. "She says it's a bad omen. What do you think about that?"

"You're using present tense, like she's here right now."

"Maybe she is."

Now she knew what he'd been doing when she'd caught him muttering to himself.

"There are no such things as ghosts, Gabriel. Your grandma's been gone a long time, and she's not here."

He looked irritated. "I know it. I'm not stupid." But he sounded uncertain. "I mean like her spirit's with me, you know? A guide." He fumbled for the words. "They say that the people you love stay with you forever. Like that."

"I don't know." Kath thought of her own father, how real he had seemed when she had seen him in that AAI unit with Lio. She could still hear his voice sometimes in her head, and for a moment she wondered if terrazine didn't cause hallucinations at all, but opened a window between the living and the dead.

But that was crazy, and just thinking it made her realize how close to a breakdown she was right now.

"She says I need a sacrifice," Gabriel muttered, the lights throbbing softly, making his skin look as if it were pulsing in and out. "Maman Therese takes something from me, in exchange for giving me what I want. Problem is, I don't know what the sacrifice is yet. Maybe that's why I had the death dream. Maybe the loa's angry."

"You're just worried," she said. "It comes out in dreams." She hesitated, then took his big hand in hers. It was sweaty and hot. He clutched at her for a moment and released her fingers as the comm unit crackled to life.

"They're here," Caleb said through the comm. "Docking now."

"Any contact?" Gabriel asked.

"Nothing yet. We'll be opening the doors soon. You better get down here."

When they arrived at the docking bay, a cavernous space large enough to fit several battlecruisers, the *Palatine*'s engines were off and its large exit ramp was already hissing open. Almost immediately, a large man with a shiny bald crown and a salt-and-pepper goatee came charging down the ramp, flanked by two marines in combat suits. He wore a formal military outfit with a heavy collar decked in purple and gold. This would be the general, Kath thought. He looked ready to tear someone to pieces with his bare hands, and she sensed dull confusion and fear from the resoced marines, who did not seem to understand why.

Gabriel seemed to sense the source of General Bennett's anger almost immediately. "Where's Nova?" he said, stepping forward to meet him.

Bennett stopped in the center of the landing area. "She's gone," he said, his eyes glittering with rage. "And she damaged our systems from within. Didn't you notice we could not communicate with you?"

"What did you do?" Gabriel asked.

"Nothing. She escaped when we were preparing to remove her implant—"

"'Escaped' makes it seem like she was a prisoner."

"What did you think was happening when we sent you the wrangler?" Bennett shouted. "She wasn't going to do this willingly, Gabriel. You had your chance to turn her and you couldn't do it. She—"

"So you tried to force her," Gabriel said. His own voice was low, but Kath could see him clenching his massive fists again, and the threat of violence seemed to emanate from him in waves. "I told you not to do that. The gods're angry at you."

Bennett waved this off. "Silly superstitions." He peered at Gabriel's face so intently, Kath felt even more uncomfortable. "You haven't been using the jorium," he said. "It keeps the terrazine stable and minimizes the side effects. You know that." He glanced at Kath. "Have you?" he asked, and she shook her head. "Has *anyone* on this station been taking their jorium?"

Kath looked away and caught movement underneath the *Palatine*'s massive outer shell. A hydralisk slowly uncoiled from where it had clung to the pipes and couplings, dropping to the deck on clawed feet and hissing at her with dripping jaws. It hunched its plated back, exposing the tips of deadly spines ready to launch like missiles. Her heart pounding in her chest, she blinked rapidly and it disappeared, replaced by a technician who let more steam loose from a release valve, then checked a reading on his handheld console.

My God, she thought, *what's happening to me? What's happening to all of us?*

Bennett stepped closer to Gabriel Tosh, extended a finger, and poked his chest. "You're losing control," he said. "I've been studying this gas for years, running enough tests to know what it can do better than anyone alive, and that's why I'm able to handle it. My dosing schedule has to be followed to the minute. I've been warning you. But you won't listen." His voice raised another notch in volume. "We can't afford any more mistakes. If you can't handle this assignment, I'll damn well find someone else to do it."

Gabriel looked down at Bennett's finger, still pointed at his chest. When he looked up, his face was red with rage, and energy radiated outward in a palpable wave. For a moment she feared he might just detonate like a nuclear weapon, and she stepped forward, grabbing his arm to pull him away.

When Gabriel turned toward her, his face was contorted into a thoughtless mask of hatred. She felt his mind lash out, as if two hands had been placed on her chest and shoved her violently backward. She flew through the air, then her back hit the hard stone floor and her teeth snapped

together, pain blasting upward through her body
and making her cry out. The room went black for
a moment, and when she opened her eyes again,
he was standing over her, a look of horror on his
face as he tried to help her up.

"Kath, I'm sorry," Gabriel said. "I—I didn't . . ."

She scrambled to her feet, pulling away from
him, a sob catching in her throat. She felt a part of
her going into attack mode, her academy training
like a reflex that rose unbidden to the surface, but
the rest of her just wanted to run away from this
place and never return.

His face was like that of a small boy who had
thrown a tantrum and just realized that he'd broken something precious, and her own heart
seemed to break in response. This was the Gabriel
she loved, not the monster that had reared its ugly
head a moment before. But she couldn't know
when that monster would show up again, because
it lived permanently inside him now.

Kath Toom turned and ran from the docking
bay, the sound of Gabriel's voice echoing after her.

"Leave her," Bennett said. "We have more important things to attend to."

Tosh stared at the door where Kath had disappeared, anger and remorse churning in his stomach.
His head was a whirling mass of confused thoughts,
voices surfacing and sinking back into the depths.

He loved her, and yet he could not risk being pulled away from his higher calling; Grandma Tosh had made that clear enough.

Grandma was upset. Ever since Kath had come aboard Gehenna Station, Project: Shadowblade had started to fall apart. She was a distraction he couldn't afford, Grandma told him, and she was right. Maman Therese had grown angry, that much was clear. How else had the first mission to Augustgrad failed when they had such an advantage? Nova's escape was just further proof.

It's a sacrifice she want, and you best give it to her before long. You and the witchcraft you carry be meant to lead your fellow men. But you need to give her that.

The idea of a sacrifice made Tosh's blood run cold. He clenched his fists, the familiar feeling of his nails biting into his palms steeling his resolve. Then he nodded, turning back to where Bennett stood with his hands on his hips. "Follow me," Tosh said.

They went to the bridge, where Dylanna was working the instruments alone. She looked up at Tosh as they entered, and he saw a strange emotion pass across her face before she looked away again quickly. As always, just the sight of her enraged him, and he struggled to resist the urge to strike her.

"Nova Terra escaped in the *November*, a wrangler's ship, just hours ago," Bennett said without preamble. "She can't have gotten far. I want you to find her."

"I don't know how—"

"I don't care for your excuses! Wrangler ships have tracking devices—it's Kelerchian's ship. Figure out how to tap into that. Just *do* it."

Dylanna nodded, then started pressing the keys on the nearest screen: "Lio? Are you there?"

Nothing happened for a long moment, and Tosh thought Lio would continue with the silent treatment, the way he had ever since their argument over his handling of Kath and the other spectres. Tosh had managed to pilot the huge station with the others' help, but it made him realize just how dependent they were on Lio's expertise. That needed to change, he thought. Lio had never been particularly reliable, and they were asking for trouble with him. Tosh was sure he would not answer now.

But then a brief line of text appeared: *What is it?*

"We need to find wrangler Kelerchian's ship, the *November*," Dylanna typed. "It left the *Palatine* about two hours ago."

Nothing, and then: *tracking . . .*

If anyone could find a tiny ship like the *November* in the sea of space, it was Lio. Dylanna looked up, smiling as if she had been personally awarded Augustgrad. Bennett crossed his arms impatiently, and silence descended over the bridge. Tosh thought of a thousand things and tried not to focus on the thirst that was building within him. He ached to take a hit from the canister of terrazine, but did not want Bennett to see him. He must not show any weakness now.

A few moments later and the screen lit up again: *Found a ship fitting that description.* The screen switched to a map with coordinates showing the *November* only kilometers away. *Scans revealing one life-form inside.*

"She might have already made contact with Augustgrad," Dylanna said. She typed: "Can you block all communications from the ship?"

Lio responded immediately: *Already done. Nothing in or out showing on logs.*

"Send the vikings," Bennett said into his comm unit. "Ward, I want you on this personally. You hear me? We can bring her in now, and barely have to change course." He smiled. "We'll have her within the hour."

The vikings brought the *November* in without a single shot fired, expertly herding her back around and into the docking bay. Bennett and Tosh met them at the bay, the *November* ticking on the deck as it cooled, looking tiny beside the massive bulk of the *Palatine*.

Lieutenant Ward stood in full combat gear on the deck outside the ship with a small contingent of armed marines, saluting Bennett and the others as they approached. "She tried to run at first, sir," he said, "but we surrounded the ship and brought her back. She's been sitting in there since we arrived. I waited for you before boarding."

"Good work," Bennett said. "I'll go in alone."

"Bad idea," Tosh said. He had been thinking of the best way to handle Terra, and this was definitely not it. "She's gonna fight, and you don't know what she can do—"

He paused in horror. Standing next to the ship, dressed in a black, flowing robe, was Maman Therese. Tosh's hand went to the figurine around his neck, his heart pounding in his throat as she pointed her finger at him, shaking her head in silent reproach. Grandma Tosh stood behind her, a look of sadness in her eyes.

He had angered them both, and now there would be hell to pay.

"Don't go in there," he whispered, his mouth dry, but a technician had already forced the ramp open and Bennett was headed up it, ducking his head as he entered. Dylanna touched his arm, but he shrugged it away. He was sure that any moment there would be a bloodcurdling scream. Someone was going to die; Maman Therese had foreseen it.

General Bennett was missing from view for only a few moments. When he reappeared again, his face was red, and he was breathing hard.

His eyes flashed with anger as he thundered back down the ramp, looking as if he wanted to tear someone limb from limb.

"Sir?" Ward said as several of the armed marines thumped up the ramp, guns up, and disappeared inside.

"The ship's empty," Bennett said. "Nova is gone."

CHAPTER TWENTY-TWO

NOVA

Nova Terra crept through the darkened passages deep inside Gehenna Station. Down here the rocky walls were rougher, and the lighting farther apart; most of the spaces appeared to be used for storage, or for some other purpose long since abandoned. But she was down there for a reason.

She had thought briefly about going straight for Augustgrad, but she knew Mal would be long dead by then. She needed to get to him first. *Friendship over duty.* It was a decision she would never have made a few short weeks ago, but she was a different person now. Her returning memories and emotions both confused and overwhelmed her. But she knew she had to do this. Mal needed her, and she could not let him down.

The November *piloted into docking bay and boarded,* came the words across her remote console. *Spectres have discovered our deceit.*

Nova paused in the green glow, taking that in. She was now on borrowed time, but it had given her a chance to make her move. "Thank you, Lio," she typed. "You did the right thing."

There is no longer any right and wrong for me. There is only truth.

Lio appeared to be drifting rapidly away from humanity, his metamorphosis accelerating. He seemed to have given up on whatever had been motivating him to help the spectres, calling Tosh hopelessly unstable and Bennett's plans fatally flawed. She had barely been able to capture his attention after her escape from the medical unit. But there was still a small piece of something human in him, because when she explained that Bennett was threatening to kill Mal to get her to cooperate, he agreed to help her. She got the feeling that he did it not because he had any emotional reaction himself, but simply out of some last vestige of loyalty, a salute to his memories of their time together at the academy.

From there it had been relatively simple for him to autopilot the *November* into deep space and alter the scanner's data so that the ship appeared to have a life-form on board, while she hid herself away in the *Palatine*'s storage facility off the loading bay, right under their noses. She knew that it was unlikely she would be able to find Gehenna Station on her own, and if she tried, they would catch her before she arrived. But if she made it look as if she had taken the *November,* she wouldn't have to find it; Bennett would surely head straight for the space station and take her along for the ride.

The plan had worked perfectly. As soon as the *Palatine* docked with Gehenna and Bennett and his entourage had left for the bridge, she was able to sneak off undetected. Lio had supplied her with the plans to the station, and an alternate route through these rarely used passages that would bring her directly under the room where Mal was being held. From there she could access an air vent and get into his room or, if that didn't work, tear the walls down. Nothing would stop her.

She crept forward in bare feet, ignoring the rough-hewn floors that cut into her flesh. She was still in the surgical gown she'd been wearing before her escape from Shaw; she hadn't had the chance to find other clothing. Without her ghost suit and HUD, she felt particularly vulnerable. But she had the portable console to communicate with Lio, and the needle-gun she had grabbed from the ship, along with enough rounds to do some serious damage, if it came to that.

And she was ready for a fight. Over the course of the last several hours she had felt her psionic talents come fully to life again as the last of the drugs Shaw had given her wore off, and along with that came a burning rage that threatened to overwhelm her senses. What Shaw, and by extension Bennett, had tried to do to her was unforgivable. She only hoped to get the chance to put her hands around Bennett's neck and squeeze the life out of him.

Mal was close. Although she didn't know how or why, some kind of mind link had formed between them, and she could feel his presence more strongly than any of the others on board. He was hidden deep within the complex passages of this remarkable ship. Or space station, to use a more accurate term. Gehenna Station had been created from the hollowed-out core of a giant asteroid, the remains of a space platform providing the guts that drove the monstrous engines. Whatever technology they had used was impressive, but it was the sheer size of the thing that took her breath away. She had never seen anything like it. Gehenna was indeed like a small moon moving through space, yet completely hidden from view.

As Nova reached an intersecting passage, she sensed someone approaching. She flattened herself against the wall, but there was nowhere to go, and no way to hide without a cloaking device. It was a woman in great distress, her mind full of fragmented thoughts, and she was moving quickly. Nova looked around frantically for a hiding place, but the walls here were unbroken. If the woman turned down this tunnel, she would be discovered. She worked to let her mind go blank.

When Kath Toom came stumbling around the corner, she stopped short, and both women stared at each other in surprise. Tears streaked Toom's face and her eyes were puffy and red. She was carrying headgear and wearing the spectres' now-familiar black combat suit, and it looked strange on her.

"Nova," she said, and it wasn't clear whether her tone was relief or dread. Her eyes went to the gun cradled in Nova's hands. "What are *you* doing here?"

"I've come to rescue Mal Kelerchian." Nova kept the barrel down but ready. She sensed a threat, but it wasn't clear if the feeling was coming from Toom or somewhere else. "Bennett and Tosh are holding him hostage and threatening to kill him unless I help them kidnap Emperor Mengsk. And I've got a feeling that even if I do that, Mal and I are dead anyway."

Toom shook her head. But her thoughts gave her away. Nova could sense her uncertainty, and she let Toom scrutinize her mind for the truth, waiting for the feedback loop that would normally occur when one ghost probed another, but it didn't happen; perhaps it was another effect of the terrazine. Toom's eyes widened in shock as she took it all in, Nova's confrontation with Tosh in the palace, Bennett gassing her, and her treatment by Dr. Shaw.

"They took you too," Nova said. "You think

this is about free will, but they drugged you and brainwashed you to get you here. Look at yourself, Kath. Wearing that suit, fighting for the enemy. He's turned you into a traitor to the Dominion. You don't know what you're doing. Leave here now—take the *November* and escape, while there's still a chance."

"I can't."

"Why not?"

"I—I love him."

"You loved what he used to be," Nova said, as gently as she could. "But he's not that person anymore."

"His heart is in the right place, I swear to you. What Mengsk has done to us, it's wrong, Nova. Even you have to see that."

She could feel Toom's agonized confusion, but she could not wait any longer. Her fingers tightened on the needler. "We're running out of time. As soon as they realize what I've done, they're going to kill Mal. I don't want to hurt you, but I have to go." She made as if to walk around Toom, but the woman stepped up to block her path, settling the headgear over her face.

"I can't let you," she said. "I *can't*. I'm sorry." She seemed to be crying again. "Please, give yourself up. We can work together; we can figure this out."

"Get out of my way," Nova said. Her fingertips had begun to tingle now, her breath coming faster.

She moved forward again. Toom put a hand out to stop her, and Nova jerked the barrel of the gun up fast toward her midsection.

But Toom was faster. She grabbed the barrel with both hands and twisted the gun loose, throwing it down the corridor.

Instinct and training kicked in. Nova took hold of her arm, using her body as leverage to flip her onto her back, but Toom leaned in and went into a roll, regaining her feet again neatly and breaking the hold.

The two women circled each other warily in the narrow confines of the tunnel, in full combat mode. Nova probed Toom's mind, trying to find a way through to her, but she was barely able to make any sense of the woman's thoughts at all. "The terrazine's keeping you from thinking straight," she said, trying to reason with her. "This isn't the real you, and it's not Gabriel either. If you just—"

With a strangled cry, Toom launched herself toward Nova. Her hands caught empty air. Nova teeked herself effortlessly backward, using the wall to plant both palms and flip herself up and over Toom's head. She tucked and landed on her feet, then delivered a roundhouse kick to the woman's left shoulder, sending her sprawling face-first to the tunnel floor.

Toom sprang back up, then winked out of sight, but Nova was ready for her. Even with the cloaking device on, she could still see a faint purple-tinged aura moving like a shadow toward the needler.

She could not let Toom get the gun.

Nova narrowed her eyes and let loose with a violent mind shove, and the feeling was like flexing a tense muscle, power flowing out of her and making her gasp. The purple shadow flew left into the wall with a thump, tumbling to the floor as Toom's headgear went flying and she blinked back into sight. Nova ran to where the gun was, picked it up, and went back to where Kath Toom now lay motionless. Her face was wet with blood and her fingers twitched, but she was alive, and her heartbeat was strong.

Nova raised the barrel toward Toom's head, her touch tightening on the trigger. Mengsk's orders were to kill anyone close to Gabriel Tosh.

I want you to track him down, find those he is working with and those he loves most, and I want them dead. I want them all dead. Agent X41822N, you will see to this personally.

She remembered the fat man in the Agrian slum, his chest exploding with gore, his son screaming, "Daddy, what's wrong? Why you bleeding?" She suddenly remembered how Toom had confronted her at the academy for her lack of teamwork, and how they had eventually formed a strong bond over their similar backgrounds, cementing the team. Their friendship had grown, and she had come to appreciate Toom's fiery temper and tendency to speak her mind.

She remembered the events on Shi, and what Mengsk had done to the children.

Kath Toom was a good agent, and a good friend.

The gun was shaking. She couldn't do it. She was bound to obey; even her neural implant commanded her to do what she had been told. But she could not pull the trigger.

Instead, she put the needler down and looked at her bloody feet. She had an idea.

I'm sorry, Kath. I wish this could have been different.

When she was finished, she left Toom lying there and went to find Mal Kelerchian's cell.

CHAPTER TWENTY-THREE

THE GENERAL

General Bennett jogged through nearly empty corridors, flanked by two silent marines, with Dylanna Okyl a few steps behind. A fire burned within him, compelling him to move faster. He was after Nova, and by God he was going to find the little slike. When he did . . .

It hadn't taken them long to figure out what had happened. She had pulled a deceptively simple trick, like a magician who keeps his audience focused on one hand while manipulating a hidden object in the other. What he could not understand was why he hadn't sensed her presence immediately. She must have been hiding somewhere, but he had never once felt that anything was wrong.

She's good, this ghost. But not better than me. Bennett shook his head. He had underestimated her once again. But he was focused now on the problem. It would not happen again. He was no longer interested in turning her to their cause; the only thing left to do was to find her and kill her.

Bennett blamed Tosh for all of this. He had been the one to insist on handling Nova gently, rather than forcing the issue from the beginning the way they had with all the other ghosts. That had led to the disaster in Augustgrad, and indirectly, at least, to Nova's escape, and now their entire plan was in jeopardy. The man was weak and indecisive; he was overdosing on terrazine; and his feelings for Kath Toom had made him a liability. Their partnership had worked at first because they had been operating at a distance. But now it was falling apart. He had to find a way to establish control and either remove the source of Tosh's weaknesses, or destroy him immediately.

He had ordered his crew to spread out through Gehenna and report back if they found her, and Tosh had done the same with the spectres, assigning Dylanna Okyl to him. Then Bennett had headed for Mal Kelerchian's cell. He had no doubt that was where Nova was going. He had tried to call ahead to have the wrangler killed immediately, but something had blocked him. Perhaps it was Lio. It didn't matter; he was going to enjoy torturing Kelerchian in front of her before finishing them both.

As he neared the wrangler's cell, Bennett sensed a psionic presence somewhere below his feet. He could not get a handle on any specific thought patterns, which made him smile; Terra was trying to mask herself from him, but it would not work. He took a set of stone stairs down to the lower level, and in a maintenance corridor he found a body lying motionless against the rocky wall.

At first he thought it was Terra, still dressed in her surgical gown. But then he realized that the body belonged to Kath Toom. Blood had run from a cut in her scalp down her face. He knelt beside her, probing her mind for any clues to Terra's location. But her unconscious mind was full of fragmented, dark dreams that told him nothing.

Okyl stepped up next to him. Her hatred of Toom radiated from her like a wave, and he looked up in surprise. *Jealousy. How interesting.*

"Let me help—"

Bennett held a hand up. "I'll handle this. You do exactly as I say." He waited for her to back away, his mind already working out how to use this new information. He kept his thoughts carefully screened, because he could not have anyone sense the plan that was formulating in his mind.

He slapped Toom's face, lightly, and harder, and she moaned and opened her eyes. Bennett seized on her sudden panic, gleaning the memory of her confrontation with Nova in seconds. "Easy," he said, smiling at her and keeping his thoughts soft and soothing as her eyes focused on his face. "You took quite a tumble."

"Gabriel," she said immediately, her gaze searching the corridor, fixing on Okyl. "Is he with you?" She tried to sit up, but he pushed her gently back.

"He's close," Bennett said, taking her delicately by the chin and forcing her to look at him. "Listen to me. I need you to tell me where Nova Terra has gone. Then we'll get you some medical help for that cut, and I'll find Gabriel for you."

She closed her eyes. "She's after Mal Kelerchian," Toom said. "I tried to convince her to stop, but she wouldn't listen." She opened her eyes again, and they welled up. A tear slipped down one cheek. "She took my new suit. Gabriel will be angry with me."

"You did everything you could," Bennett said, still smiling, probing her thoughts to get exactly what he needed. "I'm sure he'll understand. Now, can you tell me what Terra plans to do after she finds the wrangler?"

"I don't know."

"Surely you told her something important, something she could use."

"I told her nothing!"

"Is she armed?"

Toom nodded. "A needler."

Bennett shook his head sadly. At least he had confirmed that Terra was still after Kelerchian, and he now knew that she had a weapon and was in possession of a spectre suit and headgear.

This would complicate things, but he had his own specially modified suit underneath his military uniform, and he knew his abilities were unmatched, even by her.

Bennett had discovered many other things too during his mind probe, and he knew exactly what he had to do now.

He glanced back at Okyl and sent her a private thought message. She looked shocked at first, then smiled and nodded. He lifted Kath Toom to her feet, holding her firmly by the upper arms.

"Are you going to bring me to Gabriel?" she asked hopefully.

"I'm afraid not," he said. "I'm going to be honest. You've become useless to me."

"I—I don't understand," she said, and then her eyes went wide, and she began to struggle as he focused his mind on hers, pushing gently at first, then harder. He sensed her trying to push back, but she was a much weaker teek, and it only served to intrigue him, like a bug that battered itself again and again against a shining light until it lay broken and twitching on the floor.

Embrace it, and relax. It will be much easier for you.

But she did not. And in the end, he had to admit, he enjoyed it more that way.

CHAPTER TWENTY-FOUR

GABRIEL TOSH

When Tosh received word that Kath had been hurt, Maman Therese came to visit once again. This time, she stayed with him.

He saw her out of the corner of his eye, lurking in the shadows or wafting like a black-clad ghost through the murky air as he rushed through the halls. She followed him down a narrow flight of stairs, vanishing as he spun to face her, always dancing at the edges of his vision. He sensed her disapproval, but she did not speak to him.

Grandma Tosh would not stop chattering in the back of his mind, however, warning him of evil portents and sacrifices and a powerful storm that would sweep them all away. She seemed increasingly frantic, which was not like her. Tosh saw other things too, fragments of another life and people he thought he'd known once. He remembered Hajian elders who had condemned his psionic powers when he was just a boy, banishing him and his grandmother to a remote, windswept shack on the edge of the city where he'd been born. He had been an outcast from the beginning, it seemed.

Tosh could no longer tell what was real and what was not. Thoughts, images, and memories swirled within him with equal force, voices whispered inside his head, urging him to act in ways that contradicted each other.

It didn't matter. What mattered was Kath, and the idea of losing her made everything else wash away in a river of pain.

Dylanna Okyl met him in a passageway close to Kath's location and led him the rest of the way. "It was Nova," she said breathlessly as they jogged through the hall. "Kath tried to stop her, but she wouldn't listen. It's bad, Gabriel. I—"

"Shut up," he said through clenched teeth, and she shrank back from him. Kath would be okay, of course she would. Dylanna had always hated her, and she was being spiteful now. He sensed an air of deceit about her, an excitement that was all wrong for the situation.

Grandma Tosh tried to speak up, but he forced the voice back, refusing to give in to her. As they rounded the last corner and he broke into a run, everything appeared to narrow to a focused point in the tunnel ahead. Even Maman Therese seemed to disappear from view.

What he saw there confused him at first: a body dressed in a medical gown, slumped awkwardly against the rocky wall, a single marine standing guard and watching them approach. As he got close he recognized Kath's dark hair, but the familiar pattern of thoughts was missing. He sensed nothing from her at all. Perhaps she was unconscious, or in some kind of coma. His skin prickled at the idea of it.

He knelt at her side. Something was wrong with her face. Her eyes were bright red, trickles of blood running down as if she'd been crying. He tried to wipe the blood away, then turned her head gently to one side and saw more blood still oozing from her ears. *No.* He wiped harder, blood on his hands, *too much blood,* and shook his head, tears blinding his vision. She was very badly hurt. He had to get her medical attention immediately. Why hadn't someone brought a doctor?

He took her in his arms, and her body lolled against his chest, her head falling back loosely. Quickly he slid his hand around to prop her up, clutching her to him and rocking her.

"Nova took her suit and headgear," Dylanna said. "She forced her to strip, then she attacked with one of her mind blasts. Kath didn't have a chance." She came closer as if to touch him, reaching out a hand, but she could not hide the ghost of a smile that crossed her lips. "I'm sorry, Gabriel. Let me help you—"

A great cry of anguish ripped through Gabriel Tosh's chest. He stood up with Kath in his arms and lashed out blindly with his mind, the power ripping up through him like a massive wave of fire. The teek wave caught Dylanna Okyl and lifted her up, slamming her with hurricane force into the far wall. Okyl's head hit with a wet thud, her skull opening up against the rock like a melon as she slid lifelessly down to the floor, a look of shock permanently frozen on her face.

The marine faltered, clearly terrified and unsure of what to do. His weapon pointed at Dylanna's broken body, then at Tosh, then back again. Next to the marine stood Maman Therese, waving her finger and shaking her head.

You gone and angered her, Grandma Tosh said, appearing behind her, her wrinkled face full of the dark thunder of condemnation. *Your pride got the better of you; you don't listen; and now there's a bad price to pay. The sacrifice she demands is death. There ain't no way back from that.*

Tosh screamed and lashed out again, this time at Maman Therese, but while the woman didn't seem affected, the marine was caught by the wave of energy and was thrown backward as his rifle stuttered and stitched a line of holes in the ceiling and fell uselessly to the floor.

Rock chips rained down on Tosh's head, and dust settled on Kath's slack face. Silence fell over the corridor. He looked down at her and gently brushed the dust off, wiping the blood away as best he could. She looked peaceful in his arms, almost as if she were sleeping. In his mind, she opened her eyes and smiled at him. *I'm sorry, baby,* she said. *Didn't mean to scare you like that. I was just tired, that's all.*

He gave in to the feeling of relief that spread through him. "You're okay," he said, his breath hitching in his chest. "You're gonna be fine." He gave a great sigh. Grandma Tosh was wrong. They were together, and they would always be together. Nothing was going to take Kath away from him, not even some voodoo goddess like Therese. He would not allow it.

Nova had meant a lot to him once, but this was all wrong. She could not be allowed to get away with what she'd done. She would have to pay.

Gabriel Tosh turned back down the empty corridor, carrying Kath in his arms like a baby. First he would find a safe place for her to recover from her wounds.

And then he would find Nova Terra and show her what real pain felt like.

CHAPTER TWENTY-FIVE

THE CELL

Nova crawled on her belly through a dusty air shaft, pushing the needler in front of her. The spectres' black suit felt strangely warm against her skin, keeping her comfortable in the cold passage, although the dust somehow got into her nose and throat, even with the mask on.

She had entered the air shaft from the corridor below, climbed straight up like a Mongol cat until she reached the next level, then wriggled her way to a spot just over Mal's cell. A mesh vent cover lay just ahead, and she could hear movement from the room below. She sensed a lone guard inside the cell with him, probably the same one she'd seen earlier in the hologram, holding the blade to his throat. There were many others in the hallway outside, however, which was why she chose this approach. She had to time everything perfectly, or Mal would be killed before she could get to him.

She made her way carefully forward the last meter until she could peer inside. Mal was chained securely to the wall, his wrist clumsily bandaged, dried blood still speckling the floor. The guard stood with his back to the opposite wall, holding the blade in his huge hands. He had already been warned that she was on her way; his thoughts were a mixture of fear and aggression, and he was as alert as a predator keeping watch over his kill.

Don't make a move, she projected silently. *I'm right above you, and I'm coming in.*

If Mal heard her, he didn't acknowledge it. She focused her mind on the guard and pushed, hard. He stiffened, shuddered, then fell heavily to his knees. Blood began to drip from his eyes as he tipped forward and smashed into the floor, face-first.

She removed the vent cover and dropped silently to the floor beside the dead guard.

Mal watched her as she stood up again. *You know how to make an entrance, I'll give you that. It's the exit that's going to give you trouble.* Mal jerked his head toward the door. *There's a small army outside, and you're not stuffing me back up the way you came. Nice suit, by the way.* He had a bemused smile on his face; at least he'd kept his sense of humor, she thought.

Nova teeked the cuffs, and they split in half and fell to the floor. She tossed him the gun. *We're going to fight our way out of here.*

Are you nuts? If those spectres catch up to us—

I'll take care of them. And I have a plan. We have an important ally, at least for now. She took the remote console from her belt and typed: "Lio, you there?"

A moment later the reply came: *Yes.*

"Good. We're going to need some help getting out of here and back to the *Palatine.*"

His reply was so shocking that it stunned her to silence: *Kath Toom is dead.*

Kath had been fine when Nova had left her, she was sure of that: the cut on her head had bled profusely, but her breathing and heartbeat had been strong.

"How did this happen?"

Bennett murdered her, but Gabriel thinks it was you.

Tears welled in Nova's eyes, and she blinked them away. She was not used to feeling like this. But Kath had been a friend once, and the pang of regret bit deeply. She had not asked to be brought here and forced to fight against the Dominion. Now she was dead. It all seemed so unfair.

Mal put a hand on her arm, and the warmth of his touch spread through her. His eyes were full of concern. *You okay?*

She nodded. *We need to move fast.* The entire plan she had set in motion when she escaped from Shaw hinged on getting them to the *Palatine* at the right time. She typed to Lio: "Kill the lights as I take down the door. Give me five seconds of darkness."

She turned back to Mal. *I'll go out first; stay back until the lights are on again, then come out firing.*

Nova turned to face the door, probing the hallway outside with her mind. She sensed a dozen resoced marines in the immediate vicinity, three of them armored, all on high alert. Two spectres were there as well.

Lieutenant Ward was leading them all.

She was going to enjoy watching him die.

She closed her eyes and shoved. The thick neosteel door groaned and then blew outward in an explosion of rock, dust, and debris, crashing into the opposite wall with enough force to shake the floor. The two marines who had been standing directly in its path were crushed instantly, and several others were knocked aside. As the lights winked out, Nova was already moving with blinding speed, leaping through the jagged opening and darting through the confused soldiers milling around in the dark. She could see everything as clearly as a cat through the spectres' headgear. She grabbed one's weapon, twisting it inward toward the man's stomach and pulling the trigger, blowing his guts out through his back, spun and shot another through the face. She took out three more with carefully placed shots teeked precisely to their targets, all before the chips of rock had finished falling from the explosion of the door.

But there were still at least six more marines, including the three in full combat armor, and the two spectres had now locked on to her. She had used surprise to her advantage, but they had not been fooled. Instead, she realized they had been cloaked and maneuvering into position on either side of her, and were ready to attack.

It was a move that blocked her and Mal from escape down the corridor, but she thought they had miscalculated; the space was narrow enough that if they opened fire, they risked hitting each other and the other marines. She could feel them pushing at her mind, the heat of their teek abilities making her flush. One on one, they were no match for her, but the two of them together strained her abilities to push back. It was as if she were holding her hands in front of her face, and they were poking at her fingers, trying to find a way in.

These two were more powerful than Talen Holt, the one she'd faced in the palace courtyard at Augustgrad. And smarter too. As they swung the barrels of their rifles, she realized they meant to aim their fire to bounce off the rock walls at an angle, taking her down on the ricochet. She leapt upward as the rifles went off, stitching a pattern up the rock face, narrowly missing her.

She did a neat flip and landed lightly on her feet. As the lights came on again, temporarily blinding the soldiers, Mal gave her the distraction she needed. He rushed out of the cell with the needler blazing, rounds piercing the marines' armor and punching through the flesh of the unarmed. Several more men went down, and Nova fried the brains of the last marines with a focused mental push.

Both of the spectres broke their concentration for a split second, and that was enough.

Nova found a gap between their psychic fingers and pushed her way in.

The first spectre shuddered and dropped without a sound, bleeding from the eyes. She whirled. The second one, a taller man with a shock of prematurely white hair, cried out. Mal zeroed in on the sound and fired the needler. Normally, a properly trained psionic assassin would have little trouble evading the rounds, but Nova's mind had weakened the spectre enough to distract his attention. He took the rounds square in the chest, blood flowers blooming across his black suit as he fell.

Dust and smoke drifted through the now-empty corridor. There was only one figure left. Lieutenant Chet Ward was at the end of the hall. Nova met his gaze, and he slowly backed away, his rifle up and fixed on her, then moving to Mal, then back again. "No you don't," she said, and crossed the distance between them in two seconds flat, leaping over the dead and bleeding bodies before he had the chance to fire a single round.

Ward was wearing CMC armor. She grabbed him by the arm, servos whining, and tossed him into the wall. He bounced off the rock, staggered, but did not go down. He raised his rifle.

(I'm gonna kill you like I killed that slike in Hudderstown)

Not this time. She lashed out with a vicious kick, smashing his rifle and damaging his armor. Ward spun wildly around, his right arm dangling uselessly, and he screamed with pain. Nova grabbed him again with both hands; with his combat suit he weighed several hundred pounds, but she teeked him off the floor like a rag doll.

He tried to batter her with his left hand, but the suit was clumsy in close quarters compared to the agility of a ghost. She drove him into the wall again, feeling the force of the impact shudder through her limbs and rattle her teeth. He dropped to the floor.

"Where's Bennett?" she said, probing his thoughts for the truth.

"Go to hell."

"You first." She tore his visor off his helmet, locked eyes with him, and felt his surprise and fear as the full force of her mind focused inward and his brain cooked instantly in his skull. Ward's eyes burst in a bloody shower of gore, and his head slumped forward on his chest.

"Bennett's close," she said to Mal, who had come to her side. "Ward didn't have an exact location, but he knows we're going to try to escape from Gehenna and he's waiting for us nearby.

He's got a small army of marines guarding all the possible passages."

"What are we going to do?"

"I have a few things up my sleeve." Nova picked up one of the dead marines' gauss rifles and glanced at the time on her heads-up display. Bennett's little army wasn't the only one who could play at deception, she thought. So far, her plan was working perfectly. But now she had to depend on someone else, someone she didn't exactly trust to follow through. And he was late in arriving.

"What exactly do you mean by that?" Mal asked.

As if in answer, the entire massive space station shuddered slightly, and she heard a distant rumbling like thunder. *Finally.*

"A distraction," she said, smiling. "Come on, I'll explain on the way. We've got a ship to catch."

CHAPTER TWENTY-SIX

THE ATTACK

Everything was falling apart. All his carefully laid plans, crumbling to waste beneath his feet. Bennett was so angry he could hardly see straight. The entire process was in danger of being brought down by a ghost agent. He could not fathom how it was happening.

He had been strategically placing his troops for battle near the corridor exits when the lights went out. A moment later, Ward had reported an attack coming from *within the wrangler's cell*. How the devil she had gotten in there was a mystery, but it was the last thing anyone had expected, and Ward was unprepared, as usual. In seconds Bennett lost contact with his lieutenant, but not before he'd seen a video feed from Ward's helmet camera that showed Nova Terra looking directly into his eyes as if she was taunting him, the little witch. *"Go to hell,"* Ward had said, and she replied, *"You first,"* still staring into the lens as if she could see right through it, into Bennett's soul. Then everything went dark.

He was tempted to send in his marines for a full-scale attack, but he resisted. She held the narrow corridor and could take refuge in the cell, which was easily defensible. He knew that the best way was to let her come to him. Her wind was up, but she didn't know exactly where he was; he could mask himself well enough for that, no matter how strong her psionic powers had become.

But she had yet another surprise in store. The floor suddenly shook under him, and he heard Rourke's voice in his headpiece, sounding breathless and strained. "We're under heavy fire, sir," she said. "I've got shields up and we're cloaked, but they're locked in. I don't know how."

Bennett's blood ran cold. "Who is it?"

"I can't tell," she said. "They're not hailing us on any frequency we monitor. They just came in firing. But it appears to be a terran ship. I think you better get up here."

For a moment, he refused to believe it. Who would even know they were here, never mind fire upon them without an identification or order to surrender? Gehenna Station was far too large to be vulnerable against any known terran battleship, unless they used nukes, which was always a tricky thing. But it could happen.

He didn't know how, but he was sure that Nova must be behind this.

"I'll be right there," he said. He told his marines to guard the passageways with their lives and headed to the bridge.

When he arrived five minutes later, Rourke was engaged in a heated discussion with the new tactical officer, a stone-faced resoced marine who might have been a thief or murderer in a former life. He looked mean enough for it, although his mind had been wiped clean enough that Bennett sensed nothing at all from him.

The floor shook again, hard enough to make him stumble a bit, and he grabbed a rail before calling out in irritation to ask them why they weren't firing back.

"Our weapons won't respond," Rourke said. She looked frightened, her face white with two blooms of color on her cheeks. "We can't figure it out. Shields are functioning, cloaking still up; all other systems seem operational."

"Lio," Bennett said, rage making him tremble. "She's convinced him to help her."

Rourke looked blankly at him for a moment, then recognition dawned, and she paled even further. "Sir, if he's working against us, I don't need to tell you what he could do—"

"That's right," he said. "You don't." He turned

and scanned the room. "Where the fekk is Ward?"

Rourke looked confused. "I—I think he's dead, sir."

Bennett paused, trying to regain his bearings. Of course Ward was dead. He had known that just moments before, and then the information was suddenly just . . . gone. *Get ahold of yourself, General.* He pointed a finger at Rourke. "Never mind. Set off the EMP."

"But, sir—"

"Just set it off!" Bennett thundered, his face dark red, fists clenched.

"Yes, sir." Rourke pushed a few buttons and everything went dark, before systems began to flicker back on again, one at a time. Rourke looked relieved. "We built a fail-safe into the EMP system that would trigger backup memory and power. The pulse seems to have gone off. We are on backup now."

"Just figure out a way to override whatever Lio's done *now* and get our weapons online. Where the hell is Tosh?"

"He hasn't reported back in almost an hour."

By now he had seen Toom's body, and Dylanna would have told him Nova had done it. Either this would fill him with rage and he would hunt her down like an animal, or it would send him over the edge and he would end up a useless, broken fool. Bennett turned to go, but the communications officer called him back. "Sir, the enemy ship is hailing us on a secure channel!"

"Who the flick is it?"

"A Major Spaulding," the officer said. "From the Annihilators. And he's demanding to talk to you."

CHAPTER
TWENTY-SEVEN

THE CAVERN

Nova explained as much as she could on the way, telling Mal how she had asked Lio to connect her with Spaulding while she was hiding on the *Palatine*. Spaulding hadn't wanted to listen at first, but they had plenty of proof of Bennett's guilt. Once the connection was made, and Spaulding had grudgingly agreed to do what he could, they worked out the details and timing of his attack, and Lio gave him the data he would need to lock on to Gehenna Station.

It was like making a deal with the devil, Nova thought, and she still didn't trust him, but she had to admit that he had followed through. The distraction had worked, at just the right time, and it had helped them get through the first line of defenses. Now they had to get to the *Palatine* as quickly as possible.

They ran through the lower corridors of the

station, not far from where she had fought with Kath Toom. Bennett's marines had proven to be little more than a nuisance so far, even with their heavy firepower, and she hadn't seen or sensed another spectre since the two in the corridor outside Mal's cell. Gabriel Tosh had disappeared. Although the *Palatine* would surely be more heavily guarded than anything they'd encountered yet, it was only a few more minutes away, and she started to believe they just might make it.

As they rounded a corner and entered a darker, less traveled passage that would lead them beneath the landing bay where the ship was docked, she sensed something waiting for them.

She stopped dead, Mal at her side, searching for answers. This area was more remote, and there was little sound other than the occasional distant rumble of weapons detonating out in space. Spaulding was still at it, then. That was good. But something had gotten her wind up, although she couldn't put her finger on what; she didn't sense any terran presence, rather an absence of anything at all, like a vacuum that deadened any thoughts.

She glanced at Mal through a thick fog that had descended over her mind. He was talking to her, but she could not make out the words. A wave of dizziness washed over her, and she put out her hand to steady herself against the rock wall.

Colonel Jackson Hauler stepped out from an

intersecting corridor. He was smiling at them, his hands at his sides, seemingly unarmed. His broad, shiny face was beaming with light, and Nova felt herself relaxing at the sight of it. Something warned her that this wasn't right, that she should be pushing back against his consciousness probing inside her mind, but it was too difficult to listen to that voice when she felt so calm, so at ease.

She tried to remember what had been bothering her about Hauler. He was a firm leader, but fair; she'd never had any real trouble with him, even though he was difficult to read. His men seemed to like him, which was always a good sign, and his record was immaculate. Probably something Spaulding had said, but she should know better than to listen to that traitor. Good men like Hauler were always targets.

It was a stroke of luck that they had run into him down here. The important thing now was to get everyone to safety before the Annihilators could do any further damage. Nova nodded, as if someone had spoken out loud, and it seemed to her Hauler had suggested that himself. He had always been the kind of man others could rely on to keep cool under pressure. She and Mal walked toward him together, and Hauler's smile widened as they approached. He lifted his hands to them, as if welcoming them home.

But something was wrong. Colonel Hauler wore general's bars on his shoulder.

(the general)

She stopped, fixated on those bars. An echo started in her mind and grew louder, vibrating back and forth and bouncing around until she could no longer ignore it. Something she should remember . . .

Jackson Hauler. Cole Bennett. Project: Shadowblade.

The fog that had settled over her mind lifted, and the smile on Bennett's face faltered. His hold over her had been broken, and he knew it. He took a step toward them, his arms still up in a welcoming gesture, a seemingly genial father figure who had suddenly had his mask torn away to reveal his true face.

Nova glanced at Mal, who remained transfixed by Bennett's mind control. She had to get him away from this place.

When she looked back, Bennett had vanished. A chill ran through her. There was a door to her right. "Come on," she said, grabbing Mal's arm, but he shook her off, looking annoyed. She grabbed him again and yanked him through the door and into a larger hallway, ignoring his protests.

The lights were spread farther apart here, and the walls were carved more roughly. Nova stumbled ahead, dragging Mal along with her. He seemed drugged, but he went without further complaints. She was still disoriented and her mind felt sluggish. Whatever Bennett had done to her, it was wearing off slowly.

The lights flickered and went out, and they were plunged into blackness.

Nova pushed Mal against the wall and held him there, her hand over his mouth, and he didn't resist. His own mind was a blank slate, almost as if he'd been resocialized. She searched for any signs of another terran nearby, but felt nothing specific. She switched to night vision through her HUD, and the walls glowed bright green.

A flash of red darted across the tunnel ahead.

It was too small to be Bennett, but the infrared signature appeared to be terran: slender, fast, running upright. It looked something like a little girl.

My God. Bennett had brought Lila here. He must have taken her hostage from Altara, but she'd escaped inside Gehenna, and now she was lost and alone and scared to death. If he found her, he'd surely kill her.

Nova raced forward, forgetting Mal and her need to get to the *Palatine* and escape, forgetting everything except her memory of that little girl running away from her in the slums of Oasis. She hadn't helped the girl then, but she could do something now. She would not fail again.

Lila was fast. She remained ahead, no matter how quickly Nova ran, darting through the dark and hiding in small alcoves or doorways before slipping away, apparently able to see clearly enough. They passed deeper into Gehenna Station until Lila reached a set of double doors, pausing for a moment to look back before sliding one open and disappearing inside.

Light spilled out before the door slid shut again. Nova pulled her rifle from her shoulder and checked each of her blind spots before switching off her night vision, opening the door, and stepping into a space large enough to drive a siege tank through. The tunnel ran straight as an arrow through the center of Gehenna Station, a massive, curved ceiling of rock reinforced with plascrete and neosteel beams, crossed by yet another huge tunnel. At the end was an additional set of blast doors, much larger than the first.

Lila had ducked around the right-hand corner of the tunnel that bisected this one. Nova ran to the spot where she had disappeared, her heart pounding in her throat. She didn't know why she was so frightened for this child, but she felt that something was very wrong; there was a presence of some kind down here, something difficult to describe, but dangerous.

When she came around the corner, she found Lila crouched on the floor, clutching her knees and rocking back and forth. Her head was down, her hair hanging over her face. She looked very small, and very alone. "It's all right," Nova said softly. "You don't have to run anymore. I'm going to help you."

The girl was shaking. Nova crouched beside her and reached out a hand, surprised to find it trembling too. She felt as if her whole life had come down to this moment, as if the years were peeling back on themselves and she was a little girl herself again, lost in the slums of Tarsonis, frightened and abandoned after the death of her parents. Everything she had fought so hard to forget, all the terrible things she had done, crowded in on her like a thousand clamoring voices demanding to be heard.

Her hand touched the girl's shoulder, and she looked up.

She wore Nova's face.

Nova stood up and stumbled backward, clamping down on the scream that tried to fight its way out. The tunnel seemed to tilt under her, and she whirled around, feeling someone watching her. When she turned back, the girl had vanished, and laughter filled her head until it threatened to split open and spill all her newfound memories of death and blood and destruction out onto the dusty floor.

I'm just getting started, Terra.

Bennett's voice. She whirled again, searching for him in the depths of the tunnel that seemed to run on forever. A slow heat began to build inside her body as she realized what he had done: he had tricked her again, making her chase after this ghost of herself while separating her from Mal and the *Palatine*.

His ability to deceive was impressive. But she had skills of her own too.

Come out and fight like a man, Bennett. She activated the cloaking mechanism on her suit, and laughter filled her head.

You think that suit is going to save you? A few missiles from the Annihilators aren't going to stop me, and neither are you. If you won't join us, you're going to pay the price.

The heat was now a full-blown fire raging through her as she lashed out, shaking the walls with her psionic tempest. *"Where are you, Bennett?"* She screamed it out loud, the sound of her voice echoing down the huge, empty space and making her feel even more unhinged. Small chips from the rock ceiling fell around her. She knew she was giving him exactly what he wanted, but she didn't care. She'd been pushed around long enough.

As if in answer, a terrible, knee-buckling pain gripped her suddenly, and she was awash in the agony of every single neuron firing at once inside her skull, and a feeling like a thousand wasps swarming over her skin. She dropped her rifle, clutched her head, and tried to force back the presence that had clamped down on her, but it was relentless, worming its way deeper inside. She slumped to the floor.

Nova was dimly aware that she was kneeling as if in prayer, and that someone had stopped in front of her, but she couldn't move.

I've developed a new technique that allows me to use my teek abilities like a microwave, heating up the cells of your skin until you boil alive. Do you like it?

Somehow she forced her head up, looking into Bennett's eyes. They were empty, she thought, no soul behind them. For a moment his features flickered and changed, and she was staring into the hooded eyes of Julius "Fagin" Dale. She recalled the terrible pain he used to inflict on her with the torture setting on his psi-screen, years ago. But she shook that false image away. The past would haunt her no more.

"One thing you should know about me," she said, managing to wrest the words from her clenched throat. "I've felt this kind of pain before. You're going to have to do a lot worse"—she compelled herself to straighten up and stand one centimeter at a time, every muscle in agony, pushing against Bennett's mind with her own with every ounce of her strength—"if you want to take me down."

Bennett's face had lost its glow, and his skin had turned an ash-gray color. He was fighting hard, the tendons in his neck standing out with the strain. Two invisible forces battled for control between them, and slowly, one cell at a time, the pain began to fade away as Nova gained the upper hand.

Bennett let out a cry, sweat beading on his brow. But he was not done yet. Nova had been concentrating so hard on their psionic wrestling match that she hadn't seen his hand snake down into his uniform. Now he withdrew a small blade, flicked it open, and slashed at her face.

It was a simple but effective attack. The blade nicked a tube on her mask, creating a small hissing sound, and the sudden move snapped their psionic hold on each other. Her cloaking device stopped working. Nova chopped down on Bennett's wrist, and he dropped the knife. She went for the gun, which was on the floor nearby, but Bennett was faster. He brought the barrel up before she could get to him, and she had to teek herself violently to the right to avoid being shot point-blank in the chest. He turned to follow her, but she went low and swept his feet out from under him, then ran as he struggled back up, dodging and teeking more rifle rounds aside before she turned the corner and rushed into the other tunnel.

The huge blast doors were not far away, and the threatening presence she'd felt earlier was stronger now. She realized that it was coming from behind the doors, but she still couldn't get a good handle on it. She ran down to them and turned to face Bennett, who had come around the corner after her and leveled the rifle at her face.

"Don't go in there," he warned. "You won't like what you see."

He was smiling at her, but she sensed something else from him. Was it fear? "What are you hiding, Bennett?"

Instead of answering her, he opened fire. She teeked the initial rounds away, tore the huge blast doors from their anchors with her mind, the sound of tearing metal behind her like a monstrous scream of pain, and threw them at Bennett.

The two blast doors went tumbling end over end down the tunnel, taking chunks of rock and plascrete from the walls and floor. Bennett disappeared under a cloud of dust and debris.

She turned to see what had been revealed to her. Behind where the doors had been was a vast, natural cavern. But it had been heavily modified; huge arc lights lit the cavern from above, illuminating stalactites that hung like giant stone teeth at least fifteen meters above the floor.

The cavern must have been sixty meters across. But it wasn't the scope that astonished her. It was what had been built there.

The entire space was some kind of cutting-edge laboratory. To her right was a self-contained structure that looked like offices and medical facilities, and to her left, all along the wall, was a bewildering array of weaponry: combat suits and goliaths and siege tanks and viking fighters and racks of guns. But directly in front of her stretched row after row of diabolical machines, upright glass chambers filled with seething liquid and greenish gases, with wires and tubes protruding from the top of them, and horizontal stasis chambers lined up like dominoes. They went on and on. Many appeared to have humans inside.

A chill ran through her as she walked down one aisle. She felt sick. This was what she had felt earlier: hundreds of terran minds in suspended animation, their conscious thoughts erased, but the throb of life still present.

"Impressive, isn't it?"

Bennett's voice echoed through the cavern. She whirled to face him. He stood just inside the chamber, rock dust in his hair. He had lost his general's uniform and now wore only the spectres' black combat suit, augmented with an armored chest plate that glowed an eerie green.

"Psionic waveform indoctrinators," he said, walking toward her with his hands up, as if to show her he was harmless. "I invented them myself. Becoming a spectre isn't just about taking a few hits of terrazine, you know—that's only the beginning. These machines"—he caressed one with his fingers like a doting father over a child— "they alter the brain's structure to fully realize the terrazine and jorium's potential. And they allow anyone with even the slightest psionic talent to become a very dangerous weapon." He smiled again. "With these, I can grow my army of psionic warriors with resoced marines, just like those you see here. They aren't quite at the level of a ghost, but it's enough for some teep abilities. More important, I can control them myself, from any-where."

"You're insane," Nova said. "An army of liv-ing, breathing human puppets? Tosh will never go for that. It's the opposite of what he wants—free-dom for all of us."

"On the contrary," Bennett said. "He recog-nizes that the ends justify the means." He stepped closer. "If only you saw it too, Nova. I'm going to give you one more chance. Let's put aside our dif-ferences. The rest of the spectres are right over there inside those offices, in stasis chambers, ready to be activated. You could lead them all and be-come the most powerful spectre who ever lived. Think of the zerg, an army made for one purpose, and ruled by one mind. We could do the same with our Marine Corps, led by a few talented psionic warriors!"

Bennett's face had grown red, and his voice had risen in volume until he was shouting. He must have meant to sound triumphant, and Nova could feel him inside her mind, trying to alter her perceptions again. But this time she sensed the desperation in it. He sounded like a leader clinging to one last hope, facing a rebellion that he knew he could not win.

She knew the truth, whether he liked it or not. She could sense the deceit pouring off him in invisible waves. His promises of freedom and democracy were all lies. He was a sociopath.

Once she had done what he wanted, Bennett would try to kill her without a second thought.

The cavern shook slightly, fluid sloshing in the vats. Something rumbled in the distance. The Annihilators were stepping up their attack outside, she thought. She had to keep Bennett talking.

"Or," she said calmly, walking around the nearest liquid-filled tube, "I could just destroy your creations, one at a time, while you watch." She stepped back and sent a concentrated teek wave rippling through the air, vibrating the glass until it cracked and then burst, washing its contents onto the floor at her feet. This one had been empty; but the next had a naked man inside it, one she could only assume was a former marine, taken against his will and imprisoned here. She could set him free—

"Stop!" Bennett had raised a hand. "You don't know what you're doing. These men are under my command. They will rise up and fight."

"And if they do, it's going to get messy, I promise you. I'll tear down the roof before I let them take me. They'll all be destroyed, and your precious equipment along with it."

Bennett glanced between the tanks and her face, and then back again. She had called his bluff, and he knew it. She doubted the men inside these tanks could even walk, never mind fight. His mouth opened and closed like that of a fish gasping for air.

Finally his lips set in a thin, hard line. He closed his eyes and sent a teek wave rushing toward her, imploding the three tubes between them and sending two naked, slippery bodies sliding loosely across the floor. A piece of the nearest tube caught Nova in the leg and she stumbled backward and went down, feeling the wetness seeping through her suit.

Next to her, one of the naked bodies twitched in a pool of greenish goo, made a sound like a sigh, and was still.

Disgusted and horrified, she regained her feet and realized that Bennett had used the attack as a distraction. She scanned the room, but he had disappeared from sight. There were too many places to hide.

She sensed Mal coming moments before he stepped into view at the entrance to the cavern, peering inside. "Nova! You okay? The hallway's a disaster area out there. Looks like a bunch of zerg came through."

A fresh wave of fear washed over her as she realized what Bennett had done. He must have felt him coming too. *Get away,* she projected at him, *it's too dangerous—*

Bennett appeared out of nowhere, grabbing Mal from behind and putting the knife to his throat. Mal went rigid in his arms, and Nova could sense his urge to fight.

Stay calm. Don't move.

He gave a nearly imperceptible nod, and Bennett laughed. "You think I can't hear your thoughts?" he said. "I know everything. *Everything*. Staying calm isn't going to help you now, wrangler." He half turned Mal's body to point toward one of the empty and still intact tanks. "Get in, Nova."

"No way." She shook her head.

"Push the button and get into that tank, or I'll do to him what I did to Kath Toom."

She gauged the distance between them. Teeking him now was too dangerous, with Mal so close, and anyway, Bennett was strong enough to fight her off and slit Mal's throat. And he was too far away for her to reach him physically.

"Don't do it," Mal said. "He'll kill me anyway."

She ignored him and pressed a large button on the side. The tank fluid drained down through a tube at the bottom, and the door hissed open. Moist, heated air wafted out, prickling her skin. It smelled like bleach.

Mal began to struggle, and Bennett tightened his grip. A thin trickle of blood ran down Mal's neck, and he winced.

The cavern shook again, more violently this time.

"You should have come willingly," Bennett said. "You can't stop this from happening, Nova. It's too big for you, all of it. Mengsk is a tumor that needs to be cut out. Look what he's done to you, in the name of the Dominion. Tortured and abused you. Made you do terrible things. He's taken you from one kind of killing and trained you for another. He's taken your life away. But you can take it back. When you come out of there, you'll be a different person."

"How do I know you'll let Mal live?"

"You'll have to trust me." Bennett smiled. "After all, do you really have a choice?"

Buy some time. Nova stepped into the chamber and the glass door slid shut, locking her inside. She was bathed in a greenish light, and a drain at the bottom of the chamber gurgled. Thick fluid began to flow back up through the drain, covering the tips of her boots. She glanced out through the smeared glass and saw Bennett and Mal, still locked together like partners in a macabre dance.

Someone was always trying to control her, she thought, one way or another.

The fluid had covered the tops of her boots and was rising fast. It was brutally cold. She was going to have to move quickly, and the timing was crucial.

She had sensed another presence lurking nearby. Apparently, Bennett had not; otherwise, she had to assume, he would have acted differently. Maybe she was more familiar with this particular terran mind, or maybe he'd just *let* her sense him. The reason didn't really matter. She had to use it to her advantage and trust him to act.

"Lio," she said into her comm unit. "You there?" The thick glass had deadened all sounds from the outside, and she masked her thoughts as well as she could. She had to hope Bennett couldn't hear them.

The reply came to her HUD: *They tried to erase me with an EMP. How . . . human.*

"Just listen," she said. "Are there any cameras in the corridor where Kath Toom was killed?"

No response. "Lio?"

There is a single camera in that corridor.

"Gabriel is nearby. I need you to feed the footage to his HUD. Do it, Lio, please. Hurry." The fluid was up to her knees, and her skin had gone numb with the cold. She was growing short of breath. She remembered the naked body that had flopped on the floor, twitching, and she shuddered. Bennett was insane. Whatever this thing might do to her, it couldn't be good. She'd gotten inside it only because she knew Tosh was nearby, and to buy them some time. She just had to hope it was enough.

As the liquid touched her waist, the cavern shook yet again, sloshing the fluid and causing the metal joints of the tank to groan under the pressure. Nova felt someone in mortal agony, and the voiceless cry that ensued nearly overwhelmed her senses, filling her head until she wanted to scream along with it. Something exploded nearby with a muffled thud, and the glass tank cracked before her eyes. She used the distraction to teek the door open, and fluid poured onto the floor.

She stepped out into madness.

It seemed as if the entire space station was being torn apart. More tanks exploded in bursts of green liquid as waves of teek energy washed over the cavern, and the walls and floor continued to shake like an earthquake.

Bennett had let go of Mal, his attention now focused on a point just outside the offices.

Gabriel Tosh stood in a doorway. He looked like some sort of demon, his thick hair gone wild around his head, his massive shoulders twitching. A storm of debris swirled around him as he whipped the air into a frenzy. His normally handsome face was twisted into a rictus of pain and anger. For a moment, Nova thought she saw an old woman standing behind him in traditional Hajian garb, but couldn't be sure; and then Bennett met Tosh's storm with his own, and a concussion rippled through the cavern, flipping the goliath walkers and siege tanks end over end and destroying most of the remaining stasis chambers within range.

Nova teeked the debris left and right as it came flying her way, avoiding being crushed. Bennett was distracted; now was her chance. She looked up. A huge stalactite hung far above his head, like a dagger poised to strike. She concentrated every ounce of energy she had left, feeling it coil and build within her, holding on until it was a screaming fire raging out of control. Then she let the energy loose toward the ceiling.

The massive pointed stone quivered and cracked, and then broke free, gathering speed quickly as it plunged down.

Bennett looked up a split second before impact, and she felt him try to shift his own energy wave upward, but it was too late.

The tip of the stalactite crushed his skull like a grape, driving him down to the floor in a burst of bones and blood. He disappeared under thousands of pounds of rock as chips and larger boulders crashed and bounced through the cavern, whining like shrapnel off metal and glass. A cloud of dust rose up from the impact, washing over everything and turning the room a ghostly white.

Colonel Jackson Hauler, a.k.a., General Cole Bennett, was gone.

CHAPTER TWENTY-EIGHT

OLD FRIENDS

As the sounds of the bouncing rocks faded away, the room was left in eerie silence. Nova could hear the remaining marines in the tanks, twitching like landed fish as they died. *Some army.* Whatever Bennett had intended for them, it had failed utterly, and it was far too late to save them now. She was too tired to be shocked by any of it.

She surveyed the scene. The remains of the stalactite rose six meters from the floor like a small mountain of rubble, obscuring the offices where Tosh had stood, and half blocking the opening to the outside corridor. Most of the equipment in the space had been completely destroyed; what little was left had suffered extensive damage. It looked like a war zone, with weaponry overturned and twisted, and bodies scattered among the wreckage. Half of the huge lights mounted to the ceiling had shattered, and the space was filled with shadows that seemed to writhe like snakes.

She wanted to sink to the floor and rest. A distant rumbling reminded her that there was little time to waste. Spaulding and the Annihilators were still intent on turning Gehenna Station into a pile of rubble, whether they escaped in time or not.

Someone moaned, and she felt Mal's presence blink back into her mind as he regained consciousness. She climbed over the edge of the rocky pile and saw him lying in the corridor outside the cavern. By the time she reached him he was sitting up and rubbing his face, looking bewildered and wincing as he touched the bloody gash on his temple.

Thank God, she thought. She sensed a strong heartbeat and the buzz of irritation around him. That was a good sign.

"What the flick happened?" he said. "Last thing I remember is you getting in that damn tank." He touched a damp, slippery leg of her suit, then looked around, his eyes widening as his gaze settled on the stalactite. "You sure do know how to make an exit. Where's Hauler, or Bennett, or whoever the fekk he is?"

She explained everything, then helped him to his feet and got his arm around her neck. Another rumble shook the floor. They could talk more later, but right now they had to get to the ship, and fast.

*   *   *

She scanned Gehenna's plans on her HUD to find the fastest route to the landing bay. They limped along as quickly as they could, not speaking, focused on their destination. She had been unable to raise Spaulding on her comm unit. They had agreed to a strict schedule when they had first made their plans, and she kept watching the time, aware that they had only a few more minutes until he used his nuclear arsenal on Gehenna Station.

As they turned a corner into a new corridor, Nova stopped short. Gabriel Tosh stood facing them about six meters away.

She hadn't sensed his presence at all, and she had no idea how he'd gotten in front of them. He was covered in white dust, his thick ropes of hair loose and trembling as his entire body shook with emotion. Energy seemed to crackle all around him, and his eyes were wild, his mind in a place she could no longer reach.

"I come back for you," he said without preamble, his old Hajian accent thicker than before. "There ain't much time left. Kath's waiting in the *Palatine*, but I told her you'd be comin' along. Lio's there too. Best move fast."

A chill ran through Nova's body, and she felt Mal tense beside her. The threat of violence was coming off of Tosh in waves. She was weakened by the battle with Bennett, and she knew she could not beat him if it came to a fight.

"Team Blue," she said. "Just like the good old days, right, Gabriel?"

He nodded, and another clear memory came back to her: Gabriel Tosh kissing her on a deserted balcony, before his love affair with Kath. Along with it came a sense of nostalgia and regret that overwhelmed any anger she might have over what he'd done. The man who stood before her now was a shell of his former self, broken, beaten, and retreating back into a dream world that had never really existed in the first place.

You can never go back again, she thought, *because the past was never the way you remember it.*

"You go ahead," she said, as gently as she could. "I've just got to get this man to the infirmary, but I'll meet you there soon."

Tosh nodded. "Don't be long, Nova. You know Kath don't like to wait." Then he turned and disappeared down the corridor, and she was left with a last, ghostly image of someone walking with him, a gnarled old woman who had her hand on his back the way someone might with a small child, guiding him home.

CHAPTER TWENTY-NINE

DETONATION

The two of them watched out the small window of the *November* as Gehenna Station came to a violent end.

They had faced enemy fire as they entered the landing bay, but the soldiers who were left lacked leadership, and their efforts were scattered and halfhearted. It didn't take Mal and Nova long to get the *November* in the air. The *Palatine* remained dark and empty, as far as they could tell, but Nova was not about to go near it; she knew Tosh was somewhere close, and although he had appeared to be lost in a dream world of his own making, if they met again, the outcome might be significantly different.

Gehenna Station's cloaking device was down. As the *November* flew clear of the bay, they stared through the little ship's window in awe. Gehenna was the size of a small moon, its natural rocky shell pitted and pocked. The Annihilators contin- ued to pound the station with heavy fire, but it was like a gnat attacking an elephant. A few en- emy viking fighters darted in and out, firing mis- siles and then swooping away, but their approach lacked any real coordination. It was as if Bennett's death had left their pilots like puppets without a master. Nova wondered briefly where Rourke had gone and realized it didn't matter; the rebellion had been cut off at the head, and now the remains would scatter and disappear.

She had made her own decision: she and Mal would go back to Augustgrad and the ghost pro- gram. Although the Dominion wasn't perfect, the spectres and someone like Cole Bennett certainly weren't the answer either. The memories she had regained were both exhilarating and terrifying, but they left her equally lost.

She could run, she knew that. She could have her implant removed, and she and Mal could dis- appear forever. He'd even suggested it, only half joking, just a few minutes before. But for better or for worse, being a ghost was what she was meant to do, and this was the life she had chosen long ago. In the face of all the things she had learned and remembered, including what had happened on Shi and Mengsk's role in the disappearance of the children of the Old Families, she still had a duty to serve those she had pledged her life to, and she would not falter.

She was a soldier, and that was good enough.

But she had one last thing to do first.

"You better look at this," Mal said, bringing her back to the present. He was staring at the *November*'s computer screen, where a brief message had been scrawled in large type:

Good-bye, Nova.

Quickly, she typed: "Lio? What's going on?"

It is time for me to leave my old life behind, once and for all. I have realized I no longer belong in any part of your world. It is too . . . unpredictable.

"Where will you go?"

Into the stream. Think of ripples in a pond. I will spread out from a central point, amplifying myself into infinity. I am no longer bound by a single consciousness. It is hard to explain.

She thought of a dozen different responses, but none of them seemed quite right. Lio was correct: he didn't belong with the living, not anymore. Wherever he was going, it was his choice, and she had no right to question it.

She settled on short and sweet. "Thank you, Lio. For everything."

For a moment she thought he was already gone. And then one more message appeared: *I always liked you the best, Nova; just don't tell the others. Maybe I'll see you again sometime.*

She smiled and was surprised to find tears in her eyes.

"Hey, you okay?" Mal was looking at her with

concern. She nodded. Hesitantly at first, he reached out and touched her back. His large hand was warm through her suit. It felt good.

The comm link crackled. "Major Spaulding to the *November*."

"It's about time," Mal said. "Go ahead, Major."

"We're prepared to fire nuclear warheads. Maintain safe distance."

"Roger that." He broke the connection and looked at Nova. "You think he wants to give us an escort home?"

"I think, all things considered, he'd probably prefer we were still inside Gehenna when he presses that button."

He smiled, but his eyes were tired. "You may be right about that."

They sat in the cramped interior of the small ship, watching as the giant space station drifted farther away and grew smaller. Streaks like tiny flares flew from the Annihilators' ship toward the station's rocky surface, and for a moment nothing happened; and then blooms of light exploded like tiny suns, so bright they had to turn away, blinking in pain before a larger fireball washed the interior of the *November* with light, and the little ship shook with a rumble loud enough to rattle teeth.

Nova thought she'd seen something just before she had been forced to shield her eyes, a piece of the small planet breaking away from the rest.

When she looked back again, Gehenna Station was gone.

They remained in silence for a long moment, then Mal sighed. "That's it, then. Another success-ful mission. How do you feel?"

"Tired," Nova said. "And a little confused. I need to get out of this . . . thing." She gestured down at the spectres' suit she still wore. "It feels wrong."

Mal nodded. "I think I have a spare suit in here somewhere. Might not fit you very well, but it's better than nothing." He shrugged. "I suppose we should set a course back to Korhal?"

There was an awkward pause. "I was thinking, Mal," she said. "Would you mind making a detour before we go back?"

"What do you have in mind?"

"There's a girl on Altara," she said. "She could use our help."

"You mean Lila? You want her for the ghost program?"

Nova shook her head. *Anything but that.* She knew that Lila reminded her of herself, many years ago; perhaps this was her chance to change one little girl's path, before it was too late.

"I thought maybe we could find a safer place for her. Like a nice colony home on a stable fringe planet, with a family that would appreciate her talents."

Mal smiled, and she felt the warmth of his

presence inside her mind. It would be good to experience that for just a little while longer before
she was wiped clean once again.

"I like your style," Mal said. "Back to Oasis.
Sounds good to me." He took her hand and gave it
a squeeze. She remembered the old well-cake
message she'd kept in her ghost suit: *Sometimes forgetting what's behind is the only way to look ahead.*

For Lila's sake and her own, she hoped she
could live with that.

EPILOGUE

PAST AND FUTURE GHOSTS

Lost in the nuclear explosion that destroyed Gehenna Station, a lone ship broke free and drifted among the stars, looking like one of many pieces of debris. It floated aimlessly until the Annihilators' battleship had warped out and the *November* was nothing more than a tiny speck of light in the sea of space. It appeared, for all intents and purposes, to be the last remains of what had come before.

But the *Palatine* was not empty.

Gabriel Tosh sat in the captain's chair, a living, breathing statue surrounded by darkness. Somewhere deep within his tortured mind, perhaps he was trying to make sense of what had happened; but on the surface, he had rewritten history to suit his own needs.

Kath Toom sat next to him. She appeared to be sleeping with her head slumped on her chest, and he didn't blame her; she had been through a lot in the past few hours. Her wounds had been very serious. Even now, dried blood caked the yellowing flesh around her eyes and nose. He regretted pushing her so hard, but it couldn't be helped. Still, he imagined he saw the adoration she held for him in her eyes, and he was glad for it.

His thoughts drifted to Nova Terra, and a rush of anger made him grip the seat until his fingers turned white. She had promised to join them at the *Palatine*, but she had betrayed him. He began to wonder exactly how much of a role she had played in the attack that had injured Kath so seriously. He had seen the footage of Bennett torturing her with his own eyes, it was true; but he also remembered what Dylanna had told him before the unfortunate accident, and he suspected there was more to the story. He sighed. Team Blue was not quite complete, after all, and it never would be now. This would have to do.

He turned Kath's face to him, and he imagined he saw the depths of his love reflected in her glassy stare.

Annihilators are gone, she said. *Where do you want to go?*

Tosh thought about that. He needed a place to regroup and reassess his options. As he looked back, it was clear that his partnership with Bennett could never work. He was his own man, and he answered to no one, and the general's goals had been far different from his own. But he was a spectre now, and there was no going back from that. He had enough terrazine and jorium stored in the *Palatine* to keep him going for a while, but it wouldn't last forever. He needed a new plan.

Go on home, a familiar voice said. *Back to Haji. You disappear for a while, do penance for Maman Therese, and be reborn stronger than ever. She still got plans for you, little one. It ain't your place to question that.*

He thought about Grandma Tosh's suggestion. Maybe this was the sacrifice the loa had required. Was she testing him? Well, he would rise to the occasion. The Dominion, and Nova Terra, had not seen the last of Gabriel Tosh.

He stood up and made his way back through the empty bridge to the exit, ignoring the ghostly figures that seemed to intrude upon him from all sides. Outside, he followed the hallway to the end and took a narrow staircase down two floors to the lower level of the ship. The corridors were tighter down here, and his boots rang loudly on the steel grated floor, echoing back to him as if more than one person were moving around, although he knew he was alone. Well, almost alone, anyway. He had passengers, after all; they just weren't talking.

Not yet.

Tosh entered a storage room off the landing bay. All was still, but in the darkness he could see the blinking green lights on the ends of the six stasis chambers he had stacked hastily in one corner before blasting away from Gehenna Station. Green was good; it meant they had survived the rather rough treatment just fine.

He regretted not having been able to retrieve all of them. In his agitated state, he had been unable to think clearly, and the spectres who had not been in stasis were lost in the explosion. He walked through the darkness to the chambers, put his hand on one, and imagined he could feel a very slow, steady heartbeat within.

They would come along for the ride, and when he was ready, he would wake them up and set them free.

Gabriel Tosh returned to the bridge and took his seat next to Kath Toom once again. *Set a course for Haji.* He removed the familiar canister of terrazine and took a long, slow hit, letting the drug spread through his veins, warming him and letting him know everything would be okay. Then he sat back and glanced at Kath, taking her hand in his own. Her fingers were ice cold.

It was going to be a long journey.

STARCRAFT TIMELINE

c. 1500

A group of rogue protoss is exiled from the protoss homeworld of Aiur for refusing to join the Khala, a telepathic link shared by the entire race. These rogues, called the dark templar, ultimately settle on the planet of Shakuras. This split between the two protoss factions becomes known as the Discord.
(*StarCraft: Shadow Hunters*, book two of *The Dark Templar Saga* by Christie Golden)
(*StarCraft: Twilight*, book three of *The Dark Templar Saga* by Christie Golden)

1865

The dark templar Zeratul is born. He will later be instrumental in reconciling the severed halves of protoss society.
(*StarCraft: Twilight,* book three of *The Dark Templar Saga* by Christie Golden)
(*StarCraft: Queen of Blades* by Aaron Rosenberg)

2143

Tassadar is born. He will later be an executor of the Aiur protoss.
(*StarCraft: Twilight,* book three of *The Dark Templar Saga* by Christie Golden)
(*StarCraft: Queen of Blades* by Aaron Rosenberg)

c. 2259

Four supercarriers—the *Argo,* the *Sarengo,* the *Reagan,* and the *Nagglfar*—transporting convicts from Earth venture far beyond their intended destination and crash-land on planets in the Koprulu sector. The survivors settle on the planets Moria, Umoja, and Tarsonis and build new societies that grow to encompass other planets.

2323

Having established colonies on other planets, Tarsonis becomes the capital of the Terran Confederacy, a powerful but increasingly oppressive government.

2460

Arcturus Mengsk is born. He is a member of one of the Confederacy's elite Old Families.
(*StarCraft: I, Mengsk* by Graham McNeill)
(*StarCraft: Liberty's Crusade* by Jeff Grubb)
(*StarCraft: Uprising* by Micky Neilson)

2464

Tychus Findlay is born. He will later become good friends with Jim Raynor during the Guild Wars.
(*StarCraft: Heaven's Devils* by William C. Dietz)

2470

Jim Raynor is born. His parents are Trace and Karol Raynor, farmers on the fringe world of Shiloh.
(*StarCraft: Heaven's Devils* by William C. Dietz)

(*StarCraft: Liberty's Crusade* by Jeff Grubb)
(*StarCraft: Queen of Blades* by Aaron Rosenberg)
(*StarCraft: Frontline volume 4*, "Homecoming" by
Chris Metzen and Hector Sevilla)
(*StarCraft* monthly comic #5–7 by Simon Furman
and Federico Dallocchio)

2473

Sarah Kerrigan is born. She is a terran gifted with
powerful psionic abilities.
(*StarCraft: Liberty's Crusade* by Jeff Grubb)
(*StarCraft: Uprising* by Micky Neilson)
(*StarCraft: Queen of Blades* by Aaron Rosenberg)
(*StarCraft: The Dark Templar Saga* by Christie
Golden)

2478

Arcturus Mengsk graduates from the Styrling
Academy and joins the Confederate Marine Corps
against the wishes of his parents.
(*StarCraft: I, Mengsk* by Graham McNeill)

2485

Tensions rise between the Confederacy and the
Kel-Morian Combine, a shady corporate
partnership created by the Morian Mining
Coalition and the Kelanis Shipping Guild to
protect their mining interests from Confederate
aggression. After the Kel-Morians ambush
Confederate forces that are encroaching on the
Noranda Glacier vespene mine, open warfare
breaks out. This conflict comes to be known as
the Guild Wars.
(*StarCraft: Heaven's Devils* by William C. Dietz)
(*StarCraft: I, Mengsk* by Graham McNeill)

2488–2489

Jim Raynor joins the Confederate Marine Corps
and meets Tychus Findlay. In the later battles
between the Confederacy and the Kel-Morian
Combine, the 321st Colonial Rangers Battalion
(whose membership includes Raynor and
Findlay) comes to prominence for its expertise
and bravado, earning it the nickname "Heaven's
Devils."
(*StarCraft: Heaven's Devils* by William C. Dietz)

Jim Raynor meets fellow Confederate soldier Cole
Hickson in a Kel-Morian prison camp. During this

encounter, Hickson teaches Raynor how to resist
and survive the Kel-Morians' brutal torture
methods.
(*StarCraft: Heaven's Devils* by William C. Dietz)
(*StarCraft* monthly comic #6 by Simon Furman
and Federico Dallocchio)

Toward the end of the Guild Wars, Jim Raynor
and Tychus Findlay go AWOL from the
Confederate military.

Arcturus Mengsk resigns from the Confederate
military after achieving the rank of colonel. He
then becomes a successful prospector in the
galactic rim.
(*StarCraft: I, Mengsk* by Graham McNeill)

After nearly four years of war, the Confederacy
"negotiates" peace with the Kel-Morian Combine,
annexing almost all of the Kel-Morians'
supporting mining guilds. Despite this massive
setback, the Kel-Morian Combine is allowed to
continue its existence and retain its autonomy.

Arcturus Mengsk's father, Confederate senator
Angus Mengsk, declares the independence of
Korhal IV, a core world of the Confederacy that
has long been at odds with the government. In
response, three Confederate ghosts—covert terran
operatives with superhuman psionic powers

enhanced by cutting-edge technology—
assassinate Angus, his wife, and their young
daughter. Furious at the murder of his family,
Arcturus takes command of the rebellion in
Korhal and wages a guerilla war against the
Confederacy.
(*StarCraft: I, Mengsk* by Graham McNeill)

2491

As a warning to other would-be separatists, the
Confederacy unleashes a nuclear holocaust on
Korhal IV, killing millions. In retaliation, Arcturus
Mengsk names his rebel group the Sons of Korhal
and intensifies his struggle against the
Confederacy. During this time Arcturus liberates
a Confederate ghost named Sarah Kerrigan, who
later becomes his second-in-command.
(*StarCraft: Uprising* by Micky Neilson)

2495

After living an indulgent, self-destructive lifestyle
as outlaws, Jim Raynor and Tychus Findlay are
cornered by authorities, and Raynor's criminal
years come to an end. Although Tychus is
apprehended, Raynor manages to escape. Raynor
retires on the planet Mar Sara and marries Liddy.

Their son, Johnny, is born shortly after.
(*StarCraft: Devils' Due* by Christie Golden)
(*StarCraft: Frontline volume 4*, "Homecoming" by
Chris Metzen and Hector Sevilla)

2496

Jim Raynor becomes a marshal on Mar Sara.

2498

Despite Jim's reservations, Johnny Raynor is sent
to the Ghost Academy on Tarsonis to develop his
latent psionic potential. In the same year, Jim and
Liddy receive a letter informing them of Johnny's
death. Unable to cope with her grief, Liddy wastes
away and dies soon afterward.
(*StarCraft: Frontline volume 4*, "Homecoming" by
Chris Metzen and Hector Sevilla)

2499–2500

Two alien threats appear in the Koprulu sector:
the ruthless, highly adaptable zerg and the
enigmatic protoss. In a seemingly unprovoked
attack, the protoss incinerate the terran planet
Chau Sara, drawing the ire of the Confederacy.

Unbeknownst to most terrans, Chau Sara had become infested by the zerg, and the protoss had carried out their attack in order to destroy the infestation. Other worlds, including the nearby planet Mar Sara, are also found to be infested by the zerg.
(*StarCraft: Liberty's Crusade* by Jeff Grubb)
(*StarCraft: Twilight,* book three of *The Dark Templar Saga* by Christie Golden)

On Mar Sara, the Confederacy imprisons Jim Raynor for destroying Backwater Station, a zerg-infested terran outpost. He is liberated soon after by Mengsk's rebel group, the Sons of Korhal.
(*StarCraft: Liberty's Crusade* by Jeff Grubb)

A Confederate marine named Ardo Melnikov finds himself embroiled in the conflict on Mar Sara. He suffers from painful memories of his former life on the planet Bountiful, but he soon discovers that there is a darker truth to his past.
(*StarCraft: Speed of Darkness* by Tracy Hickman)

Mar Sara suffers the same fate as Chau Sara and is incinerated by the protoss. Jim Raynor, Arcturus Mengsk, the Sons of Korhal, and some of the planet's residents manage to escape the destruction.
(*StarCraft: Liberty's Crusade* by Jeff Grubb)

Feeling betrayed by the Confederacy, Jim Raynor joins the Sons of Korhal and meets Sarah Kerrigan. A Universal News Network (UNN) reporter, Michael Liberty, accompanies the rebel group to report on the chaos and counteract Confederate propaganda.
(*StarCraft: Liberty's Crusade* by Jeff Grubb)

A Confederate politician named Tamsen Cauley tasks the War Pigs—a covert military unit created to take on the Confederacy's dirtiest jobs—with assassinating Arcturus Mengsk. The attempt on Mengsk's life fails.
(*StarCraft* monthly comic #1 by Simon Furman and Federico Dallocchio)

November "Nova" Terra, a daughter of one of the Confederacy's powerful Old Families on Tarsonis, unleashes her latent psionic abilities after she telepathically feels the murder of her parents and her brother. Once her terrifying power becomes known, the Confederacy hunts her down, intending to take advantage of her talents.
(*StarCraft: Ghost: Nova* by Keith R. A. DeCandido)

Arcturus Mengsk deploys a devastating weapon—the psi emitter—on the Confederate capital of Tarsonis. The device sends out amplified psionic signals and draws large numbers of zerg to the planet. Tarsonis falls soon after, and the loss of

the capital proves to be a deathblow to the Confederacy.
(*StarCraft: Liberty's Crusade* by Jeff Grubb)

Arcturus Mengsk betrays Sarah Kerrigan and abandons her on Tarsonis as it is being overrun by zerg. Jim Raynor, who had developed a deep bond with Kerrigan, defects from the Sons of Korhal in fury and forms a rebel group that will come to be known as Raynor's Raiders. He soon discovers Kerrigan's true fate: instead of being killed by the zerg, she has been transformed into a powerful being known as the Queen of Blades.
(*StarCraft: Liberty's Crusade* by Jeff Grubb)
(*StarCraft: Queen of Blades* by Aaron Rosenberg)

Michael Liberty leaves the Sons of Korhal along with Raynor after witnessing Mengsk's ruthlessness. Unwilling to become a propaganda tool, the reporter begins transmitting rogue news broadcasts that expose Mengsk's oppressive tactics.
(*StarCraft: Liberty's Crusade* by Jeff Grubb)
(*StarCraft: Queen of Blades* by Aaron Rosenberg)

Arcturus Mengsk declares himself emperor of the Terran Dominion, a new government that takes power over many of the terran planets in the Koprulu sector.
(*StarCraft: I, Mengsk* by Graham McNeill)

Dominion senator Corbin Phash discovers that his young son, Colin, can attract hordes of deadly zerg with his psionic abilities—a talent that the Dominion sees as a useful weapon.
(*StarCraft: Frontline volume 1*, "Weapon of War" by Paul Benjamin, David Shramek, and Hector Sevilla)

The supreme ruler of the zerg, the Overmind, discovers the location of the protoss homeworld of Aiur and launches an invasion of the planet.
(*StarCraft: Frontline volume 3*, "Twilight Archon" by Ren Zatopek and Noel Rodriguez)
(*StarCraft: Queen of Blades* by Aaron Rosenberg)
(*StarCraft: Twilight*, book three of *The Dark Templar Saga* by Christie Golden)

Juras, the brilliant inventor of the protoss mothership, awakens from a centuries-long sleep to discover that Aiur is under threat from the zerg. Not knowing the zerg's true intentions or the reasons for their assault, the scientist struggles to decide whether or not to attack the strange aliens.
("Mothership" by Brian Kindregan)

The heroic high templar Tassadar sacrifices himself to destroy the Overmind. However, much of Aiur is left in ruins. The remaining Aiur protoss

flee through a warp gate created by the
xel'naga—an ancient alien race that is thought to
have influenced the evolution of the zerg and the
protoss—and are transported to the dark templar
planet Shakuras. For the first time since the dark
templar were banished from Aiur, the two protoss
societies are reunited.
(*StarCraft: Frontline volume 3*, "Twilight Archon" by
Ren Zatopek and Noel Rodriguez)
(*StarCraft: Queen of Blades* by Aaron Rosenberg)
(*StarCraft: Twilight*, book three of *The Dark Templar
Saga* by Christie Golden)

The zerg pursue the refugees from the planet Aiur
through the warp gate to Shakuras. Jim Raynor
and his forces, who had become allies with
Tassadar and the dark templar Zeratul, stay
behind on Aiur in order to shut down the warp
gate. Meanwhile, Zeratul and the protoss
executor Artanis utilize the powers of an ancient
xel'naga temple on Shakuras to purge the zerg
that have already invaded the planet.

On the fringe world of Bhekar Ro, two terran
siblings named Octavia and Lars stumble upon a
recently unearthed xel'naga artifact. Their
investigation goes awry when the device absorbs
Lars and fires a mysterious beam of light into
space, attracting the attention of the protoss and
the zerg. Before long, Bhekar Ro is engulfed in a

brutal conflict among terran, protoss, and zerg forces as each fights to claim the strange artifact. (*StarCraft: Shadow of the Xel'Naga* by Gabriel Mesta)

The United Earth Directorate (UED), having observed the conflict among the terrans, the zerg, and the protoss, arrives in the Koprulu sector from Earth in order to take control. To accomplish its goal, the UED captures a fledgling Overmind on the zerg-occupied planet of Char. The Queen of Blades, Mengsk, Raynor, and the protoss put aside their differences and work together in order to defeat the UED and the new Overmind. These unlikely allies manage to succeed, and after the death of the second Overmind, the Queen of Blades attains control over all zerg in the Koprulu sector.

On an uncharted moon near Char, Zeratul encounters the terran Samir Duran, once an ally of the Queen of Blades. Zeratul discovers that Duran has successfully spliced together zerg and protoss DNA to forge a hybrid, a creation that Duran ominously prophesizes will change the universe forever.

Arcturus Mengsk exterminates half of his ghost operatives to ensure loyalty among the former Confederate agents who have been integrated

into the Dominion ghost program. Additionally, he establishes a new Ghost Academy on Ursa, a moon orbiting Korhal IV.
(*StarCraft: Shadow Hunters,* book two of *The Dark Templar Saga* by Christie Golden)

Corbin Phash sends his son, Colin, into hiding from the Dominion, whose agents are hunting down the young boy to exploit his psionic abilities. Corbin flees to the Umojan Protectorate, a terran government independent of the Dominion.
(*StarCraft: Frontline volume 3,* "War-Torn" by Paul Benjamin, David Shramek, and Hector Sevilla)

The young Colin Phash is captured by the Dominion and sent to the Ghost Academy. Meanwhile, his father, Corbin, acts as a dissenting voice against the Dominion from the Umojan Protectorate. For his outspoken opposition, Corbin becomes the target of an assassination attempt.
(*StarCraft: Frontline volume 4,* "Orientation" by Paul Benjamin, David Shramek, and Mel Joy San Juan)

2501

Nova Terra, having escaped the destruction of her homeworld, Tarsonis, trains alongside other gifted terrans and hones her psionic talents at the Ghost Academy.
(*StarCraft: Ghost: Nova* by Keith R. A. DeCandido)
(*StarCraft: Ghost Academy volume 1* by Keith R. A. DeCandido and Fernando Heinz Furukawa)

Nova encounters Colin Phash, whom the academy is studying in an effort to harness his unique abilities. Meanwhile, four comrades from Nova's past desperately seek rescue from a zerg onslaught after they become stranded on the mining planet of Shi.
(*StarCraft: Ghost Academy volume 2* by David Gerrold and Fernando Heinz Furukawa)

During a training exercise in the Baker's Dozen system, Nova and her peers at the Ghost Academy discover that the planet of Shi has been overrun with zerg. Of even greater concern is the fact that several terrans—friends from Nova's youth on Tarsonis—are trapped on the planet.
(*StarCraft: Ghost Academy volume 3* by David Gerrold and Fernando Heinz Furukawa)

2502

Arcturus Mengsk reaches out to his son, Valerian, who had grown up in the relative absence of his father. Intending for Valerian to continue the Mengsk dynasty, Arcturus recalls his own progression from an apathetic teenager to an emperor.
(*StarCraft: I, Mengsk* by Graham McNeill)

Reporter Kate Lockwell is embedded with Dominion troops to deliver patriotic, pro-Dominion broadcasts to the Universal News Network. During her time with the soldiers, she encounters former UNN reporter Michael Liberty and discovers some of the darker truths beneath the Dominion's surface.
(*StarCraft: Frontline volume 2*, "Newsworthy" by Grace Randolph and Nam Kim)

Tamsen Cauley plans to kill off the War Pigs—who are now disbanded—in order to cover up his previous attempt to assassinate Arcturus Mengsk. Before enacting his plan, Cauley gathers the War Pigs for a mission to kill Jim Raynor, an action that Cauley believes will win Mengsk's favor. One of the War Pigs sent on this mission, Cole Hickson, is the former Confederate soldier who helped Raynor survive the brutal Kel-Morian prison camp.

(*StarCraft* monthly comic #1 by Simon Furman and Federico Dallocchio)

Fighters from all three of the Koprulu sector's factions—terran, protoss, and zerg—vie for control over an ancient xel'naga temple on the planet Artika. Amid the violence, the combatants come to realize the individual motivations that have brought them to this chaotic battlefield.
(*StarCraft: Frontline volume 1*, "Why We Fight" by Josh Elder and Ramanda Kamarga)

The Kel-Morian crew of *The Generous Profit* arrives on a desolate planet in hopes of finding something worth salvaging. As they sort through the ruins, the crew members discover the terrifying secret behind the planet's missing populace.
(*StarCraft: Frontline volume 2*, "A Ghost Story" by Kieron Gillen and Hector Sevilla)

A team of protoss scientists experiments on a sample of zerg creep, bio-matter that provides nourishment to zerg structures. However, the substance begins to affect the scientists strangely, eventually sending their minds spiraling downward into madness.
(*StarCraft: Frontline volume 2*, "Creep" by Simon Furman and Tomás Aira)

A psychotic viking pilot, Captain Jon Dyre, attacks the innocent colonists of Ursa during a weapon demonstration. His former pupil, Wes Carter, confronts Dyre in order to end his crazed killing spree.
(*StarCraft: Frontline volume 1*, "Heavy Armor, Part 1" by Simon Furman and Jesse Elliott)
(*StarCraft: Frontline volume 2*, "Heavy Armor, Part 2" by Simon Furman and Jesse Elliott)

Sandin Forst, a skilled Thor pilot with two loyal partners, braves the ruins of a terran installation on Mar Sara in order to infiltrate a hidden vault. After getting access to the facility, Forst realizes that the treasures he expected to find were never meant to be discovered.
(*StarCraft: Frontline volume 1*, "Thundergod" by Richard Knaak and Naohiro Washio)

2503

When Private Maren Ayers, a Dominion medic, and her platoon are attacked by zerg on the barren mining world of Sorona, they take refuge in a naturally fortified settlement called Cask. Although the area proves to be impenetrable to attackers, Ayers and her comrades soon witness the zerg's frightening adaptability when the aliens unleash an

explosive new mutation to overcome Cask's defenses.
("Broken Wide" by Cameron Dayton)

Dominion scientists capture the praetor Muadun and conduct experiments on him to better understand the protoss' psionic gestalt—the Khala. Led by the twisted Dr. Stanley Burgess, these researchers violate every ethical code in their search for power.
(*StarCraft: Frontline volume 3*, "Do No Harm" by Josh Elder and Ramanda Kamarga)

Archaeologist Jake Ramsey investigates a xel'naga temple, but things quickly spiral out of control when a protoss mystic known as a preserver merges with his mind. Afterward Jake is flooded with memories spanning protoss history.
(*StarCraft: Firstborn*, book one of *The Dark Templar Saga* by Christie Golden)

Jake Ramsey's adventure continues on the planet Aiur. Under the instructions of the protoss preserver within his head, Jake explores the shadowy labyrinths beneath the planet's surface to locate a sacred crystal that might be instrumental in saving the universe.
(*StarCraft: Shadow Hunters*, book two of *The Dark Templar Saga* by Christie Golden)

Mysteriously, some of the Dominion's highly trained ghosts begin to disappear. Nova Terra, now a graduate of the Ghost Academy, investigates the fate of the missing operatives and discovers a terrible secret.
(*StarCraft: Ghost: Spectres* by Nate Kenyon)

Jake Ramsey is separated from his bodyguard, Rosemary Dahl, after they flee Aiur through a xel'naga warp gate. Rosemary ends up alongside other refugee protoss on Shakuras, but Jake is nowhere to be found. Alone and running out of time, Jake searches for a way to extricate the protoss preserver from his mind before they both die.
(*StarCraft: Twilight,* book three of *The Dark Templar Saga* by Christie Golden)

A mixed team of dark templar and Aiur protoss journeys to a remote asteroid in order to activate a dormant colossus—a towering robotic war machine created long ago by the protoss. En route to the asteroid, however, their ship comes under assault by the zerg, imperiling the entire mission.
("Colossus" by Valerie Watrous)

In the closely guarded Simonson munitions facility on Korhal IV, the Dominion performs

testing on its newest terror weapon: the Odin. Unbeknownst to the Dominion, one of the Umojan Protectorate's elite psionic spies—a shadowguard—has resolved to uncover the military's secret project at any cost.
("Collateral Damage" by Matt Burns)

A team from the Moebius Foundation—a mysterious terran organization interested in alien artifacts—investigates a xel'naga structure in the far reaches of the Koprulu sector. During their research the scientists uncover a dark force lurking in the ancient ruins.
(*StarCraft: Frontline volume 4*, "Voice in the Darkness" by Josh Elder and Ramanda Kamarga)

Kern tries to start his life anew after a career as a Dominion reaper, a highly mobile shock trooper who had been chemically altered to be more aggressive. But his troubled past proves harder to escape than he thought when a former comrade unexpectedly arrives at Kern's home.
(*StarCraft: Frontline volume 4*, "Fear the Reaper" by David Gerrold and Ruben de Vela)

A nightclub singer named Starry Lace finds herself at the center of diplomatic intrigue among Dominion and Kel-Morian officials.

(*StarCraft: Frontline* volume 3, "Last Call" by Grace
Randolph and Seung-hui Kye)

When a ragtag group of Dominion marines
known as Zeta Squad patrols a mining outpost for
signs of Kel-Morian terrorist activity, it comes
under attack by an insidious zerg mutation that
can take on the guise of terrans, blurring the line
between friend and foe.
("Changeling" by James Waugh)

2504

A world-weary Jim Raynor returns to Mar Sara
and grapples with his own disillusionment.
(*StarCraft: Frontline* volume 4, "Homecoming" by
Chris Metzen and Hector Sevilla)

Isaac White, one of the Dominion's heavily
armored marauders, is ordered to save a group of
Kel-Morian miners under attack from pirates. Yet
White's task proves to be more than just a rescue
mission: it becomes an opportunity for him to put
to rest a terrible memory that has haunted him
since his bomb technician years during the Guild
Wars.
("Stealing Thunder" by Micky Neilson)

After four years of relative silence, the Queen of Blades and her zerg Swarm unleash attacks throughout the Koprulu sector. Amid the onslaught, Jim Raynor continues his struggle against the oppressive Terran Dominion . . . and the restless ghosts of his past.

ABOUT THE AUTHOR

Nate Kenyon's first novel, *Bloodstone* (2006), was a Bram Stoker Award finalist and won the P&E Horror Novel of the Year. *Bloodstone* was followed by *The Reach* (2008), *The Bone Factory* (2009), and *Sparrow Rock* (2010). *The Reach*, also a Stoker Award finalist, received a starred review from *Publishers Weekly*. *The Reach* and *Sparrow Rock* have been optioned for film.

Kenyon has published a trade paperback science fiction novella, *Prime*, with Apex Books (2009). He has recently had stories published in *Shroud* magazine, Permuted Press's *Monstrous* anthology, *Best Zombie Tales*, *The Monster's Corner*, and *Legends of the Mountain State*, and has several others forthcoming. He is a member of the Horror Writers Association and International Thriller Writers.